IRRESISTIBLE
ATTRACTION

W WINTERS

A

SINGLE

GLANCE

I saw her from across the bar.
My bar. My city. Everything in that world belonged to me.
She stood out from the crowd, looking like she was searching for someone to blame for her pain.

That night, I felt the depths of my mistakes and the scars they left behind. With a single glance, I knew her touch would take it all away and I craved that more than anything.

I knew she would be a tempting, beautiful mistake.
One I would make again and again... even if it cost me everything.

Dedicated to both TJ and Gem. In no particular order.
Your love for my books and these characters knows no bounds. You
have no idea how happy it makes me to hear you guys fighting over
who licked Jase first. I love you both... and I'm staying out of this one!

MUAH!

PROLOGUE

Bethany

I'VE LEARNED TO LOVE THE COLD. TO LOVE THE HEAT THAT COMES AFTER. To love his touch. Whatever bit of it he'll give me.

Only when we're in this room though. Outside of it, he's still my enemy. And I'll never forget that. But when I'm tied down and waiting for him to use me as he wishes… I live for these moments.

The edge of the knife drags down my body, the blade running along my bare skin and taking the peach fuzz from every inch of me. It doesn't cause pain, but it leaves a sensitive trail that awakens every nerve ending it passes. Making me feel alive, so desperate and so conscious of how good it feels to long for something.

The knife travels down my collarbone carefully, meticulously, leaving a chill in the air that dares me to shiver as the sharp knife glides lower, down to the small mounds of my breasts. It's so cold when he's not hovering over me. The icy bite of the air alone has never brought pleasure, but knowing what's to come, the draft is nearly an aphrodisiac.

All the heat I need is buried between my legs, waiting for him to move the knife lower, bringing with it his hands, his breath… his lips.

The desire stirs deep in my belly, then lower still. With my legs spread just slightly, my thighs remain touching at the very top, closest to my most bared asset. The temperature in the room is low, low enough to turn my nipples to hardened peaks. Sometimes he drags the tip of his knife up to the top of my nipples, teasing me, and when he does this time, I let my head fall back, feeling the pleasure build inside of me. The smallest touches bring the largest thrills.

He tortures me just like this; he has for weeks. At one point, it did feel like suffering, but I crave it now. Every piece of it. I only feel lust when I think about being at his mercy.

"I love you naked on this bench." Jase's deep voice is so low, I barely hear him. But I feel his warm breath along my belly as he moves his tongue to run right where the blade has just been.

He does this first every time, teasing me with the knife, shaving any trace of hair before moving on. He always takes his time, and part of me thinks it's because he doesn't want this to end either. Once the flames have all flickered out and darkness sets in, and the loud click of the locks in the barren room signal it's over, that's when reality comes rushing back.

The war. The drugs. All of the lies that leave a tangled web for me to get lost in.

I don't want any of it.

I want to swallow, the need is there, but I know to wait until the blade is lifted, leaving me cold and begging for it back on my skin. Teasing me. It's only once he pulls it back that I dare to swallow the lump in my throat and turn my head on the thick wooden bench to look at him.

Jase Cross.

My enemy. And yet, the only person I trust.

Fear used to consume me in these moments, but as the rough rope digs into my wrists, not an ounce of it exists. His dark eyes flicker, mirroring the flames of the fireplace lining the back wall of the room.

My gaze lingers as he swallows too, highlighting the stubble that travels from his throat up to his sharp jawline. That dip in his neck begs me to kiss him. Right there, right in that dip, as if he's vulnerable there.

With broad shoulders and a smoldering look in his dark eyes, Jase is a man born to be powerful. His muscles rippling in the fire's light as he looks down at me force my heart to flicker as well.

The gold flecks in his irises spark, and I'm lost in a trance. So much so that I freely admit what I never have before as I say, "I love it too."

I swear I see the hint of a smile tugging the corners of his lips up, but it's gone before I'm certain.

I shouldn't have said that. I shouldn't have given him more power than he already has.

Jase Cross will be my downfall.

CHAPTER
1

Jase
One month earlier

I T'S A SLOPPY MISTAKE. I NEVER MAKE A MISTAKE LIKE THIS. *NEVER*. YET, staring at the bit of blood still drying on my oxfords, I know I've made a mistake that could have cost me everything.

And it's all because of her. She's a distraction. A distraction I can't afford.

The thick laces run along my fingertips as I untie them, and as I do, a bit of blood stains my fingers. Pausing, I contemplate everything that could have happened if I hadn't seen it just now. I rub the blood between my fingers, then wipe it off with a napkin from my desk. Carefully, I slip off my shoes, shoving the napkin inside of one before grabbing a new pair from behind my desk and putting them on.

The pair with evidence of my latest venture will meet the incinerator before I leave my bar, The Red Room, tonight. Where all evidence is meant to be left.

"What do you think?" Seth asks me, and I turn my attention back to him. Back to the monitors.

She's gorgeous. That's what I think. With deep hazel eyes filled with a wild fire and full lips I'd silence easily with my own, even if she's screaming on the security footage, she's nothing but stunning.

Her anger is beautiful.

The bar and crowd would normally take my attention away from her, but I was there that night and I only saw her. The patrons from last week get in the way of seeing her clearly on the security footage though. I can barely make out her curves… but I do. Even if I can't fully see them here, I remember them. I remember everything about her.

If I hadn't been with my brother at the time and in a situation I couldn't leave, I would have been the one to go to her. Instead, I had Seth throw her out. No one was to harm her, which isn't the best example to set, but I wanted to tempt her to come back. I needed to see her again. If for nothing more than to serve as a beautiful distraction.

Running my thumb over the fleshy pads of my fingertips, I lean back in the chair, crossing my ankles under my desk and letting my gaze roam over every bit of her as he leads her out.

My voice is low, but calm as I comment, "She's different here than she is in the file."

"Anger will do that. She lost her fucking mind coming into your bar talking about calling the cops."

Although my lips kick up into an asymmetric smile, a heaviness weighs down on me. There's too much shit going on right now for us to handle any more trouble.

She's a mistake waiting to happen. A delicate disaster in the making.

"How many days ago was this?" I ask, not remembering since the days have melded together in the hell that this past week was.

"Eight days; she hasn't come back."

"What do you want me to do?" Seth asks when I don't respond.

"Show me the footage again."

He's my head of security at The Red Room, and over the years I've come to trust him. Although, not enough to tell him what I really want from her. How seeing her defy the unspoken rules of this world, seeing her slander my name, curse it and dare me to do anything to stop her… I'm harder than I've been in a long fucking time.

"She's irate about her sister," Seth murmurs as the screen rewinds, then plays the footage of her parking her car, storming into the place, and demanding answers from a barkeep who doesn't know shit.

None of them could have given her the answer she wants.

I recognize every movement. The sharpness of her stride, the way her throat tenses before she even says a damn thing. I bet she can feel each of her words sitting on the tip of her tongue, threatening to silence her before she's even begun.

Even still, I find her beautiful. There is beauty in everything about what she did and how she feels.

"She lost her fucking mind," he mutters, watching along with me.

Seth is missing something though, because he doesn't know what I know. He doesn't see it like I do.

She's not just angry; she's lonely. And more than that, she's scared.

I know all about that.

The days go by so slowly when you're lonely. They drag on and bring you with them, exaggerating each second, each tick of the clock and making you wonder what it's all worth.

I can't deny the ambition, the desire for more. There's always more. More money, more power, more to conquer. And with it more enemies and more distrust.

It's a predictable life, even amidst the chaos.

"I can understand why she's looking for someone to blame." I pause to move my gaze from the screen to Seth, and wait for him to look back at me. "But why us?" I ask him, emphasizing each word.

He shakes his head as he skims through the file he's holding, an autopsy report and photographs of a body catching my eye in particular, although you can barely tell that's what she was after washing up on shore. Dental records were needed to identify her, the poor woman.

"She thinks you and your brothers are responsible."

"No shit," I answer him, waiting for his attention before adding, "but why would she think that?"

Again he shakes his head. "There's nothing here that would lead her to that conclusion. We didn't touch the girl. Her sister wasn't a threat to anything that we know of."

My fingers rap on the desk as I think about Jennifer, the girl who died so tragically. I met her once, and I can imagine she got into far more trouble than she could handle.

"I'll figure it out, Boss," Seth tells me and I immediately answer, "Don't go to her."

His brow raises, but he's quick to fix the display of shock. "Of course," he replies.

"I'm arranging to see her shortly. Dig up everything you can on her and on her sister's death."

"Will do," Seth says as he slips the papers back into the folder and then glances at the monitors once again. The paused image of Beth shows her leaning across the bar midscream, demanding answers. Answers I don't have for her. Answers she may never get.

"The other reason I wanted to see you... I have those papers you wanted," Seth says, interrupting my thoughts.

"What papers?"

"The ones about your brother."

My brother.

There's always someone to fight. Someone to blame.

It never stops.

CHAPTER
2

Bethany

PEOPLE MOURN DIFFERENTLY. MY MOTHER WOULD TURN IN HER GRAVE IF she knew I went to work last night instead of going to my sister's funeral. My sister, Jennifer, was the only family I had left.

And instead of watching Jenny be put in the ground, beside my mother who's been there for a decade, I worked.

Yes, my mother would turn in her grave if she knew.

But that's because my mother had never been able to stand on her own two feet whenever there was a loss, or any day of the week, really. Let alone take on a sixteen-hour shift to avoid the burial of a loved one. The last loved one I had.

As I let out a flat sigh, remembering how she used to handle things, I watch my warm breath turn to fog. It's not even late, but the sun has set and the dark winter night feels appropriate if nothing else.

The laughter coming from inside my house doesn't though.

My heart twists with a pain I loathe. *Laughter*. On a night like tonight.

Gripping the door handle a little harder than I need to, I prepare myself for what's on the other side.

Distant relatives chattering in the corner, and the smell of every casserole known to man invade my senses.

The warmth is welcoming as I close the door behind me without looking, only staring straight ahead.

Even as I lean my back against the cold door, no one sees me. No one stops their unremarkable conversations to spare me a glance. Bottles clink to my right and I turn just in time to see a group of my sister's friends toasting as they throw back whatever clear liquor is in their glasses. *My glasses.*

With a deep breath, I push off the door. Focusing on the sound of my coat rustling as I pull it off, I barely make eye contact with an aunt I haven't seen in years.

"My poor dear," she says, and I notice how her lips purse even while she's speaking. With a wine glass held away from her, she gives me a one-armed hug. "I'm so sorry," she whispers.

Everyone is so, so sorry.

Offering her a weak smile, and somehow not voicing every angry thought that threatens to strangle me, I answer back, "Thank you."

Her gaze drifts down to my boots, still covered with a light dusting of snow and then travels back up to my eyes. "Did you just get done with work?"

I lie. "Yes. Did the scrubs give it away?" The small joke eases the tension as she grips my shoulder. This isn't the first time I've ventured to the bar before coming home. Although, this is the first time the house isn't empty. And it's the first time I've felt I truly needed a drink. I need something to numb... *all of this.*

"Would you like a drink?" she offers me and then tells a group of people I've never met goodbye as they make their way out of my house.

"How about some red wine. A nightcap, since it's almost over?"

It's. Is she referring to the evening? Or the wake?

The tight smile on my face widens and I tell her, "I'd like that." My gaze wanders to the living room and I spitefully think that I'd like the four-year-old rummaging through the drawer of my coffee table to get out. They can all get out.

That thin smile still lingers on my lips when she brings me a glass and I nod a thanks, although I don't drink it. Not because I don't need one, but purely out of spite.

"Did the caterers bring everything?" I ask her politely, nodding a hello at a few family members who offer a pathetic wave in return. My mother was the black sheep of the family. Because of that, I couldn't name half of the people in here even though I recognize their faces. She got a divorce when my dad skipped out on us, and the family essentially divorced her for not "trying harder" in her marriage.

So the majority of the people here, I've met only once or twice... usually at funerals.

"They did," Aunt Margaret answers and I'm quick to add, "I'm glad everyone could come."

I hate lies, but tonight they slip through my lips so easily. Even as the emotions make my throat swell up when I see the same group of girls doing another round of shots.

Maybe it makes me a hypocrite, seeing as how I just came from drowning myself in vodka and Red Bull at the bar down the street, Barcode. I tend to swing by after a lot of hard shifts, but that particular group doesn't need any more drugs added in the mix.

"The funeral was beautiful." My aunt's words bring a numbness that travels down my throat and the false expression I'm wearing slips, but I force the smile back on my face when she looks up at me.

I take a sip of cheap Cabernet and let the anger simmer.

Beautiful.

What a dreadful word for a funeral.

For the funeral of a woman not yet thirty. A woman who none of these people spoke to. A woman I tried so desperately to save, because at one point in my life, she was my hero.

The glass hits the buffet a little harder than I wanted.

"Sorry I didn't make it. I'm glad it went well." My voice is tight.

"It was really kind of you to pay for everything... I know there's nothing in the estate or..." she says, but her voice drifts off, and I nearly scream at her. I nearly scream at all of them.

Why are they doing this? Why put on a front as if they cared? They didn't come to visit any of the times she was in the hospital. They didn't pay a cent for anything but their gas to attend the funeral and come here. And whatever those fucking casseroles cost. All the while I know they were gossiping, wondering about everything Jenny had done to land herself in an early grave.

They're from uptown New York and all they do is brag on social media about all their charity events. All their expensive dresses and glasses of champagne, put on full display every weekend for the charity that they so generously donated to.

I'm sure that would have been so much better.

Or maybe this alternative is their charity for the weekend. Coming to this fucking wake for a woman they didn't care about.

I could scream at myself as well; why open my door to these people? Why tell my aunt the reception could be held here? Was I still in shock when I agreed? Or was I just that fucking stupid?

They didn't see what happened to her. How she morphed into a person I didn't recognize. How my sister got sucked down a black hole that led to her destruction, and not a single one of them cared to take notice.

Yet they can comment on how beautiful her funeral was.

How lovely of them.

"Oh dear," my aunt says as she hugs me with both arms this time and I let her. The anger isn't waning, but it's not for them. I know it's not.

I'm sorry they didn't get to see those moments of her that shined through. The bits of Jenny that I'll have forever and they'll never know. I feel sorry for them. But her? My sister? I'm so fucking angry she left me here alone.

Everyone mourns differently.

The thought sends a peaceful note to ring through my blood as I hear footsteps approach. My aunt doesn't pull away, and I find myself slightly pushing her to one side and picking up a cocktail napkin to dry under my eyes.

"Hey, Beth." Miranda, a twentysomething string bean of a girl with big blue eyes and thick, dark brown hair, approaches. Even as she stands in front of me, she sways. The liquor is getting to her.

"Do you guys have a ride home?" I ask her, wanting to get that answer before she says anything else.

She blinks slowly, and the apprehension turns into hurt. She shifts her tiny weight from one foot to the other. Her nervousness shows as she tucks a lock of hair behind her ear, swallowing thickly and nodding. "Yeah," she croaks and her gaze drops to the floor as she bites the inside of her cheek. "Sorry about last time," she barely whispers before looking me in the eyes. "We've got a ride this time."

It's when she sniffles that I notice how pink her cheeks are – tearstained pink – not from drinking. Fuck, regret is a spiked ball that threatens to choke me as I swallow.

"I just don't want you guys getting into another accident, you know?" I get out the words quickly in a single breath, and pick up that glass of wine, downing it as Aunt Margaret turns her back on this conversation, leaving us for more… proper things maybe.

Miranda's quiet, looking particularly remorseful.

I don't mention how the accident was in front of my house, five fucking feet from where they were parked. Miranda passed out after getting drunk with Jenny and some other people nearby. Her foot stayed on the gas and revved her car into mine, pushing both cars into my neighbor's car until mine hit a tree. She could have killed them all. All four of them in the car, high and drunk and not caring about the consequences. Consequences for more than just them.

Her voice is small. "Yeah, I know. I'm sorry. It was a bad night."

A bad night? It was a bad month, and the start of me losing my sister. That night, I couldn't turn a blind eye to it any longer.

"I just wanted to say," she begins, but raises her voice a little too loud and then has to clear her throat, tears rimming her eyes. "I wanted to tell you I'm really sorry." Her sincerity brings my own emotions flooding back, and I hate it. "I loved your sister, and I'm…" This time I'm the one doing the hugging, the holding.

"Sorry," she rasps in a whisper as she pulls away. I look beyond her, at the groups of people in the dining room and past that to the kitchen. There are maybe twenty or thirty people in my house. And not a single one looks our way. They're too busy eating the food I paid for and drinking my alcohol. I wonder if they even feel this pain.

"She had this for you." Miranda pushes a book into my chest before running the sleeve of the thin sweater she's wearing under her eyes. Black mascara seeps into the light gray fabric instantly. "Right before she went missing, while she crashed at my place, she couldn't stop reading it."

It takes me a moment to actually take the book from her. It's thick, maybe a few hundred pages… with no cover. The spine's been torn off and my name replaces it. *Bethy*. That's what Jenny used to call me. The black Sharpie marker bled into the torn ridges of what the spine would have protected.

"What is it?" I ask Miranda, not taking my eyes from the book as I turn it over and look for any indication as to what story it is. I can feel creases in my forehead as my brow furrows.

Miranda only shrugs, the sweater falling off her shoulder and showing more of her pale skin and protruding collarbone. "She just kept saying she was going to give it to you. That you needed it more than her."

My gaze focuses on the first lines of the book, skimming them but finding no recollection of this tale in my memory. I have no idea what the book is, but as I flip through the pages, I notice some of the sentences are underlined in pen.

He loves like there's no reason not to. That's the first line I see, and it makes me pause until the conversation pulls me away.

"Before she died, she told me things." Miranda's large eyes stare deep into mine.

Jenny told me things too. Things I'll never forget. Warnings I thought were only paranoia.

As Miranda's thin lips part, my boss, Aiden, walks up to us in a tailored suit and Miranda shies back. My lips pull into a tight smile as he hugs me.

"You're dressed to the nines," I compliment him with a sad smile, not bothering to hide the pain in my voice. Miranda leaves me before I can say another word to her. She ducks her head, getting distance from me as quickly as she can. My eyes follow her as Aiden speaks.

"You okay?"

My head tilts and my eyes water as I reply, "Okay is such a vague word, don't you think?"

He's older than me, and not quite a friend, but not just a boss either. The second my arms reach around his jacket, accepting his embrace, he holds me a little tighter and I hate how much comfort I get from it.

From something so simple. So genuine. My circle is small, but I like to keep it that way. And Aiden is one of the few people in it. He's one of the few people I can be myself with.

"I heard you didn't go… that it was today?" he asks me, although it's more of a statement, my face still pressed against his chest.

I won't cry. I won't do it.

Not until I'm alone anyway. I can't hide behind anger then. There's nowhere to hide when you're lying in bed by yourself.

"I couldn't bring myself," I tell him, intending on saying more, but my bottom lip wobbles and I have to pull away.

He's reluctant, but he lets me and I find my own arms wrapping around myself. Looking back to where Jenny's friends were, I notice they're gone, along with a lot of the crowd.

Maybe they heard my unspoken wishes.

"You need to take time off." Aiden's words shock me. Full-blown shock me.

My head shakes on its own and I struggle to come up with something to refute him. Money seems like the most logical reason, but Aiden beats me to it.

"There was a pool at work, and the other nurses are giving you some of their days for PTO. You have your own banked, plus the bereavement leave. And I know you have vacation time too."

"They don't have to do that…" My voice is low, full of disbelief. At Rockford, the local youth mental hospital, I know everyone more than I should, especially the night shift. But I wouldn't ever expect any of them to give me their time off. I don't expect anything from anyone.

"They can't do that. They'll need those days for themselves." They don't even know me really. I'm taken aback that they would do such a thing.

"It's a day here and a day there, it adds up and you need it."

"I'm fine-"

"My ass you are." Aiden's profanity draws my gaze to his, and the wrinkles around his eyes seem more pronounced. His age shows in this moment. "You need time off."

Time off.

More time alone.

"I don't want it."

"You're going to take it. You need to get your head on right, Fawn." His voice is stern as my body chills from a gust of air blowing into the dining room when my front door opens once again. More *guests* leaving.

"How many days?" I ask him, feeling defeat, so much of it, already laying its weight against me.

"You have six weeks," he informs me and it feels like a death sentence. My heart sinks to the pit of my stomach as my front door closes with a resounding click.

With his hands on my shoulders he tells me, "You need to get better."

Holding back the pain is a challenge, but I manage to breathe out with only a single tear shed. Six weeks.

The next breath comes easier.

I tell myself I'll take some time off, but not to get better.

My breathing is almost back to normal at my next thought.

But to find the men responsible for what happened to my sister.

⟨ɕ⟩⟨ɕ⟩

My eyes are burning and heavy, but I can't sleep.

I'm exhausted and want to lie down, but my legs are restless and my heart is wide awake, banging inside of me. I need to do something to take this agony away. Staring back at The Coverless Book beside me on the side table, I lean to the left, flicking on the lamp while still seated on my sofa.

The Coverless Book
Prologue

I'm invincible. I tell myself as I pull the blanket up tighter.

My heart races, so fast in my chest. It's scared like I am.

Jake is coming.

He's going to see me here in my house, and then where could I possibly hide from him? Where could I hide my blush?

Maybe behind this blanket?

"Miss?" Miss Caroline calls into the room, and I perk up.

"Yes?"

"Your guest is here," she announces and I give her a nod, feeling that heat rise to my cheeks and my heart fluttering as she gives me a knowing smile and I hide my brief laugh. Caroline knows all my secrets.

Before I can stand up on shaky legs, he's standing in the doorway, tall and lanky as most eleventh-graders are. But Jake is taller. His eyes softer. His hands hold a shock in them that gets me every time he reaches for my calculator in class.

"Jake." His name comes from me in surprise as I struggle to lift myself.

"Emmy." The way he says my name sounds so sad. "I heard you were sick."

I read the prologue and the first chapter too before falling asleep on the old sofa that used to belong to my mother. I'm cocooned in the blanket I once wrapped my sister in when the drugs she'd taken made her shake uncontrollably.

The only sentence Jenny underlined was the one that read, "I'm invincible."

Jenny, I wish you had been. I wish I were too.

CHAPTER
3

Bethany

MY EYES FEEL SO HEAVY. SO DRY AND ITCHY.
Rubbing them only makes it hurt worse.
I would have slept better had I worked. I know I would
have.

My gaze drifts back to the book. I'm only a few chapters in, but I keep walking away from the pages, not remembering where I left off and starting over each time.

Knowing I can't focus on work, knowing it's been taken away, has brought out a different side of me.

The side that remembers my sister.

Not the way she was in the last few years, but the way she was when we were younger.

When we were thick as thieves, and my older sister was my hero. Those memories keep coming back every time I read the chapters written from Emmy's perspective. She's young, and sweet, but so damn strong. My sister was strong once. Held down by no one.

Once upon a time.

Letting out a deep breath, I stretch my back, pushing the torn-up book onto my coffee table. I sit there, looking out the front bay window of my house. The curtains are closed, but not tightly and I catch a glimpse of a car pull up.

A nice car. An expensive one.

All black with tinted windows. Jenny came home in a car like that once, shaken and crying. Back when all of her troubles started. My blood runs cold as the car stops in front of my house.

If it's someone she was associated with, I don't want them here.

Anger simmers, but it's futile. You can only be angry for so long.

Once it's gone, fear has a way of creeping into its place.

My pace is slow, quiet and deliberate as I head to my coat closet and reach up to a backpack I haven't used in years. I figured it would be the perfect place to hide the gun. The one Jenny brought home for me, the one she said I needed when she wouldn't listen to me and refused to stay. I was screaming at her as she shoved it into my chest and told me I needed to take it.

It was only weeks ago that my sister stood right here and gave me a gun to protect myself, when she was the one who needed help. She needed protecting.

Jase

I can't handle one more thing going wrong.

My keys jingle as the ignition turns off and the soft rumble of the engine is silenced.

Wiping a hand over my face, I get out of the car, not caring that the door slams as my shoes hit the pavement. The neighborhood is quiet and each row of streets is littered with picture-perfect homes, nothing like the home I grew up in. Little townhouses of raised ranches, complete with paved driveways and perfectly trimmed bushes. A few houses have fences, white picket of course, but not 34 Holley, the home of Bethany Fawn.

Other than the missing fence, the two-story home could be plucked straight from an issue of *Better Homes & Gardens*.

Knock, knock, knock. She's in there; I can hear her. Time passes without anything save the sound of scuttling behind the door, but just as I'm about to knock again, the door opens a few inches. Only enough to reveal a glimpse of her.

Her chestnut hair falls in wavy locks around her face. She brushes the fallen strands back to peek up at me.

"Yes?" she questions, and my lips threaten to twitch into a smirk.

"Bethany?"

Her weight shifts behind the door as her gaze travels down the length of my body and then back up before she answers me.

The amber in her hazel eyes swirls with distrust as she tells me, "My friends call me Beth."

"Sorry, I'm Jase. Jase Cross. We haven't met before... but I'll happily call you Beth." The flirtatious words slip from me easily, and slowly her guard falls although what's left behind is a mix of worry and agony. She doesn't answer or respond in any way other than to tighten her grip on the door.

"Mind if I have a minute?"

She purses her full lips slightly as the cracked door opens just an inch more, enough for her to cautiously reply, "Depends on what you're here for."

My pulse quickens. I'm here to give her a single warning. Just one chance to stay the hell away from The Red Room and to get over whatever ill wishes she has for my brothers and me.

It's a shame, really; she's fucking gorgeous. There's an innocence, yet a fight in her that's just as evident and even more alluring. Had I met her on other terms, I would do just about anything to get her under me and screaming my name.

But after this past week with Carter and all that bullshit, I made my decision. *No distractions.*

The swirling colors in her eyes darken as her gaze dances over mine. As if she can read my thoughts, and knows the wicked things I'd do to her that no one else ever could. But that's not why I'm here, and my perversions will have to wait for someone else.

I lean my shoulder against her front door and slip my shoe through the gap in the doorway, making sure she can't slam it shut. Instead of the slight fear I thought would flash in her eyes as my expression hardens, her eyes narrow with hate and I see the gorgeous hue of pink in her pale skin brighten to red, but not with a blush, with animosity.

"You need to stay out of the Cross business, Beth." I lean in closer, my voice low and even. My hard gaze meets her narrowed one, but she doesn't flinch. Instead she clenches her teeth so hard I think they'll crack.

With the palm of my hand carefully placed on the doorjamb and the other splayed against her door, I lean in to tell her that there are no answers for her in The Red Room. I want to tell her that my brother isn't the man she's after, but before I can say a word she hisses at me, "I know all about Marcus and the drugs and why you assholes had her killed."

The change in her tone, her expression is instant.

My pulse hammers in my ears but even over it, I hear the strained pain etched in her voice. Her breathing shudders as she adds, "You'll all pay for what you did to my sister." Her voice cracks as her eyes gloss over and tears gather in the corners of her eyes.

"You don't know what you're talking about," I tell her as the rage gathers inside of me. *Marcus.* Just the name makes every muscle inside of my body tighten and coil.

The drugs.

Marcus.

Before I can even tie what she's said together, I hear the click of a gun and she lets the door swing open, throwing me off-balance.

Shock makes my stomach churn as the barrel of a gun flashes in front of my eyes. She leans back, moving to hold the heavy metal piece with both hands.

Fuck! Lunging forward, still unsteady as dread threatens to take over, I grip the barrel and raise it above her head, shoving her small body back until it hits the wall in her foyer and she continues to struggle, pushing away from me and getting out of my grasp.

Bang!

The gun goes off and the flash of heat makes the skin of my hand holding the barrel burn and singe with a raw pain. Her lower back crashes into a narrow table, a row of books toppling over and a pile of mail falling onto the floor as I stumble into her and finally pin her to the wall.

My chest rises and falls chaotically. My body temperature heats with the adrenaline racing through me.

Her small shriek of terror is muted when I bring my right hand to her delicate throat. My left still grips the gun. I can't swallow yet, I can't do anything but press her harder against the wall, smothering the fight in her as best as I can.

She struggles beneath me, but with a foot on her height and muscle she couldn't match no matter how hard she tried, it's pointless. Her heart pounds hard, and I feel it matching mine.

"Knock it the fuck off," I grit between my teeth.

She yelps as I lift the gun higher, ripping it from her grasp. Both of her hands fly to the one I have tightening on her throat. On instinct, like I knew she would. Did she really think she could get one over on me?

"You tried to shoot me." I practically snarl the words, although they're nearly inaudible.

Struggling to catch my breath, I don't let anything show except the absolute control I have over her. The door is wide open and I'm certain someone could have heard, although it's a Monday and during work hours. It's why I chose this time to pay her a visit.

A faint breeze carries in from behind and I take a step back, pulling her with me just enough so I can kick the door shut and then press her back to the wall. Her pulse slows beneath my grip and her eyes beg me for mercy as her sharp nails dig into my fingers.

The way she looks at me, her hazel eyes swirling with a mix of pain, fear and anger still, makes my chest ache for her, because I see something else. Something that fucking hurts.

She doesn't want mercy. She wants it to end. I can see it so clearly. I've seen it before, and the unwanted memory is jarring in this moment.

A second passes before I loosen my grip just enough so she can breathe freely.

Through her frantic intake, I lean forward, crushing my body against hers until she's still. Until her eyes are wide and staring straight into mine. The sight of her, the fear, the desperation... I know I'm not letting her go. Not yet.

"You're going to tell me everything you know about Marcus." I lower my lips to the shell of her ear, letting my rough stubble rub along her cheek. "And everything you know about the drugs."

My mind is whirling with every reason I should walk away. Every reason I should simply kill her and leave this mess behind. She tried to kill me; that's reason enough.

But I don't want to. I need more.

With a steadying breath, my lungs fill with the sweet smell of her soft hair that brushes against my nose.

I comb my fingers through her hair and let my thumb run along her slender neck before I lean into her, letting her feel how hard I am just to be alive. Just to have her at my mercy.

"And because of that little stunt you just pulled, I'm not letting you go."

CHAPTER
4

Jase

FUCK! THE PALM OF MY HAND BANGS ON THE STEERING WHEEL, SENDING A sharp pain radiating up my arm. Fuck! Over and over I slam my hand against the wheel while gritting my teeth to keep from screaming out profanities.

Even with the adrenaline still racing and the anger still present, I force myself to sit back in the car, listening to the dull thuds coming from the trunk.

I shouldn't have done that. *What the fuck was I thinking?*

I put cuffs around her wrists, her ankles too, and then gagged her to keep any more screams for help from crying out between those beautiful lips of hers.

I backed my car into her garage and dealt with the kicks and her feeble attempt to fight back as I forced her into the tight space.

I can only imagine what she's thinking with the handcuffs digging into her wrists as she's trapped, dark and alone and having no idea what's going to happen.

Thump. The sound reminds me—I shouldn't have done that shit.

Her garage door opens with an abrupt, jerky motion and then slowly rises, bringing with it a vision of the suburban street, lit by the warm glow of the inevitable evening. A sarcastic huff leaves my lips as I pull away, gently stepping down on the gas and blending in.

Knowing she's bound and gagged in the trunk, unable to do a damn thing until I decide what to do with her, time slips by as I drive down her street, thinking about how the hell I'm going to fix this shit.

The second I give her freedom again, she'll go to the cops, which is fine, since they're in our back pocket.

Every way I look at this, I know she's going to have to go. A threat is a threat is a threat. I underestimated her, but now that I know what she's willing to do, there's no excuse for keeping her alive.

No reason except for that look in her eyes.

The blinker ticks as I round the corner, turning right out of her neighborhood and down the main drag. I'm not taking her to the back of The Red Room. I don't want a damn soul to know about her pulling out a weapon. She's merely a nuisance, nothing more.

No one can know. If they find out and I don't silence her, they will.

"Call Seth." I give the command and instantly the cabin of the sedan fills with the sound of a phone ringing. Before it finishes the second ring, Seth answers.

"Boss," he greets me.

"I need you to do something."

"I'm listening." I can hear the shuffle of papers in the background and then it goes quiet on the other line.

"Drive out to the address you gave me yesterday. You know which one?" I ask him and keep my words vague. I'm careful not to risk a damn thing, not when calls can be recorded and used against me.

"Of course," he answers and I can practically see him nodding his head in the way that he does. Short and quick, with his eyes never leaving mine.

"I went over there and I may have made a mess."

"Just clean it up?" he asks. "Anything in particular to look out for?"

"The hinge on her door broke, and there's a bullet hole in her ceiling, but everything's fine otherwise. No one will be there, so lock it on your way out." A thought hits me as I get closer to my own home and my fingers slide down to my house key, dangling from the ignition. "I'm going to need you to make me a copy of a key too."

"For the address I gave you yesterday?" he clarifies and I nod while answering, "Yes."

"Anything else?" he asks and I'm silent for a moment, thinking about the next step and the one after it.

Seth is a fixer. Every fuckup I make, or better yet, any fuckups from my brothers, he cleans up. He's also my right-hand man when I want to keep things from Carter.

"If anyone asks or comes looking, let them know you were hired to fix it."

"No problem."

Thump, thump, THUMP! My gaze lifts to the rearview mirror as I listen to Beth trying to escape. The trunk can't be opened from the inside; she'll learn I'm smarter than that. She caught me off guard once, but it won't happen again.

CHAPTER
5

Bethany

M Y HEART WON'T STOP RACING. IT'S POUNDING HARD AND FIGHTING back from inside my chest; I can't imagine I'll survive this.

It's throbbing so loud, it takes me a moment to realize the car's stopped. The hum of the engine has vanished and there isn't a damn sound other than my own chaotic heartbeat.

I hear a crunch, I think, and my head whips around to the side, so sharply it sends a bolt of pain down my already aching shoulder. Traveling up and down my shoulders is a dull fire that blazes. Between the way I was forced in here, practically thrown in, and lying on my arms with them cuffed behind my back, my shoulders are in absolute agony. The metal bites into my wrists and ankles, and I know I'll have bruises on my knees from slamming them as hard as I could into the top of the trunk. My entire body is cramping.

Every trunk has a latch somewhere on the inside. It's to save children from being locked within and trapped. I know because I once played hide-and-seek with my sister and tried to get in the trunk, only to have my mother scream at me. She said it was dangerous, and the neighbor girl we were playing with told my mother what her mother had told her. That there was a latch on the inside. Sure enough, there was. My mother still didn't let me hide in the trunk though and after she grabbed me by the hand and brought me inside, I didn't want to play anymore.

Since being dumped in here, I've spent all my energy maneuvering through the pain to search for the latch. I can't fucking find it. So I resorted to bucking my body in a desperate attempt to force the trunk open or to kick out a taillight. Anything. Anything at all to get the hell out of here.

No luck. And now it's too late.

It's funny what you think of while you're waiting for the inevitable. Maybe it's a coping mechanism, a way to take your mind elsewhere when darkness is looming. Or maybe my memory was simply triggered by the lack of a handle and how I learned such a thing should be here because of hide-and-seek. Maybe that's why as I close my eyes and listen for something, for anything at all, my mind takes me elsewhere. I hear my sister call my name down the hall of our childhood home.

I'm in the closet upstairs, and it's so hot. I buried myself under all the blankets my mother stored on the floor in there and carefully laid them on top of me, hoping that when Jenny opened the door, searching for me, she wouldn't see me.

She was always better than me at everything—every game, every sport, every class. But today, when she opened that door, and I waited with bated breath, she closed it and continued silently searching the house.

With the smugness to keep me company, I stayed there under those blankets and I must have fallen asleep. It was Jenny's voice that woke me and when I came to, I felt so hot. I was absolutely drenched in sweat and the blankets felt so much heavier than they did before.

"Jenny," I cried out for her, feeling an overwhelming fear that didn't seem to make sense, but I knew I needed to get out from under the blankets. I couldn't shove them forward though, the door was closed and I couldn't lift them up because a shelf was above me. "Jenny!" I cried out again. Louder this time, as I tried to wiggle my way free under the weight of the pile. I didn't have to free myself alone though; Jenny opened the door and helped me out, telling me I was okay all the while and when I did crawl out into the hallway, I knew I was okay, but it didn't feel like I was.

I never hid there again. I don't think I ever played hide-and-seek again at all.

There's another loud crunch, and another. My eyes pop open and suddenly I am very much in the present, leaving the memory behind. I'm listening to the sound of shoes walking along small pieces of gravel maybe. The beating in my chest intensifies and I can't breathe as I hear the steps get closer. I even squeeze my eyes shut, wishing I could make myself disappear, or go somewhere else. Like I used to do when I was a child. As if this could all just be a dream or I had somehow gained impossible abilities.

I would try to scream, but the balled-up shirt in my mouth is already threatening to choke me as every small movement sends it farther into my mouth. Any farther, and I think I'll throw up.

When the trunk swings open so loud that my instincts force me to look up, the light's bright, almost blinding.

I wish I could beg; I wish I could yell. I wish I could fight back when I see him towering over me and taking his time to consider me.

"That looks like it hurt," he says as if he finds it funny. The words come out with condescension as he reaches down to let his fingertips glide over my already bruised knees. Even the small movement makes me buckle, forcing my weight back onto my shoulders and it starts a series of aches cascading throughout my body all over again.

The agony begs me to cry, but in place of tears, I find myself screaming the words, "Fuck you," over the gag in my mouth. The soft cotton nearly touches the back of my throat, and for a moment I think, if I were to vomit right now, I'd choke on it.

I won't die like this. Not like this.

My gaze doesn't leave his as he angles his head, reaching up to grip the hood of the trunk with both of his hands. The sun's gone down and wherever we are, there are trees. Lots of trees.

Staring up at him, searching for a clue as to where we are, it's hopeless. Yellow light slips through the crisp dead leaves above us, giving way to a deep blue sky that'll soon turn to black night, and there isn't a damn thing else to see.

Nothing but his handsome face, and the way his broad shoulders pull that jacket a little too tight.

Let him think you've given up. Don't die like this. Use him. Use him to find out what happened to your sister.

The voice in my head comes out as a hiss. And with the reminder of Jenny, tears prick at my eyes. Through the glossy haze, I see the man's expression change. Jase's hardness, his cockiness, it all dims to something else.

My breathing slows, and the adrenaline wanes.

My fight isn't over, but I'll give in for now.

"We're going to have a conversation, Bethany." Jase's words sound ominous and they come with a cold gust of wind from the late fall air. Both send a chill down my spine and leave goosebumps in their wake.

"Nod if you understand." His hardened voice rises as he gives me the command. Loathing him and everything he stands for, I keep perfectly still, feeling the rage take over anything else. His eyes blaze with anger as he grips the hair at the nape of my neck, pulling my head back with a slight sting of pain and forcing me to look at him. "You need to play nice, Bethany." If I could punch him in the throat right now, I would. That's how *nice* I'm willing to play.

He lowers his head into the darkness of the trunk, sending shadows across his face that darken his stubbled jaw and force his piercing gaze to appear that much more dominating.

A heat flows in my blood as my breathing stutters and he brings his lips down to my neck. They gently caress my skin and with the simple touch, a spark ignites down my body. A spark I hate even more than I hate Jase himself.

His next words come with a warm breath and another tug at the base of my skull as he whispers, "You're going to listen to me, Bethany. You're going to do what I tell you... *everything* I tell you." The way he says the word everything dulls the heat, replacing it with fear, and for the first time, I truly feel it down to my bones. Standing up a little straighter, but still keeping his grip on me, he asks with a low tone devoid of any emotion, "We're going to have a conversation, isn't that right?" He loosens his grip on the back of my neck as he waits for my response.

I wish his gorgeous face was still close to mine, so I could slam my head into his nose.

With a tremor of fear running through me and that image of him rattling in my head, I nod.

As a small smile drifts along his lips and he nods his head in return, I welcome the cold gust that travels into the trunk.

He may think he can use me, but I swear to everyone, living and dead, I'll be the one using him.

CHAPTER
6

Bethany

HOPE IS A LONG WAY OF SAYING GOODBYE.
I told that to Jenny a few weeks ago. No, it was longer than that. It doesn't matter when, because by then, I'd lost my faith in her. Disappearing for days on end and talking about a man who had what she needed … my sister was never going to get help. I begged her to come back home, and she just shook her head no, and told me to hold on to hope.

I wanted her to stay with me. To get better.

I could have helped her, but you can't help those who don't want to be helped.

I can still feel her fingers, her nails just barely scratching the skin down my wrist as I ripped my hand away.

The memory haunts me as I think in this moment – this terrifying moment of waiting for his next move - I think, *I need to have hope that it's not over.* I need to have hope that I can get the fuck away from this man. That I can make him pay if he had any part in her death. *Jase Cross will fucking pay.*

The last thought strengthens my resolve.

"You'll be quiet," he tells me as if he's certain of it, a hint of a threat underlying each syllable, and I nod.

I nod like a fucking rag doll and try not to show how much it hurts when he rips the duct tape off my face in one quick tug. The stinging pain makes me reflexively reach for my mouth, but I can't; that act only exacerbates the cuts in my wrists, still cuffed behind my back. I try not to heave when he pulls the wet cloth from my mouth, finally giving me the chance to speak, to scream, to fucking breathe.

My body trembles; it's not from a cold breeze or the temperature though, and not from the fear I know is somewhere inside of me. Instead it's from the anger.

His eyes stay fixed on mine as he reaches down and lifts me into his chest before heaving me over his shoulder.

My teeth grit as he slams the trunk shut, turning to the side and giving me a view of a forest. All I see is a gravel drive and trees. So many trees. My heart gallops, both with that tinge of fear and with hope. *I could run.*

Fuck that.

I'm not running. I'm not giving up this chance to find out more about the family name I've heard so much about lately.

Somewhere in the back of my mind, I see my sister, and I hear her too. *The Cross brothers,* she whispers. She mentioned them so many times on the phone. He knew her. Or one of his brothers did.

As time stands still while I wait for the verdict I'm about to receive and what this man has in store for me, I remember the week my sister first went missing. I started with Miranda to try to figure out where my sister had gone. It made the most sense because Jenny told me she'd crash at a friend's place whenever we got into a fight. Miranda and she were close. But Miranda didn't have any idea what happened to her, only that she went out for drinks at The Red Room before she disappeared, a place I'd heard Jenny mention before. A place I knew I was headed to next.

All I had were two names and a single location. One name, Marcus, proved elusive—no one had any information on him at all. Not a single person inside The Red Room had any idea who he was. They wanted a last name, and I didn't have one. He was a dead end.

I'd spent hours at that bar, waiting for something. Waiting for anything. Any sign of her, or for anyone who knew them. Everyone knew of Jase, but no one *knew* him. They couldn't tell me anything about him. Nothing more than the dirt I dug up online.

They said he was one of the Cross brothers. The owner of The Red Room.

They said you don't cross a Cross; they laughed when they said it, like it was funny. Nothing was funny to me then.

And when two men appeared from the back of the club, heading toward a side entrance, the woman next to me pinched my arm and pointed as the side door was opened for them.

"Those are the Cross brothers," she said and then bit down on her bottom lip as she sucked it into her mouth. She was skinny like a model, with the straightest black hair I'd ever seen. Her icy blue eyes never left the two of them and I stared at her for far too long, missing my chance to catch the Cross brothers. The thick throng of people kept me from making it to them, and by the time I got outside, they were nowhere in sight.

I stalked that place for four days straight, waiting for Jenny to show up. An aching hollowness in my heart reminds me how it felt, sitting there alone at the bar, praying she'd walk up to me or someone would message me that they found her.

It was late on that last night, and hopelessness was counting on me to give up so it could take over, but I never would.

It was 1:00 a.m.; I remember it distinctly because I had an early shift the next morning, and I kept thinking I wouldn't make it through my twelve-hour shift if I stayed out any later.

All the time I'd spent in the bar hadn't given me any new information. Countless hours had been wasted, but I didn't know what else to do or where else to go.

It was that night I got a better view of Jase. Only his silhouette, but it grabbed my attention and held me in place. The strength in his gaze, accompanied with a charming smile. He was handsome and beautiful even. I remember thinking he was the kind of man who could lure you in so easily and you wouldn't know what hit you … until he was gone. He had that pull to him, a draw that made you want to go to him just to see if he'd look your way.

He came and he went and I sat on that stool, knowing my sister wasn't coming.

That was then. This is now.

A grunt of pain slips from me as he hoists me up higher on his shoulder, one hand wrapped around my waist to keep my body from falling backward, and the other hand swinging easily at his side.

Every step hurts, and the agony tears through me with my hands still restrained behind my back. Biting down on my bottom lip, I don't scream, and I don't try to fight him. Not like this.

I'll be good until I'm uncuffed. Then this fucker will get what he has coming to him.

His hand splays on my ass, immediately heating my core as I hear the jingle of keys. Craning my neck, I get the first view of where he's taken me.

A house in the forest. A big fucking house, to boot. It's three stories with white stone leading all the way up. My body reacts on its own; the need to run takes over, as if I could still run, cuffed like I am.

"Don't struggle." Jase's words come out hard, and I bite down harder on the inside of my cheek to keep from telling him to go fuck himself. If I could struggle, really struggle, I would.

He holds me tighter with both of his hands this time, and the sharp metal of the keys digs into my thigh. Even when I keep myself perfectly still, he doesn't let go.

With a tight throat and resentment flowing through my veins I attempt to answer him, but I can't think of anything to say. Maybe it's the blood pooling in my head, or maybe it's the pain finally taking over, but I have to close my eyes just to keep from passing out. The moment I do, he takes his hand away and I hear the keys scrape into the lock along with a beep from something that startles my eyes open, followed by the telltale sound of a door opening.

The beep... There's some sort of alarm beyond the key. It's then that I see my purse swinging. He brought it with him, and I force myself to think about everything in that bag that can be used as a weapon.

Knowing that and gathering information keeps me calm. Anything that can help me fight.

The warmth is welcoming, even as I bid farewell to the forest that leads somewhere to freedom. I intend for the goodbye to be temporary anyway.

I don't expect him to be careful as he sets me down in what looks like a foyer. But he is.

Thud. My heart flinches as the jangle of keys being tossed somewhere to my right hits me. And then I see him again.

His back is to me as he removes his jacket, revealing more of him. Everything is in place. The cuff links, the neatly trimmed hair on the back of his neck. He screams wealth, power… sex appeal.

My eyes close slowly at the thought, hating myself for recognizing that primal urge. They open just as slowly when his footsteps grab my attention. Even the sound of his steps hints of elite status. He walks toward me and my eyes stay on his, even though the depth of his stare dares me to defy him.

My stupid heart races, dying to get away.

He makes me feel weak and I hate him for it.

"I hate you." The hoarse words come from my throat unbidden. The fact that they only make him smirk as he crouches in front of me, pisses me off that much more. It hurts, though. I can't deny it does more than aggravate me to be at the mercy of this man.

Craning my neck and straightening my back so I can bring my eyes to his level only forces more weight onto my hands.

I seethe through clenched teeth, giving away the pain and that's when he breaks his stare.

I turn away from him to my right as he reaches behind me and uncuffs my hands first. He reaches for the pair on my ankles, but pauses.

"How much?" he asks me, his voice deep and husky.

My gaze flickers to his as I pull my hands into my chest, my fingers gripping around the small cuts, trying to rub some feeling back into my wrists. I hesitate only for a moment, confused by his question. "How much what?"

"How much do you hate me?" he asks, and my heart does it again. It scrambles in my rib cage, wanting so desperately to escape. The heart is a wild thing, meant to be caged after all.

I try to swallow, swallow down the spiked lump, but I can hardly do it. Staring into his eyes, I answer him, "It depends."

"On what?" he asks, letting his fingers drift over the metal cuffs, his eyes roaming from mine down my body. He tilts his head, looking back at me once again when I answer, "Whether you tell me the truth or not."

Thump, thump. My heart hates me.

"You're in no position to question me."

"What makes you think I'm not?" Somehow my words come out evenly; controlled and daring. I revel in it as his dark eyes flash with the heat of a challenge, but then he moves his hand away from the cuffs, the small key still resting in his palm.

I could try to reach for it, but I wait.

When he peers down at me, I stare back without flinching, but the second his eyes are off of me, my gaze scatters across every inch of this place. Every window, every door. Every way out.

"You're not getting out of here until I let you out," Jase says absently when he catches me. So casually, as if he doesn't care.

My lips purse as I wait for more from him. If he thinks I won't try to get out, he's dead fucking wrong.

"You don't believe me?" he asks with a trace of humor lingering in his tone. I can feel my heartbeat slow, my blood getting colder with each passing second.

"There's always a way out." My words come out low, barely spoken, but he hears them and shakes his head before crouching in front of me again.

"Every window and door requires a fingerprint and a code, Bethany." The way he says my name sounds sinful on his tongue. I wish he'd take it back. I don't want him to speak my name at all.

My jaw clenches as I take in this new information and then ask him, "What do you want from me? Are you going to kill me?" The second question catches in my throat.

He runs the pad of his thumb along his stubbled jaw and then up to his lips, bringing my eyes to the movement as he says, "I went to your house with decent enough intentions. I wanted to tell you that you weren't going to get anywhere and whatever rabbit you were chasing was only going to lead you down a dead-end road and get you hurt, or worse."

I have to grab on to my fingers, squeezing them as tight as I can to keep from slamming my fists into his chest, to keep from slapping him or from punching him in his fucking throat as he gets closer to me.

"I don't have the answers you're looking for. I'm sorry about your sister," he says and my stomach drops, it drops so quickly and so low I feel sick. "I don't know how she died and I sure as shit didn't play a part in her death…" He pauses and inches closer to me, a hint of sympathy playing at his lips before he adds, "She owed us far too much money for me to kill her."

Dread is all-consuming as he stands, leaving me with a chill and turning his back to me. "I was being nice, giving you a warning and then you tried to shoot me."

He takes three steps away, three short steps while staring down at his own shoes as if contemplating. The hard marble floors feel colder and more unforgiving as I struggle with whether or not I believe him.

He's a bad man. Jase Cross, all of the Crosses are bad men. I don't believe him. I believe what Jenny told me.

She'd said the name Cross over and over again. Cross and The Red Room were my only real clues to go by. At that thought, there's a prickle at the back of my neck and I struggle to stay calm as the exhaustion, the sorrow, and the hate war with each other.

"I don't believe you," I whisper weakly but with his back to me, he doesn't hear me.

"I'll be nice again. Only because you remind me of someone I once knew." Looking up through my lashes, I wait for him to continue.

His dark eyes pierce me, seeing through me and causing both the need to beg for mercy and the need to spit on him, simply for not having the answers I crave.

"If you're lying to me… you'll pay," I utter and keep going. "I'll… I'll," I attempt a threat, but my last word cracks before I can finish.

Without warning, Jase closes the distance between us in foreboding steps I both loathe and refuse to be intimidated by. So I react. All I've been doing is reacting. I spit in his face the second he lowers himself to tell me off.

The shock from what I did is enough to outweigh the fear as Jase wipes his face, his expression morphing into fury as he stares at my spit in his hand.

Before I can say anything, he grips my throat. His large, hot hand wraps tightly around my neck, and my own hands reach up to his in a feeble attempt to rip his fingers off of me.

The heat from his body engulfs my own as I struggle to breathe. My nails dig into his fingers. His body is heavy against me, practically burning me. His entire being overshadows mine with power.

"I'll allow you to ask questions," he says and pauses, letting the air leave my lungs and the panic starts to take over, thinking there's no air to fill them, "but you will never," he pauses again for emphasis, staring into my eyes as they burn while he concludes, "threaten me again." Small lines form at the corners of his eyes as he narrows them, gazing at me and squeezing just a little tighter. So tight it hurts, and I struggle, scratching at my own throat in an effort to pry his grip loose.

My head feels light as my body sways in his grasp.

Just as I think he's going to kill me, that I'll die like this, he releases me.

Heaving in deep gulps of air, my shoulders hunch over.

I practically suffocate on the sudden rush of oxygen. My clammy palms hit the cold floor and my body rocks on its own.

"Don't make me regret this, Bethany." He does it again, saying my name like he had to spit it out of his mouth.

I grind my teeth against one another so hard that my jaw aches from the pressure. I have to stare intently at the spiral staircase behind him to keep from saying anything.

Time passes, the ticking of my heart somehow finding its normal rhythm once again in the silence.

"Your sister owed a debt, and you're going to pay it."

CHAPTER
7

Jase

L IES. I HEAR THE WORD IN MY HEAD OVER THE SOUND OF THE ARMOIRE
crashing to the bedroom floor. I turn the speakers down, but
continue to watch her trash the guest bedroom.

I'm not surprised she's destroying everything she can.

As I dragged her to the guest bedroom, she never stopped fighting,
and I never stopped hearing the hiss in my head. *Lies.*

Never tell a lie, my younger brother, Tyler, once told me. I was fucking around with him about something when we were kids. I don't remember what, but he looked up at me and the words he spoke stuck
with me forever.

A lie you have to remember. So never lie, it will only fuck you over.

I can still see the smug look grow on his face as I felt the weight of
his words. He was an old soul and had a good heart. *Never tell a lie.* He'd
be ashamed of the man I became.

The screaming that comes from the faint sound of the speakers
brings me back to now, back to the present where I keep fucking up.

One mistake after the other, falling like dominos.

I stare at her form on the screen as she pounds her fists against the
door, screaming to be let go. Bethany Fawn's throat is going to hurt tonight. It already sounds sore and raw from her fighting.

It's useless. Part of me itches to hit the release on her door to let her roam throughout my wing, struggling with every locked window, with the doors that will never open for her. Just to prove a point.

I can't blame her though and as she falls to her knees, violently wiping away the tears under her eyes as if they're a badge of dishonor, I hurt for her. For the woman she is, and for the woman I once knew who did the same thing.

She fought too. She fought and she lost.

It's so easy to hide behind anger, but it gets you nowhere. I can help her though. I need this too. The very thought of what I could do for her makes my blood ring with desire.

"I hate you!" Bethany's words are barely heard through the speaker, seeing as how I've turned them down so low.

In an attempt to ignore the thoughts and where they're headed, I check my phone and notice a flurry of texts, coming one after the other.

I text my brother, Carter, back without reading much of what he wrote. *I'm busy. Can we talk tonight?*

His response is immediate. *We need to talk about how we're going to deal with this situation.*

This situation … meaning Romano. The next name on a list of men I'll put ten feet in the ground.

A grunt barely makes its way through my clenched teeth as I write him back. *Push him out of his window, his own property.*

Let his body fall onto the spiked fence surrounding his estate.

Make an example of him.

I keep messaging him as the thoughts come, one line after the other.

Carter's answer doesn't come for longer than I'd like. My gaze is drawn again to Bethany, lying exhausted on the floor, and covering her face to hide the pain.

Fuck. I don't know how the hell it came to this.

Finally, he answers. *It's not that easy. There are complications.*

I stare at my phone, but my attention is brought back to the security monitors when Bethany finally stands, making her way to the bed. She stares at the door for a long time, sitting cross-legged and tense.

Jase, we need to wait for this one.

I don't have time for complications. I don't have patience for this. I don't have a desire for any of this. He should be dead already.

I turn off the phone, unwilling to spend another second dealing with this shit.

I want to get lost and find myself somewhere else.

Glancing at the screen, I watch Bethany pull a book into her lap. She must've gotten it from her purse. I went through the contents of her bag before I retrieved her from the trunk. Everything's there, except for her keys and a pen. I've seen both used in more violent ways than one could imagine.

She brushes the hair away from her face, showing me her vulnerability as she closes her eyes, and calms herself down.

I can get lost in her.

I lock the door to my office as I make my way to her, letting the keys clink against one another. My thumb runs along the jagged teeth of the key to the guest room as I think about stealing the fight from her, dragging it out of her and giving her so much more.

I'm careful with the lock, even more careful as I silently push open the door to her room. I don't stop at a crack, I keep pushing until the door is wide open and I can easily step through the threshold. It's quiet, so quiet in fact, that at first I don't see her.

Her small form is still on the bed, and only the sound of a page turning alerts me to where she is. With the overturned dresser, splintered wood and ripped curtains, she could have been hiding anywhere in here.

She ripped out every drawer. She threw two across the room, denting the drywall and cracking the walnut furniture.

Fragments of wood litter a corner of the room where she demolished a drawer, slamming it on top of another.

What a waste of energy. She should've saved it for this moment.

Instead the poor girl is still, curled up in a ball, and has her nose buried in the book.

She still doesn't see me, not even as I take a step forward, carefully stepping over a broken drawer.

The empty dresser, thick damask curtains and neatly made bed with bright white linens were all that were in the room. And now the fabric is heaped on the floor, the curtains ripped from the oil-rubbed bronze finishings and the armoire is … wrecked.

And little Miss Bethany sits in the middle of the bed, worn out and oblivious.

Her hair's a chaotic halo around her shoulders. The faint light from the setting sun casts a shadow around her, but it highlights her hair and when she tucks a strand behind her ear, it hits her face. Her fair skin's so smooth, it tempts me to brush my fingertips against it. The light falls to the dip in her neck, to the hollow there and it dares me to kiss her in that spot.

My cock hardens as I wonder what sounds would spill from her lips if I were to do just that.

"Looks like you had some fun." My voice comes out harder than I anticipated, startling her. She practically screams and slams her book shut as her body jostles.

She stands abruptly, backing off of the bed and clutching the book to her side as she squares her shoulders. "Let me go."

The huff comes back to me, but this time it's with a hint of humor.

"You're good at making demands when you have no authority, aren't you?" I question her, feeling a smirk play at my lips.

Silence. It's so fucking silent in this room, I think I can hear her heart pounding.

"Did you think destroying your room would … upset me?" I ask her with a deliberate casual tone to my question. Rounding the bed, moving closer to her, I kick a scrap of broken wood away from me. I follow her gaze as she glances at it, and then to the chunk of wood she left on the bed where she was sitting.

"Leave it there." I give her the command and watch her resist the urge to lunge toward it.

Her plump lips tug into a feigned smile. It's faint, but it's there. She is a fighter. There's no denying that.

"Did you want to anger me, Bethany?"

She flinches every time I say her name. That hint of a smile vanishes and the smoldering hate returns.

"I don't care what you do with this room. I won't be cleaning it up." I shrug as I add, "I hope it calmed you down to make such a mess."

With a gentle shake of her head, she huffs a humorless laugh at me then says, "Whatever you do to me, know that it won't hurt me. Whatever it is, I'll give you nothing."

She practically sneers her words, even as her eyes gloss over.

"We need to come to an agreement, and seeing as how you've gotten some of your… displaced anger out of the way-"

"Fuck you. I'm not agreeing on a damn thing with--"

"Not even to get the hell out of here?" I ask and cut her off.

The anger wanes from a boil to a simmer as her glare softens. "Just like that?" she asks skeptically.

"I don't want to keep you locked up… breaking all my shit." I make a point of kicking a piece of broken wood to the side. "I didn't plan this. And I want something else."

"So you're going to just let me go?"

"Once we come to an agreement, that's exactly what I plan on doing."

Shock lights her eyes, but so does skepticism.

"Do you think you can be reasonable this time?" I ask her, feeling I have the upper hand via the element of surprise.

"You fucking kidnapped me," she scoffs, the control leaving her in an instant. I watch as her knuckles turn white from how she grips the book so damn hard.

I take another stride forward to the end of the bed, and now only a few feet and a puddle of cotton linens stands between us.

Bethany takes a half step back, but when she tries to take another, her heel hits the balled-up curtain on the floor behind her. The wall is next.

"You tried to shoot me." My words cut through the air, leaving no room for negotiation as I add, "You should be dead for trying something so stupid."

At my last word, she steps behind the bundle of fabric at her feet, pressing her back to the wall. Her body trembles even as she utters the words, "Fuck you."

"I'm sure a well-read woman such as yourself has a wider vocabulary to choose from," I taunt and then nod to the book in her hand. "What is it?"

She breathes in and out, staring at me and refusing to speak.

"What book are you reading?" I ask her with less patience.

"I don't know," she answers, not taking her eyes from me.

"Now you're deliberately pissing me off," I tell her without any attempt at hiding the irritation.

"I don't know," she repeats, raising her voice, and her words come out hoarse. All that screaming she did caused more harm than good.

"Bullshit," I grit out and reach for the book, pissed off that she's being so stubborn, so resistant. With a single lunge forward, I grip the book in my hand, the other finding her hip to pin her against the wall.

"No!" she screams out at me, ripping the book away, and the thin pages on top nearly rip off without the cover to shield them. She turns her small body away from me as I press my chest against her. Barely managing to turn herself to face the wall, she cradles the book against her chest with both hands, concealing it from me. "It's my sister's." Her words are more of a cry than anything else, but the tone of them holds her explanation. "It's the last thing she gave to me," she bellows against the wall.

"I just got it yesterday; I don't know what book it is." Her voice lowers as her shoulders shudder. "There's no cover and I don't know what it is."

So this is what it takes to make her cower? An attempt to steal a book from her?

She's a trapped, scared, wild creature with nowhere to run and not sure how to fight, holding on to defiance because she has nothing else. I see her so clearly.

One breath, and then another. I stand there and just let her breathe.

"I believe you. Calm down."

"Calm down?" she shrieks at me, her voice wavering.

"Lower your voice or you'll stay in this fucking room until I feel like letting you out." I practically hiss the low threat, backing away slightly, but still remain close enough that she doesn't turn around. "Let me see it," I demand, holding out my hand. "I'll give it back."

She's still and quiet for a long moment as my hand hovers in the air.

"There are times to fight and times to give in," I say calmly and then add, "I might know what book it is."

Thump. My heart pounds in my chest as she still doesn't react. Hope starts to wane, but before I have to decide what to do with her, she turns to face me, and hesitates only a second more before giving me the book.

"Do you read a lot?" she asks me as I skim the first page and then turn it over to examine the back.

Before I can reply, a small sigh of amusement erupts from her lips and then she covers her mouth. I can't help but to watch as her fingers trail down her lips before she lets her hand fall to her side. "Sorry," she says. "That's a ridiculous question."

"It's a ridiculous situation, so it's a fair question," I answer her evenly, letting her see how easy it could be if she just gives in.

Holding the book out to her, I shake my head and say, "I don't anymore, and I don't recognize it either."

Her fingers barely brush against mine as she takes the book back, and the heat in her touch is electrifying. So magnetic, I nearly slip my hand forward, desperate for more. Her lashes flutter as she moves away from me, pulling back as much she can and wrapping her arms around herself. "What do you want from me?"

The immediate response is disappointment, and something else. There's a twisting feeling inside that feels like a loss, but I would have had to have possession of her in the first place to justify this feeling deep in the pit of my stomach.

"I have an offer for you and then I'll let you go," I tell her simply, acutely aware of the way each word sounds controlled.

"Is that a promise?" she asks as her gaze lifts to mine and she shakes her head in disbelief.

"Only because you'll be coming back."

In return she bites her bottom lip, effectively silencing herself, but the rage is clearly written on her face.

"You want to hate me." I address her anger before anything else.

"Yes," she answers quickly and honestly.

"That's only going to hurt you." The rawness in my words comes from a place I don't recognize.

She answers me, but she chokes up as she says, "I'm fine with that."

The twisting in my gut gets sharper. The seconds pass, and the air changes subtly between us, each of us staring at the other and waiting for the next move.

"What do you know about Marcus?" I ask her pointedly.

She shrugs like none of this matters, as if she isn't breaking apart. "I heard my sister say his name. He had something for her."

"What else?" I push her for more.

"Nothing." She looks me in the eyes and says, "All I had was his name and yours when she left."

"Nothing else?" I finally ask her when I judge her response to be sincere. "Nothing about the drugs?"

"You're all drug dealers," she bites back.

"Now Marcus is a drug dealer?"

"He must be. Just like you must be."

"Why do you say that?"

"Because my sister bothered to learn your name."

"What name is that?"

"Cross."

"So when you said you know all about Marcus and the drugs…"

"I wanted to …" She can't finish. Her lips press into a thin line before she finally says, "I wanted it to sound like I had you."

Time moves quickly as I stare at her and she stares back.

"I wanted you to feel like you weren't going to get away with it," she whispers, breaking the silence and rubbing her arms.

"That's all you know?"

"One of you had her killed." She croaks the quick response and I can see the frustration on her face from not being able to keep it together.

"It wasn't me or anyone who works for me," I tell her calmly, keeping my voice low and steady and looking her in the eyes just like she did me.

When she doesn't react, I add, "You have questions; I can give you answers."

"What happened to my sister?" she asks me without allowing a second to pass.

"I don't know exactly, but I can find out. And more importantly, it's not going to happen like this. I have a way of doing things and a desire to handle things in a certain manner."

She stares at me like I'm the devil and she's searching for a way to escape. There's no escaping from this though.

"You'll get the answers you want and pay off the debt your sister owed."

"What do you get?"

"It will be tit for tat. I seem to remember you mentioning Marcus and something else about drugs?" I press and she blanches. "But I like things done a certain way. When I have questions to ask and I need to make sure the person giving me an answer is telling the truth."

"What way is that?" she asks in a single breath. The nerves are making her shoulders shake slightly.

There's no way I can tell her; I have to show her instead.

"Every ten minutes is a hundred dollars." I make up the amount on the spot and before I can calculate anything else, she questions, "Ten minutes of what?" She doesn't bother to hide the trepidation in her voice.

I can see her nervousness, the anger barely hidden.

"I'm not going to lie, Bethany. One of the reasons I didn't kill you where you stood in your foyer is because I find you…" I trail off as I debate on the next words I want to say, but take a risk.

"I think you're beautiful and I love the way you fight me."

Her lips part, her breathing coming in short gasps, and her chest flushes with a subtle blush that trails up her neck. The compliment leaves her more amenable. Her eyes widen, the depths of the darkness taking over as what I want sinks in.

"And what do you expect me to do?" she asks and her words are rushed as if she doesn't already know.

"You'll see."

"I'm not a whore." Her barb is immediate and raw. "I don't care what my sister owed you." She lowers her voice to add, "I don't owe you anything."

A smirk tugs at my lips and I lean forward, letting my palm rest against the drywall just above her right shoulder. Bringing my lips to her ear, I tell her, "I don't have to buy sex and if and when we do fuck, it will be because you're begging me to be inside of you."

"Fuck you."

"Those words again." I tsk and then add, "You do owe me."

"I don't owe you shit. The person who killed my sister owes you, not me."

With her raised voice, the tension rises as well until I tell her, "Three hundred thousand dollars."

"I don't… my sister…" She struggles to finish her sentence, choking on her words, letting the number hit her. *Three hundred thousand dollars*.

That's more than she'll make in five years of working her ass off at the mental health hospital. I know what she makes, and every cent she has to her name was in the file Seth gave me.

I can see the way number piles on top of her; the very idea that she would have to pay that amount suffocates her. Stealing the life from her for only a moment before she tries to back away from me, but there's only the wall behind her. Nothing more, and nowhere to go.

"You have no choice."

"Jenny couldn't have…" It's not the debt that causes grief to settle in the depths of her eyes, it's the very idea that her sister owed that much money to men like my brothers and me.

"You have questions and want answers. I want my bar to be free of your bullshit." Although my words are harsh, my voice is calm, as soothing as it can be given the situation.

Her gaze whips up to mine, and she battles the need to hold on to the anger as my eyes roam down her body. The sleeve of her shirt is ripped, probably from her own doing. Her nails are chipped—again, probably from the way she's struggled in all of this and then destroyed everything she could get her hands on.

"You have aggression and you need a release; I can give you that."

She breathes a little heavier then says, "I want to leave."

"I want an answer."

Silence.

"You have a debt, an inherited debt and I'm giving you a way to pay it, free and clear."

"I don't owe you shit," she whispers, her pain laced in between each word, woven in the air between us. But more than that… I can hear the consideration evident by the lack of her animosity.

"It's your house, Thirty-four Holley Drive? Your sister was on your deed, wasn't she? I'm guessing she helped you get the loan before she fell down the path that took her away from you?"

I'm an asshole, a prick. I'm going to fucking hell for this. With every second that passes, Bethany struggles more and more to fight, because she can barely hold herself together. "She used your home as a marker for this loan. It's going to be paid."

It's cruel how I stand here, watching these words strike Bethany over and over. Each time taking a larger piece of her sister's memory and changing it. Changing how she remembered her. And how she feels about her now.

I am the devil she thought I was.

"It's not about the money for you though."

My statement brings her gaze to me as I add, "And I'm not interested in taking from you what you don't want to give."

Her lips part, bringing me closer to getting what I want.

"You want to do it, Bethany. You will do this. The curiosity will win out. And if you don't go through me, if you go back to pounding down doors and calling the police…" I let the unspoken threat dangle in front of her, allowing her to come to her own conclusion. "I'm a powerful man, but even I can't save someone from themselves."

My words seem to strike a chord with her, stealing what's left of her composure.

"I just want- "

I cut her off and say, "I can give you what you want. And you can give me what I want too. Or you can pay me three hundred thousand by the due date, which is in…eleven days." I make up a date, and then regret the fact that I didn't say tomorrow.

CHAPTER
8

Bethany

I DON'T KNOW HOW LONG I'VE SAT HERE, WONDERING WHY HE LET ME GO. I know I should be dead after what I did. He's a criminal, and he could have done whatever he wanted with me. Before or after I shot that gun. He's strong enough to, and he has the means to do it. I've learned that much.

The sun's gone down, leaving my small living room bathed in shadows. My eyes burn, and my left ankle is numb from sitting on it for so long.

There's a bus that runs from the next block over all the way to Jersey City. I've been thinking about that too. And whether or not I would be able to use my credit cards, or if he'd be able to track me. I don't have enough cash to live without cards. I barely have any cash, in fact. There's a lot of debt in my name if I were to run and somehow try to come up with a fake ID.

I guess I can add three hundred thousand more to that debt. My stomach sinks at the thought, somehow finding its way to my throat even though it's in the opposite direction.

I've been waiting for some miraculous plan to smack me in the face. An easy way out, or even a difficult one. Something tells me Jase Cross will find me though. He'll find me wherever I run.

I can hear my back crack as I slowly rise from the sofa. My body is so stiff and sore, an obvious reminder of what happened. I need to give in to sleep and rest, but I can't bring myself to do it. To go lie in my bed when I'm so fucked.

Three hundred thousand dollars. What did you get yourself into, Jenny?

I have nothing. No money saved, only debt from school and from bailing Jenny out countless times. No answers to what happened.

He has answers. The nagging voice reminds me of that fact as I walk around my coffee table, leaving the book where it sits, and heading to the kitchen.

He wants to use me and pressure me into this when I don't deserve this shit. And he's the one with all the power. The one with all the answers.

Answers that belong to me. If he wants that debt to be paid, he'd better hold up his end of the deal. He'd better give me answers.

Grabbing a glass from the dishwasher and one of the many open bottles of red wine from my fridge left by all my unwelcomed guests, I decide on a drink. A drink to numb it all.

It's what I relied on last night too, after hours of searching my sister's old room for anything at all. Drugs she could have bought, cash she stored somewhere. I have no fucking idea how she owes so much, but her room was barren.

When Jase Cross dropped me off and told me he'd be seeing me soon, that was the first thing I did. Then I searched everywhere else. I searched and dug until my body gave out. And then I drank, somehow finding a moment of sleep, only to wake up with a pounding headache and that sick feeling still in my gut.

The way he said he'd be seeing me soon, before unlocking the car doors and walking me to my front door, the way he said it was like a promise. Like a promise a long-lost lover makes.

Not at all like the threat it really is.

The cork pops when it comes out, that lovely sound filling the air, followed by the sweet smell of Cabernet.

One glass quiets the constant flood of questions and regrets.

Two glasses numb the fears and makes me feel... alive. Free? I don't know.

Three glasses and I usually give in and pass out and everything's better then. Until I wake up and have to face another day with nothing to take this emptiness inside of me away.

He has answers.

Jase fucking Cross.

Ever since he let me go, my wrists and throat have felt scarred with his touch, and his voice has lingered in the back of my thoughts.

I hate that he makes me feel so much. There's a spark between us I can't deny. He doesn't hide it, and that only makes this all hotter. It's in the way he talks to me, his candor and tone. The way his gaze seems to see through me while also seeing all of me, every bare piece of me. There is nothing that isn't raw in the tension that ties us together. Raw and thrilling... and terrifying.

I shouldn't find the arrogant prick so hot. He's a criminal and an asshole.

It doesn't matter if I want to fuck him. I still hate him. I hate what he does to earn a living and what he stands for. I hate that in her last months, he may have seen my sister more than I did.

Hate doesn't do what I feel toward him justice.

He has to know there's no way I can pay him three hundred thousand dollars.

He has to know and that's why he's given me this "out" – it's coercion at best. I could take him to court, but I already went to the cops. And going to them got me nothing. Not a damn thing but Jase fucking Cross knocking at my door.

"I don't trust him," I whisper to no one, letting my fingertip drag along the edge of the wine glass before tipping it back, gulping down the chilled liquid. "I don't trust anyone anymore."

I almost called the cops. The very second I shut the front door after saying goodbye as if he was an old friend, not a bad man wrapped in a good suit, and pushed my back against it. I almost did it and then I remembered doing the same damn thing yesterday, and the day before and the day before that. No one can help me.

Jase has answers. The voice doesn't shut up. I slam the glass down hard on the counter. Too hard for being this sober. Barely caring that the glass isn't broken, I grab the bottle and pour the rest of it into the glass. It's more than enough to help me pass out and to leave me with a hangover in the morning.

With both of my hands on the counter, I lean forward, stretching and going over every possibility.

If I stay, he's either going to try to fuck me or kill me. And I must be insane, because I think it's all worth it if I get answers.

I'm willing to risk it just to feel something else – something other than this debilitating pain. "I've lost my fucking mind."

Just as the words leave me, I hear a ping from the living room and turn my head to stare down the narrow walkway of my kitchen.

My gaze moves from the threshold, to the fridge and I purse my lips before making my way to where the other bottles are hiding from me.

My bare feet pad on the floor and it's the only sound I hear as I grab the next partially drunk bottle from the fridge, the glass from the counter, and move back to where my ass has made an indent in the sofa.

Pulling the blanket over my lap, I sit cross-legged and read the text. I'm trying to prepare myself for any number of things. The trepidation, the anxiety, both are ever constant, but dampened with yet another sip of the sweet wine.

It's only Laura, though. Seeing her name brings a small bit of relief until I read what she wrote.

Where the hell are you?

Home. What's wrong?

I went there yesterday. What happened to your door?

That sick feeling creeps up from the pit of my stomach and rises higher and higher until I'm forced to swallow it down with another gulp. This wine is colder, and it gives me a chill when I drink it.

Lie.

Just lie.

I know I should. I need to. I won't bring her into this bullshit. It's my problem, not hers.

You know I'm Italian, I answer her. Hoping the bit of humor mocking my hot-tempered heritage will lighten her mood.

You broke your door?

Italian and Irish, can't help it. Even I smirk at my answer. My mom used to tell us we're mutts, a mix of Italian and Irish, so people should know we'll hit them first if they're coming for us, and we won't stop hitting until we hit the floor. She was a firecracker, my mom.

The memory of her, of us, stirs up a sadness I keep at bay by filling my glass again. Three glasses, in what, twenty minutes? Even I can admit that's too much.

What happened? Laura asks.

Staring at the full glass, but not taking a sip, I settle with a half-truth. *My boss told me I have to take time off.*

Is it paid?

I get a little choked up thinking about how everyone chipped in to donate their PTO and debate on telling her the details, but hell, I can't deal with all this shit right now. I've never felt so overwhelmed in every way in my entire life. So I keep it simple.

Yeah. It's paid.

I miss you, she writes back. Thankfully, not continuing a subject that's going to push me over the edge.

I'm teetering on the wrong side of tipsy, exhausted, mourning, angry and in denial of fear and loneliness. And being coerced into … probably sex, by a man I thought was going to kill me.

Fuck any kind of therapeutic conversation right now. Whether it's with Laura or anyone else. I don't have the emotional energy for it.

I miss you too.

We should go drunk shopping next weekend. Laura's suggestion sounds like a good way to have a minor public breakdown and max out my credit card. Which is fine if I do decide to leave town on the bus to Jersey City.

We can start at the mall, hit the restaurant bars in between the depart-ment stores? she suggests. The best times I've had with Laura were on the edge of a barstool holding a bag in one hand and a drink in the other, all while laughing about old times.

Hell yes, I answer her, because that's how I always answer her. Whether I'm going or not, I'll let her think I am so she feels better.

I promised I'd make you go out, so boom. Look at me keeping my commit-ment. I can practically hear the laughter in her voice from that text.

Who would have thought drunk shopping was a commitment you could keep, I joke back.

Seriously though, we haven't talked. How are you? Do you need me to come over? Laura's message makes me pause. But I can't hesitate for too long. She's sent me that message before, *do you need me to come over,* when in reality she was five minutes away and already headed here. She's notorious for just dropping in on people like that and thinks it's cute. In all honesty, I'm glad she's done it in the past, but I can't tonight. I will break down and tell her everything.

Don't come, I'm fine. I think I needed the time off, I admit to Laura after writing several messages and deleting them all.

If she came over… it would be disastrous.

Life moves too fast. It's whirling around me, demanding, taking, and I don't even have time to do an inventory of what's left of me. I don't know how to be okay, and I want someone to hurt for what happened to Jenny. I want someone who deserves it to be in this pain.

Someone other than me. It's so easy to blame myself. I deserve some of it. I can admit it.

I don't tell Laura any of that though. A small part of me knows she already knows I blame myself. No matter how many times she's told me you can't help someone who won't help themselves. It doesn't change the fact that Jenny was my sister. It doesn't change the fact that I keep thinking if only I'd been with her, or if I'd followed her, if I'd pushed her more, maybe she'd still be with me.

I don't even realize I'm crying until I feel the tears on my cheeks.

Angrily, I wipe them away and toss my phone across the coffee table. It makes the glass clatter against the table as I cover my face with my hand and force myself to calm down.

I just need to know what happened. I need to know.

Jase Cross will get me answers.

The very thought has my eyes opening, and the need to mourn subsiding.

My gaze wanders to the foyer. To the small table that sits right where it should, but was pushed to the side only hours ago. To the wall he pushed me against. The scene plays out in my head, complete with the bang of a gun and his husky voice whispering against the shell of my ear.

As I remember his words, shivers run down my shoulders. I'll blame some of them on the wine.

He may not have hurt her, but he knows who did, or he knows

someone who can find out. He knows *something* about the side of my sister I never fully knew.

I want it. I need it. I need to know.

As my phone pings with another text, there's a knock at my door.

Fucking Laura. I love her, but I cannot deal with life right now. I don't bother picking up the phone to see what she wrote this time.

Instead I'm focused on one glaring thought that won't leave me alone as I stand up. I know nothing about the world my sister inhabited. I know nothing about the life she led.

All I know is this, my work, my small circle, and the daily patterns that haven't changed in years.

But Jase Cross knows it all.

Making my way to the door, I come up with every excuse I can to make her go away; looking down past my baggy pajama shirt all the way to the stains on my old sweatpants, my very appearance is excuse enough. I need to pass the hell out and be alone.

I'm already telling her to go home when I open the door, wide and easily, not even considering for a second that it isn't her.

"You aren't touching my wine-" I start to joke with her, but then my jaw drops open and my heart stutters. My body heats with both fear and desire, making my grip on the doorknob slip as Jase stares down at me.

He's taller than I remember; how is that even possible? His shoulders are wide and dominating as he stands in my doorway. A ribbed black Henley under a thick wool coat and dark jeans are all he wears this time. For some reason, comparing the two sides of him, this casual man with an edge of seduction and the buttoned-up powerful man of control... it stirs a heat in my core.

"What do you want?" My words are rushed and I try desperately to hold on to what little sense I have.

"You look surprised." His voice is smooth like velvet, caressing every one of my senses.

"What are you doing here?" I question him, feeling panic rise inside of me.

With a sexy smirk kicking up his lips, he runs the pad of his thumb down the sharp line of his jaw before telling me, "I'm here with your contract."

CHAPTER
9

Jase

S HE'S LESS THAN SOBER. THE WINESTAINED LIPS TELL ME THAT.
She hasn't slept, judging by her messy hair and the darkness under her eyes.

And I can tell by the response of her body when she looks into my eyes that she needs to be fucked. Hard and ruthlessly. Fucked into her mattress until she can't do anything but sleep away everything that plagues her.

Good fucking timing for me. I've never given in to these desires. It's only been a fantasy. I know she's hurting and so am I. There is a certain kind of pleasure that can soothe such a deep pain. I fucking need it. Right now.

The thoughts run wild in my head as I wait for her to let me in.

The foyer is just how I remembered it. A classic '50s house with a mix of modern and antique furniture that give it a comfortable feel. She's eclectic. Or at least her belongings are.

The chill of the winter air moves with me as I take a long stride inside, forcing Bethany to take a step back. Her stride is shorter though and she bumps her ass into the hall table, turning around as she startles, and I take the moment to close the door.

"I didn't say you could come in." She breathes out her words and stumbles at finding her anger and her strength to keep me away. I almost feel bad catching her off guard. But then again, that's how she caught me yesterday.

"We got off on the wrong foot." I ignore her statement, taking a step toward her but making sure to be as nonthreatening as I can. With my hands slipping into my front pockets I meet her questioning gaze, and each passing moment it heats with an anger she's barely concealing.

"I apologize," I offer, seeing that fight come and go inside of her. She has no idea what to do, and my apology gives her whiplash.

Her lips part, but no words come out. Her hands move behind her, gripping the small table and I swear I can hear her heartbeat loud and clear. As if it's pounding inside of her just for me.

Still no words have come but her lips stay parted, and her gaze remains questioning.

"I shouldn't have come in here like I did, making demands. I think we can come to terms in a civilized manner."

A crease mars her forehead as Bethany brushes the hair from her cheek and tucks it behind her ear.

"You're a criminal," she speaks lowly to the floor, but her eyes rise to mine as she adds, "You think you can force your way into getting what you want and if that doesn't work, charm will?" Although she poses the statement as a question, I know she believes what she said wholeheartedly.

She's not wrong, but I won't give her that satisfaction.

"I've never been called charming, Bethany," I tell her, playing with the way I say her name. Softening it, letting it fall from my lips gently, as if simply whispering it allows it to hang in the air, hinting at all the things we're leaving unspoken.

It takes her a moment to say anything at all. The force in her words is absent, and she doesn't look me in the eyes.

"Apology accepted, please leave."

"We have unfinished business." My response is immediate.

I watch as she swallows, hating me but knowing I push more boundaries than just anger.

"I stand by what I said, you owe a debt." Her gaze snaps to mine and her exhale is forceful. I continue before she can object. "I wrote up a contract I think you'll find agreeable."

She's silent as I pull out the folded paper from my back pocket, along with the pen I lifted from her purse.

Her gaze narrows as she recognizes it. "You'll need to sit down for this. Standing in the hallway isn't how I conduct business."

Silence.

Ever defiant.

I fucking love it. I relish standing here while she makes me wait, as if she could actually control what happens next. Our story is already written, and she knows it. She'll give in. She knows that too.

Without saying a word, she stalks to her living room, her arms crossed over her chest until she sits.

Although I haven't been in the living room, I've already seen it. And the kitchen and dining room. I'm prepared for what's in every drawer. Seth took care of that for me.

There's a heavily poured glass of wine on the table, and she pours it back into the bottle rather than downing it like I thought she was going to do when she grabbed it.

"You can sit wherever you want, intruder."

"Intruder?" I question her and the only acknowledgement I get is a firm, singular nod in time with the glass being placed gently on the coffee table.

"All right then, *attempted murderer*," I quip back and take a seat on the armchair beside the sofa.

Her mouth drops open and then slams shut, her jaw tense as she stares back at me as if I've said something offensive. "Just calling a spade a spade," I say and hold her gaze as I raise my hands, palms toward her in defense.

She hesitates to respond and I know I see remorse in her eyes. I know what it looks like; I see it every fucking day.

"I would have done the same, just so you know," I confide in her and her tense shoulders ease a bit. Only a fraction though. "I don't blame you."

She's still silent for a moment, assessing me and everything she's dealing with.

I'll be gentle with her, I'll give her what she needs. I can be that man for her. And she can be what I need.

"What do you want?" she asks after a moment. "What contract?"

Leaning forward, I rest my elbows on my knees and lace my fingers together. "You have questions, needs, and so do I. You owe me a debt, whether you like it or not, and I can give you something you never knew you wanted."

Her thighs tighten as she swallows thickly, tensing her neck. She pulls the blanket closer to her and asks, "Did you know my sister?"

"Not personally, but I know things she was doing. She got into some trouble."

The reaction is immediate, her expression falling and for the first time I came in here, the pain shows, but she's quick to hide it.

"I'll answer your questions," she says softly, gaining control of her composure before looking at me and finishing her negotiation. "And you'll answer mine?"

A sorrowful smile plays at my lips. "That's not how this works." Her bottom lip wavers and her fingers dig into the comforter on her lap. "I want more."

The tension thickens between us with every passing second of silence.

The paper crinkles in my hand as I unfold it and read it to her.

"For the payment of three hundred thousand dollars, not a penny will be paid in currency. The party agrees that sessions will take place, in which Bethany Fawn allows Jase Cross to question her as he sees fit, questions she will answer honestly to the full extent of her knowledge, and in a manner that will entail no physical harm whatsoever to Miss Fawn. The ability for Bethany to stop all proceedings whenever she wishes, verbally, will halt the session, allowing Miss Fawn to leave as she wishes."

I watch her expression, noting how she squirms uncomfortably and pushes her hands into her lap and she then reads the last line.

"Every ten minutes is equivalent to one hundred dollars."

"That's thirty thousand minutes total, that's five hundred hours," Bethany says aloud with no indication in her tone as to what she makes of that sum.

"Correct."

"I couldn't possibly… that's a full-time job for a quarter of the year. I won't let this interfere with my job."

"It won't. We can add in a line if you'd like, stating that it will come second to your occupational needs."

"I would be in debt to you for a year at least."

"Yes," I say, and there's no negotiation in my tone.

"What about my questions?"

"They're yours to ask, but not a part of this contract."

"That's-"

I cut her off. "Not necessary to be included in a contract regarding how you'll be paying me back." I lean forward, holding her gaze. "I choose to answer your questions as a gesture of goodwill."

"And you'll continue to?" she pushes.

"I don't have a single problem answering every question you have. Tit for tat." She gives a small nod of acknowledgement, but nothing else.

Time passes and Bethany chooses not to push for that to be in writing.

"How will you be questioning me?" she asks and a warmth flows through me, the tension lighting slowly, crackling between us like a smoldering fire.

"Sign first," I answer, swallowing thickly as I pass the paper to her, followed by the pen. Her fingers brush against mine, gentle but hot. The sensation travels from my knuckle all the way up my arm, the nerve endings coming alive with heat.

My throat's dry and my blood hot just thinking about her allowing me to show her.

"You realize I'll never believe I owe you anything?" she questions me, a simple statement, so matter of fact.

"You owe me your life for that stupid shit you pulled. Whether you want to believe that or not."

She picks at some indiscernible fuzz on the blanket before whispering, "I'm sorry."

Remorse and conflict swirl in her gaze, but she's quick to hide it from me.

"I like that you're less angry."

"That happens when I greet the bottom of a green glass bottle with a label that reads Cabernet." Her tone is muted, but she gives a small huff of a laugh, and lets a smile kiss her lips for only a moment.

"I need to know what you're going to do to me," she says before clearing her throat. "I'm not naïve. I know … I know you can do what you want. I know you may lie to me, hurt me, fuck me, whatever it is you intend to do, I'm not stupid." I can hear her swallow and then she adds, "But what if I did go along with it? Would you really tell me what happened to her?" Her eyes gloss over and her voice softens.

"A question for a question," I tell her. "An answer for an answer."

"You're going to be disappointed with my answers," she says with a weary note to her voice. "She barely told me anything. I was speaking out of anger when I saw you."

"You came to my bar, you looked for my family. You tried to shoot me." With every sentence, she cowers more and more. "There's a reason for those actions." She nods solemnly.

"What are you going-"

"Just sign," I cut her off and she moves her focus to the empty glass. My pulse is racing, my nerves on edge. And yet, she looks so … unaffected by the weight of what's to come. Like some part of her has given in.

"I need this as much as you do."

Her huff is nothing but sarcastic. Easy, I remind myself. Go easy on her now. It will be different later.

"It will be an escape from the pain if nothing else. You need it," I tell her and this time her expression changes slightly, as if she's so very aware of the agony that mourning is. It's also an aphrodisiac. There is never a more relevant time to be touched, or to be loved than when someone you love is gone.

"You want another glass?" I offer with a slight teasing tone to lighten the mood, an asymmetric grin pulling at my lips when she peeks up at me through her thick lashes.

"I may have had more than enough already."

The sofa groans as she leans back on it, reading the single sheet of paper once again.

The faint light from the disappearing sun kisses her skin as the loose shirt slips down her shoulder and she has to readjust it. She doesn't look back at me as she does. With her legs bent, her bare feet resting on the edge of the sofa and a thin blanket thrown over her lap, she looks far too casual for this moment.

As if that exposed skin of hers wasn't everything I've been thinking about since I first saw her across the bar. As if I don't want to rip that shirt off of her and devour every inch of her body with open-mouth kisses, dragging my teeth along her skin and making her that much more sensitive for what I'm going to do to her.

There are moments in time, pauses in your reality, where you realize this instant will be a memory forever. Something that will never leave you. I'll remember this one forever.

I hope I never forget how the adrenaline is rushing through me, how eager I am. I want to remember it all. Every single detail.

I'll remember it, and I'll have to, because I'm going to lose her. She's not meant to be mine.

That doesn't mean I won't take her, though.

"If I say no?" she asks, her wide hazel eyes searching mine for something.

"It doesn't happen." There's no hesitation in my answer.

"If I say stop?"

"It stops."

"Why do it then? Why would you do this?" she asks with her brow furrowed.

"Because I know you want it. I know you need it." She's silent in return.

"This would never hold up in court," she says, finally breaking the quiet.

"I have no desire to ever see you in a courtroom, Miss Fawn. I didn't even intend to write this down; I only did it because I thought you would respond better, maybe even listen to what I'm offering, if it was written in black and white."

"And what is it you're offering exactly, Mr. Cross?"

"Answers, and an escape, a way to pay a debt I know you can't afford." My gaze stays on hers, holding her in place until she gives me an answer. "This is a world you know nothing about, Bethany, and I'm willing to bring you into it. I'm willing... and you'd be wise to take this deal."

"Call me Beth." She corrects me without looking at me as the pen scribbles her signature, right on the line next to mine.

Desire sinks into my blood in an instant, surging through every fiber of my being as the paper and pen find themselves on the coffee table. Signed on the dotted line.

"I'll go easy on you," I tell her as I stand up, preparing myself to show restraint. She stays where she is, pretending not to be affected in the least.

"Is that right?" she asks as I pour a glass of wine. She stares at the dark liquid swirling before speaking out loud. "I'm already a little further than the right side of tipsy, Mr. Cross."

I fucking love the way she said my name. My cock stiffens, immediately hard just from having her obey me, having her speak to me like this. There's something about a fiery woman submitting that makes me lose all control and focus, giving it all to her.

"It's for me," I point out and take a sip. It's cheap wine, but decent enough.

"Don't confuse me going along with this for something it isn't," she says a little harder, with more resolve than I expect.

"Oh, and what isn't it?"

"I'm not just going to let you do what you want and get away with it. I'm not that easy, and I'm not submitting to your every wish if that's what you think this is."

A beat passes before I ask her, "Then what are you doing?"

"I'm simply learning the ropes of your world, Mr. Cross."

"This is how you'll learn. You'll do what I say. I ask the first question, then once I'm satisfied with your answer, you can ask me whatever you want. Those are the ropes, Miss Fawn."

Her long brown hair brushes against her shoulders as she nods, making her shirt fall once again and a shiver run across her skin. She's quick to lift the thin fabric back into place, as if it will be staying there.

"Lie down." I give her the first command and just like yesterday, in the guest bedroom when I waited for the book she held so tightly, she hesitates, testing me before obeying.

"I'd like to address an important matter first," she states innocently enough, arching a perfectly plucked brow at me.

"What's that?"

"It's seven seventeen," she tells me and I grin, letting the rush of desire take over.

"I already started the clock at six fifty-two when I pulled into your driveway."

Surprise widens her eyes.

"Lie down."

"I'll say no if you tell me to spread my legs for you."

The determination in her voice is surprising, considering how badly she wants me.

Although I don't speak the sentiment out loud, I make her words a personal challenge.

"You'd spite me to deny yourself a basic need?" I ask her and before she can respond I add, "I have no intention of fucking you today, but I know you need to be fucked long and hard … both that mouth of yours and your cunt."

Indignation flashes in her eyes, darkening them, which only makes the golden hues that much more vibrant.

"If I put my hands between your thighs, would I find you hot and wet for me?" My voice is calm, although my dick leaks precum, throbbing from the very idea that her cunt is ready for me.

"You'll never know," she says offhandedly before lying down, covering herself with the blanket and resting her head on the one pillow that was tucked in the corner of the sofa.

"I asked you a question." My words are hard, and her hazel glare whips to mine. "Is your cunt soaking wet for me?"

"No." She answers savagely and begins to ask her own question, but I tell her, "I'm not satisfied with that answer."

I drop to my knees one by one to get closer to her, feeling her heat, but not touching her. Not yet.

Somehow I keep my voice low and controlled when I repeat my question, "Is your cunt soaking wet for me?" My breathing is short, my palms hot with desire raging inside of me.

Give in to what's to come, my cailín tine.

The Gaelic phrase fits her, everything about her, perfectly. My cailín tine. My fiery girl.

Lifting her head and staring boldly into my heated gaze, she answers, "You're an attractive man, Mr. Cross. I've been wet for you since you pinned me against my foyer wall." Her blink is slow and deliberate. When she opens her eyes, she stares at the ceiling as if her heart isn't racing out of her chest, as if the blush on her cheeks is only from the wine. With her hands on her chest, she gently places her head on the pillow and asks politely, "Is it my turn to ask a question?"

Sitting back, I rest my hands on the rustic wood floors on either side of my thighs, forcing myself not to touch her. It's so cold, and a much-needed reminder of how hot I burn for her.

"You aren't in the position I want yet, but yes, I did say I would go easy on you this first time."

"Who killed my sister?" Her words are blurted out and her body tenses. "I want a name," she adds quickly.

"I don't have a name, but I'm looking into it and when I do – which I will, I promise you – when I do have a name, I will tell you."

"So you're saying you had nothing to do with it?"

"That's another question, Miss Fawn. I'll gladly answer it now, but then I get two in a row."

Her wild eyes search mine for a moment as she clenches her jaw before nodding in agreement.

"Not only did I have nothing to do with her death, neither did my brothers or anyone who works for me. I have no idea why she was killed… yet."

She swallows thickly and her forehead scrunches as she wars with whether or not to believe me.

All I can think about is the one night at The Red Room. I bet her sister told her about that night and that's why she came searching for me and knew to go to my club.

"Move your hands above you, to here," I say then reach up and pat the arm of the sofa. She's slow to obey, but she does. Her nails sink into the fabric and that loose shirt slips down her shoulder again, showing me more of her soft skin. I run a finger along the curve of her arm, leaving goosebumps along my path.

"I don't know-"

I cut off her objection. "I want to know when you're lying to me, and I'll do as I see fit." My words are barely spoken, because my focus is on how flushed her skin is already from such little contact.

I take my time, moving her hair to the side so I can see her slender neck and the dip in her collar.

Reaching into my left back pocket, I pull out a simple, black silk tie and tell her, "Your wrists will be bound." Her eyes flash to mine, and I take another sip of her wine. It's so much sweeter the second time, not unlike herself.

Although she watches as if she'd like to object, she doesn't. Instead all she says is, "Seven thirty-four."

"One thing you'll find benefits you greatly in this arrangement is that I enjoy taking my time," I tell her, picking up her left wrist, wrapping it and then the other before tying the two together. "Your body will tell me if you're lying to me. Your body will tell me *everything.*"

All the while I watch her body. How her back arches slightly, how slowly she's blinking, how quickly she's breathing. I'm captivated by her and I couldn't give two shits if every word out of her mouth is a lie.

"You said you'd stop if I want you to?" she asks me and I answer with a question of my own. "Are you already having doubts?"

"Just checking," she whispers as I tighten the knot and place her wrists back on the arm of the sofa, above her head. The nervousness colors her every move. She can't hide anything from me like this.

I don't ask her or warn her before I pull the blanket down, exposing her to the cool air, so at odds with her heat.

I'll go slow. I'll be gentle this first time and ease her into what I want.

Her hips dig into the sofa as if she's trying to get away or hide, before ultimately relaxing. Her thighs are pressed firmly together, all the way down her legs to her ankles, barely covered by the thin sweatpants. With her shirt pulled up from the way she's laying, there's a sliver of her midriff exposed.

"Let me tell you a secret." My fingers fall to just above the exposed skin, playing along the hem of her shirt and gently lifting it higher. "I often have to get answers from people. It's what I do; it's what I'm good at."

It's because of me that Carter was able to create this empire so quickly. Everyone had secrets and I was able to get them all. With a knife and ruthlessness he didn't have quite yet. Power is limited if you don't have the knowledge to enforce it.

Her body stiffens and the breath she releases is strained.

"When someone is put in a state where they can't control their body, their emotions," I say, watching her as she stares at the ceiling, waiting for her eyes to find mine before continuing, "their pain or their pleasure, they give so much away." I let my words linger in the air before my fingers finally fall to her exposed belly. I run the tips of my fingers just inside the waistband of her sweatpants. Just barely venturing lower. "I intend to tie you down, to push your limits, and to enjoy every detail you give me about whatever it is I want to know."

"I can say no," she gasps as I slip my hand lower, finding the elastic band of her underwear. The way her shoulders rise and hunch with every quick breath reveals her desire just as much as it displays her need to run.

"Of course you can, but why would you deny yourself if you have nothing to hide?"

"I don't have anything to hide."

"Prove it," I tell her.

"You just want to touch me." Her words fall carelessly from her lips.

"I want to do more than touch you," I admit to her and feel a pang in my chest. A longing that's desperate to be spoken. "You aren't the only one in this room who's in need."

At my words, her gaze drifts lower, down to my zipper and I'm sure she can tell how hard I am for her. Her mouth parts slightly and she looks away, not commenting but showing her cards all too easily.

My gaze wanders to the crook of her neck, and as she breathes, a lock of hair falls right where I'm looking.

Leaning forward, I brush it to the side and bring my lips closer to her ear. Intent on whispering, intent on sharing a part of me I haven't shared with anyone.

I want to run my lips along her neck, kissing and sucking and confessing all my sins, begging for forgiveness.

Her chest heaves as if she knows I want to kiss her.

None of that happens though, because she turns her head just as I start to make my move, and she steals the kiss from me.

Her lips brush against mine at first, soft and hesitant. Yet she nips my bottom lip before I can deepen it. The gentleness of her touch is at odds with how my hands reach up to her hair, gripping it at the base of her neck and pulling her head back to expose more of her throat.

With my breath stolen, once again caught off guard, and with the desire running rampant in my blood, I stare down at her. Her eyes half lidded, her breaths coming in short pants as if I'd just devoured her and it wasn't at all a tempting taste of a kiss.

I'm drunk off her.

Breathing in her lust and not breaking her gaze, I lower my fingers to her swollen nub, spreading her arousal up to it, and then circling it. "What was that for?" I ask her and she tells me, "I wanted to take it first. I deserve that much at least." Her last word skips in the air, like a flat rock thrown across a summer lake. Her speech moves from a higher pitch to a whisper as I move my fingers lower, playing with her and watching every reaction she gives me.

"How many lovers have you had?" I ask and my question catches her off guard as she struggles to hold back her gasps.

"Few," she answers in a strained voice as I circle her clit again.

"Recently?"

"Not since college."

"Did they touch you like this?" I ask her, imagining a younger version of her under the sheets in a dorm room, letting some dumb fuck put his hands on her.

"Yes," she breathes with her eyes closed and I gently press down on her clit and then smack it.

She sits up and when she does I aim for another kiss, but she bites down hard on my mouth. Her teeth plunge into my bottom lip, the bite sending a pain shooting through my body. It's hard enough to draw blood and I swear to God it does nothing but make me that much harder for her.

She releases me all too soon, sucking in a deep breath with her mouth still open, her chest heaving and her eyes pinned on me.

Lifting my fingers from her heat, I bring them to my throbbing lip.

"No blood," she murmurs and a soft smirk plays on that pouty mouth of hers. "Don't get the wrong idea, Mr. Cross. Even if the thought of you getting me off makes me all hot and bothered, I still hate your fucking guts."

My dick responds, getting harder by the second as she utters the threatening words so sensually, words that would get others killed.

Her anger's at war with her desire, but it's losing the battle. Maybe it's the wine, maybe it's the exhaustion, but I can give her desire the upper hand.

I watch her every move. The way she clenches her hands and struggles to keep them motionless above her head. The way her skin flushes and goosebumps run up her chest, then down her arms. She's fucking gorgeous like this. Bared to me without reluctance. Without a single hint suggesting she's hiding a damn thing.

She's lost in the lust.

I spread her arousal around her swollen nub before bringing my middle finger back to her opening. With a gentle press, her lips part, and the word *stop* is there, just behind her clenched teeth. The hiss of an S was coming.

I push her, barely sliding the tip of my finger into her hot entrance, and her jaw drops open, the word lost somewhere and remaining unspoken.

Bringing my fingers back to her clit, I let her come down from the high, simply toying with her as she regains her composure.

"That's your limit?" I ask her, bringing my fingers back up to her clit, watching as her eyes go half lidded and she exhales with pleasure. My fingers drift back down and press against her slick entrance slightly before she nods a yes to my question.

Her control is as surprising as my restraint. If I hadn't decided I wasn't going to fuck her tonight, not until she truly begs for it, she'd be screaming my name as I ravaged her on the carpet beneath me. Maybe bent over the coffee table to leave bruises on her hips as a reminder. Making sure she'd feel it tomorrow, so it would be all she could think about.

I need to be gentle today. I'll ease her in until she's drowning in the pleasure I'm so desperate to give her.

She can barely breathe. Her gasps and held breaths are making her body tremble just as much as my touches are.

"Cum." My singular word bites through the air as I land a hard smack on her clit and then capture her scream of pleasure with my own kiss. My kiss is more ruthless than hers as I let my tongue delve into her hot mouth. It's quick like hers though; I pull back both the kiss and my touch, just as soon as it began.

She can barely keep herself still, her body begging her to move away from the sensation, but she needs more. Pulling her shirt down, I move her bra so it pushes her breast up, and before she can object I lean forward and swirl my tongue around her nipple. Her thighs move together and stagger to the side.

Still sucking on her, I smack her thigh with the back of my hand, pushing her legs open and moving my hand to cup her pussy.

Letting her nipple out of my mouth with a pop, I pull back to tell her, "Your cunt is soaking wet for me," and rub ruthless circles around her clit, making her brow pinch, her mouth open and her body shudder with another climax.

Her entire body spasms with the second orgasm. And I can barely fucking stand to watch with how hard I am. Everything in me begs me to shove my cock down her throat.

Still panting and struggling, Bethany lets her hands fall forward and then quickly moves them back into place on the arm of the sofa. Her eyes search mine for direction with a desperate apology to forgive her swimming in their darkness.

In answer, I pull the tie loose. She came, she let me touch her. I need to get the hell out of here before I fuck her and ruin it all before it's even begun.

"Next time will be more intense. You should prepare yourself."

Her first words as I reach for the contract, still on the table, bring a genuine smirk to my lips. "You didn't ask your question."

"I know."

It's quiet for a moment as I tuck the contract into my back pocket.

"Why are you doing this?" Her bright eyes are wide and full of fire. Full of an intense desire and a curiosity that are addictive. Every look she gives me brings out more life, more heat, more passion in me to coax more of this from her. She burns like wildfire and I want to add fuel to her flame.

"I wanted you to see why I let you live. What I wanted from you against that foyer wall after you pulled that trigger." Although her chest rises and falls rapidly, the memory of yesterday adding fear into the cocktail of emotions she's drunk on, the golden flecks in her hazel eyes stay lit. Her lips part slightly, and I know the memory only gets her off just like it does to me.

"It was an accident," she admits to me.

My smirk widens into an asymmetric grin. "Is that supposed to make me feel better about it?" I ask her and she simply shakes her head, pulling her shirt down and reaching for the thin blanket to cover herself. Her skin is still flushed, the pleasure still rocking through her, but her eyes are focused on the digital clock below her television.

Ever a reminder.

My smile falls as I tell her, "You're reckless."

"You're the one who was almost murdered by someone like me. So who's really reckless?"

"Maybe I'm just reckless for you," I answer without thinking, barely hearing my words before recognizing them.

I warn her, "Next time I won't ask for your boundaries."

"I would have--"

"Next time I'm going to fuck you like both of us want me to."

CHAPTER
10

Bethany

I FEEL LIKE I'M DROWNING. LIKE I'M IN OVER MY HEAD, AND I DON'T KNOW how I ventured into the dark abyss of the ocean, sure to swallow me whole.

I dreamed of him. I dreamed of Jase fucking me, taking me ruthlessly on the sofa. I dreamed of telling him no, only to have him pin me down and take me regardless.

The thought sends a blush of desire to grace my skin, kissing it and leaving a shiver in its wake. The way Jase did last night. Every small touch brought more and more heat, more sensitivity, more life. I felt alive under him.

And I want more. I'm not ashamed to admit I want more of Jase Cross.

Bringing my fingertips to my lips, I remember the kiss I drunkenly stole—thank God I can blame it on the alcohol. He tasted like bad decisions and lust. A sin waiting to happen.

When did my life become like this?

Working every day has kept my thoughts at bay. And now I have nothing to occupy my time. Nothing but a debt to Jase Cross and unanswered questions I have no way of answering on my own.

The only thing I've been working on is looking up every detail I can on Jase Cross. Hardly anything comes up at all about any of his brothers. All I can tell is that they were a poor Irish family, raised in the hellhole that is Crescent Falls. Back then they were nothing. And now they're everything.

There are only four pictures of Jase that I could find. Two had the same woman in them. In one, she's in the background, laughing at something. It's a candid photo and it seems harmless enough. But in the second, her arm is around him. It was taken nearly five years ago, and Jase looks much younger.

I have no fucking clue who she is.

Although, she looks a little like me in this picture, the second one. Only slightly. But the resemblance spreads an eerie chill over my body when I think about it.

Is this who I remind him of?

Was he with her? The fact that I feel any hint of jealousy is ridiculous.

I haven't been touched since college, and I haven't wanted a damn thing from a man since that catastrophe.

Maybe I've always been jealous like this, and I just didn't know it because I had nothing to be jealous of. It only took the strike of a single match to ignite a blazing desire to overtake every piece of me.

Maybe this is what it was like for Jenny. One small change, and everything fell from there. Addiction is like that, isn't it? No matter what your addiction is.

The sound of my phone vibrating on the kitchen counter saves me from the downward spiral of my thoughts.

It's only Laura, checking in again since I didn't respond to her last night.

A few quick texts and I'm free of her prying questions, plus I've booked a date with a bottle of tequila, her, and the outlet mall next weekend.

The phone clatters on the kitchen counter when I toss it down, staring at it and wondering what that night will end up being. A few drinks, and I'll tell her the sordid details.

I know I will.

I can see it unfolding in front of me.

She won't judge me, seeing as how she's had a few one-night stands.

She's gone backstage with an out-of-town band before, only to be seen again at 2 p.m. the next day, walking a little funny but smiling so hard that it didn't matter.

It's not the judgment that concerns me. I couldn't care less about what people think of me.

If Laura thinks I'm in danger though, she'll get involved. The very thought makes me let out a slow quivering breath, calming the rush of anxiousness.

I can't keep Jase my dirty little secret, but some things will have to be just that. A secret. I'll let him use me, and I'll use him. Every encounter with him is a step closer to the world my sister lived in before I lost her. It's closer to where she was and closer to finding out what happened. At least the thought is somewhat calming.

Knock, knock, knock.

Three raps in quick succession sound through the first floor of my house. I've never been so grateful for a distraction before.

Looking out through the peephole, I see a man in a gray wool coat, a man I don't recognize.

Maybe he has a package, or maybe he's a neighbor. I hesitate to open the door, my hand gripping the knob tight as I consider getting the gun. That didn't turn out well last time though, and I refuse to live in fear.

It's just a man. Not everyone is a villain.

The last thought firms my resolve and I pull open the door halfway, wincing when I feel the sharp coldness in the air.

"Hello," I greet him easily, immediately struck by how handsome he is.

Classically handsome with striking blue eyes and a charming smile. This man has definitely left broken hearts behind in his wake.

The small smile from the thought fades.

Nervousness pricks along the back of my neck. Every hair is standing on edge when I glance behind him, only to see a cop car.

He's a fucking cop.

"Ma'am, I'm Officer Cody Walsh," he tells me, taking off his gloves and reaching out his hand to shake mine.

Every ounce of me is consumed with fear, nausea, and the

suspicion that this is a setup. I shake his hand without thinking, without considering a damn thing.

Even though he was wearing gloves, his strong hand is ice cold and I feel the chill flow from his touch straight to the marrow of my bones.

It's not until I swallow my nerves, nearly ten seconds after shaking his hand while he only stares at me curiously, that I'm able to speak.

"Could I see your badge?"

He's quick to take it out, passing it to me and when he does, his fingers brush against mine. The physical contact is a little too close I think at first, but then I peek up at him and he's all business. It's all in my head.

"Sorry, I just didn't expect to see any more cops now that the funeral's passed," I tell him, whipping up the excuse on a dime and praying it explains my hesitation as I pass back his badge. Again his fingers brush mine and although I'm well aware of that fact, he doesn't show any sign that he noticed.

"The funeral?" he questions and I feel the blood drain from my face.

"My sister's; isn't that why you're here?" My voice is calm but drenched in sorrow. Real sorrow. I stand there pretending I know nothing of the past few days but my grief. I think back to what I felt the night my estranged family left me alone and I had to sleep knowing Jenny was really gone. That the world has accepted that, and I needed to as well.

I'm only a sister in mourning. That's all I choose to be right now.

"I'm sorry to hear about your loss." He clears his throat, bringing his closed fist to his mouth as he looks to his right, away from me and then adds, "I'm here on different matters."

Finally, he looks back at me, and at the same time I feel my heart pounding, filling with so much anxiety, it feels as if it will burst.

As I grip the edge of my door, letting him see the nerves and apprehension, he asks, "Do you mind if I come in?"

A second passes as I look past him to his cruiser. The pounding inside my chest intensifies.

I don't know what to do, and I'm terrified to make the wrong decision.

"Is this a bad time?" he asks when I don't answer, his voice carrying my attention back to him.

The light blue eyes that pierce into me tell me it's all right, there's a kindness there, a caring soul somewhere deep inside. A small voice inside my head is screaming at me to tell him about Jase. The voice says I'll be safe. There will be no debt, and all of this will be over.

But a bigger side, the side of me that's taken over, the side I don't recognize, isn't ready for this to end. Already I love being touched by Jase Cross. I crave for that powerful man to use me, and I'm determined to use him in return to get answers.

I can practically hear his sinful voice, luring me into a darkness I may never come out of.

And that's why I tell him, "I'm sorry, it's just a bad time. I wasn't expecting anyone."

The officer nods his head in understanding, but his eyes are assessing and my body tenses. *Just go. Please, go.*

"I'm new here," he tells me. "I came down from upstate New York."

I nod, blinking away the confusion. I anticipated him saying goodbye and apologizing, but instead he shuffles his feet on my porch, shoving his hands into his pockets as he speaks.

"I wanted to come to a smaller city, somewhere with fewer problems and a slower pace."

A genuine, soft sound of amusement comes from me, forcing the semblance of a smile to my lips. "You aren't going to find that here," I tell him.

"So I noticed. Born and raised?" he asks, and I nod.

"My mom moved here when she was pregnant with my sister, before I was born. It was just us three for the longest time."

"Your sister who just passed?" he asks, inflecting his tone with an appropriate amount of sympathy as his voice lowers, and again I only nod. With the small movement comes a pang in my chest. Every reminder of her is like hearing the news that she's missing all over again. Or worse, the news that they found her and my worst fear was realized.

"I'm sorry. I lost my brother a while ago. We were close, so I can understand the loss."

I have to look up to the sky, letting out a slow exhale to keep from tearing up. He doesn't know. No one could know what we went through this past year.

"I'm getting the lay of the land here, and it seems like there may be a bit of trouble from a man who owns a vehicle spotted at your address recently."

My teeth sink into my bottom lip and I try to keep my expression neutral until I can ask, "Who would that be?"

"Jase Cross. His entire family and a few others are associated with murder and drug rings, along with other criminal activity."

Silence.

It's a long moment that passes, a frigid gust of wind traveling between us before I tell him, "Like I said, this isn't a good time for me."

Officer Walsh takes a large step forward, coming close enough to startle me. Staring into my eyes as my lungs are paralyzed, he lowers his voice and says, "I can help you, Bethany. All you have to do is tell me that's what you want."

Thump. Thump.

Staring into his light blue eyes, feeling the authority that comes off him in waves, I can't speak. I only know when I do say something, no matter what I say, there's a very large probability that I'm going to regret the words that come out of my mouth.

CHAPTER
11

Jase

THE DOOR OPENS BEFORE THE KNUCKLES OF MY LOOSELY CURLED FIST can even hit the hard wood. The bite of the cold night nips at my neck at the same time the warmth of Beth's home welcomes me into 34 Holley Drive.

I'm only slightly aware of either, and neither could beckon me inside the way Bethany's eyes do. Wide and cautious, but curious more than anything. In this split second, the way she's breathing, heavy with anticipation—nothing's ever made me so fucking excited.

"Jase." She murmurs my name, but not in a greeting. It's more like an omen.

As I take a step inside, dropping the duffle bag just inside the foyer, she takes a step back, releasing the door and allowing me to close it. It's quiet; the only sound is the foreboding click of the door shutting.

Bethany nervously picks under her nails as she waits silently.

"You scared?" I ask her and she responds with a huff of a sarcastic laugh and the faintest hint of a smile that comes and goes.

"Is that your question?" she asks me and it's then that I catch something's off. Something happened. Squaring my shoulders, I peek behind her. The front hall leads to the kitchen in the back, with the living room to the left and the dining room to the right. It's all quiet, all dark with the exception being the living room.

"If it's my turn to ask a question … who do I remind you of?"

My gaze returns slowly to her. I let it travel down her body, noting that she's in sweats and a baggy t-shirt that reads, *Coffee Solves Everything*.

"No questions yet," I answer her and then brush her thick locks of gently curled hair behind her back. "You need to see what I want from you first."

She leans her weight onto her left heel, tilting her stance and the nervousness wanes some. That's better.

"I think I got a good idea of that last night," she says and tries to hide the breathiness that came with "last night" and the rosy blush that slowly rises to her cheeks.

My smirk kicks up, and a warmth flows through me. I knew she needed it. I knew she'd love to be played with.

Lowering my lips to hers, but just barely keeping our mouths from touching, I look her in the eyes and tell her, "That was hardly a nibble of what's to come."

Instead of stepping back slightly as I expect her to do so I'm not in her space, she stands her ground and shrugs as she replies, "No need to hold back tonight." Her words caress my face, causing a longing desire to travel down my body, all the way to my cock.

Keeping my gaze pinned on her, I stand up straighter and gesture to the living room. "After you then," I offer.

"Not in the bedroom?" she comments under her breath as she walks ahead of me, and I don't hesitate to grab her hip in my left hand and pull her back into my chest. Her yelp of surprise only makes me harder.

With my lips at her ear, I whisper, "The bedroom is reserved for the nights you beg me the second I walk in to fuck that pretty little cunt of yours."

The second the words are spoken, I let her go and she falls forward slightly. Barely catching herself although she plays it off, just like she tried to hide her lust for me as she walks ahead of me. I watch her wide hips sway and grab the black duffle bag I'd dropped by the door.

"What's that?" she asks when she sees it, taking a seat on the sofa easily. As if she's not nervous at all, and that moment a few seconds ago never happened. It's cute that she thinks she's playing hard to get when she's nothing but eager.

"Rope, for starters." Her eyes flash, but she says nothing more.

The bag drops with a thud and as the sound of the zipper opening fills the room, she leans closer, attempting to peek inside.

"Ethanol?" she questions with a hint of hesitancy as I pull out several feet of thin nylon rope.

"I'm not sure we'll need that tonight," I tell her absently as I let the rope fall to a puddle on the floor and move the coffee table out of the middle of the room. It drags along the floor, and in true Beth fashion she focuses on the bag, walking to it and taking into account everything inside.

A bottle of ethanol, a lighter, candles, a torch, balm, four sections of nylon rope, two large flame-retardant blankets, a weighted blanket, and last but not least, a knife.

Her lips purse as she stiffens by the bag. The worst thing that could happen is that I scare her off. I've never wanted anything more than I want this right now.

"Don't be scared," I tell her softly with a bit of humor I know will challenge her.

"I'm not," she bites back, even though she is. I can see it.

"If you could supply a bucket of ice, I think you'll be grateful for that."

At my words, she turns her head slowly toward me.

"What exactly is this?" she asks softly, backing away from the bag.

"I'm going to show you."

Her eyes move to the digital clock and she says, "Eight fourteen…"

"We'll start the clock at eight if you'd like," is all I offer her.

When I stand up, the coffee table now repositioned, her arms are crossed and she's staring down at the bag.

"Your reluctance is understandable, but I promise you, you want this." My last word hisses in the air, the tempting snake that led Eve to the apple.

"I want at least one question answered first," she tells me, lifting her gaze from the bag to meet my own.

"One."

"What kind of business is done at The Red Room?" she asks and a glimmer of a smile pulls at my lips.

"Once you're tied up with your hands behind your head, I'll allow you to ask the question again, and I'll answer it completely."

The skepticism is there, the hesitation, but slowly she stands tall and leaves the living room, heading to the kitchen. Presumably she's getting the ice.

I lay down the first flame-retardant blanket and leave the second within reach.

Beth makes her way back into the room holding a glass wine decanter filled with ice. "I don't have an ice bucket," she admits to me while I'm still on my knees, fixing the corner of the blanket.

"You nervous?" I ask her, reaching for the decanter.

"You fucking know I am." She rushes her words like she can't get them out fast enough, and a deep, rough chuckle leaves me.

"I'm going to need you naked for this," I tell her as I set the ice down next to the folded-up blanket.

"Of course you are," she says skeptically, turning away from me and breathing out deep as she shakes out her hands.

"If you want to stop, it stops. I'll learn your limits. You'll still get your answers and your debt paid." I start with addressing her logical concerns, but move to the other side of her thoughts. "The exotic becomes the erotic. Have you ever heard of that?" I ask her.

"I understand temperature play and that this is meant to be …" she trails off and swallows as she turns to face me, her features riddled with a mix of nervousness and fear. "Why like this?"

"Because I crave this," I admit to her without thinking twice. "It soothes a part of me that isn't easily kept at bay. I will enjoy every second of this. It's worth more to me than secrets and a debt." I didn't realize how much I needed this, how much I coveted her body beneath mine as I brought out the most intense reactions from her until those words were spoken.

Her eyes close and her body trembles.

"Does this excite you?" I ask her and when I do, her hands move under the hem of her baggy shirt, to the top of her sweatpants and she slowly pushes them down, stepping out of them and then opening her eyes.

Her lips part slightly, ready to answer. But she closes herself off, shutting her mouth and balling her hands into fists at her side. Clearing her throat, she looks away and I remind her, "I'll answer your question tonight, the single question. But after tonight, it's tit for tat. Tonight is so you can see what I want."

She nods her head once and then again, standing only feet from me in nothing but her socks and a t-shirt. "Yes, it excites me," she finally answers and as she does, the radiator kicks on behind her, making her jump slightly.

"And it scares you?" I ask, although it's more of a statement. She doesn't waste a second to answer, nodding furiously.

"I don't like not being in control. Tied up and..." She doesn't finish her thought, and swallows thickly.

"You're thinking too much," I tell her and her gaze narrows. All the jitters leave her in that instant and I have to smile. "There you go, just remember how much you hate me and this should be easy."

With her lips pressed in a thin line, she removes her socks first and then reaches behind her back to unhook her bra, revealing a simple white cotton bra with no lace, no frills, no padding.

And with her arms crossed in front of her, she prepares to lift her shirt over her head, but I stand abruptly and stop her, gripping her wrists.

Her skin is hot to the touch.

"I want to do it," I tell her softly. Slowly, she releases her grip on the hem and I circle her, taking my time to observe how the shirt, hitting just below her ass, is more tempting than I'm sure she thought it would be.

"You didn't try to impress me, did you?" I ask, although the light in the room shines off her freshly shaved legs, smooth and glimmering.

"This is business, Cross," she tells me and I simply nod.

"It is."

Making sure not to touch her skin, I grip her hem and lift the shirt above her head, revealing one inch of skin at a time. The movement is achingly slow. Her body quivers as I let a single finger run along her side. The lone touch causes such a strong reaction in her, and it only makes me that much harder for her.

She doesn't look at me; instead she stares straight ahead, but she doesn't cover herself either.

She's fucking beautiful. Every inch of her. From the freckle on her lower stomach, to the pale rose pink of her nipples. Her hips are wide enough to grip during a punishing fuck, and her ass begs me to smack those perfect curves.

Time ticks as I circle her one more time. "You're beautiful," I whisper and the small compliment does wonders in relaxing her stiff posture. "How long has it been since someone's told you that?" I ask her, standing in front of her and allowing my gaze to roam to her hazel eyes.

She blinks and her lashes seem thicker, her lips fuller, her chestnut hair ready to be fisted as I kiss her. Everything about her is fuckable and desirable.

"I don't know," she whispers. Her eyes drift to the blanket and then look back to me. "It's been a long time."

I search her expression for an idea of just how long, but she doesn't give an answer.

"Lie down on the blanket."

Her shoulder brushes my arm as she obeys.

The blanket moves under her slightly, but her entire body is positioned in the center of it.

Using the longest section of the thin rope, I lift up her thighs, making her knees bend so I can lay the middle of the rope under her ass. I secure her hands with the remainder of the rope on either side of her with a simple bondage knot. I'm effectively making sure she won't be able to reach up. Half the rope is knotted around her left wrist where it slips under her thighs, right below her plush ass and the other half is knotted around her right wrist. Perfect.

"I'm going to put a weighted blanket across your ankles," I tell her as I pull it out of the bag, reaching past the sealed bottle of ethanol and one of the two candles.

"Why?" she asks, and I answer easily in an attempt to calm her nerves. "So you'll have a resistance to lifting them up. It'll make everything feel more intense."

With the weighted blanket laying across her ankles, she's bared to me, bound and somewhat calmer than I imagined.

"You fought very little tonight," I note.

"Learning the ropes," she answers softly, opening her eyes for the first time since she looked down and saw the rope twined around her wrists.

"You're going to enjoy this," I tell her, lightly brushing my fingers down her stomach. When I do, I hear the weighted blanket rustle, but her legs stay still, immobilized from the weight. Her shoulders shudder and her head lifts slightly before falling back down into a halo of brunette hair.

"I'm ready for you to answer my question," she says confidently. As if we're in an interview and she's not bound on her living room floor, available for me to do whatever I'd like to her.

Her breasts are perky and full; taking them in my hand, I play with their weight and bend down to suck her nipple into my mouth. I moan around her nipple and then let my teeth drag up them. One, and then the other.

Bethany lets her back arch and her body sways to the side, moving further from me as she puts her weight on her left hip. Pushing her back down on the blanket, I blow across her nipple, chilling the moisture I left there and she sucks in a shuddered breath, her head falling back and a sweet sound of rapture leaving her lips.

"I'm going to take my time touching you, playing with you," I say without acknowledging her earlier remark. "Does that scare you?"

"What are you going to use from the bag?" she asks me and a slight laugh slips from my lips.

"That doesn't answer my question."

"My answer relies on it." Her eyes darken, her pupils dilating as she answers me honestly. I can see the plea in her eyes to not push her boundaries, to not touch the bag of supplies.

She should know better than that.

"Everything, Bethany. I intend on taking full advantage of tonight."

Bethany

I'm scared, I can't deny that. My entire body is alive with both fear and something else. Something sinful.

Every tiny hair on my body, from head to toe, is standing on end.

My nipples have hardened and every touch from Jase sends a trail of goosebumps down my body that makes me shiver with hunger for more.

More of his warm breath on my chilled skin, more of his fingers barely touching my sides as he brings them down to my hips.

But only if he answers me. He'd better fucking answer me. *We have a deal.*

"What kind of business do you do at The Red Room?" I ask him as he turns his attention away from me and reaches to the decanter of ice.

He makes me wait for my answer, but not too long.

"I first created The Red Room as a place to conduct other business. My brother's business, really."

His voice is far too low, too soothing and seductive for the information he's relaying. The ice clinks in the glass before he places a single piece at my lips.

I part my lips, intent on sucking the ice, but he moves it too soon, tracing my lips and then bringing it lower. A cold sensation flows over my skin in a wave.

"Eager thing, aren't you?" he teases me.

"Fuck you." The words come out quickly but his are just as quick as he says, "Only when you beg me, cailín tine." I don't know why he calls me that, *cailín tine*. Or what it means. And I hate that I swallow down my curiosity rather than ask him. But I want him to answer my damn question.

"My brother was dealing. Drugs, guns, all sorts of things," he tells me and my focus returns to the one reason I have to allow this. The one logical reason I'd ever willingly put myself in this situation. *Jenny.*

I ready myself for another question to clarify, but Jase places a finger over my lips. His touch is so hot compared to the ice. "I'm still answering. Let me tell you everything," he whispers.

He runs another cube from the dip just below my throat, down the center of my chest. His hand brushes my breast until he brings the ice farther, all the way to my belly button, circling it and then moving lower still, letting it sit just where my thighs meet.

The ice itself is numbingly cold, sending a spike of awareness through my body. But it's the path that I'm so highly aware of. Each trail leaves a bit of water behind and the air cools it, causing every nerve ending there to prepare to spark.

Even though he lets the ice linger at the top of my pussy, he's quick to repeat the pattern, and I don't know how it's possible, but it makes my body feel even hotter. My toes curl on the third round, and my core heats.

All I can do is turn my head, close my eyes and my fists, and try not to let the ice excite me.

It's an impossible feat, though.

In between every round, he gives me more information, and occasionally asks me insignificant things. Things I don't mind answering, all the while Jase promises to tell me more. It's not quite tit for tat, since he's giving me more and more information about The Red Room and what happened to make it become what it is, all while asking me simple questions that don't require more than one-word answers. But he's gauging how my body reacts when I tell the truth. Taking the time to learn my body. My only response to that is that I'm not a liar. I don't have the time to tell him that though as he continues to feed me information.

"I enjoyed the control. Knowing when and where everyone would meet up. Giving them a space where they could enjoy themselves, and observing them in the meantime. I wanted to know the ins and outs of every partner we had. I wanted their secrets…"

I can barely breathe as he gives me his past so easily, all while bringing the mostly melted ice down farther than he ever has to my pussy, and gently pushing it inside of me. My lips make a perfect O as every nerve ending in my body lights.

He continues his story as my lips part, feeling the rush of desire spark inside of my body. "So we could blackmail them. I used the bar to set everyone up to owe us in some way, or to have information we could use against both our partners and our enemies. In this industry, everyone is an enemy at some point, and we would be ready the second anyone thought they could turn their backs on us."

It's exhilarating.

Both his touch, and the tale of how they rose to power. Creating a place for divine pleasures and allowing everyone to taste, for everyone to fall into their grasp to be controlled and their actions predicted so easily.

He lowers his lips to the crook of my neck, letting his warm breath be at odds with the chill that's slowly melting at my core, being consumed with his criminal touch.

"I sell every addiction possible and I don't have rules within those walls." As he speaks, he pushes his fingers inside of me, dragging them against my front wall and bringing me closer and closer to the peak of an impending orgasm. I close my eyes tight, trying not to give in although I know it's useless. My toes have curled and the pleasure builds inside of me so quickly like a raging storm, unstoppable and demanding its damage be done.

"Every corner of that place is defiled; every square inch has been touched by sin. That's the kind of business I conduct in The Red Room."

My neck arches as I give in to the need, a wave of pleasure rising from my belly outward, followed by another, a harsher, more severe wave crashing through me. I can't move an inch as Jase grips my throat with his free hand and continues to torture me, fucking me with his fingers and drawing out every bit of my orgasm. I wish I could move. I want to get away from the third wave threatening to consume me, but I'm paralyzed as it rages through me.

Every nerve ending in my body ignites, my body shuddering and trembling as my release takes its time, wandering through my body and slowly dissipating. Jase removes his fingers carefully, and I gasp in pleasure as he circles my clit before bringing his fingers to his mouth.

My arousal shines on his fingers as he sucks it off, one by one. I can't bring myself to look away when he groans in sheer delight.

Even as my heart races and adrenaline and excitement race through me, fear freezes my body when Jase picks up a knife from his bag. It's only a pocket knife.

It's just to get the ropes off, I tell myself. It's amazing how the sight of it destroys the previous moment. I close my eyes, waiting to hear the sound of the blade sawing at the rope, but Jase doesn't allow me to.

"I need your eyes open for this. You need to stay still and I don't want the touch to startle you." He sounds so calm and in control as he splays a hand on my chest. His elbow rests on my shoulder and pins me in place as my heart lurches inside of me, ready to escape.

My gaze begs him to explain, to stop, to reconsider whatever he's doing as he brings the knife closer to me.

"It's only to shave the small hairs from your body," he says, answering my unspoken questions. "I won't hurt you," he tells me soothingly as the blade just barely touches my skin. He drags it slowly across my breast, all the way down my mound and then back up, avoiding my sensitive, swollen nub.

"Can I let you go?" he asks me, gently lifting his elbow. "Or are you going to move?"

I can only swallow, I can barely even comprehend what he's saying since the panic is so alive within me.

"If you move, it will cut you," he tells me.

"I'll be still," I whisper and as the blade lowers to my skin I consider the word, stop. So easy to say. I could say it; it's right there, waiting to be spoken. But Jase drags the knife along my chest before I can utter it and then he kisses the sensitized skin. An open-mouth kiss that feels like everything. Like this is the way a kiss is meant to be, and every other way is wrong.

My head's fuzzy and a haze clouds it as he scrapes the knife along my body, leaving a pink path occasionally, but his kisses and the ice make the evidence vanish.

It's all overwhelming and agonizingly slow. By the time he gets to my pussy, I'm on the edge of another release. My impending orgasm is waiting for the knife, for his touch, for a kiss. But it doesn't come.

After the longest time, my body feels his absence and I open my eyes. He pours ethanol onto a rag, then wipes down my body in one swift stroke and before I can say anything, a flame lights on a candle and he lowers it to the ethanol, lighting my skin ablaze.

The scream is trapped in the split second, but before its escape, his hand follows the path, quenching the heat and leaving me wide eyed and breathless.

So hot, and then so cold.

With a pounding heart, I take in the reality. "You lit me on fire."

"No, I lit the alcohol just above your skin on fire." He does it again and this time hot wax drips with it and I suck in a tight breath, my hands turning to fists from the slight pain, the immediate heat, and the cold absence that comes afterward. My head thrashes from side to side as he does it again and again. The pain morphing to unmatched pleasure makes my body feel alive in a way I never knew was possible.

Every climax feels higher and more unbearable than the last. My words fail me as Jase moves down my body, not sparing any inch of my skin.

The alcohol, the fire, his touch. Over and over. He massages the wax onto my breasts before using the knife to pick it off, and the third time he does it, I cum violently.

The pleasure rages through my body with no evidence of it even approaching until the blinding pleasure rocks through me, from my belly to the tip of my toes and fingers.

It's as if my body has rebelled, choosing his touch and this heat over any sense of calm. It prefers the chaos, the unknown, the absence of all control and stability.

With my bottom lip still quivering and my belly trembling as the tremors of the aftershock subside, Jase kisses me, madly and deeply. I feel all of him in this kiss and it kills me that I can't lift my hands up, keeping him where I want him.

I'm at his mercy. Fully and truly, and that very fact plays tricks on me. Telling me I love it. Telling me he knows what I need more than I do.

With every pleasure still ringing in me, he pulls away and stands up, removing his shirt and the light from the candle plays along the lines of his defined muscles. I can see his thick length pressing against his zipper and when he palms it, I have to look away. I'm so close to another orgasm. My clit is throbbing; I feel swollen and used, but he's hardly touched me there.

The sound of a zipper makes me look back at him and the instant I do, his pants, along with his belt, drop to the floor with a clink and a thud and his dick is all I can see.

His girth is so wide I'm not sure I could wrap my hand around him. I can practically feel the veins pressing against my walls and pulling every ounce of pleasure from me, practically imagine his rounded head sliding back and forth over my clit. Oh my God. He's massive. He grabs his cock and rubs the glistening precum over the head and that's when I lose it.

Cumming again, and he didn't even touch me. That's how much power he has over me. Just the thought of what he could do to me, how he could ruin me, how he is so much more than any boy I ever thought of letting touch me... all of it is fuel that ignites a raging fire inside.

Jase groans deep in the back of his throat, dropping to the floor so quickly and so hard, I know it will leave bruises on his knees. "Cum again," he commands me breathlessly, leaning over my body to kiss and bite the crook of my neck as he pushes three fingers inside of me and ruthlessly fucks me with them.

The waves of my last release have barely left me when the next orgasm crashes through me, harder and higher than any of those before. My scream is silent, my body stiff as it commands attention from all of me. My body, my soul.

And Jase doesn't stop, even as my arousal leaks down my ass, he continues. Even as I feel myself tighten around his fingers, he doesn't stop.

I can't. I can't take it. I can't breathe.

I can't move. I can't speak.

I'm helpless and consumed by fire and lust.

I try to focus on Jase when he whispers in my ear, but my body won't stop shaking and my neck is rigid. "When you look at me, know this is what I want from you. Only I can give you this." His words hiss in the air, crackling and demanding to be burned in my memory.

Jase Cross destroyed me and what I thought was pleasure.

And where I thought my boundaries lied with him.

CHAPTER
12

Bethany

MY EYES OPEN QUICKLY, THE DARKNESS CONSUMING ME EXCEPT FOR the moonlight from the bedroom windows. My heart's racing and it's then that I realize the trembling isn't a dream. I can't stop shaking and I'm so fucking cold.

"Shhh." Jase's voice is anything but calming. After the initial shock of realizing he's in bed with me, I barely turn around before the bed groans and he pulls the weighted blanket up and around my entire body.

Frantically I try to recount it all, every moment that I can remember.

"What did you do to me?" I ask, and the question comes out viciously. I'm fucking freezing, and I can't stop trembling.

"I brought you to bed," he says lowly, a threat barely there, warning me to be careful but fuck that.

"What did you do?" The words are torn from my throat. It's not even the fear that's the most overwhelming. As my throat dries and a sinking sensation in my stomach takes over, I look him in the eyes and realize how much trust I had in him. It wasn't just business. I gave up more than I should have, and he did something to me. He hurt me.

How could you? I want to say the words, but I can't bear to bring them up and admit to the both of us that I thought he wouldn't hurt me. That I was that fucking naïve.

Jase's arm is heavy and pulls me closer to him, even though I attempt to push him away as he says, "It's just the endorphins crashing." Although his words are drenched with irritation, there's something else there, something buried deep down low in his words that I can't decipher. "You're okay," he nearly whispers and then pulls me in closer, dragging my ass to his groin, my back to his chest and nuzzling the nape of my neck with the tip of his nose. "It's okay, I've got you."

His voice is a calming balm. Even as I continue to shake. As my fingers feel numb and then like they're on fire. Cold again. "I'm so cold."

I almost expect my confession to turn to fog in front of me. Like warm breath in the winter air.

"You were on a high," Jase tells me and then presses his arm against mine, pushing it closer to me and acting as if I'm not trembling uncontrollably. "It's all coming down. I thought you may have a little aftershock. That's why I stayed," he explains.

Aftershock. Endorphins.

He didn't drug me. It's not drugs. I can barely swallow for a long moment, trying to make it stop, but my body's not listening.

"Does this happen all the time?" I ask him, attempting to let go of the anger, swallowing my regret that I immediately assumed the worst of him. It was my first instinct, and shame hits me hard as I realize he did quite the opposite.

I'm a bitch. I am an asshole. An embarrassed asshole.

With sleep lacing his words he tells me, "Not often, but I imagine that was your first?" and I instantly clench my legs. Remembering the ice, the cold, his touch, the fire.

My shoulders beg to buck forward, my eyes closing at the memory and the heat flourishing in my belly.

"Was it?" he teases me, nipping my neck and just that small touch threatens to push me over again.

"I can't," I say, and the words leave me in a single breath. A single plea. Instantly a chill creeps up my neck, the open air finding its place there as Jase moves his head to the other pillow.

A shaky breath leaves me as I turn my head to peek at him, craning my neck as my back is still positioned firmly against his chest. "Did we have sex?" I ask him, feeling a weight press down on my chest.

Jase merely gazes back at me. The depths of his dark eyes deepen as I stare into them. Licking my lower lip first, I explain, "I don't remember everything."

"We didn't. No," he answers me, and his expression remains guarded. "I told you, you'd have to beg me for it."

His warmth calms me and slowly I stop trembling as hard. Very slowly, but the tremors are still there.

"For all I know, I did tell you to fuck me," I tell him.

"You could barely look at me, let alone speak."

"Holy shit," I murmur beneath my breath.

"When I fuck you, trust me when I say you'll remember it."

His words force a shiver of pleasure through me when I remember I saw ... I saw *all* of him. "Why am I shaking so much?"

"From you getting off so many times. Your body can only handle so much."

"I can't believe it can feel like that," I say, thinking out loud.

"Sometimes the things that cause you pain can bring you so much pleasure."

"Not everything that brings you pain." The hollowness in my chest expands at my thought, drifting to darker places.

The shaking and trembling stop altogether, but Jase doesn't let me go and I'm happy for that. There's so much comfort in being held right now.

"Tell me something," I ask Jase, resting my cheek into the pillow, feeling the warmth come back to me and the lull of sleep ready to pull me under once again.

"Tell you something?" He ponders and then readjusts on the bed, making it shake slightly. "What do you want to know?"

"Anything," I answer as my eyelids fall heavily without second-guessing and my eyes pop open wider, remembering all the bits and pieces he told me about The Red Room. "Maybe about your brothers?"

Once again Jase's lips find my neck, and this time he leaves an open-mouthed kiss there. I'm starting to love those kinds of kisses. I think they're my favorite. "I had four brothers, now I have three and I recently learned that my younger brother, the one I was closest with..." He hesitates and again that small space on my neck feels the prickle of the air instead of his warmth. "I found out his death wasn't an accident; it was murder. And it was supposed to be me, not him."

"Oh my God," I whisper, completely shocked. My heart breaks in half for him. I know the pain of losing a sibling, the agony of blaming yourself. But knowing it was supposed to be you instead? "I'm so sorry." I put every ounce of sincerity into my words and pray it doesn't come out the way everyone else says, like the people who say it simply because they don't know what else to say. "I'm really sorry."

Jase doesn't say anything at all. Not for a while until he requests the same from me. "Tell me something."

"I can't figure you out, Jase," I answer him almost immediately.

"You already know who I am, cailín tine. Don't let me fool you."

I look over my shoulder to ask him, "What's that mean? Cailín tine?"

He gives me one of those smirks, but it's almost sad and short lived. "Fiery girl."

My entire body betrayed me earlier, and so does my heart in this moment, beating just for him with a warmth I've never felt before.

As I nuzzle back down into the pillow, I remember Officer Walsh and I spit out the words before I hide them forever. "A cop came asking about you today. He knocked at my door."

Nerves prick down my neck, but Jase's touch remains soothing and his voice calm when he asks, "What was his name?"

"Cody Walsh," I answer and then feel Jase's nod as his nose runs along my neck.

"He won't be a problem. He's just new."

"Don't you want to know what I told him?"

"If you want to tell me."

"I didn't tell him anything."

His response is to kiss my neck. Then my jaw. He tries to lie back down, leaving my lips wanting but I take them with my own. Reaching up to grip the back of his neck, and pulling myself off the comfort of the bed.

It's a quick kiss, but it was mine to have. And mine to give.

"What was that for?" he asks me, and I answer him honestly. "I wanted you to have it."

Turning my back to him, I lie back under the covers. There are no more questions or conversations. With my eyes wide open, I pretend to sleep. After a short while, the bed protests under the weight of him moving, the covers are shrugged off behind me and I listen to him leave. Across the wooden floorboards, down the stairs. I can only faintly hear him in the living room, but I recognize the sound of the front door opening and closing.

All the while, there's this vise wrapped around my heart. Keeping it still, not allowing it to move the way it used to.

CHAPTER
13

Jase

"WHAT HAPPENED TO HER? TO JENNIFER PARKS?"

Seth hesitates. Seated across from me, he slides forward to readjust before leaning back into an auburn leather armchair. It's silent in the back of The Red Room. Not a single beat of the music or murmur of the guests makes its way through these doors.

Nothing makes it out of them either.

It's a decadent but vacant space. A simple, but too-fucking-expensive iron and driftwood desk with no drawers stands in the middle of the room. My chair is at one end, while two matching chairs are on the other side. Not a damn thing else in the room.

The stubble on my jaw is rough; I'm way past due for a shave as I run my hand along my jaw as I wait for Seth's answer.

"I'm still working on it, but let me tell you what I've got so far."

"Are you fucking kidding me?" The rage is inexplicable as I slam the edge of my fist down on the desk. It jolts and I clench my jaw, hating that something like this can get to me.

I focus on calming my shit down, ignoring the irritation and Seth's questioning gaze.

All day I've been on edge. Ever since I left Bethany's place, the second the sun rose.

"It goes deeper than you think, Boss." His voice is low, testing my patience and apologetic even.

"Let me have it," I speak and gesture for him to get going.

"She went missing on December twenty-eighth, but before then she was in and out of her sister's home and several friends' places. It was January seventeenth that the burned remains, including several of her teeth, were found in a trunk at the bottom of the Rattle River on the west side of town."

I remember the flash of an image I found myself, searching through the archives at the downtown station hard drive. It was all the information Kent, one of the detectives we keep on our payroll, had to give.

"Fucking brutal," I murmur. The remains were charred, but some of the bones were broken before being burned.

"She was tortured, but time of death couldn't be determined."

"I already know this. Get to something I don't know."

He starts to speak, but before he can even suck in the air needed for the first word, I ask, "Did you find anything on the sister?"

My fingers rap on the desk, one at a time with brief pauses, one after the other. As if it's only a casual conversation.

"Bethany Fawn?"

At my nod, he begins. "Jennifer was born out of wedlock to a Catherine Parks. Shortly after her birth, her mother and father got hitched, then conceived Bethany. Not long after her birth, the father took off. Leaving their mom with no job, a toddler and an infant."

"Where did he go?"

"Nebraska, where he died of a heart attack in a casino three years ago."

"Did they keep in touch?"

"Not a word," Seth answers professionally, but his eyes are questioning.

"Go on."

"Bethany Fawn, the younger of the two, did well in school. And it seems like that was all she was interested in. She's a nurse on the psych ward at Rockford. She's worked there since she graduated. Apparently her mother had issues in the last years of her life and she chose this path because of it. Her sister--"

"What issues?" Again, I cut him off midbreath.

"Alzheimer's."

"How old was she?"

"Bethany? Twenty. Her mother was fifty-two when she died."

I watched my mother die slowly, but I was young. Cancer is a bitch. I can only imagine being more aware and having to go through that. Being old enough to understand. Back when I was a kid, I was sure Mom was going to get better. Knowing there is no getting better and having to watch someone you love slowly die? That's a cruel way to live. A cruel way to die as well. But that's life, isn't it?

"One thing you may find interesting is that she was spotted with you recently," Seth says and sits back further in his seat. It's the only note on her in the entire department. *"A possible associate."*

"And who put that in? Our new friend, Walsh?" I surmise.

"You got it," he says and snaps his fingers. "And you two aren't the only ones doing some digging. Miss Fawn's search history is interesting … limited, but interesting."

"Is that right?" I ask, bringing my thumb up to run along my chin.

"Little Miss Fawn was looking you up and Officer Walsh after he paid her a visit."

I shrug impatiently, and Seth continues.

"She didn't find much, obviously, since there's nothing on the internet to find… although it seems she's interested in Angie. She's searching for pictures of her, doesn't look like she knows her name. *Jase Cross with brunette. Jase Cross lover. Jase Cross date.* Things like that."

"Angie?" The only piece of information that surprises me so far is this. "Why?"

"I guess she saw her with you in pictures online. But she doesn't have her name, or any information on her."

Who do I remind you of? I remember her question last night. That's why.

"Shit." I breathe out the word. "Anything else?" I ask him, ignoring the dread, the regret, the deep-seated hate for myself because of everything that happened four years ago. All of those ghosts belong in the past. They can stay there too.

Seth passes me a folder; opening it up reveals six profiles. All are of women in their late twenties, and two I recognize from the club. Jennifer is the first. The second is Miranda. She's gotten thrown out a handful of times. Too high to know she was messing with the wrong guys. Causing problems that aren't easy to fix.

"She ran with quite a crowd," I comment as I sift through the papers, reading one charge after the next and notes about the men they each were associated with. Men I don't trust or like.

"You could say that. It was all recent though. She only came into the scene this past year," Seth comments and leans back in his seat. The leather protests as he does. "College grad who struggled to keep a job after school. Taking one after the next. All had nothing to do with her degree."

"Quit or fired?"

"She quit them all. Everyone I talked to said they loved her, but they knew she wasn't going to stay long. It wasn't *interesting* enough for her," he says but forms air quotes around the word "interesting."

"You think that's why she quit them? Boredom?"

"I'm guessing she just needed to pay her bills." He shrugs. "From what I gather she was eccentric and wanted to solve the world's problems. The last job she had was working at The Bistro across the turnpike."

That particular information catches my attention and I look up from the papers to see Seth nodding. "Romano's place?"

"The one and only."

Just hearing that name makes me grit my teeth. "He's a dead man." My throat tightens as I speak. All I can see when I hear the word Romano is the picture of Tyler, dead on the wet asphalt; the water soaked into my hoodie he wore that day.

It was supposed to be me.

"Damn right," Seth says and I check my composure. Refusing to let that fuck get in the way of this conversation.

"So, The Bistro," I say to push Seth to continue the conversation, picking at the pages in the folder, and trying to rid my mind of the sight of Tyler. He was a good kid. That's the worst part. No one really deserves to die, but if anyone in this world could have been spared, it should have been him.

Tossing the folders down onto the desk, I lean back, letting the information sink in. "So she's got debt from college, can't get the right job yet so she's bouncing around to pay the bills. She lands a job at The Bistro and something there's leading these girls down a dark path.

"We have eyes down there; what'd they say?" My voice rises on its own, demanding information.

Seth winces slightly before telling me, "You aren't going to like this."

"Don't be a little bitch," I tell him, losing my patience.

"They said she was there and gone. She was friendly and nice, but then up and quit. Miranda was working there at the same time and quit with her. No reason. She didn't stand out and nothing did about the two of them leaving. Just two open waitress spots to fill when they left."

"So they've got nothing?" I ask as my heart rate rapidly increases and the blood rushes in my ears. "We have a group of women," I enunciate each word and Seth takes the opportunity to butt in.

"Two of them working there at the same time and quitting at the same time," he adds and I meet his gaze, daring him to interrupt me again.

"A group of women with no prior history of any of this bullshit, getting hooked on some shit, all of them racking up charges in the past year and some of them stepping foot into my club. And you're telling me the boys we're paying to watch that shithole have no fucking idea what happened, or who influenced this shit?" I slam the bottom of my oxfords again on the inside of my walnut desk, kicking it as hard as I can on impulse. Needing to get out the rage. My muscles are tense, my body's hot and I need to beat the shit out of something.

I have no fucking impulse control, no restraint today. Not a damn thing keeping me under control.

Moving my chair back into place, I set my elbows on my desk, lower my head and smooth my hand over the back of my neck.

"I'm losing my patience," I tell him. Staring at my desk, I admit the obvious. "I don't like not having answers when I want them. She's one girl. A girl we've seen; a girl we've watched before. We should know who the fuck killed her and why."

Seth grips the armrest, looking away from me, toward the blood-red leather walls that line the room.

"It's like someone's hiding it," Seth speaks quickly.

"Hiding?"

"I can't find a damn thing on her after she started working there other than what we had already with the sweets," he says, and his frustration grows with each word.

"We know she was buying our shit in bulk, high on what was obviously coke. She gave the name of a fake brother when we questioned her, that was early December. Then there's not a trace of her."

"She ever come back after that night?" I ask him. I remember that night. Carter came down here, looking for answers about his drug. It hardly sold shit, it's something that puts you to sleep. We only push it on addicts that can't handle any more. It knocks their asses out as they go through withdrawal. They always come back though, but never for the sweets.

Not until recently.

"No. She never came back and the demand for the sweets dropped simultaneously."

"She was buying for someone," I remark. "Someone who backed off when they found out we were onto them…. maybe that's who did this? He wanted her silenced so there were no loose threads?"

"It's not Romano, we have ears on him, we would know. I've been through every fucking recording from December twenty-seventh to the fucking week she was discovered. He didn't say a word about it. I don't think she's on his radar."

"So it's just a fucking coincidence that all her shit starts going downhill when she starts working for him?" I raise my finger, feeling the lines in my forehead deepen with anger.

"He got her hooked; I think he did. Or someone there did. I think that's when it started, but her dying… whoever it was, they got to her at his place, and Romano doesn't know about it or even realize someone's taking those girls from him."

The pieces of the puzzle fall slowly into place, giving me the rough edges of a watered-down image someone doesn't want me to see.

"It would be easy if it was Romano; he's already a dead man."

"As soon as this new cop is off our fucking backs, he's dead," I tell him, opening up the folder again to see Jennifer's profile on top and Beth's name listed as her only living relative staring back at me in black and white. "If Officer Cody Walsh doesn't watch his step," I say and lift my gaze from Beth's name, where the tips of my fingers still linger to tell Seth, "he's a dead man too."

CHAPTER
14

Bethany

The Coverless Book

Third Chapter

I'm pretending not to be tired. Like the weight and pull of sleep isn't a constant battle tonight. Every day after seeing the doctor, it's like this. Well, every day for the past five years except today. Today will be the exception, because of Jake. He makes me smile, and just smiling reminds me I still have so much left in me.

"I'm really happy you do this for me," I tell Jake, pulling the blanket around my shoulders a little tighter. We're having a picnic in the backyard over-looking the hill. The spring air brings a strong scent of lilac and I breathe it in. As much as I can, and for as long as I can.

This is what living feels like.

"The soups were perfect," he comments and adds, "I didn't know it'd get this cold at night."

"The summer nights are warmer," I tell him easily and then feel embar-rassed. Of course they are, I think inwardly and my stomach stirs with nerves.

"We'll have to do it again in summer then."

The nerves turn to something else and they spread higher up to my chest at Jake's words.

"I'd really like that." I almost whisper the words and then have to clear my throat. As he picks two blades of grass, no doubt to whistle with them again like he showed me earlier, I take a chance.

"Maybe even before summer?" I ask him and lean close to nudge his shoulder with mine. Just a nudge, then I sit back upright, but he's quick to nudge mine against his.

"Definitely before summer too."

Time passes and the sun sets too quickly. I know time is almost up, and that's so bittersweet.

"Are you really sick? Like... like, sick sick?" Jake's question pulls the smile from my face in a single swoop. And the nerves settle back in my stomach. I pick two blades of grass, thinking maybe I could whistle too. But instead I let them fall, and the wind takes them.

"The doctor said I was sick years ago..." Instead of letting any bit show of what I felt that day Mama cried and cried in the car, I actually let out a small laugh. It's only a huff of laughter. Even though I'd like to pretend I'm not affected by the pain of the memory, my eyes gloss over.

"Why are you laughing?" Jake sounds truly concerned, and I'm quick to put a reassuring hand over his. That small move changes everything. The electric spark, the sudden heat. I'm quick to take my hand back.

"Sorry, it's just a little joke I tell myself," I explain, shaking off both the memories and the touch with a quick sip of water.

"What do you tell yourself?" he asks skeptically as I set the cup down. I can't take my hand off of it as I nervously peek at him and answer, *"That I'm invincible."*

His smirk is slow to form, but it grows quickly, turning into a grin. *"I like that."*

His smile is contagious, and I find myself telling him, *"I like that you like it."*

I'm still biting down on my bottom lip and hoping I'm not blushing too hard when he looks me in the eyes and responds, *"I like you, Emmy. I think I more than like you."*

Three days came and went. I got lost in the pages of The Coverless Book, falling in love with both Emmy and Jake, rooting for them as he fell in love with her and she with him. I spent all of yesterday checking in with my patients at work before Aiden told me that wasn't what my leave was for. I spent every waking hour trying to occupy my thoughts and time. All so I wouldn't think about Jase Cross or my sister, and every moment in the months that I lost her.

Every moment I wish I could have changed.

Between the two, I thought about Jase the most. Because it felt better to think of him than her. Choosing pleasure over pain.

Three days went by, and I thought of him every morning and every night. I started to think I'd made it all up because I didn't hear from him, not one word. Not until this afternoon when I got a text from a number I didn't know, giving me an address signed with "J." Followed shortly by the number of hours we'd already spent together. Eleven. I imagine he must've included the time he was in bed with me. One hundred dollars every ten minutes, six hundred dollars an hour, so I've barely made a dent in the time I owe him.

And I haven't gotten anywhere. I have no new information that sheds light onto what happened to Jenny. He says he didn't do it; I already knew The Red Room was a place for drug deals and a criminal hangout.

Nothing new. Time is stagnant and I can't hold on much longer. I can't rely on someone who isn't coming through.

I made it down the long winding path around the massive estate and parked in the back where Jase told me to; I made it all that way without breathing.

Maybe that's why I feel faint as I shut my car door, the thud echoing in the depths of the thick forest I stared into only days ago. The dark greens are covered by a slight dusting of white as the snow falls gently, creeping into the crevices of everything.

Pulling my scarf a bit tighter, I take the steps one by one to the front door.

Answers. I will get answers. Even if it's only one question at a time. *He has to know something.*

The bite from the wind creeps up quickly as I raise my fist to knock on the door, only to hear a beep and a click before I even touch it. Someone else grants me entry. *He already knows I'm here.*

Warily, I push the large, carved wooden door open, and it glides easily with the softest of pushes.

Thump. My heart slams as I remember the last time I gazed at this wood, but the engravings were upside down as I dangled from Jase's shoulder.

It's only been days, but it feels like everything's changed.

The massive foyer greets me with warmth, but not much else. The lighting of the wrought iron chandelier reflects on the shiny marble floor, radiating wealth with the spiral staircase, but that's all this room contains. It's empty and even in the warmth, even coming in from the blustery weather, it's cold in here.

Click.

The door shuts behind me, and the small sound startles me. My quick gasp echoes in the room.

Clenching my fists, I inwardly scold myself. *Pull it together.*

He's only a man. A man with answers. A man who will bring me justice. Justice Jenny deserves.

A man who is not here. I have no idea where he is. But I'm alone in the foyer.

My lips purse as I breathe out, letting my heavy bag drop to the floor. It's topped with the weighted blanket Jase left.

My gaze moves from window to window, to the heavy front door.

I can't help but to test Jase's statement. That the doors are locked on the inside and there's no way out. Something about Jase makes me feel like he wouldn't lie. Like he doesn't make threats, only promises of what's to come.

I think it's the severity of his presence. The confidence in his banter. Everything is always just so with him. It's how he wants it to be, and everything is exactly that. How he wants.

It's the impression he gives me and that impression is why I pull off my gloves and shove them in my coat pocket. Gripping the knob with both hands, I turn and pull. I yank it harder when it doesn't give, feeling the stretch in my arms from tugging on an unmoving door.

Huffing the stray hair out of my face, I glance up at a small black square, smaller than the size of a sheet of notebook paper. It's digital. Whatever lock he uses, it's digital.

"Fingerprints and hand scans," Jase's voice bellows from the empty hall behind me, forcing me to whip around to face him, my hand on my chest. "That sort of thing," he adds, slipping his hands into his pockets.

"Jesus fuck," I gasp with contempt. "Are you trying to give me a heart attack?"

My heart thumps a *yes*, my core clenches with affirmation and my gaze drifts down his body, agreeing with the two of them.

He's not wearing a suit today. And he looks damn good in his perfectly fitted suits. In jeans and a t-shirt stretched tight across his shoulders, showing off those corded muscles in his arms... he's doing that shit on purpose.

Swallowing down my heart, I try to relax again. "Just testing what you said..." My explanation dies in the air as he stalks closer to me with powerful strides and in a dominating way that almost has me stepping back, bumping my ass into the door. Almost, but I hold my ground.

"Well then, I'm relieved you weren't leaving already," he comments, the words spoken lowly as he stops right in front of me.

The air between us crackles like a roaring fire.

How does he do this to me?

"I like it better when you're an asshole," I speak without thinking. I'm rewarded with a charming smile, and a deep rough chuckle.

"I'll remember that, cailín tine." Holding out his hand, he commands me, "Come."

As I reach for my purse, Jase leans down, grabbing the handle before I can. His blanket is in plain sight on top and before I can speak, he comments, "You could have kept it with you; it may help you sleep."

One step in front of the other I follow him, with only the sounds of our footsteps keeping us company while I try not to think too much about what he said and why.

He doesn't care about my sleep.

He doesn't care about how I'm feeling.

He wants to get his dick wet. He wants to tie me up and do with me what he wishes.

All of this is simply to keep me amenable.

Jase Cross may have the upper hand, but I'm doing this for me.

The echoes of my footsteps get louder in the narrow corridor as I think, *I'm doing this for Jenny.*

One step, one beat of my heart, one tick of the clock.

I have my questions lined up in a pretty row. Without warning, Jase halts and unlocks a door, but how? I don't know. It simply clicks the moment he stops in front of it and with a flick of the handle, it opens.

I've never seen wealth like this before. And I imagine it shows in my expression, judging by the smug look on Jase's face when he opens the door wider and says, "After you."

"Where would you like me?" I ask him the moment he opens the door and I step in before taking a look. "Oh," I murmur, and the word leaves my lips without my conscious consent.

The click of the door closing behind me is followed by a dull thud of a lock, some sort of lock, moving into place.

My belly flips in a way I don't understand. Almost like when you're driving down a hill too fast, or on a roller coaster. The anticipation of the fall, the sudden drop of reality making your stomach somersault.

As I spot the table in the middle of the room, that's exactly what I feel. Followed by the same exact cold prickling I remember so well from three nights ago traveling along my skin.

"What do you think?" Jase asks me, and at the same time he reaches up to my shoulders to take my coat. I anticipate the feel of his fingers trailing along my skin as he does, but he's careful not to touch me. I think he does it on purpose.

I think he does more things with intent than I first realized.

"It's not at all like your foyer," I comment and then drag my eyes back to the wooden bench in the middle of the room. It's at odds with the large plush carpet that takes up most of the space. I have to look out further to the edge to note that under it is a barn wood floor, or something like it. A darker wood, with wide planks. The cream rug is the brightest thing in here, and thank goodness it's large. Even with the three chandeliers at varying heights with a mix of iron and wood, the room has a soft, airy feeling. Dim and romantic even.

As my coat falls off my shoulders, I take a half step forward and touch the wall. It's a thick wallpaper in a damask cream, but it's darkened by the blood-red pattern within it.

Besides the bench and a matching dresser, there's a whiskey-colored leather chaise lounge and a white crystal fireplace that would certainly be the focus, if not for the wooden bench dead smack in the center of it all.

With the flick of a switch from behind me, I hear the gas turn on and the fireplace roars to life. Jase's hand is still on the switch when I peek behind my shoulder.

I dare to step forward and touch the edge of the wooden bench, noting it's lined with padding upholstered in a soft black leather.

"It's beautiful. It's primitive and raw. Elegant, yet seductive in a way that borders on decadence."

He doesn't respond to my comment, although his eyes never leave me as I walk around the table. "The wood won't catch on fire?" I ask him, remembering how the flames felt like they consumed everything. I've never felt so alive.

"It's for fucking, not fire play." Jase's words come with authority and a heat that could match that raging from the fireplace behind me.

My lungs still as I'm pinned by his gaze. "Is that what you think you'll be doing today?"

Thump, thump, thump. The pace picks up.

"I think you'd enjoy it and my temperament hasn't been… appropriate. I'd appreciate a good fuck."

"I can say no," I remind him, feeling the warring need to give in, to have it all, and to keep my head on straight.

"You could." His dismissive nature would piss me off if it weren't for the way he looks at me. Like he can see right through me, but he doesn't want to. He wants to see *me*.

"I don't fuck every man I find attractive. Even if I'm willing to admit," I pause a moment, wondering if I should say it out loud. It brings the truth to life when you speak it, but he already knows. This cocky bastard is well aware of what's between us. "Even if I'm willing to admit there's chemistry between us and I like what you do to me. If it weren't for the fact that I have questions and a debt you're holding over my head… I wouldn't give you the time of day."

The heat sizzles between us, although the nerves rack through my body. He intimidates me. Maybe it's something I hadn't admitted to myself before, but in this moment, as he stares down at me, making me wait for a response, I'm so sincerely aware of how much he intimidates me.

"Business then?" Jase asks with an arched brow; his expression doesn't hold a hint of emotion, or amusement. He's a man in control and nothing more.

Standing toe to toe with him, I swallow as I nod. "It's business."

"I have the first question, you have the next." He speaks as he turns his back to me and strides to the dresser, laying my coat over the top of it. He stands there a second too long. The silence is only broken by the pop of the fire to the left of him. The bright light sends shadows down the side of him, and when he turns around those shadows make his jawline seem sharper, his eyes darker and every inch of his exposed skin looks taut and powerful.

He exudes raw masculinity.

"Strip." He gives the command and whatever hint of defiance had come over me flees in an instant.

I have to lean down to unzip my leather boots, then slip them off. I'm ashamed to say I put more effort into this outfit than a woman with self-respect would. The dark denim skinny jeans take a little more effort to shimmy out of, and all the while Jase stands there with his muscular arms crossed in front of him as he leans against the dresser, watching in silence.

I can't even look at him as I second-guess everything in this moment.

I'm not a whore, but that's exactly what I feel like. I can't pretend it's anything else.

When I'm left in nothing but my silk undershirt and lace bra, both covered by an oversized, cream cashmere sweater, Jase's steps destroy the distance between us. It only takes three steps until he's in front of me, his hands at the hem of my sweater. I'm quicker than he is, my hands wrapping around his powerful wrists. My arms are locked and my nails nearly dig into his flesh as I glare into his prying gaze.

"I can do it myself," I say, pushing the words through clenched teeth.

"I'm paying very well for this time with you. I intend to enjoy every minute. If you'd like for it to stop, you know how to tell me just that."

There's no reason I should feel a sudden stab of emotions up my throat, drying it and tightening it. Or the hollowness that grows in my chest.

"It's just business, isn't it?" he questions and with another thump of my treacherous heart, I release his wrists, waiting for him to undress me like he wishes.

Whore. Whore is the first word that comes to mind, and how I made it this long without feeling like one is beyond me.

"May I ask a question then? I know you have yours first, but I'd like to ask one, if you'll … allow it." I keep my tone professional as I can, holding back the desire to smack my hand across his arrogant, handsome face.

Jase doesn't touch my sweater. Instead he walks around me to stand behind me, leaving only the fire for me to look at. His voice hums a "mm-hmm" behind me. His chest is so close to my back, I can feel the vibrations of it, even if he's not touching me.

"Are you looking in to who did that to my sister? If she owed anyone anything?" My words waver in the air and I wish I could hold them steady. I wish I could sound as strong as I feel on my best of days. Not in this moment, not when I'm acutely aware that I'm whoring myself out to this arrogant bastard who could be using me, lying to me and toying with me just for his own sick pleasure. All so I can chase the ghost of whoever hurt my sister. Whoever took her from me.

"I already told you I was." His answer is clear and lacks the arrogance and dismissiveness he's given me so far today. I don't have to ask him to expand on his answer, since he does that himself. "Her death has caused ripple effects. When I have a name and a reason, you will too."

I can't help that I flinch when he lays a hand on my shoulder. I can't control the way I feel, and I struggle to hide that from him.

I'm so alone. In a room with this man I've been thinking about for days, I feel so fucking alone. Maybe I made the memory of that night more than what was actually there.

I stare at the flames lingering among the pure white crystals. I let them mesmerize me and tell myself I don't have to go through with this. I don't have to rely on Jase Cross.

But the alternative crushes me; I can't risk never knowing what happened and having to say goodbye without giving her justice.

His left hand finds my hip and he rubs soothing circles there over the sweater. Which only makes me hate him more until he lowers his lips to my ear and whispers, "Does it make a difference to you... if I admit I feel that chemistry too? That I have a desire to be near you?"

With a gentle kiss on my neck, that hard wall around me cracks and crumbles.

"It's no longer only business for me, cailín tine."

His words are a soothing balm. One I didn't realize I needed. My hand covers his, and I lean back into his chest, where he holds me. This man holds me because he wants to do just that. And I lean into him, because I want to do just that.

"I like it when you touch me," I whisper into the room, hoping it will keep my secret.

"And I like touching you," he says softly and runs the tip of his nose down the back of my neck, causing my eyes to close, my head to loll to the side and the pain to drift away slowly.

I don't want to be alone. I almost speak the realization aloud.

"I promise you, I will find out who hurt her." His words cause my eyes to open and when they do, I stare at the fire as Jase pulls my sweater over my head. It falls to the floor and then he whispers against the shell of my ear, "I will make them pay for what they did. And you will know every detail."

CHAPTER
15

Jase

WHEN SHE TURNS IN MY ARMS, I DON'T EXPECT HER TO DEVOUR me with a kiss full of need and hunger. She can only hold up the hate routine for so long before her arms get weak and tired, and her body gives in to what it needs.

Pressing her lips to mine and spearing her fingers through my hair, she pulls me lower to her, standing on her tiptoes and holding her body against mine.

My tongue dives into her hot mouth, feeling the heat and need and lust she has to offer.

Her head falls back so she can breathe, deep and chaotically. I don't need air. I need to devour her.

With my arms wrapped around her and my lips traveling down her neck, down her bare shoulder, I take in every inch of her. Inhaling her sweet scent, memorizing the alluring sounds she lets slip from her lips. Dragging my teeth back up her neck, I hear her hiss my name, "Jase."

"Make me forget," she whimpers against my lips before I can ravage her.

Make me forget.

I don't speak the only response I can give her. *I will, if you do the same for me.*

Slamming my lips against hers, I grab her ass and lift her into my arms. Her legs straddle my waist as I carry her to the table.

Her hips need to be nestled against the padding, and the strap is meant to keep her in place. But I have no time for any of it. The urgency of our heated kiss fuels a primitive side of me with the need to have her under me as soon as possible.

With her heels digging into my ass, spurring me on, I groan in the hot air between us, "I need to be inside of you."

Her lips part, and I can almost hear her say the words. I know what she's going to say before she says it, *I need you too.*

But her gaze lingers, time pauses and the truth is lost in a haze of want and need.

Instead she kisses me, long and deep. Massaging my tongue and taking everything she wants with our kiss.

With her ass supported by the bench, I unbutton and unzip my jeans, letting them fall as I stroke my cock.

"I need you," she whispers into my mouth and then kisses me reverently again.

She's already wet, but so tight. Pushing two fingers inside of her, I stretch her until she can take three. "Your cunt was made for me to fuck," I tell her as I drag my knuckles against her front wall.

Her grip on the edge of the table nearly slips as her pussy spasms around my fingers.

I don't stop fucking her until her release is passed and her chest heaves for air and her face is flushed.

"Flip over," I command her but it's unneeded. I take the task on myself, gripping her hips and butting them against the bench.

Moving the head of my cock to her core, I press against her gently, not pushing in just yet.

A deep groan leaves me as I bend over her, my chest against her back. "You feel so fucking good," I whisper against her and just as she lifts her head to respond, I slam myself inside of her. Every inch of me in one swift stroke.

Her mouth drops open with a scream and her nails dig into the wood. Fuck, she's tight, so tight it almost hurts and I have to clench my jaw and force myself to slam into her over and over again.

Her small body jostles against the table and I know there will be bruises tomorrow. I'll be a happy man if she can't even walk.

A strangled noise leaves her as she gets impossibly tighter, cumming all over my cock.

"Jase," she moans my name, arching her back and scratching the wood as her body stiffens with her release.

With one hand on my shoulder, keeping her arched, and the other on her hip to pin her against the table, I ride through her release, taking her savagely and with no mercy.

It's more than just fucking her, this is about owning her and I don't know when that happened.

She adjusts to me soon enough and my thrusts pick up, my balls drawing up with the need to release, but I can't give in just yet.

A desperate moan, loud and uncontrolled, fills the air. In an attempt to silence it, Beth covers her mouth with both hands as I thrust again and again.

"Don't you fucking dare." The words leave me at the same time that I grab her arms, pulling her hands away as I continue to fuck her with a ruthless pace.

Her upper body sways with every hard push of my hips against her ass.

"I want to hear every fucking sound." The words come out rough, from deep in my chest. "Scream for me."

CHAPTER
16

Jase

"I THINK I SHOULD LEAVE." BETHANY'S CADENCE IS SOFT AND INNOCENT, and it doesn't hold any of the regret I'm sure she's feeling.

She's been silent since I brought her into the bedroom. Limp, well fucked, and sated.

And questioning everything.

I know the war that rages inside of her. I feel the same.

It's not just business. And there's no justification for the two of us being together.

She knows it. I know it. It's easy to get lost in each other's touch, but when it's over, what's left?

Beth turns in my bed, careful not to disturb the sheets to face me. Her small hand rests against my chest and I lift mine up to hers, holding her hand and bringing it to my lips so I can kiss her knuckles.

I don't know what this is. Or where it's going. All I know is that we shouldn't be doing it. She knows it too.

"Do you mind if I use your bathroom?" she asks, not even looking me in the eyes.

I nod, forcing her to peek up at me, and the well of emotion I'm feeling sinks deep into the soft browns and hints of green in her gaze.

I move to lie on my back as she scoots to the edge of the bed and quietly picks up her sweater from the pile of clothes we carried in from the den. I watch the dim light kiss the curves of her body until it's covered by the soft fabric.

Listening to her bare feet pad on the floor, then the flick of the light switch and the running water, I stare at the ceiling, knowing I need to give her an answer to her unspoken question, but the moment I do, I may lose her forever.

"You take medication?" Beth's question brings my attention to her as she stands in the threshold of the bathroom. One hand on the door, the other on a bottle of unmarked pills.

"No," I answer her, feeling the tension thicken.

Her weight shifts from one foot to the other. "So… you just keep your product in your bathroom then?" she dares to speak.

"My product?" I'm quick to throw off the covers and stalk toward her. My shoulders feel tense, hearing the confrontation in her voice. Maybe she just wants to pick a fight. Something she knows will end whatever it is between us and she can go back to pretending, *it's just business*. Bull-fucking-shit. I won't allow it.

"For a moment, I forgot. For a moment," she says under her breath, shutting the medicine cabinet. She turns around before I get to her and looks me in the eyes as she takes a step forward to meet me. "I was looking for Advil. And I thought…" She trails off and swallows hard, pulling her hair into a ponytail before continuing to speak. "For a moment, I forgot and I don't know how that's fucking possible."

I expect anger, but all I see in her features are disappointment and sadness. "Of course you have drugs here. You're a drug dealer."

Even as she stares at me, her eyes gloss over. She's so close to the edge of breaking. Looking for anything to push her over so she doesn't have to deal with the real cause of her pain.

Reaching around her, I open the medicine cabinet door and pull out the pills. "They're for sleeping," I tell her, and my voice comes out hard.

She tries to maneuver around me, but with my other hand, I grip her hip and keep her right there. "That's all they are. I don't do drugs and I don't like what I do, but I have to do it."

"You don't-"

My finger over her lips silences her. Her eyes spark and rage, but beneath the anger there's so much more.

"You don't have to understand." She pulls my hand away from her mouth just then.

"Yes, I do," she says and shakes her head. "You don't understand. I am not okay." Her last word cracks. "I don't know when I became this woman, or if I was always like this and never knew it because I was too busy solving someone else's problem. But right now, I have nothing." She swallows thickly, holding on to her strength. "I feel like my life is on the precipice of changing forever. And I don't want to go back to the girl I was, but I don't like where this is headed either. I don't have answers, and I need answers."

Her hand is still firmly gripping my wrist, and I stare at it until she loosens her hold.

"What answers do you need?"

My patience with her is higher than it should be. I'm softer and more willing to be gentle with her.

"I don't like what you do."

"That's not a question to be answered."

"Well I don't like it. I don't like that I like you."

I let her raised voice and condescension slide. For now. Only because it's true. She's only being honest, and I get it.

"Someone's going to do it, Bethany. There will always be someone in my position. You can't stop that. I can at least have control if I'm that someone."

"You sell drugs?" she asks, staring at the door to the bathroom before looking me in the eyes.

"You know I do. That answer isn't going to change."

"Why?"

"It's a long story," I say, keeping my voice firm.

"I have time."

"I don't want to tell it right now."

"Why are you making me pay Jenny's debt?" Her wide eyes beg me to give an answer that will calm her fears. I can see it clearly. "You didn't mention it when you came to the house. It wasn't until after you brought me here. And you don't need the money, that's for damn sure." Her gaze searches mine, looking for the only words she wants to hear.

"I wanted to let it go," I lie, hating myself for every word that comes out of me.

"How could she even owe so much? What did she use the money for?" she continues, not finding my answer satisfying enough.

Every question is another cut in the deepening gouge.

"You already got a question. Mine first." It's the only thing I can think of to hold her off for a moment. She quiets, watching me and waiting. Willing to give me whatever answer I need.

"How did you know about The Red Room? Why is that where you went to find answers?"

I already know the truth, so all while she speaks, I grasp for what answer I can give her in return.

"Jenny; she used to talk about it. The back room of The Red Room. All the time. I heard her on the phone."

"Who was she talking with?"

"I don't know." She's quick to add, "That's another question."

"Semantics."

"Answer my question!" Bethany pushes her hands into my chest. Not to hit me, not to push me, but to get my attention, to demand it. My blood simmers simply from her touch. "Why did she owe you so much money?"

"She owed it to Carter," I answer her, unable to deny her at this point. Blaming the debt on someone else like a coward. "He didn't want to let the debt go and be made to look like a fool."

"I don't understand what she did with all that money," she nearly whispers, looking past me as she searches through her memories for answers. Answers she'll never find.

"Debt adds up fast." I try to keep my tone gentle as I speak. "I can tell you I met her once," I add, and my confession brings her gaze to mine. "She was looking to buy that drug you just had."

"Sleeping pills?" She looks confused.

"Sweets is what they call it. Sweet Lullabies. We mostly use it for addicts to wean them off, put them out during their withdrawal." Bethany stares up at me, hanging on every word as I speak. I only wish this story had a better ending for her.

"She was strung out on coke; every telltale sign was there. And she was buying too much of the sweets. It didn't make sense. It wasn't for her. When we questioned her, she said it was for her brother. She left and never came around again."

"We don't have a brother."

"I know. We could tell she was lying to us, so we sent her away."

"That's what you know of my sister?" Shame and sadness lace her words.

"That's the only time I met her," I answer her and her gaze narrows, as if she can see through my truth to the lies I just told her moments ago. But this is the truth.

"I don't know who she was buying it for, or if it has anything to do with why she was killed."

I've lost a piece of her in this moment. I don't know how, but I did.

"Don't judge me, Beth. I'm the one who will pay for this."

She stares up at me, but she doesn't say a word. Still assessing everything I said, or maybe trying to see her sister as she was in her last days.

"You've got to calm down."

"I don't just calm down," she says, wrapping her arms around herself and I think she's done, but she tells me a story. "I was a preemie when I was born, and I almost died. My mother told me she thought it was God punishing her. She hadn't wanted my sister; she almost gave her up. Not that she was a bad person," she adds, quick to defend her mother. "She didn't think she'd be a good mom to her, and had broken up with my father just before she found out she was pregnant. She came very close to giving her up, but my father came back around and wanted to try to make things work. And then a few years later, they wanted to have me. And she told me she'd thought God was going to take me away. My lungs didn't work and the hospital couldn't do anything, so they put me in a helicopter and sent me away to a hospital that could save me. My mom couldn't come at first, because she lost a lot of blood.

"My grandfather used to say I came into this world fighting and I never stopped. He told me once, 'You'll leave this world fighting, Bethy. And I'll still be so proud of you.'" Tears cloud her eyes, but she doesn't shed them. Not my fiery girl; she holds on to every bit of her pain.

"It's okay," I tell her, rubbing her arm and then holding her when she falls into my chest.

"I'm sorry I'm a bitch," she tells me, sniffing away the last evidence that she may have been on the verge of crying. "I don't know why I'm always ready to fight. I just am."

"It's okay, I already told you that."

"Why is it that when you say that, it feels like it really is?" The way she looks up at me in this moment is like I'm her hero. It's nothing but another lie.

"Because I'll do everything I can to make sure it is okay, maybe that's why?"

She sniffs once more and takes a step back to the counter as she says, "I should leave."

"I want you here. I don't want you to leave tonight."

"Why?" she asks. "Why do you want me to stay?"

"Do you really want to go to bed alone?"

"No," she whispers.

A moment passes between us. The look she gave me a moment ago is coming back.

"Jase, promise me one thing."

"What?"

"Don't hurt me."

I lie to her again, knowing that I hurt everyone I touch. Knowing I've already hurt her, although the truth of that hasn't revealed itself yet. "I won't hurt you," I tell her. I would have told her anything. Just to get her to stay.

CHAPTER
17

Bethany

ONE THING THE KIDS AT THE HOSPITAL DO ALL THE TIME IS LIE. They lie about taking their medication. They lie about their symptoms. They lie for all sorts of reasons all the time.

It's my job to know when they're lying. I can't save them if I don't know the truth.

When Jase looked me in the eyes hours ago, he lied to me.

I don't know what piece of the conversation contained the lie. I don't know how much was a lie. I don't know why.

But I know he lied to me. And I can't let it go. The nagging thought won't let me sleep. He fucking lied to me. I put it all out there, allowed myself to be raw and vulnerable. My imperfect, broken, bitchy self. And he lied to my face. The worst part is that I'm sure it had to do with my sister.

That's what hurts the most.

Every minute that passed after seeing that look on his face when he lied, every minute I thought of how I could get it out of him. How I *needed* to get it out of him. How I was failing Jenny by letting it happen. How I was failing myself.

I'm careful as I slip off the sheet. I haven't slept at all, but he has. His breathing is even, and I listen to it as I gently climb out of the bed. My body is motionless when I stand up, listening to his inhales and exhales.

I already have my excuse ready in case he wakes. I never got that Advil, after all.

Every footstep is gentle as I move to the dresser, opening a drawer as silently as I can. The first drawer proves useless and as I shut it, Jase breathes in deeper, the pace of his breathing changing. I stand as still as I can, holding my own breath and praying he falls back asleep.

And he does. That steady, even breathing comes back.

With the rush of adrenaline fueling me, I move to his nightstand quietly, slowly, wondering if I've lost my fucking mind. I'm so close to him that he could reach out and grab me if he woke up. I watch his chest rise and fall as I open the drawer. The sound of it opening is soft, but noticeable. All the while, Jase sleeps.

I watch his chest for a steady rhythm; I watch his eyes for any movement. He's knocked the hell out.

The faint light from the room is enough to reflect off the metal of the set of cuffs. I only have two, but if I can get one wrapped around his wrist and linked to the bed, I'll have him where I need him.

Trapped, until he tells me the fucking truth.

I almost shut the drawer, almost, but then I realize he would be able to reach it, and nestled inside are both a gun and a knife.

The metal gleams in the night and I carefully pick up both weapons and move them to the top of the dresser on the other side of the room, away from his reach.

Thump. Thump. The heat of uneasiness creeps along my skin. My own breathing intensifies, my hands shake slightly and the metal of the handcuffs clinks in the quiet night.

Freezing where I am on the other side of the bed, I wait. And wait. Watching him carefully. If he woke up right now, I don't even know what he'd do to me.

But it's better to suffer that consequence than to accept him lying straight to my face, all the while, I fall for him … him and his lies.

It's what my mother did. She accepted my father's lies. And it left her a lonely woman. I won't be with a liar. I don't care about any debt or any other bullshit reason. I can't trust a liar.

I don't realize how angry I've become, not until Jase rolls over slightly in bed and my heart leaps up my throat.

The thought runs through my mind not to do it. That I'm out of my element and this world is more dangerous than I can handle. This isn't the person I am.

But he lied to me. ...About Jenny.

Biting down on my bottom lip, I creep back up onto the bed and close one of the cuffs around an iron post of Jase's bed. There are four metal posts that surround his bed. The soft clink of the locks goes by slowly, *clink, clink, clink* and I swear he'll hear it, but his chest rises and falls evenly while he shows no signs of waking.

As I lean closer to him, closer to the other side, and ready to slip the other cuff through the post on that side of him, I gaze down at his face. In his sleep, he's still a man of power. But even with his strong stubbled jaw, there's a peacefulness I haven't seen.

He's only a man.

It fucking hurts to look at him. When someone can hurt you, it means you care. I have lived my life making sure not to care, so that I won't be hurt. And yet, Jase Cross pushed his way in, only to lie to me.

It solidifies my decision. I'll be damned either way.

Clink, clink, clink. With both handcuffs in place, I know securing the one on the left to his wrist will be easy. His wrist is close to the first cuff already. I'm sure he'll wake and then I'll be fucked, but I have to try. I'll have him where I want him.

With that thought, I go through with it, not second-guessing a thing.

I grab his wrist and it's by sheer dumb luck that he wakes up and grabs my throat with that hand. His dark eyes open wide and he stares daggers at me. Pinning me with a fierce look, the fear I knew I held for him deep down makes me still.

The look he shows is of startle and shock, and I don't let it distract me, even if I do scream out of instinct.

I drop my head down, shoving my face into the headboard, feeling the burn rising over my head from hitting my nose, and slip the metal around his wrist, scraping it against his skin as he screams at me, locking it into place.

"What the fuck are you doing?" his voice bellows in the room. His grip tightens for a moment, right before releasing me altogether.

I can still feel the imprint of his hand on my throat, the power he has to hurt me. I can feel it as I kick away from him, fighting with the sheets to get far enough away.

Scrambling backward, I fall hard off the bed onto my back, gasping for breath as my heart attempts to climb out of my throat.

Jase rips his arm back, yelling in vain as the metal digs into his wrist and the bed shakes, but he remains attached to it. Cuffed to the bed. He does it again and again and each time I lie on my back like a coward, my elbows propping me up on the floor as I wait with bated breath to see if I have trapped the beast.

"What the fuck did you do?" he jeers. "Where's the key?" he asks in a snarl.

Silence. *Did I really do it?* Thump.

"Where's the fucking key!" he screams until his face turns red. The anger seeps into the air around us as I slowly stand.

"I have the key," I manage to say somehow calmly, still in disbelief. He blinks the sleep from his eyes, breathing from his nostrils and slowly coming to the realization of what's happened. The way he looks down at me, like I betrayed him—I'd be a liar if I said it didn't kill something inside of me.

I ruin what I touch. I should have known this would end with him hating me.

"Give it to me," he requests with an eerily calm tone, one that chills me to my bones.

"No," I say, and the word falls from me easily. More easily than I could have imagined as I stand up straighter, walking slowly around the edge of the bed. Not unlike the way he does to me when I undress for him.

His dark eyes narrow on me. "Don't do this. I won't be mad. Just give me the key."

Thump. Thump. Fear burns inside of me. The fear of both repenting, and the fear of going through with it.

I keep walking, slowly making my way to the dresser and Jase's eyes move to it before looking back at me. "What are you doing?" he asks me, and then I hear him swallow. I hear the hint of fear creeping into his voice. "Give me the key."

I ignore his demand and pick up the gun. I don't aim it at him, I merely hold it and tell him, "Put the open cuff around your other wrist." Although I lack true confidence, the gun slipping slightly in my sweaty palms.

"And how would you like me to do that?" Jase questions, a lack of patience and irritation are the only things I can hear in his voice. Like I'm a child asking for something ridiculous.

"You're a big boy," I bite back, "I'm sure you can figure it out."

All the while I watch him and he watches me, my heart does this pitter-patter in my chest making me think it's giving up on me as it stalls every time Jase looks back. Using the pillow and occasionally leaning down to hold the cuff between his teeth, he struggles to lock it. I don't trust him enough to do it myself though. There's no way he wouldn't grab me.

My heart beats faster with each passing second as he attempts to close the cuff himself.

Every moment his gaze touches mine, questioning why I'd do this, I question it myself.

"I don't want to hurt you," I whisper when I hear the cuff finally pushed into place. He rests his wrists against the iron rod, pushing it tighter and securing it.

"Then put the gun down," he urges me and I listen. I set it down on the dresser where it sat only minutes ago and hesitantly turn to him, each wrist cuffed to his bed.

"You can still uncuff me," he suggests with more dominance than he should have. Especially because I lift the knife at the end of his sentence.

"More cuffs." I speak the words and fight back the bile rising in my stomach from knowing my own intentions.

Jase's eyes stay on the knife as he answers me, "In the top drawer of the dresser. To the right side… with the ropes." His voice is dull and flat. "You're going to cuff my ankles?" he guesses correctly and I nod without looking at him, simply because I can't.

Thump. Thump. My heart feels like it's lagging behind as I pick up the cuffs from the drawer, right where he said they were.

"Why are you doing this?" he asks me; any hint of arrogance or even anger is gone.

I can barely swallow as I move toward him. With the sheet barely covering him but laid haphazardly over his groin still, the rest of him is fully exposed. He is Adonis. Trapped and furious, but ultimately mortal.

"I want answers," I say, and I don't know how I'm able to speak. "You lied to me. I know you did."

His only response is to stretch out his legs, not fighting, not resisting. Putting his ankles close to the rods.

He's helping me. Or it's a trick. I decide on the latter, moving closer, but hesitantly.

"Go on," he tells me, staring down at me.

I stand back far enough away from the footboard, cautious as I click the first cuff into place.

"Go ahead, cailín tine," he tells me, staring into my eyes. His nickname for me breaks my heart. Even as I look away, feeling shame and guilt consume me even though I know I have a good reason to do this. But it doesn't make it hurt any less.

With the last cuff in place, and Jase half sitting up in bed, leaning against the headboard and staring at me, I observe him from where I stand.

"What are you going to do now?" I ask him.

"Wait."

"You lied to me." I whisper the ragged words and turn the handle of the knife over in my hand.

"When?" he questions, and the muscles in his neck tighten.

A sad laugh leaves me and I'm only vaguely conscious of it when I hear it.

"So you did lie?" I ask weakly, feeling the weight against my chest. "And here I was hoping I was just crazy."

"I'd be hard-pressed in this moment to call you sane," Jase comments, and my eyes move to his. "Yes, I lied to you."

"What was a lie?" I ask him and take a step closer to the bed. The floorboard creaks under my step and I halt where I am, taking it as a warning.

"I don't want to tell you. It doesn't matter." He speaks a contradiction.

Wiping my forehead with the back of my hand, still holding the knife, I walk closer to him, gauging his ability to move, even though he's still as can be.

"I don't think you could do anything," I start to tell him as I stand right in front of the nightstand, "if I stand right here." Holding out my arm, I gently place the blade of the knife on his chest, not pushing at all, but letting him see how far away I can be while still capable of hurting him. "What do you think?" I ask him, wondering if I truly am crazy at this point.

"What do you want to know?" he asks, not answering my question.

"What did you lie about?"

"It's irrelevant."

"Anything relating to my sister is relevant." I grit out the words, pushing the knife down a little harder. Enough so the skin on his pec surrounding the knife, tightens under the blade.

"Did you hurt her?" The words come out unbidden.

"No, I told you that."

"And you told me you lied," I counter.

"I lied to protect you, Bethany." He almost says something else, but instead he rips his gaze away from me, gnashing his back teeth to keep him from talking.

Before I can continue, he tells me, "I have a name, but it's useless." His dark eyes lift to mine. "We think he got her hooked, intentionally or not, but he can't be tied to anything else. Nothing ties him to her death."

"Give me his name." The strong woman inside of me applauds my efforts, rejoicing in the fact that it took this much to make him speak and that I was able to push myself to this point.

And that I have a name.

I have someone I can blame and punish, someone I can make pay for what they did to my sister. They tortured her. Broke her body. She was gone for so long, I don't know how long it went on. And then they burned her. They left nothing of her for me.

There will be nothing of them left when I find them.

"No." His answer dies in the tense air between us. It takes me a long moment to realize what he's even saying no to. My mind has gone to darker places, and tears streak down my cheek thinking about what she went through and that I wasn't there. I couldn't save her.

"Tell me who it was," I say as I move a bit closer, holding the knife with both hands, barely keeping it together. I let the tears fall with no restraint, and no conscious consent either. "I want his name!" I raise my voice and even to my own ears it sounds violent and uncontrolled.

Jase stares straight ahead, ignoring me, not answering.

"I don't want to hurt you." The confession sounds strangled.

"You don't have to," he answers.

"Give me the name, Jase!"

"You'll get yourself killed!" he yells back at me and the sound bellows from deep within him.

"You don't understand what they did to her!" I scream at him, feeling the well of emotion filling my lungs. I remember the fear when she went missing. "She would text me every day when she woke up, regardless of what time that ended up being. Sometimes she forgot. But every day, there was at least one text…" I trail off, remembering how angry I'd been when she messaged last. She wouldn't come back after I made her admit she had a problem. She refused to come back and get help. But she still messaged me every day. Until she didn't.

"And then there was nothing," I speak so softly, using what's left inside of me as the tears fall freely down my face.

"For days and then weeks, there was nothing but fear and hope. And fear is what won. Every day she didn't text me. The fear won." As I try to regain my composure, I wipe haphazardly at my face and focus on breathing.

"I waited in silence for nothing. The first forty-eight hours, no one did anything at all," I say and my words crack. "Why would they? She was reckless and headed down the wrong path."

The knife is still in my hands, still pressed to his skin when I tell him, "I knew something terrible had happened to her, and I could do nothing. She was still alive then. I know she was. I remember thinking that. That she was still out there. That I could feel her."

I'm brought back to my kitchen, crying on the floor, hating myself for pushing her away, regretting that I yelled at her, all alone and praying. Praying because God was the only one left to listen to me. Praying he could save her, because I couldn't.

"I had no name. No one had a name for me. But you do." I twist the knife just slightly, and suddenly feel it give, but I don't dare look. I don't look anywhere but into Jase's eyes, even as he seethes in pain.

"Give me the name."

"He'll kill you, Bethany." Sorrow etches his eyes and I know his answer already even before he says, "I won't do that."

I scream a wretched sound as I pull back the knife. It slices cleanly, so easily, leaving a bright red line in its path. Small and seemingly insignificant, but then blood pours from the wound and he bites back a sound of agony.

It's bright red. And it doesn't stop.

What have I done? Jase's intake is staggered but he doesn't show any other signs of pain.

"Fuck!" The word leaves me in a rush. "Jase," I say, and his name is a prayer on my lips. "No," I think out loud as my hand shakes and the knife drops to the floor. There's so much blood. There's so much soaking into the bed as it drips around his body.

It doesn't stop.

"Jase," I cry out his name as I ball up the bed sheets and press them to the laceration.

He breathes deep, staring at the ceiling. Silent, and ignoring me as I press more of the cotton linens to his chest, only for it to be soaked a half second later.

There's so much blood.

"I'm sorry," I utter as I rip the sheets out from under him, desperate to make it stop. "I'm so sorry."

The blood soaks through the fabric within seconds, staining my hands.

Staring down at the blood that lines the creases of my palms, I take a step back and then another.

What have I done?

CHAPTER
18

Jase

I't's like when you wake up from a nightmare. There's a moment where it all feels real and then, sometimes slowly, sometimes quickly, reality comes back to you. The horror stays, the damage done, the terrors in your sleep lingering as you walk down the steps of your quiet house to get a drink of water. And sometimes those monsters stand behind you. You can still sense them, even when you know they're not real.

That's what this feels like as the slice on my chest rips agony through my body. Like I can't get away from the ghosts in her eyes, even if she's woken from her dream. Even if disbelief and regret are all she feels, all she sees, all she recognizes.

The ghosts will still be there, waiting in the dark.

Every time she presses the sheets to the wound, a renewed sense of pain spreads through my body, but I refuse to make a sound. My hands turn to fists and I pull against the cuffs, feeling the metal dig into my wrists.

"I'm so sorry. I don't... I didn't mean..." she says, choking on her words.

"I told you I would tell you," I remind her, flexing my wrists and breathing through the pain. I've had worse shit done to me. "When I know who it was, I will tell you and I will make them pay."

Besides, I fucking deserve this.

"I'm not going to give you a name without knowing for sure," I confess to her, letting her believe that's the only thing I've withheld, the only lie I've spoken. "I promise you."

Her beautiful hazel eyes lock onto mine, begging and pleading for forgiveness but more than that, an out. A way out of the nightmare she's in.

There's no way out of this shit though. This is what life is. It's what mourning is. A waking nightmare.

"I'm sorry," she blurts out before turning her back to me and running to the bathroom.

I hear her open the medicine cabinet and when I do, I push the escape lock on the cuffs with my thumb. It would be all too fucked up for her to have found the cuffs in my car; the ones I put on her, the ones I keep in my car. And not these safety cuffs I intend to use when I light her ass on fire with my paddle. The ones for play sold at sex shops.

Maybe I shouldn't have let it go on for as long as I did, but I think she needed this. She needed to get it out of her system.

I'm quiet as I unlock the ones on my ankles, taking my time to put them away, gritting my teeth every time the sharp pain reminds me that she cut me.

With the drawer open, I drop the cuffs in, one by one when I hear her close the cabinet and I wait.

Her gasp is telling and I turn around slowly to see the halo of light surrounding her from the bathroom door. A bandage and gauze in one hand, and hydrogen peroxide in the other.

Horror plays in the depths of her eyes as she freezes where she is. She's a beautiful, broken mess.

I take a single step toward her; the floor groans and the only other sound is the hushed gasp she makes.

"Jase," she pleads, not hiding her fear. She doesn't hide anything; it's a big part of what I admire about her.

"Jase," she says again and this time my name is strangled as it leaves her. So much begging in only a single word as I take another step.

She trembles where she stands. I reach out for the bandages, and her arm drops dead to her side as she awaits her sentence. I place the bandage over the cut without sparing it a glance and wipe up the remaining blood with the gauze before tossing it behind her into the bathroom and onto the floor.

And she flinches from the movement. From my arm moving her way.

It fucking kills me. My chest doesn't feel a goddamn thing from the cut. But it feels everything knowing that she thought I was going to hit her. That I would strike her.

Everyone deserves punishment for their sins. And I accept mine. But I won't accept losing her.

Her eyes never leave mine, and mine never leave hers.

She doesn't beg for mercy; she doesn't try to run.

The world is full of broken birds and pain. I won't add to it.

Not her. Not my fiery girl, my *cailín tine*.

"Jase." She says my name thickly and swallows after a second passes of silence. Just the two of us knowing the other's pain, knowing what's happened wasn't a nightmare, it was real.

"I'm sor-"

I cut her off with my own apology. "I'm sorry I can't bring her back." The emotion wells in my throat as I add, "If I could, if I had that power, I wouldn't be feeling the same shit you are."

The tense air changes, and everything falls around us. For me it does. Nothing else exists for me but her.

"If I could, I would," I tell her as I brush her hair off her shoulder and lower my lips to hers. It's all done slowly. I'll be sweet with her tonight.

Her lips brush against mine gently and then she deepens our kiss.

Her fingers are hesitant at first, as if she's still expecting me to snap like she did.

I have all the time in the world for her tonight. To see what's really here. To know what's between us.

I can show her, and I do. Slowly, gently, and with every small touch, I chip away at any armor she has.

I don't want the hate; I don't want the fight.

Not tonight.

Tonight I make her feel loved.

A part of me knows it's selfish, because I don't deserve her or any of this. But tonight I need to feel loved too.

CHAPTER
19

Bethany

The Coverless Book
Fourth Chapter

"Do you think Mama will be okay with it?" I ask Caroline, nervously peeking up at her. The silk is like water under my fingers. So smooth and easily flowing. "I've never worn anything like it."

"It's perfect for your first date," Caroline tells me with that sweet Southern charm.

I turn around fully to face her, repeating my question, "But do you think Mama will be okay with it?"

Caroline's expression falters.

"I think your mama would love it, Emmy," Caroline says, forcing that false smile to her lips. She's worked for our family since just before I got sick. I know all her tells and that smile she's plastered on her face is only there to hide the truth. She hates my mother, but I don't know why.

"She's sick too," I whisper defensively. "That's why she's not here." The excuse falls flat, just like it does every time.

"She's not sick like you. She's just in pain," Miss Caroline corrects me.

Those in the most pain, cause pain. My mother told me that once. It was a while ago and she said that's why she doesn't see me very much. She doesn't want to hurt me. I know it kills her inside to know what's happening to me. "Pain is a sickness, isn't it?" I ask Caroline.

The false smile wavers as she reaches down to pick up the pair of shoes. "Your first pair of heels," she states and pretends she didn't hear me. She does that sometimes. She doesn't answer me when I ask questions. I know they're insignificant, but I have no one else to talk to. Some days I wonder if I've spoken when she does that.

I only know I have when I hear her sniffle. They don't like to see me like this, frail and losing weight and muscle like I am. No one does. I'm not just sick; I'm dying. That's what the doctors say.

Smoothing the ruby red silk fabric with my hand, I turn to the mirror thinking, Jake will like me in this dress. He won't mind seeing me sick. He doesn't cry when I tell him I'm invincible, not like Mama and not like Miss Caroline.

Jake thinks I'm pretty. He thinks I'm sweet.

"Soup, Emmy," Caroline calls out and I can hear the spoon clinking against the porcelain.

"Is it- "

Before I can finish, Miss Caroline nods and says, "Of course it is. I had to make your favorite for today. Drink up, baby, you need to be strong."

"I already am strong," I tell her with a smile, feeling the excitement of tonight. "Haven't I told you? I'm invincible."

The story grips me as the pages turn. A young boy and a sick girl, falling in love even though they know it won't last. I can't help but to think it's not that simple. I hate her mother and I like Miss Caroline, but I feel sorry for Emmy. It's funny how they feel so real when I curl up under the blanket and let the night disappear in between the pages of The Coverless Book.

Lines of a dark blue ink run along the pages. And with every line, I add it to the list in my notepad.

I'm invincible.

Those in the most pain, cause pain.

I don't feel sick when he looks at me like that; I can only feel cherished with his gaze on me.

Agony is meaningless; only love can relate.

There is no pattern. No reason to think there's a hidden message lying inside. But I do. I can't help but to hope that I'm missing something. Anything. I just want my sister to tell me something.

Or at least I did. Days ago.

Before that night with Jase. The night everything changed. Somehow, he took my fight away, but with it, there's relief.

It's been two days and he hasn't messaged me, and I haven't messaged him either.

I don't know how it happened, but everything feels different now.

With every thrust against his bedroom wall, he forced the air from my lungs. He took it, he made it his. The air, my body… and more.

Forgiveness and understanding can do something to a person. Especially when you don't feel worthy of it.

When I stepped out of that bathroom, not knowing what the hell I was going to do or what the hell I was thinking when I cuffed him, I wouldn't have fathomed he'd be there facing me.

What did I think would happen even if I did get a name from him?

That somehow he would let me out of his gilded cage after he admitted what he lied about? That he wouldn't hold it against me that I'd cuffed him up and threatened him?

I don't know what the hell I was thinking. I've never been sorrier for hurting someone. I can't believe I did that.

There will be consequences, I remember Jase's words last night. Just before I fell asleep, he told me the night wasn't forgiven wholly, until there were consequences.

And I accept it. Whatever those consequences may be.

I don't know what happened to make me think I could, and that I should, lay a knife to his skin.

The only way I can justify it, is that I think it happened for a reason.

I think we were meant to have that moment. The moment when he kissed me, and he made it feel okay to let go. He made me feel like if I was with him, everything would be the way it should be.

He made me feel like I wasn't as broken as I thought I was.

And I gave him everything I had to give. Even if it's not much.

I would give him everything and anything from this day forward.

His forgiveness and touch are worth more than I'll ever have.

Ping. My phone goes off with a text message, followed by another.

Are you okay?

How are you feeling?

Two different texts, from two different people. And I'm grateful for the distraction.

One's from Laura and one's from Jase.

I'm feeling good, how are you? I text them both the same thing. I don't even realize it at first.

I just haven't heard from you. Anything new? Laura writes back first.

I write a few words and delete them. Write some more and delete those too. I finally settle on, *Maybe. I'll know more when we go out this weekend.*

My heart does this little pitter-patter thing and my head tells it that it's naïve.

The three dots at the bottom left of the screen tell me she's writing something, but before she can finish, Jase messages.

I was hoping to see you tonight. But things came up. Tomorrow.

He doesn't ask. He tells.

I debate on what to say, focusing on the first part and then the second. *He was hoping to see me.* The butterflies Emmy feels … I feel them too. They kind of scare me. Everything that's happening scares me.

Before I can respond to him, Laura writes back.

What's new? I can't take the suspense. You know I thrive on instant gratification.

Shifting on the sofa, I pull the blanket up my lap, hating the draft coming from the old window and focusing on that rather than the butterflies.

I pick up my mug and take a swig of it; the decaf tea is lukewarm, but still satisfying.

I don't know exactly what it is yet, I tell Laura. *But when I do, I'll let you know.*

I press send and then realize I sent it to the wrong fucking person. The mug slams down onto the table when I realize, but thankfully my tea's almost gone so none of it splashes out.

"Fuck, fuck, fuck, fuck," I mutter under my breath, feeling my heart race.

Sorry, I meant that for someone else. See you tomorrow. I type out the response quickly, before Jase can respond. My heart's a damn war drum as I copy and paste what I sent him to send to Laura.

"Fuck a duck," I say out loud, letting my head fall back on the sofa. I am … a mess. A living, breathing mess.

Omg that's so exciting! Tell me everything! Laura writes immediately.

You don't know what "what" is? What is "what?" And who are you talking to? Jase writes back. Fuck, he knows. It doesn't take a genius to know what I'm talking about.

"Shit, shit, shit," is all I can think and say as I stare at his message.

Rubbing the stress away from my forehead, I decide they can get the same message again.

I'm heading to bed. Sorry, we'll talk later. As soon as the text is sent, I toss the phone on the other side of the sofa and stare at it as it goes off. Again and again. Taunting me every time. And with each one, I wonder if it's Jase, or Laura.

Fuck both of those conversations. It's late, and I'm obviously not with it. I'm tired, but I haven't been able to sleep. They can wait. Everything can wait.

Rubbing my eyes, and ignoring the sick feeling I have inside, I finally get up off the sofa and wonder if I should grab another cup of tea, or just pass out like I said I was going to do.

My mind won't stop with all the questions though. So sleeping is nonexistent.

I don't know what we are. Jase and me. I don't know where this is going. And I don't know how I'll be all right if I don't have Jase in my life. I owe him a debt, and the hours are numbered. It will come to an end. I'm fully aware of that, and it's terrifying.

Sleep doesn't come easy for me and with that thought in mind, I pick up the small bottle of pills from my purse. The handwriting on the back merely says, *All you need is one.*

I can add assault and theft to my résumé after what happened two nights ago.

Before I left Jase's home, I swiped the bottle of sleeping pills from his medicine cabinet. I don't know if he knows yet, or what he'll do when he finds out, but he can add them to my tab.

This goes against everything I know; everything I've ever done. Both the stealing and taking the drugs. *They're only sleeping pills,* I remind myself. And I desperately need sleep. Holding the pill up, I see it's a gel capsule with liquid inside. Just like an Advil.

But everything about this week is more than morally ambiguous. And everything has changed.

The phone pings again and I check to see what they said after getting a glass of water and a single pill.

Laura wrote back a novel. Text after text demanding I give her every detail. To which I reply, *I still love you! I'll tell you all of it soon!*

And Jase wrote back, *Sleep well.* To which I reply, *You too.* And feel far too much just from being able to tell him goodnight.

⟨꙰⟩

It's so cold here. At first I don't know where I am. Sleep came too easily. I remember feeling my entire body lift as if I'd become weightless, right before falling so deeply into darkness. Even now I can remember it, as if I could touch it and relive it. Although I know it's already passed.

I fell and fell, but it didn't feel like falling. Everything else was moving around me until I landed in this room. A small room with dirty white walls. There's a radiator in the corner with a thick coat of paint, or maybe many coats of paint. It's white too, like the walls. The thin wooden boards on the floor are old and they don't like me walking across them. They tell me I don't belong here. They tell me to go back.

But I hear the ripping.

Something is being torn behind the old chair. It's a tufted chair, and maybe it was once expensive, but faded fabric is being torn down the back of it.

Rip, another tear and I hear something else. The sound of a muffled sob. A shuddered breath and the sound of gentle rocking. Just behind the chair.

I take another step, and a freezing prick dances along every inch of my skin. It's so cold it hurts, like an ice pick stabbing me everywhere.

It doesn't matter though. Nothing does. Because I see her.

She's there, Jenny's there. Sitting cross-legged on the floor, rocking back and forth with a book in her hand. The Coverless Book.

"Jenny," I cry out her name and try to go to her, but the chair doesn't let me;

its torn fabric holds me where I am, making a vine around my ankles. My upper body tumbles forward, falling onto the back of the chair. "Jenny!" I scream as I reach out to her. But I can't reach her, and she can't hear me.

Her hair is so dirty, long and stringy now. The tears on my cheek turn to ice.

"Jenny," I whisper, but her name is lost in the cold air as I try to move from where I am. How is it holding me back? Let me go! She's my sister! She's here!

I fight against it all, but my hips are now tied down as well. I can't move to her; I can't even feel my legs. Please, let me go. I have to go to her!

The book falls, and the sound whips my eyes to her once again as Jenny covers her face to cry. Her arm has a marking, is it a quote? A tattoo?

What is it?

Her shoulders shake as tears stream down her cheeks and I tell her not to cry. I tell her it's okay, that I'm here. Her wide, dark eyes look up at me. Her pale skin is nearly as white as the fog from her breath.

It's so cold here.

"You shouldn't be here," she says, staring straight into my eyes. Both pain and chills consume me.

"Come with me," I beg her, licking my chapped lips and I swear ice coats them after. "Come with me, Jenny!" I scream, feeling the bite of a chill deep in my lungs, and she only tilts her head as if she doesn't understand.

The torturous feeling of being trapped makes me scream a wretched cry. And Jenny only stares at me.

"I just wanted them to be okay," she tells me as if she's apologizing. "Someone needs to be okay."

"Who?" I beg her for an answer. "Who did this to you? Where are you?"

Her voice cracks and she tells me repeatedly, "You shouldn't be here." Over and over in the same way, all while she shakes her head and rocks. "You shouldn't be here."

Darkness descends, like a storm brewing inside of the small room. "Jenny, come with me!" I scream again, "Jenny, come with me!" as the room stretches, tearing her away from me. No!

"Don't believe them," she whispers and I hear it as if she's next to me. As if she's whispered it into my ear.

"Don't believe the lies. They'll all tell you lies."

Even when she's gone and there's only darkness left, she tells me, "Don't believe your heart; it lies to you too."

CHAPTER
20

Jase

"WHAT HAPPENED?" I ASK HER THE SECOND I SHUT HER FRONT door. I've only just gotten here, intent on implementing consequences, and I'm already changing my mind.

Her eyes are bloodshot, and her skin is pale. Hugging her knees into her chest, she's seated on her sofa, staring at nothing.

"Nothing," she's quick to tell me. "I didn't think you'd be here in the morning. I thought you'd come at night," she adds and then wipes under her eyes as she tosses the blanket to the side of the sofa.

"I don't like it when I ask a question and you lie to me," I speak as I walk into the living room. Not a single light is on and the curtains are shut tight. It's too dark.

That gets her attention, and a hint of the girl I know shows herself when she answers smartly, "Oh, it's not the best feeling, is it?"

The sarcastic response leaves her easily, and she watches me as I narrow my gaze at her. From bad to worse, the air changes.

"Something happened from the time you left me to just now." I speak clearly, with no room for argument and Beth crosses her arms, staring just past me for a moment before looking me in the eyes.

She's in nothing but a sleepshirt that's rumpled, and dark circles are present under her eyes. Even still, she's beautiful, the kind of beautiful I want to hold on to.

"Are you going to tell me?" I ask her, not breaking our stare.

Time ticks by and I think she's going to keep it from me, but finally she looks to the kitchen and then back at me. "Over coffee," she tells me.

She turns toward the kitchen like she's going to walk there, but then pauses and looks over her shoulder. "You coming?" she asks, and I follow. Watching every detail, noticing the way her movements lag, the way she sniffs after a long exhale, like she's been crying. The way she leans against the counter after putting the coffee grinds in the pot, like she can barely stand on her own.

"What the fuck happened?" I ask her and lean against her refrigerator. Standing across from her, we're only feet apart but it feels like so much farther away. I should know everything that happens. I'll correct that mistake immediately.

"Where do we stand on the debt?" she asks and then clears her throat as the coffee machine rumbles to life.

"I wrote it down; don't have it with me." I give her a bullshit answer and ask again, but harder this time, "What happened?"

Lifting up her head to look me in the eyes, her lips pull down and she tells me in a tight voice, "I wasn't sleeping... not at all since Jenny..." She leaves the remainder unspoken. "So I took those pills you had." She crosses her arms, looking down at the coffee pot and licking her lower lip before telling me, "I'm sorry. It was shitty of me and I don't know why I'm doing so many shitty things, to be honest."

Her arms unfold and she rests her elbows on the counter, like she's talking to the coffee pot instead of me. Her fingers graze her hairline as she keeps going. "That drug doesn't work; I'll tell you that." As she speaks her voice is dampened, although she tries to keep it even. "I had the most awful dream, but it felt so real." I take a tentative step forward, getting closer to her, but am careful to keep far enough back so she won't feel threatened.

She reminds me of a caged animal backed into a corner. One who's given up and given in, but still frightened and not ashamed to admit it. One who would still try to hurt you, and you'd be the one to blame, because it warned you so.

"It was so real, Jase," she whispers and before I can ask what her dream was, she tells me. "Jenny was there, ripping the cover off the book." She turns around to face what little of the living room she can see from this angle. Her hand falls to her side as she peeks up at me.

A deep well of emotions burns in her gaze, enrapturing me and refusing to let me go. "She said I didn't belong there and she wouldn't come back with me." She has to whisper her words, her voice is so fragile. Like she really believed it happened.

"I'm sorry I stole from you, and I'm sorry I even took it. I don't know what's happening to me." Bringing the heels of her hands up to her cheeks she wipes at the stray tears and that's when I hold her, rocking her in my arms and shushing her.

"I hate crying... why am I crying?" Her frustration shows as she holds on to the pain, still not having learned to let it go.

The coffee pot stops, and I can't hear anything. She's stiff in my arms, not crying, but not getting better either.

She's stuck in that moment. The monster in her dreams, following in her shadows.

"You want to go upstairs?"

She doesn't answer right away and I add, "You need to sleep."

It takes a moment, it always does with her, ever defiant, but she nods eventually. She pushes off from the counter, leaving the black coffee to steam in the mug where it sits, knowing it'll go untouched and turn cold.

Her arms stay wrapped around her as she walks up the old stairs, and I follow behind her, listening to the wooden steps creak with every few steps.

I keep a hand splayed on her back and when we make it to the bedroom, she stops outside of the door. "You don't have to babysit me," she tells me, craning her neck to look up at me in the dimly lit hall.

"Maybe I want to lie in bed with you, ever think of that?" I ask her softly, letting the back of my fingers brush her cheek.

She takes my hand in both of hers and opens the door to her bedroom. It's smaller than mine, but nice. Her dresser looks older, maybe an antique like the vanity she has in the corner of her room.

Everything is neatly in place, not a single piece of clothing is out, nothing is askew. Nothing except for the bed. It looks like she just got out of it. The top sheet's a tangled mess and the down comforter is still wrapped up like a cocoon.

"When did you get up?" I ask her.

She shrugs and pulls back the blankets, fixing them as she answers, "I think around three... I don't remember."

"It was almost midnight when you said you were going to bed."

"Yes," is all she answers me.

"Come here." I rip her away from straightening the sheets to hold her, and she clings to me. "It wasn't real," I whisper in her hair.

"I wish..." she pauses, then swallows thickly before confessing, "I wish it was in some way, because at least I got to see her."

Her shoulders shudder in my arms. I don't have words to answer her, so I lay her in bed, helping her with the blankets and climbing in next to her.

The kisses start with the intent to soothe her pain. Letting my lips kiss her jaw, where the tearstains are. Up her neck, to make her feel more.

And she does, she breathes out heavily, keeping her eyes closed and letting her hands linger down my body.

Slowly it turns to more. She deepens the kisses. She holds me closer and demands more.

"You're still in trouble," I whisper against her lips, reminding her that she needs to be punished. Her response is merely a moan as she continues to devour me with her touch.

"Not tonight, but it's coming."

Her eyes open slowly, staring into mine and she whispers, "I know."

"Tell me what you want." I give her the one demand, wanting her to control this. Giving her something I haven't before.

"Don't make this harder on me. Please," she begs me and I nearly turn her onto her belly, to fuck her into the mattress like I've wanted to do since the day I first laid eyes on her, but then she says, "I don't want to beg you for something like... like..."

"Like what?" I ask, not following.

"I don't want to consciously ask... for... for this," she whispers and opens her eyes to look back at me.

It takes a long moment to feel how deep that cut me. Maybe it's the disbelief. "To ask for something … like for me to fuck you?" My tone doesn't hide a damn thing I'm feeling as I sit up straighter in bed. "Is it offensive? Or do you just not want to admit that you want me?"

"Jase." Bethany wakes in this moment, her eyes more alive than they were downstairs. Brushing the hair out of her face, she sits up straighter, and blinks away the haze of lust.

"Tell me what you want." I give her the request again. Waiting. Every second the fucking agony grows deeper and deeper.

"Jase," she pleads with me. But I ask for so little now. I'm trying to give her everything to make it right, but I need this. "Tell me," I say. The demand comes out hard and her expression falls.

A moment passes and she takes my hand, but her grip is weak.

"Please," she begs me, "I don't want to be alone."

"I know that, but you don't want to be with me either. Do you? We shouldn't be doing this anyway." I say the words without thinking. I know we've both thought it. That what this is today isn't what it was that night I had her sign the contract. And two nights ago, we should have parted ways. It's volatile and wrong. Being with her is going to be my downfall, I already know it.

And yet here I am waiting for her answer, because she's the only one of the two of us who has the balls to admit out loud that we shouldn't be together.

She hesitates, although she doesn't deny it. She doesn't say anything. The silence grows between us, separating us and making it seem as if the last time we were together never happened.

Thump, there's the dull pain in my chest. It flourishes inside of me as I stand there in silence.

"After what I did for you, I deserve better than that," I snap back. It fucking hurts. There's a splintering sensation in my chest as if the absence of her words truly injured me more than that cut she gave me the other night. Only one will scar.

Her lips turn down as she swallows, making her throat tight. Her inhale quivers but instead of saying anything, she shakes her head, her hair sweeping around her shoulders as she looks away.

Nothing. She gives me nothing and with that I turn my back to her, slamming the door shut behind me. As hard as I can. The force of it travels up my arm, lingering as I walk away from her.

I could tell her she still owes me; I could tell her that. But right now, I don't want to.

An awful sound travels down the hall, following me. A sob she tries to cover. The kind you hope comes out silent, but it's ragged and fierce. My footsteps thunder behind me as I take the stairs as quickly as I can.

The kind of sobs that you can't control. The kind that hurt.

Both the pounding of my shoes as I leave and the evidence of her misery, both are uncontrolled and painful.

I have seen so much brokenness in my short life. I hate it. I hate how easily everything can be destroyed and wasted. It's so useless to live day by day, not just seeing it all around you, but making it so.

Standing at the bottom of her stairs, with one hand on the wall and the other gripping the banister, I listen to her cry. Crying for me? And the pain she's caused me? Crying for herself and how alone and empty her life truly is? Crying for us?

And it takes me back to the time I heard similar cries. A time I left.

And I remember what was left of me when I came back to see the damage done.

My body tenses and my throat dries as I stand in between the man I was before and the man I'll be tomorrow.

Tonight is mine regardless and knowing that, I turn on my heels and make my way back up the stairs as quickly as I can, pushing her door open without knocking. Her wide eyes fly to mine as I kick the door shut behind me.

"Jase?" She whispers my name in the same way the snow falls around us. Gentle and hopeful the fall won't last for long.

She moves on the bed, making a spot for me easily enough although her eyes are still wide and searching for answers. She stays sitting up even though I climb in and lie down back where I was, pulling the covers over my clothes.

It's too hot, but it's better than taking the time to do something other than lie down with her.

Patting the bed, I tell her to lie down, noting how gruff my voice is. How raw.

"Are you angry?" she asks and I tell her I've always been.

Molding her small body to mine, she rests her hands on my chest, still wary, still exhausted. Still hoping for more. "I'm sorry," she whispers and I tell her so am I.

Hope is a long way of saying goodbye. Even I know that.

Her hair tickles my nose when I kiss the crown of her head. The covers rustle as I move my arm around her, rubbing soothing circles on her back.

Time marches on and with it the memories of long ago play in my mind. Making me regretful. Making me question everything.

"Why did you come back?" she asks me before brushing her cheek against my chest and planting a small kiss in the dip just beneath my throat.

I confess a truth she could use against me. Even knowing that, still I admit, "I don't want you to be alone either."

CHAPTER
21

Jase

THE SNOW'S FALLING. IT'S ONLY A LIGHT DUSTING, BUT IT DECIDED TO come right this moment, right as my brother leads his love across the cemetery.

One grave has been there for half her life. The one next to it has freshly upturned dirt. The snow covers each of the graves equally as Aria silently mourns, her body shaking slightly against Carter's chest.

I spoke to her father only days before he met his death. A death he knew was coming. A death that always comes for men like us.

The powerful man asked me to find a way. Swallowing his pride when he thought his daughter was going to die because of him.

Talvery wasn't ready to lose his daughter. She swears he was going to kill her.

That's the irony in it all.

He was a bad man. And that's the crux of the problem. She expected him to do bad things, even if she loved him in his last days, although I don't believe she did love him anymore.

She swears he was going to shoot her, but there was only one gun cocked and it wasn't her father's. She heard it, she speaks of it, but she doesn't realize what really happened and I don't have the heart to tell her.

The man who pulled the trigger confessed to me. He said in the old man's last breaths, he laid down his gun and said goodbye to his daughter. But she didn't see, clinging to a man she loved and not to the man who gave up fighting to ensure she would be loved one more day.

That's what this life brings. A twisted love of betrayal. A reality that is unjust and riddled with deceit.

Aria lays a single rose across her mother's grave, but not her father's, even though when he called me, he said he would give up everything right then and there, if I promised we'd keep her safe.

There was no negotiation we could offer.

Her father had to die. And Aria was never in harm's way. The man had nothing to barter with, not when he knew we'd take it all. I never told Carter. And I never will. The perception that her father was a ruthless crime lord past his date of redemption is what makes it okay. It makes it righteous that she only lays a rose down for her mother, a woman who betrayed everyone to benefit herself.

Watching Carter hold her hand, kiss her hair and comfort her, only reminds me of what could have been. If the gun cocked had been Talvery's and my brother was in that grave instead.

Bright lights reflect a section of falling snow. Headlights from a cop car pulling in across the parking lot I'm sitting in.

Gripping the steering wheel tighter, I take into account everyone here. It's only me, still in the driver's seat waiting for Carter to bring Aria back and the sole cop parking his vehicle across from mine.

Before Carter has a chance to look behind him, taking attention away from Aria, I message him. *I've got it. Stay with her.*

A second passes, and another before Carter looks down at the message, back at me, and then to the cop, who opens his door in that moment.

Officer Walsh.

The sound of his door closing echoes in the vacant air. It's hollow and reflects its own surroundings.

As I open my car door, welcoming the cold air, breathing it in and letting it bite across my skin, I nod at Carter, who nods in return, holding Aria closer, but not making a move to leave.

The snow crunches beneath my shoes, soft and gentle as it falls. It vanishes beneath my footprints as I make my way around to the front of my car, leaning against it and waiting for him.

As I take in the officer, a crooked smile forms on my face. We're wearing the same coat. A dark gray wool blend. "Nice coat, Officer Walsh," I greet him and offer a hand. He's hesitant to accept, but he does.

Meeting him toe to toe, eye to eye, his grip is strong.

"So you've heard of me?" he asks. I lick my lower lip, looking over my shoulder to check on Carter one more time before I answer him, "I heard someone was asking about me, someone who fit your description."

"Funny," he answers with a hint of humor in his voice, although his pale blue eyes are only assessing. "I heard the same about you."

"That I was asking about you?" I ask with feigned shock as I bring my thumb up to point back at me. "I only asked who was asking about me and my club."

"The Red Room." The officer's voice lowers and his gaze narrows as he speaks. He slips his hands into his coat pockets and I wait for more, simply nodding at his words.

Some cops are easy to pay off. They need money, they want power, or even just to feel like they're high on life and fitting into a world they could only dream of running themselves.

I can spot them easily. The way they walk, talk—shit, even the clothes they wear on their time off. It's all so fucking obvious. The only question that needs answering is: how much do I need to pay them until they're in my back pocket?

Not Cody Walsh.

"What is it that you want, Officer?" I ask him and then add, "Anything I can help you with?"

"Anything you had in mind?" he asks in return, tilting his chin back and waiting.

The smirk on my face grows. "I don't dislike having conversations with cops." I follow his previous gaze just as he looks back at me and see Carter and Aria making their way back to the car that's still running. "But I don't really like to start a conversation either."

He's playing me. Thinking I'll try to bribe him for nothing. What a fucking prick.

"Is that his wife?" he asks me, and I tell him the truth. "His fiancée."

"Aria Talvery," he comments.

"You know a lot of names for being new around here."

"It's my job," he answers defensively.

"Is it?" I rock back on my shoes as I slip my hands into my pockets. My warm breath turns to fog in the air. "You know everyone's name who you pull over then?" I ask him.

"Not unless their name is in the file of the case I'm working on."

"A case?" I ask him as the cold air runs over my skin, seeping through my muscles and deep down into the marrow of my bones. I feel the shards of ice everywhere, but I don't show it. "It's the first time I'm hearing about a case."

"A house burned down, killing over a dozen men, explosives."

"Aria's family home," I remark, acknowledging him with a nod. "What a tragedy."

"It was arson, and one of a string of violent crimes that leads back to you and your brothers."

With the sound of the car door opening behind me, indicating Carter is helping Aria into the backseat, my patience is gone.

"If you have questions, you can ask my lawyer."

"I don't have any for you," he tells me and I huff a humorless laugh before responding, "Then why come to pay this visit?"

"I wanted to see her reaction; if she was remorseful at all."

"Aria?" The shock is apparent in my tone and my expression, because I didn't hide it in the least. I shouldn't be speaking her name. I shouldn't even engage with this fucker. And that's the only reason I'm silent when he adds, "Knowing she's sleeping with her father's killer…"

He shakes his head, although his eyes never leave mine.

"Is that all then?" I ask him.

A moment passes, and with it comes a gust of cold wind. Each day's been more bitter than the last and with a snowstorm coming, the worst is yet to come.

"That's all," he says and then his eyes drift to my windshield before he adds, "And pay your parking tickets. Wouldn't want that to be what gets you."

All I give him is a short wave, right before snatching a small piece of paper off the windshield. It's not a parking ticket, it's a thick piece of yellow paper folded in half. It's been here for a while, partially covered by the snow. And knowing that, I look back to see if Walsh is watching. His eyes are on Carter, not me. Thank fuck.

I don't know who the fuck left it, but I'm not going to figure that out while under the watchful eyes of Officer Walsh.

Lacking any emotion at all, I bid the man farewell. "Have a good night, Officer."

With my back to Walsh I share a glance with Carter, who's waiting by the backseat door on the driver's side, one hand on the handle, his other hand in his pocket.

"You too," the officer calls out in the bitterly cold air, already making his way back to his car.

It's silent when I close the door. Aria tries to speak, but I hear Carter shush her, telling her to wait for the officer to leave. Peeking at her in the rearview mirror, worry clouds her tired eyes.

"Everything's fine," Carter reassures her and she lays her cheek, bright red from the frigid air, onto his shoulder.

My gaze moves from the cop car, reversing out of the spot, to the note. The sound of the thick paper opening is all I pay attention to as Officer Walsh drives away, leaving us alone in the parking lot.

A sharp ringing in my ear accompanies my slow breaths and the freezing sensation that takes over when I glance at the note, a script font I recognize as Marcus's.

How the fuck did he leave a note? And when? I read his message and then read it again. The psychopath speaks in riddles.

You took my pawn. I have another.
The game hasn't stopped. It's only changed slightly.
Just remember, the king can only hope to be a pawn when his queen is gone.

Every hair on my body stands on end after reading the note, knowing he was here. How the fuck did I not see him?

"What's wrong?" Carter asks me as I reach for my phone, needing to tell Seth and everyone else what happened and get security footage immediately.

But Seth's already texted me.

And I sit there motionless in my seat, reading what he wrote as Carter bites out my name, demanding an answer I don't have to give.

We found the sister.
She's alive.
Marcus has her.

CHAPTER
22

Bethany

I CAN'T STOP READING. WHEN I DO, I HAVE TO FACE REALITY AND I'M NOT ready to face the consequences of my decisions yet. I'd rather get lost in the pages.

Every time they kiss, I think of Jase Cross.

I think I love him.

I love my enemy.

Why couldn't I be like the characters in this book? Why couldn't I be like Emmy and fall for the boy who loves her just as much and the only thing they have keeping them apart, is whether or not they're both still breathing?

Why did I have to fall for a villain? Maybe that's what I deserve. Deep down inside though, I don't think I even deserve him.

Books are a portal to another world, but they lead to other places too. To places deep inside you still filled with hope and a desperate need for love. Places where your loneliness doesn't exist, because you know how it can be filled.

Jase isn't a good man, but he's not a bad one either. I refuse to believe it. He's a damaged man with secrets I know are lurking beneath his charming facade, a man with a dark past that threatens to dictate who he will become.

And I think I love him.

I can't bring myself to tell him that. I just had the chance a moment ago when he told me he wasn't able to come tonight because he was with his brother and Carter needed him.

But he still asked if I needed anything. I could have told him I miss him. I could have messaged him more. Instead, I simply told him I would be ready for him when he wanted me.

The constant thumping in my chest gets harder and rises higher. I have to swallow it down just so I can breathe. This was never supposed to happen. How could I have fallen for a man like him?

I'm drowning in the abyss, and he's the only one there to hold me. That's how. I need to remember that.

He made it that way, didn't he?

The sound of the radiator kicking on disrupts the quiet living room. I take the moment to have a sip of tea, careful not to disturb the open book in my lap. The warmth of the mug against my lips is nothing compared to Jase's kiss.

With my eyes closed, I vow to think clearly, to step back and be smart about all of this. Even though deep inside, I know there is no way that means I could ever stay with Jase Cross, and the very thought destroys something deep inside of me. Splintering it and causing a pain that forces me to put the cup down and sink back into the sofa, covering myself with the blanket and staring at the black and white words on the page.

It all hurts when I think about leaving him.

That's how I know I've fallen.

The Coverless Book
Eighth Chapter

Jake's perspective

"Kiss me again?" Emmy's voice is soft and delicate. It fits her, but she's so much more.

"You like it when I kiss you?" I tease her and that bright pink blush rises up her cheeks.

"Shhh, she'll hear us," she says as her small hands press against my chest, pushing me to the side so she can glance past me and toward the hallway to the kitchen.

"Miss Caroline knows I kiss you." I smile as I push some strands of hair behind her ear, but it falls slowly. It should be her mother who Emmy's afraid will catch us. But her mother is never here.

"Maybe go check on her?" Emmy asks, scooting me off the chair. "See what she's doing and if we have a little more time?"

It's her elation that draws me to her. There are some people in this world who you love to see smile. It makes you warm inside and it feels like everything will be all right, if only they smile.

That's all I can think as I round the corner to the kitchen. I've only been here to Emmy's house twice, but I know the help's kitchen is through one of these two doors. I'm right on the first guess and there's Caroline, hovering over the large pot with a skinny bottle above it. Clear liquid is being poured into the steaming pot of soup.

Although I'd planned to offer to help, just so I can gauge how much time we have, my words are stolen.

The glass bottle she's holding doesn't look like it belongs in a kitchen. I feel a deep crease form between my furrowed brows and I stare for far too long as she pours more and more into the pot. She's humming as she does. A sweet tune I'm sure would lull babies to their dreams.

Emmy has soup every night. Every night the caretaker makes her soup. And Emmy stays sick, every day.

"What did you put in there?" My question comes out hard and when Miss Caroline jumps, the liquid spills over the oven and the bottle crashes onto the floor with her startled cry.

I debate on grabbing the notebook from the kitchen counter where I left it. Just so I can add to the collection of underlined sentences. I'm reading without really paying attention, just letting the time go by.

My gaze skims the page, finding four sentences underlined this time and none of the four hold any new meaning. One is the same as it's been for a while now. *I'm invincible.*

If it weren't for the distraction of this story, the suspense and the emotion, I'd feel hopeless. I'm hopeless when it comes to Jase.

If hope is a long way of saying goodbye, hopeless can only mean one of two things. As the thought plays in my mind, my thumb brushes along my bottom lip and I stare at the page.

And that's when I see it. What I've been waiting for. What I was so sure was here.

A chill spreads across my skin as the mug slips from my hand, dropping to the floor, crashing into pieces. If the letters weren't staring right at me, I never would have seen them.

It's not the underlined sentences. *It's the lines below them.* The first letters of the sentences *beneath* the pen marks. C. R. O. S. S. She buried the message so deep, I didn't see it before.

At first it hits me she left me a message, and there's hope. And then I read the word again.

C. R. O. S. S.

"No." The word is whispered from me, but not with conscious consent. My head shakes and my fingers tremble as I stare at the evidence.

C. R. O. S. S.

She did leave a note. My blood turns to ice at the thought. Jenny left me a message in this book, and it has to do with the Cross brothers.

"No." I repeat the word as I lay the book down, although not gently, but forcefully, as if it will bite me if I hold it any longer. I nearly trip over the throw blanket in my rush to get off the sofa.

Thump, thump, thump. Ever present and ever painful, my bastard heart races inside of me.

My limbs are wobbly as I rush to the kitchen, searching for the notebook. I need to write it down. "Write it all down," I speak in hushed and rushed words as I pull open one drawer in the kitchen, jostling the pens, a pair of scissors, and papers and everything else in the junk drawer. It slams shut as I bring the notebook to my chest, ready to face the book. To face the message Jenny left me.

Knowing she wrote something about the Cross brothers.

Knowing Jase Cross lied to me.

They had something to do with her murder. Maybe even him.

Tears leak from my eyes as I stumble in the kitchen.

"No," I whisper, and force myself to stand. *It will say something else.*

I tell myself it will, and the sinful whisper in my head reminds me, *Hope is a long way of saying goodbye.*

Swallowing down my heart and nerves, I push myself to stand, only to hear a creak.

Thump, goes my heart, and this time the beat comes with fear.

I couldn't have heard that right. No one is coming. No one is here, I tell myself, even though my blood still rushes inside of me, begging me to run, warning me that something's wrong, that someone's here who isn't supposed to be.

I keep silent and hear the sound of my front door.

Thump. Terror betrays my instincts. Stealing my breath and making me lightheaded.

The foyer floor creaks again and the front door closes, softly. A gentle push. A quiet one meant not to disturb.

The creaking moves closer and I listen to it with only the harsh sound of my subdued breath competing with it.

And I'm too afraid to even whisper, "Who's there?"

Jase and Bethany's book continues in … *A Single Kiss*. Preorder now!

There are many moving parts in this world. If you haven't read Carter's saga, starting with *Merciless*, I highly suggest you do that now. His story is just as intense and a tale that will stay with me forever. I hope these words stay with you as well.

Here's to love stories keeping our hearts beating.

A

SINGLE

KISS

From *USA Today* best-selling author Willow Winters comes a gripping, heart-wrenching tale of romantic suspense that will keep you on the edge of your seat.

I should feel shame for not wanting this to end, but he doesn't want it to end either.

When the darkness sets in with the flames all flickered out, and the loud click of the locks signal it's over, that's when reality comes flooding back.

The war. The drugs. All of the lies that weave a tangled web for me to get lost in.

I don't want any of it.

I only want him. Jase Cross. My enemy. And yet, the only person I trust.

With broad shoulders and a smoldering look in his dark eyes, Jase is a man born to be powerful.

I shouldn't give him more power than he already has…

Jase Cross will be my downfall.

A Single Kiss is Book 2 of the Irresistible Attraction series. *A Single Glance* must be read first.

"Grief does not change you, Hazel. It reveals you."
—John Green, *The Fault in Our Stars*

PROLOGUE

Jase

I T'S ODD THE THINGS YOU REMEMBER IN THE MIDST OF FEAR. FOURTEEN years later, and I still recall the cracks in the cement; the sidewalks were littered with them. This particular one though... I remember it in vivid detail, probably because of what happened immediately after.

Against the old brick building of the corner store, a green vine had found its way through the broken cement and climbed up the wall. I remember thinking it had no business being there. The crack belonged, but the new life that had sprouted up and borne what looked like a closed flower wasn't supposed to be there. Nothing beautiful belonged on that street.

The dim streetlight revealed how lively it was, even that late at night. With shades of green on the perfect vine and its single leaf with the bud of a flower just waiting to bloom, it made me pause. And in that moment, I hated that it was there.

I was almost eleven and maybe that childishness is why I scraped my shoe against the leaf and stem, ripping and tearing them until the green seemed to bleed against the rough and faded red bricks. I know I wasn't quite eleven, because Mama died right before my birthday that year. It was her medicine that almost fell out of the overfilled paper bag I was gripping so tight as I continued to kick at the wall before feeling all the anger and hate well up and form tears in my eyes.

Life wasn't fair. Back then I was just learning that truth, or at least I'd felt it somewhere deep in my bones, although I hadn't yet said it out loud.

Mama was getting sicker. Dad's condition was getting worse too, although he couldn't use cancer as an excuse. Thinking about the two of them, I continued to kick the wall even though my sneakers were too thin and it hurt to do so. The bottles the clerk had given me to give my dad clinked against one another in the bag, egging me on to keep kicking until I felt a pain that I'd given myself. A pain I deserved.

All the while, the bottles clinked.

That's what I had gone out to get, even as my stomach rumbled. I had enough money left over to get something to eat, but Dad always demanded the receipt. If he saw that I spent his change, I knew it'd be bad. I knew better than to take his money. Times were hard and I would eat what I was given to eat and do what I was told to do.

I picked up the medicine and beer for my folks on the way home from dropping off something at a classmate's house on the other side of town. Maybe a book I'd borrowed. Those details are fuzzy over a decade later. I didn't have many friends but a couple of students pitied me. I was the smallest one in the class and we couldn't buy everything I needed for school. The other kids didn't mind letting me borrow their things every once in a while. I never asked the same person in the same week and I always gave stuff back promptly. Mama always smiled when I told her I'd just gotten home from giving things back to my friends. I told her they were my friends, but I knew better. She didn't though.

I'm not sure what I'd returned that night or to who. Only that I had to go by the corner store on the way home.

None of that mattered enough to remember, but the damn flower I'd killed, I remember that.

It was the shame of nearly crying that made me take that detour, right at the damaged sidewalk that was free of what wasn't supposed to be there anymore. I cried a lot and that's why everyone looked at me the way they did. The teachers, the other kids, the clerk at the corner store. They always got a certain look on their faces when they saw the dirty, skinny kid whose mother was dying.

They didn't look at my older brothers that way. They were trouble and I was just… not enough of anything other than a kid to feel sorry for.

I stalked down the alley to hide my face in the darkness, only to meet a man I thought was a figment of everyone's imagination.

He was like the boogeyman or Santa Claus; all myths I didn't believe in.

A lot of people called him the Grim Reaper, but I knew his name was Marcus. It's what my brothers called him. I thought they were messing with me when they'd told me stories about him, right up until I looked into Carter's eyes and he shook my shoulders because I wouldn't listen.

Don't ask for Marcus, don't talk about him. If you hear his name, run the other way. Stay the fuck away from Marcus.

Swallowing thickly, I remember the harsh look of fear that Carter never allowed to cloud his expression and his tone that chilled my spine.

The second I lifted up my head about halfway down that alley, staring at where I'd heard a soft cough in the darkness, in that moment, I knew it was him.

I thought I knew fear before that night. But no monster I'd conjured under the bed ever made my body react like it did when I saw his dark eyes focused on me. His breath fogged in front of him and that was all I could see as my grip involuntarily tightened on the paper bag. It was late, dark and cold. From the icy chill on my skin, down to my blood and even deeper to the core of what makes a person who they are, suddenly it was freezing.

So I stood motionless, paralyzed in place and unable to run even though every instinct inside of me was screaming for me to do so.

I remember how gracefully he jumped down from his perch atop a stack of crates, still hidden in the darkness. The dull thump of his shoes hitting the asphalt made my heart lurch inside of my chest.

"What do you want?" I braved the words without conscious consent. As bitterly cold as I'd been seconds ago, sweat began to bead on my skin. Sweat that burned hotter than I'd ever felt, knowing I dared to speak to a man who would surely kill me before answering my question.

A flash of bright white emerged in the blackness as he bared a sick grin. I could feel my eyes squint as I searched desperately for his face.

I wanted to at least see him, see the man who'd kill me. I'd heard the worst thing you could see before you die was the face of the person who ends your life. But growing up here, I knew it wasn't true. The worst thing you could see were the people all around you who could help, but instead chose to do nothing and continue walking on by.

The streets were quiet behind me, and somewhere deep inside, I was grateful for that. At least if I begged for help, no one would be there to deny me a chance to be saved. It would end and there would be no hope. Having no hope somehow made it better.

"Your brother has an interesting choice of friends."

Again my heart spasmed, pumping hard and violently.

My brother.

I was going to lose my mother; I knew I would soon. She was holding on as hard as she could, but she'd told me to be strong when the time came and that was a damn hard pill to swallow. I'd already lost what semblance of a father I had.

My brothers…. they were all I had left. I suppose life is meant to be suffered through loss after loss. That would explain why the Grim Reaper showed up, whispering about my brother.

I don't know how I managed to answer him, the man who stayed in the shadows, but I questioned, "Which brother?"

He laughed. It echoed in the narrow alley, a dark and gruff chuckle.

For years that followed, every time I heard footsteps behind me or thought I saw a figure in the night, I heard that laugh in the depths of my mind. Taunting me.

I heard it again when my mother died, loud and clear as if he was there in that empty kitchen. It was present at her grave, when I saw my closest brother dead in the street, when my father was murdered and I went to identify his body—even when I first killed a man out of vengeance when I was nineteen years old.

That demeaning laugh would haunt me because I knew he was watching. He was watching me die slowly in this wretched world and yet, he did nothing.

"Carter," he finally answered me. "He's making friends he shouldn't."

"How would you know?" I asked without hesitating, even though inside I felt like a twisted rag, devoid of air and feeling.

"I know everything, Jase Cross," he told me, moving closer to me even as I stepped back. The step was quick, too quick and the one free hand I had crashed behind me against the rough brick wall from the liquor shop. It left a small and inconsequential gash just below my middle knuckle. Eventually the gash became a scar, forming a physical memory of Marcus's warning that night. His laugh stayed in my mind after that night, and like my scar, served as a permanent reminder of him over the years.

He neared the dim strip of light from the full moon overhead, the bit that leaked into the alley, but still he didn't show himself.

I nearly dropped the bag in my grasp when he came even closer and I had nowhere to go.

"I have a message for you to deliver to him," he told me. "If he ever goes against me, your entire family will suffer the consequences."

"Carter?" I breathed his name, shaking my head out of instinct from knowing Carter hadn't done anything. "He doesn't know anyone. You have the wrong person."

All he did was laugh again, the same sick sound coming up from the pit of his stomach. I repeated in the breath of a whisper, "Carter hasn't done anything."

"Not yet, but he will." The words were spoken with such confidence from the darkness. "And I'll be watching."

He left me standing there, on the verge of trembling as he walked away. The pounding in my chest was louder than his quiet footsteps although I didn't dare breathe.

That was the first night I met the man I would now call my enemy. Whatever fear I had for him as a child has turned to resentment and spite.

That's all he is. He's only a man. A man with no face, a hefty bag of threats and a penchant for eliciting fear in all who dare to walk the streets he claims as his own.

These aren't his streets. He has no right to them, but I do.

He treats this world like a game; the lives and deaths of those around us are only pieces on a board to be lost or taken, used however he'd like.

But the mistake he made is simple: He dared to meddle and bring Bethany into this game.

She's mine. Only mine.

Not a pawn for him to play with.

It's time for Marcus's game to end.

CHAPTER
1

Bethany

FUCK. *Fuck. Fuck. Fuck. Fuck.*

A numb prickle of fear races up and down my body like a thousand needles keeping me still. All the while, my heart's the only thing that's moving. It's frantic and unyielding as it thrashes inside of me.

The floorboards creak again as someone moves toward the stairs while I keep my feet firmly planted in the kitchen. *Someone.* Who? I don't know.

No one has ever walked into my home unannounced and I know it's not Laura; I know it's not Jase. Just thinking his name sends another chill down my spine. The fear, the regret, the unknown from what I just read in The Coverless Book are all things I can't dwell on right now. Blinking furiously, I shut the wayward trail of thoughts down.

No, it's not Jase.

It's someone else, someone with bad intentions. Deep down, I can feel it.

If I'd just been back in the living room when the door opened, back there where I was a moment ago, reading The Coverless Book and using this notebook to jot down the underlined words… if I'd been there, whoever just opened the door would have seen me instantly. If I'd left the notebook in the living room, and not in the drawer in the kitchen, whoever it was, would have seen me. I wouldn't have had a chance to run.

Fate spared me, but for how long?

My fingers tremble as I silently set the notebook down on the counter, devising a plan.

Get my phone. Run the hell out of here. Call the cops.

It's as simple as that. If I can't get the phone, *just run.*

Whoever it is, they're heading upstairs and once I hear the creaking from the floorboards move from the stairs to one of the bedrooms, I'll move as quickly and quietly as possible. I can barely keep it together while I'm waiting, listening, and feeling the numbing fear flowing over my skin.

Hot and cold sensations overwhelm my body at once and I don't know how I'm even capable of breathing with how tight and raw and dry my throat is. All I know is that I can't fail. I can't let him know where I am.

My movements are measured as I release the notebook. The second I do, I hear another person open my front door. *Thump, thump, thump.* My heartbeat is louder than anything else. Another person's here. I'm not in control as I instinctively back away from the threshold of the kitchen, closer toward the back of the house.

One person and then another.

Thump, thump, thump.

Abandoning all reason, I turn my back to where they are, ready to hide somewhere as quickly as possible. *Somewhere. Where? Where can I hide?* My head whirls with panic. I need to hide.

My body freezes when I hear my phone go off. It's still where I left it in the next room over, the living room. Footsteps come closer, closer to me, closer to the threshold of the kitchen where they can see me. *No, fuck, please no.* Inwardly I beg; I plead.

I'm trapped in the narrow kitchen with three people sneaking into my home. I can't die here. Not like this. Not after everything that's happened. It would be more than cruel to make me suffer in the last weeks of my life, like this.

I know if whoever it is stops at the coffee table where my phone is, he won't be able to see into the galley kitchen, but that won't stop him from moving on once he picks up my cell. Even more, he'll know for certain I'm here. I wouldn't leave without my phone, so they'll know. *Fuck!*

Thump, thump, thump. I wish I could quiet the pulse that's banging in my ears faster by the second.

Forcing myself to calm down and think as I hear a murmur from only ten... maybe twelve feet away in the other room, I focus on anywhere I could conceal myself. The pantry is the obvious solution, but it's so full, there's no way. Plus the shelves come out too far.

With numb fingers, I pry open the cabinet door for the recycling. The bin is still outside where I left it for pickup yesterday. It'll be cramped, but I think I can squeeze myself into the small space. I don't know the chances they'd open every cabinet of the kitchen, but I don't have anywhere else to hide.

My feet are heavy and my limbs rigid. I'm not as quiet as I wish I was. But I'm quick. I'm damn quick as I cram myself inside of the cabinet, the faint scent of spilled wine that's leaked from empty bottles hitting me at full force, along with other less than desirable odors.

I couldn't give two shits about what it smells like. All I care about is if they heard. *Please, please.* The telltale sound of shoes on the tile lets me know someone's here.

The weight of the steps is heavy; they have to be from a man. Both hands cover my mouth out of an instinct to be quiet, just as my eyes slam shut tight and refuse to look. I pray he didn't hear. If he heard the sound of a cabinet... *fuck. Please, no.*

I swear whoever it is can hear my ragged breaths and the ringing in my ears that's so fucking loud I can barely hear them walk into the kitchen. Them. Multiple footsteps.

Fuck, fuck, fuck, fuck.

I can't think about it. I can't be here right now. Not my mind. The stress and fear wrap around my body like barbed wire, tightening by the second and forcing me to fight it, to move, to react. I can't be here. This can't be happening.

Go somewhere else. My own words, words I've told patients many times slip into my consciousness. *Go somewhere else.*

"Have you ever thought about what it would be like to be pregnant?" my mother asks me with a devious grin. Her knee rocks back and forth as she sits in the chair, playing with her long hair that's draped over one shoulder. "Like, to be Talia right now? Could you imagine?"

I was hoping she'd remember today, but at least she's talking. That's good, I tell myself. It's good that she's happy today, in whatever time she's living in, it was a happy one for her.

"Who's Talia?" I ask her, feigning the curiosity I think she'd expect from whoever it is she thinks she's talking to. It's never me. She never knows it's me.

"You know, the blonde in Mr. Spears's class. She's almost six months along now," my mother says, enjoying the gossip.

"Mr. Spears?"

"Tenth grade English. The really tall one and kind of young? I think he's hot."

My mother's comment makes me smile. I wish I were back in high school. She didn't have Alzheimer's then.

"So have you thought about it?" she questions again and I shake my head honestly.

"I can't imagine having kids right now."

"I can. I want a boy. A boy with James Peters's eyes and smile."

"James Peters." I repeat the boy's name and set two cups of water down on the end table.

"One day I'm going to ask him out."

"What if you have a girl?" I ask her.

"Oh no," she says and shakes her head. "Girls are too much trouble." I have to remind myself that she's only a teenager today. I'm sure all teenagers think that. They have perceptions before having kids.

I remind myself of it but still, I have to get up and get away. Just for a minute.

"Where are you going? Is class starting soon? I thought we had another half hour of lunch?"

"We do," I answer her, forcing a smile. "I just have to do something."

"You forgot your books, didn't you, Maggie?" She taunts me. "You're so forgetful."

I can feel it when I hit my breaking point. It's not getting easier like I thought it would.

Resting against the wall in the kitchen, all I can do is breathe. All I can do is hide from my mother and hide from the truth.

"Does Mom remember?" Jenny's question comes from the threshold of the kitchen. She leans against it with a mug in her hand although I can smell the

whiskey from here. I'm not sure if it's in her mug or just a leftover stench from wherever she was last night.

"No," I answer her.

She takes a sip in response and with it, I'm given an answer to my own unspoken question. It's nine in the morning and the whiskey is in the cup she's currently clinging to.

"She's talking about having kids right now. Back in high school."

"Kids," my sister repeats, rolling her eyes and taking another sip.

"Yeah, she said she wants daughters." I don't know why the lie slipped out. I think I just wanted to comfort my sister.

My sister throws the mug back, downing its contents before tossing it into the sink.

"Really? She told me the other day she'd hate to have daughters."

A bang close by brings me back to now. Back to the present. Away from my sister and away from my mother.

My eyes open unhurriedly, not wanting to see but forcing myself to take in anything I can in the dark space. Tremors run through my legs and up my spine to my shoulders, leaving goosebumps in their wake. With a single unsteady exhale, I stare through the bright slit in the cabinet door as faded, broken-in blue jeans show themselves. I can see the seams and the stitching even. He's that close to me. Just behind the door. I nearly whimper when the creak of the pantry closet proves he's searching for me.

He heard me moving around in the kitchen. I feel lightheaded for a moment, maybe from fear, maybe from holding my breath.

A buzzing from the other room makes him turn on his heels and I watch all the while with both hands over my mouth, my palms sweaty and clammy. He stands still as the other person walks out of the kitchen. They're louder now, reckless and bold as they open doors and search for something or someone.

It doesn't have to be me. Please, don't let what they're looking for be me. Be looking for something Jenny left here. Please, for the love of God, be that. Find it. Find it and get out.

The thoughts don't go unanswered. Fate lets me know the worst-case scenario is in fact my reality.

"Her car is still in the driveway. You think she heard us and ran?" A muted voice I don't recognize is coming from the living room. Another voice, one from farther away, maybe in the foyer answers, "Nah, she has to be here still. She wouldn't leave her phone."

The man just beyond the cabinet door walks away swiftly and moves toward the voice—that's when I catch a glimpse of the red stripes on his white sneakers. A single horizontal stripe runs along the length of each shoe midway up the side. White shoes with red stripes. I can hear him smack the man after a gruff response from his throat and then it's quiet again.

The man who was so close to me knows better than to talk and give away their thoughts.

Thump, thump, thump. They don't say another word as I inhale the musty smells from the cabinetry, willing my body to obey me and not betray my position.

Every time a loud bang or the crash of something being overturned startles me, my shoulders push harder against the rough wood behind my back and I bite down on the inside of my cheek to silence the instinctive scream.

My nails dig deeper into my skin on my thighs as the bangs get closer and louder. It's obvious they're trashing the place. All the while, I pray. *Please don't find me. Please leave.*

For a moment, I think they might.

The recognizable noise of the front door opening is suddenly clear. As are the sounds of them leaving, one by one, but I don't believe they're truly gone. It's too obvious. It's a trick and a trap; one I won't be caught in. Time passes, each second seeming longer and longer, gauged by the steady ticking of the clock above the kitchen sink.

All I can think about is every time a girl is in the middle of the woods running from someone in the movies. She hides behind a tree or bush—something that offers her a hidden spot—and she waits until she thinks they've run by and can't hear them anymore. She thinks they've moved on, as if they've kept running through the tall trees and didn't see her. She doesn't hear them, so she takes off.

That's when they catch her. They know she's hiding and they're just waiting until she comes out to snatch her up.

Not me. They won't catch me that way. For the first time since I heard someone come in, strength and conviction outweigh the fear. I'll stay here until I know for certain it's safe.

I don't know what these men wanted with me, but I know they were looking for me and that's all the reason I need to stay right where I fucking am.

My body stays tense for I don't even know how long. It feels like maybe ten minutes. Only ten minutes or so, maybe twenty? I can't track the sound of the clock; it's going too fast and then too slow and then it blurs together and I can't focus on it. It feels hotter and hotter in this small space, but I don't waver. Never daring to move. Not even after it's silent. With stiff legs and an aching back, I finally lower my hands and that's when I realize how my neck is bent. It hurts; everything hurts from being shoved in this small space and hunched over, crouched down. My ankle dares to stretch forward, causing my toes to brush against the cabinet door.

Did they really leave?

Not a sound is heard when the cabinet pushes open, ever so slightly. I didn't do it on purpose, I just needed to move.

Nothing happens. There's no sign they're still here and I could see myself sneaking out slowly, risking a look.

I still don't trust it though. What happens if they're right outside and they see through the windows that I'm here? A black vision passes before my eyes and my head falls back, feeling the anxiety rush through me.

Staying as still and as silent as I can be, I wait, praying for a sign that I'm safe.

All I'm given is silence. God didn't answer my prayers for my sister. Why would he answer me now?

For the longest time, there's nothing but silence. The tick of the clock goes on and on, and I endure it. Not daring to move.

And then everything happens all at once.

The slam of the front door, and then the back door to the garage. My hands whip up to my mouth to cover the silent scream as my entire body tenses and my skin scrapes against the wooden walls of my hiding spot.

The crash of glass breaking, I think a window in the back room, makes my shoulders hunch and I wish I could hide even further back. All of it is followed by the sound of tires squealing from outside my house. At least two cars. At least three men. And one with a pair of white shoes with red stripes.

I don't think I inhale the entire time. It doesn't seem like they came back in. They merely broke something from the outside. Did they throw something inside the house? A bomb? That's the first place my head goes. They threw a bomb in here and I'm going to die anyway. Still, I can't move and nothing happens.

There's no noise, no explosion. Just silence again.

Possibilities run furiously through my mind as I try to calm down. The back of my head rests against the wood as my thoughts turn dark. I think about how desperate I was to move, and how they were right there waiting. How close I was to playing into their trap.

I don't have long to drown in gratitude and the horror of what could have been. Maybe five or ten minutes go by before I hear another car. That's all the time that passes from the squeal of one set of tires leaving and then the shriek of another set slamming to a halt in front of my house.

I nearly upheave at the prospect of what they came back to do.

The front door opens, loud with intention, banging off the wall. Then I faintly hear a gun cock, followed by his voice.

Jase.

"Bethany!" Although he screams my name with a demand, his cadence is laced with panic. "Bethany, where are you?" he calls out as I hear the crunch of glass beneath his feet. "Fuck! Bethany!" He screams my name louder and still I don't move.

There's a moment where I feel relief. Where I want to run to him and get out of here, climbing into his arms and begging him to take me away from here and spilling everything.

But then I remember. The black words on cream paper with the blue underlined ink left from Jenny. All I can think about is how CROSS was in The Coverless Book. A hidden message from my sister.

The unknowing fear is crippling and the pain in my chest makes me grip my shirt, right where it's hurting.

I hear the faint sound of a phone dialing—muted and barely heard, followed by my cell vibrating on the coffee table. *They left it?*

"Fuck!" Jase screams and then hurls something across my living room that makes my entire body jostle.

My thoughts scramble, my emotions stay at war with one another, but one thing is for certain: He'll protect me. The selfish thought forces me to lurch from where I am.

I push the cabinet door open, the creaking a companion to the aching pain of my muscles screaming from being cramped up for so long. "Jase." I try to call out his name, but it comes out jagged and hoarse from my dry throat. I fall on my ass and right thigh as I make my way out of the cabinet, wincing from a cramp sending a sharp pain shooting up my side just as Jase sees me.

"Bethany," he says, and my name is wretched on his lips. Slipping out with relief and his own fears ringing through.

I'm stiff as he drops to his knees beside me, pulling me into his hard chest. Both of his arms wrap around me and he tucks my head under his chin, rocking me and kissing my hair. I can't focus on him though; my body is screaming in pain. I just want to breathe and stand up. Why do I hurt so much? I don't know what to think or what to say or what to do. It's all too much. I'm breaking down.

All I can focus on is keeping my eyes open and staying aware. He's still shushing me when I finally push a logical thought out.

"Let me go," I tell him, my words rushed. I have to clear my throat, but that just makes it more hoarse. My body's still stiff and it's then that Jase seems to notice I'm not quivering in his arms and begging for him to save me. Maybe that's what I should have done, but I've always been a bad liar. "I need to move; let me go."

The change in Jase's demeanor is immediate and palpable. His grip moves to my upper arms, his fingers digging into my flesh and nearly hurting me.

"What happened? Are you okay?" he questions and the hardness in his words echoes the look in his gaze. Piercing me, demanding information. He doesn't let go. There's no sympathy from him, and for the first time, I see the man he really is. The man who rules with fear and unrelenting force.

I try to answer him, but my throat is so dry I could choke on the words. With a heavy breath out, I feel faint, staring into his eyes. I watch as his stern expression changes slowly. Before, I felt like I'd been given a glimpse, but thought I'd imagined it. This time I know I saw it.

"Why didn't you answer me?" The words of his question waver. The guilt and betrayal flicker on each syllable and make my chest feel hollow and vacant. I'm pinned by his gaze and the nausea comes back full force.

A dry heave breaks the tension, forcing Jase to lift me to my feet and bring me to the sink. Pushing him away with one shaking hand, I turn the faucet on, my fingers slipping around the knob at first, unable to grip it tight enough. The cold water is more than a relief against my face, dripping down my neck and throat, even though it soaks into my sweater. And then drinking it from my cupped hands. I hear Jase go through a cabinet to my upper left and then he pushes a glass toward me for me to take.

One breath. And another. One breath. And another. The water swirls around the drain and I focus on two things.

1. I'm alive.
2. Jase doesn't know about the message in the book.

It's hard to remember where we were before I read those lines. It's always hard going back.

The knob protests with a squeaking sound as I turn it off, still not daring to look Jase in the eyes. Leaning my hip against the countertop to stay upright, I force myself to calm down. Still feeling dizzy and as if I don't have a grasp on anything at all, bringing my arms up to cross in front of me, I spit it out, one line at a time.

"At first one man… or woman," I breathe the words out. "I didn't know who it was but…" I trail off slowly, because that's when I remember Jase said he wasn't coming over tonight. I knew it wasn't him because he'd told me he wasn't coming.

"Why are you here?" I ask him and stare into his dark eyes as I feel how heavy my own are.

"Things changed and I wanted to make sure you were all right." Every word is spoken with a sense of calm but also forcefully. His hand on my upper arm steals my attention. Though gentle, it's demanding just the same. It strikes me that "gentle but demanding" is exactly how I'd describe this man. The knowledge makes something in the pit of my stomach flicker to life, a dull burn.

"One man came? One man did all of this?" he questions.

One breath, one beat of my heart and I move my gaze to his. "I was in the kitchen and heard someone come in. Whoever it was went upstairs and before I could do anything, two more people came in and I hid."

It sounds so simple when I say it like that. Only two sentences to describe the last half hour? Or maybe an hour? I peek at the oven and then swallow thickly at the red digital numbers staring back at me. Over an hour and a half. Sucking in a hesitant breath and closing my eyes, I tell him just that. "I hid for an hour and a half and they just left."

My eyes are still closed when he asks, "They just left? How long ago?"

The irritation that flows from my words is unjustified, but it's there nonetheless. "Yes, that's what I just said. They just left." My voice cracks as I raise it and pull the hair away from my hot face. "Minutes ago. They could come back." I lie and say, "That's why I couldn't answer you when you first came in. I wasn't sure if they were really gone yet."

He sees right through my lie; I can tell with the hint of a tilt of his head.

The realization leaves me just as it comes. Jase is here. Relief is hesitant to console me when he says, "No one's going to hurt you," instead of calling me out on the lie.

"You sound so sure of that," I speak just under my breath and finally look into his eyes. Into the eyes of a man I was falling for. A man I trusted and slept with. A man who makes me question everything now.

I have to break his gaze and let out an uneasy breath as I stare past him and see the destruction. "Oh my God." The words fall from my lips. "What the hell did they do?"

He follows me silently as I walk without thinking into the living room. The sofa is moved away from the wall, the cushions scattered on the floor. Maybe they did that when they were searching for me, but the lamp is busted, the light bulb shattered on the floor where it fell, the coffee table is overturned and that's when I realize the book is gone.

The Coverless Book. Disbelief runs through me in a wave as I fall to the floor searching for it, but knowing it's not here.

These were my mother's things and the first pieces of furniture I bought on my own. Pieces I picked out with my sister. Each and every thing in this house comes with a memory. They violated it. I've never felt like this before.

"A robbery," Jase says behind me and I shake my head. Denying the lie he speaks.

"They wanted it to look like that." I'm barely conscious of my response as I take in the place. "That's why they did it," I add as the thought hits me and I stand up, looking toward the door. "They broke the window after they left to make it look like a robbery. Like they broke the glass to unlock the door."

I feel sickened more than angered.

Pushing the hair out of my face, I try to think about what they could have been after, but it's obvious. "They came here for me, but they thought I ran, so they made it look like a break-in." I whip around to face Jase and tell him, "They knew I was here... or maybe they thought I took off. So they staged it..." My gaze falls as I swallow the lump in my throat. "They thought I took off when I heard them so they staged it as a robbery."

"It's a setup," Jase agrees, searching through things and telling me Seth is nearby watching the entrance to the neighborhood and that everything's okay now. He promises me he'll fix it, he says he'll find whoever it was and make them pay. He tells me he's happy I'm okay and tries to comfort me with his touch, but I pull away. I don't listen to his promises. I'm not in the habit of relying on promises. The seconds pass as I give myself a moment to actually process what happened.

It makes sense. All of it makes sense.

But why take the book? Every hair on the back of my neck stands up when the question echoes in my head.

My phone's on the floor, as is a stack of envelopes from the pile of opened mail, but the mail itself, is missing. They were only bills, nothing of importance. But my laptop is gone too. Fuck! I need that for work. As I halfheartedly lean forward searching through my things, I take everything into account, but the one thing that matters... It really isn't here.

"The book." I can't help but to say it out loud and when I do, my lips feel chapped and the sentence comes out raw. "They took it?" Denial is apparent. "Why take the book?" I shove everything out of the way, searching all over the living room until I get to the hallway only to see it's trashed too. My mother's vase sits perfectly where it is, thank God, but the light in the hall is broken. All the lights are broken.

They upturned the furniture, then busted the lights and stole meaningless items with no worth. Meaningless to them, but to me... "I want my book back." I'm surprised that after all this time, the back of my eyes prick and my hands ball into fists at the thought of someone coming in here and taking The Coverless Book.

I don't even realize I'm shaking until Jase holds me from behind, pulling me into his chest. And again, I'm stiff.

His embrace is calming and masculine, wrapped in warmth. It's designed to comfort, just like the small kiss he plants on my neck. But I can't relax. I can't.

"Why did they do this?" My question turns to broken pieces of whispered syllables in the air.

"Stay with me. I'll make sure we find them and get your book back." His soothing words do nothing to change what's happened and where my mind leads me.

None of this would have happened if Jenny hadn't died; if she hadn't gotten herself into this mess. It always leads back to Jenny and with her name on the tip of my tongue, tears threaten again to fall.

All the calm words and pretty promises couldn't keep the tremors at bay.

"I want to know who they were. They knew what they were doing. It's the men who murdered Jenny. That's why they took the book."

Every memory of my sister always brings out the worst in me.

Angry tears form but don't fall as I take in a heavy breath and shove Jase away. I'm good at doing that. At shoving people away.

Those bastards came here. They took her book from me, the last thing she left me and the only thing that had a message from her. The only key I had to finding out what happened to her.

"Call the cops," I demand, wiping at my eyes with the sleeve of my sweater. The words scratch my throat on their way out.

"No." He answers hard.

"Call them!" I screech, shoving my fists into Jase's chest to get him away from me. Anger is nothing compared to what I feel. He grabs my wrists quicker than I can register, forcing me to stare up at him. He can stare all he wants; he can try to hold me, try to bend me to his will, nothing will get through to me. Once he learns that, he'll leave.

It's only when I look into his eyes in this foyer, with this fear and the memories of Jenny that I realize it's just as it was a week and a half ago when he first knocked on my door. Nothing has changed.

"Just go," I seethe.

"Calm down." He grits the words through his teeth, the irritation barely contained in his voice.

"I'm calling the cops." I stare into his eyes as I speak.

"No, you're not. You're going to come with me. You're going to wait while I find the men who did this and make this right." Every word from his mouth is a demand. They strike me and dare me not to obey.

Ripping my hands away from him, I step back and then step back again. My teeth grind so hard against one another they could crack.

Jase knows better than to approach me as I reach for my shoes and then gather my phone without a word spoken. He thinks I'm obeying him. Going along with what he says and listening like a good girl.

Never in my life has someone bossed me around and told me what to do. Not until Jenny went away and Jase came storming into my life. The bitter acknowledgement stays with me as I prepare to get the hell away from here.

He walks around my place as I silently put on my shoes and grab my coat, my car keys still in the right pocket. Beneath the heavy fabric is my purse, the wallet still there.

And the knowledge is a smack in the face.

They had to know it would be obvious that it wasn't a robbery. Maybe they were counting on me not calling the police. Maybe they know about Jase. They thought I'd run to him?

A chill flows down my spine as I stare up at the man I've been sleeping with, the man I thought I was falling for. He nods toward the door, telling me he has to make a call before we leave.

I don't answer him, not trusting myself to speak.

Instead, while he's on the phone on the porch I walk right past his car and get into my own, speeding off quickly enough so that all he can do is run into the street as I stare into my rearview mirror watching him.

The deafening silence is my only companion as I run away from it all, toward God knows where. I have no idea where I'm going or how I'll find a way out of this mess. The second I get around the corner, panic takes over. Realizing this is my life; this is what my life has become.

The tires screech as I yank the wheel to the left and turn into the neighbor's long drive. Slamming on the brakes and parking, I turn off the car, feeling a sickness churn in my gut.

I did what she used to do to me.

This is what Jenny used to do when she'd leave in an angry fit. We'd get into fights about her new friends and new habits. She'd threaten to leave and I'd threaten to follow. She thought I didn't know that she would just pull in here until things calmed down and then she'd drive home. She'd drive away, just to hide down the street, all alone crying in her car. The house itself is empty. The owner lives in a retirement home and his kids aren't willing to sell it yet.

I knew. I knew exactly what Jenny was doing. Not the first time, but the time after, she was too slow and I saw. I'd drive past every time though and park a few streets down and then walk back up here, watching her cry in the driver's seat. At least she was safe.

That's all I ever wanted.

Safe is what matters.

That's what I told myself back then. As I see Jase speed down the road behind me, not glancing my way at all, that's what I tell myself now. I need to keep myself safe. Safe from everything.

I don't trust anyone.

All I know is that I need my book back.

I need to know what Jenny's last words to me were.

CHAPTER
2

Jase

THE LEATHER IS HOT AGAINST MY PALMS AS I TWIST MY HANDS AROUND the steering wheel. My knuckles are turning white with every second that passes.

I force myself to focus on every detail around me to keep from losing all sense of control.

The ringing of Seth's phone echoes in the silent car. It rings once, then halfway through a second ring before he picks up.

"Where is she?" My question comes out hard and I don't bother to hide the fury. "How the fuck did she get away?"

"Boss?" Seth questions and it only makes the irritation grow.

A seething anger is in command of every aspect of my being right now. Nothing is going right and nothing is under control. "Where the fuck is she?" I scream the question, feeling each word claw up my throat on the way out.

"Bethany Fawn's car is located at Forty-two Bayview."

"Forty-two Bayview." I breathe out the address, craning my neck beneath the windshield to look at the small green street sign and then to my left as if one of them will magically be Bayview. Neither of them are and that fact is why I slam my fist on the dashboard as I simmer with pure rage. She fucking left me. Knowing there are men after her, she fucking ran from me!

"Four streets behind you, Mr. Cross." I focus on what I can control and then finally breathe.

"Four streets?" I swallow after repeating what he said, knowing she's safe. She's within reach.

"Make a U-turn when you're able. It looks like she stayed there for..." The word stretches out as he pauses and then continues, "...two minutes. She's on the move now, backing out of the driveway." Seth uses the GPS in her car to track her and gives me directions. "I'm still at the back entrance to the neighborhood and it looks like she's coming this way. She'll be driving by me if she stays on course."

"Follow her." Resolution takes over, following a pang of regret. Running my hand down my face and pinching the bridge of my nose, I try to pinpoint the moment I lost her. Truly lost her. She shouldn't have done that. Something happened.

The break-in. I slam my head back, exhaling a tight breath and loathing the life I live. No shit, something happened. What the fuck is wrong with me?

"On her tail," Seth says over the speaker. His obliviousness to my state is a kind gift in this moment as I press my palms to my eyes and focus on what I can do to keep her safe.

"Call for backup and continue following her but keep your distance and keep me informed. I want to know where she's going and I never want her out of your sight."

"Understood, Boss."

"I'm not letting her go," I tell him. My voice is firm and resolute, although my words are more for me than for him.

"Of course not," he answers although his tone has changed. Softer, not consoling, but understanding. A sedan skirts around me, a newer Mazda with an older man at the wheel who looks at me with a crease marred into his wrinkled forehead as his car passes mine.

Forcing a semblance of a smile to my lips, I offer him a small wave and pretend to be someone just passing by. As if I could ever just pass by Bethany. I would never be able to not feel her presence in a crowded room. I could never ignore it. Let alone allow her to ignore me.

"Is everything all right?" Seth asks after a moment of quiet.

"No, I'll brief you once she's secure."

There's a pause before he asks, "Is there anything else I can do?"

"She is your only priority at the moment."

It's quiet again, but I can't hang up yet. Not without Seth acknowledging what I just said. My gaze lifts to the rearview as a man exits his front door. As he walks to the car in his driveway, the headlights flash and it's only then that I'm aware of how dark it's gotten.

It wasn't that late when I left the cemetery. I just wanted to make sure she was okay. It was foolish to think she would be.

It took me far too long to get to her. I never would have guessed when I got there that her brunette hair would tumble into a halo upon the tiled floor, followed by her small frame. My hand stings from the impact of bashing it against the dashboard a moment ago and I clench it into a tight fist, staring at the silver scar below my knuckle as I remember how she fell.

Fuck, she didn't even make a sound for the longest second.

I thought she was dead. I thought he'd killed her. I thought Marcus had ripped her away from me, getting to her first, when she fell out onto the kitchen floor. I hate that the scar stares back at me in this moment.

It's hard to ignore the splinter of pain that tears through me.

Why else would she not have responded? He'd killed her and shoved her in a cabinet for me to find. I thought it was merely her body falling and that she was already dead.

"Does she know about Jenny?" Seth's question brings me back to the present. To her running away from me.

"That he has her?" I clarify and breathe in deep, staring at the picket fence in front of me. "She doesn't know anything. I didn't tell her about the note."

She'll live her life with unanswered questions unless I can give them to her, and right now, I wouldn't be so cruel.

Even if she'd been fine. Even if she'd spilled out of that cabinet and ran to me like I wanted her to, I wouldn't tell her. She's barely holding on as it is. It's not pity I feel for her, it's worry.

"I'm not telling her that her sister's alive until I know we can bring her back." It's one mess after the other. "False hope can kill what's left of a person." That's the only explanation I give him. He knows about the note from Marcus. He knows Marcus has Jenny.

I'd rather she continue thinking Jenny's dead. Just in case that's how this all ends.

"We'll discuss everything moving forward tonight." Even as I give him the command, I hear the fatigue in my voice. The day has taken its toll. More than its fair share. "Has my brother gotten in touch with you?"

"About the men we sent out?" he asks to clarify.

"Yes."

"We have men trailing the man seen with Jenny. His name's Luke Stevens. He's driving out west. We don't know where to but he's definitely taken orders from Marcus. He's mentioned him twice on the calls taken from his car."

"Don't let him get far; I don't give a shit if we blow our cover. Have our men grab him and bring him back here."

"Consider it done."

"Good. I want him brought in and questioned. I want to know everything about Marcus. About Jenny. Everything that bastard knows… I'll get it from him." There are enemies everywhere and everything is moving quickly. "Bethany needs to stay put tonight. Let her run it off. But stay on her and don't lose her. I want an update every five minutes."

"Of course," he answers me.

Glancing at the clock, I change my mind. "Every three minutes. An update every three minutes." I give him the order as I make a U-turn and head back to Bethany's home, preparing myself for the evidence of what happened. "Briefing is tonight, war starts tomorrow."

CHAPTER
3

Bethany

I SHOULDN'T CALL LAURA. I KEEP THINKING IT OVER AND OVER AGAIN EVEN
as I stare at the bright white screen of my phone with her contact
info staring back at me.

I'm so fucking alone. After driving to nowhere in silence for an
hour, that's what I've realized more than anything. I'm so fucking alone.

It's sad when you realize there's only one person left, and you can't
reach out to them, because God forbid if what happened to me affects
her. I'd never forgive myself.

The darkness outside drifts in as I sit listless in the driver's seat.
There's not a star in the black sky and the moon is merely a sliver.
Not even the lingering snow reflects the light. It's no longer white and
bright, it's dulled and nearly vanished as well.

My teeth scrape against my bottom lip as I pull it into my mouth
and look out of my window, still strapped in to the driver's seat. From
the outside of my house, no one would ever know what happened.

Closed doors hide a variety of crimes.

Wiping under my tired, burning eyes, I then press the button to
exit my contacts to prevent myself from giving in and being weak. I
won't call her.

But that only leaves Jase.

CROSS. I can't think of him without being reminded of the book, the underlined hidden message inside it, followed by the break-in, and then Jenny. Every thought, question, and mournful memory assault me one after the other just from thinking his name. I'm so confused and lost... and alone.

I stare down at the white plastic bag on the passenger seat. The logo of Martin Hardware stares back at me in a bold red font and beneath it I know there are three packs of light bulbs, each containing four apiece. It took me a while to feel safe enough to go in. Shit, it took me a while to stop looking in my rearview mirror and keeping track of cars who could be following me. There was no one there for all the hours I've been away from my home.

There's no one here now either. It's just me and the aftermath.

All I have to do is get out of my car and replace the bulbs so I can at least turn on a light.

I have to know what happened. I have to search my place and see what they took. The puzzle keeps me from breaking down. It keeps me from remembering Jenny and the fact that she's gone. As well as Jase, and the fact that he may be to blame if the message in the book is about him.

Why did they take the book and my bills? I think back to the living room. Everything turned over, but systematically. Everything was done with the purpose of making it look like a robbery... but they didn't steal what a random burglar would take.

A long exhale and I'm able to pretend like it isn't devastating. Like I don't feel violated. Like there's no reason for me to be terrified.

My bills and mail, plus whatever other papers were in the coffee table, although I can't even imagine what else I had stored there. And my laptop.

But not my phone or my wallet.

They stole information.

Resting my elbow against the window frame of my car, I press my thumbnail between my teeth and bite down gently, mindlessly. All I can do is stare at my front door and see a man. He had to have been tall, wearing faded, broken-in blue jeans and white sneakers with a red stripe along the sides of each. My mind plays the scene for me. Him quietly picking the lock, pressing his shoulder against the door and opening it as silently as he could. Did he know I was in the living room before he stepped in? Did he peek into the curtains in the bay window beforehand?

Again the series of thoughts plays out. The break-in will always lead to Jenny.

Did he hurt Jenny? Did he know her? I can barely stand to look at the stark white door as the realization hits me.

The men I've been after, the ones I've demanded be served justice were only feet from me today. And I cowered.

My breathing comes in staggered pants as I look at my front door again and instead of seeing him, I see my sister sitting on the front step. Just as she was the last time I saw her. Bloodshot eyes full of fear staring back at me. It was the day she gave me the gun.

The image washes away as my eyes turn glossy, but the emotions are short lived.

Bright lights from a passing car distract me and the fear I can't deny takes over. It lasts only for a second as the car continues on its way, never even turning down this street.

The sliver of strength I had pulling into the driveway is long gone.

The adrenaline doesn't wane though. And I know there's no way I can go back inside.

I can't sleep here.

I'll never feel safe in this house again.

My thoughts aren't cohesive when I call him. I don't even realize what I've done until Jase's phone is ringing with my cell pressed to my ear. He doesn't make me wait long to answer. Which is a damn good thing, because I nearly hang up on the second ring.

"Bethany." He says my name with a quiet emotion I can't quite place. Longing is evident though and somehow that makes me feel like it's all going to be okay. But how could it ever be okay at this point?

Time goes by and words evade me. Jase doesn't speak either.

"Are you angry?" I eventually ask him and I can't fathom why. It shouldn't matter if he's angry at me or not. My life does not revolve around this dark knight. I won't allow it. I don't want this life.

"I'm disappointed."

"You sound like my mother," I answer with feigned sarcasm and not really meaning it. It just seems like something someone would say in response to, *I'm disappointed.*

All I can hear is a huff on the end of the line followed by a resigned sigh. "I keep having to remind myself that you're going through a lot, but that doesn't mean you can do this shit, Bethany."

Shame heats my cheeks and my throat dries, keeping me from being able to swallow as I look back to the house. With every passing second, I'm sinking deeper into the dark pit of emotions that's expanding around me.

"You don't know what I'm going through," I tell him simply. And all the voices I've heard before at the hospital echo in my mind. So many people think no one else feels the way they do when they're mourning, when they're sick. When life has got them by the throat and they have nowhere else to turn to but a mental hospital.

"I know people have it worse, people have more pain and more tragedy… but that doesn't mean I'm not handling things the best way that I can." Dignity is slow to greet me and I strengthen my voice to tell him, "I'm trying to just hold on right now." As I finish, my words crack and it's then that I feel as crazy as my patients. I'm losing it. I'm losing everything, watching it all slip through my fingers like the sand of an hourglass.

"Why did you run?" he asks me, not commenting on a word I've just spoken. Somehow, I'm grateful for that.

"I wasn't in the right mindset to be bossed around and whisked away." It's semi-honest. At the very least, it's not a lie.

"And now?"

"I don't know what to do," I admit, feeling the insecurity and the weight of what's happened push against my chest. "And I'm scared," I add. The confession barely leaves me; I don't know if he heard me or not. Another car passes down the street that crosses mine, forming a T-shaped intersection. This time I'm not as scared, but I'm conscious of it. I'm conscious of everything around me.

"Do you want to stay with me?" he asks.

"No," I say, and it hurts to answer him honestly. Physically hurts and drains me of what little strength I have left. I should add that I don't trust him after what I read in the book. But without the book, I can't be certain that I shouldn't trust him. Which makes everything all the more complicated.

"Why is that?" There's no hint of what he's feeling in his question; it's only a string of words asked for clarity. And that makes it easier, but not easy enough to tell the truth. How could I tell him I saw his last name in a coded message in The Coverless Book? I already feel like I've gone insane. I don't need someone else to confirm it.

"I'm just confused and I want to be alone." Nodding to myself although he can't see me, I repeat the sentiment, "I'm not sure exactly what I want right now, but I think I'd really like to be alone."

"I'd prefer you weren't alone right now... And you still owe me time." He adds the second statement when I don't respond to the first.

"I can always say no."

"I never should have put that in the contract."

His response forces a weak smile to my face. It's just as tired and sad as I am. "Your contract is bullshit." Our quips are a quick tit for tat. The rough chuckle from the other end of the line eases a small piece of me. As if slowly melting a large sheet of ice that encases and presses against me constantly.

"You're not going to be happy." He pauses after his statement and I simply wait for what's next, not responding until I know what he's getting at.

"Seth is behind you. He's parked a few houses down. I'll have him flash his lights for you." *Thump*, my heart squeezes tight, so tight it hurts and I actually reach up to place a hand over my chest as bright white lights shine behind me and then disappear.

"How long?"

"The entire time. Did you think I'd risk anything happening to you?"

Gratitude is a strange thing. Sometimes it feels warm and hugs every inch of you. Sometimes it strangles you and makes you feel rotten and unworthy. The latter is what I struggle with as Jase continues to tell me what to do.

Follow Seth to a hotel.

Stay there tonight.

Meet Jase tomorrow for dinner.

He ends the rattled-off list of things I'm required to do with, "We need to have a conversation."

The pit of my stomach sinks as I take in my current reality.

"I was a fool to think I'd outrun you, wasn't I?" My words are whispered and as they leave me, Seth's car comes to life. As he pulls up in front of my house, his eyes meet mine in the faint darkness. I rip my gaze away.

"You're far from a fool, but running from me … it won't be tolerated, Miss Fawn."

CHAPTER
4

Bethany

THERE'S A SAYING ABOUT LIFE AND HOW IT CAN BE ANYTHING YOU WANT it to be. I forget how it goes exactly. Not that it matters, because the saying is a fucking lie. You can't just decide one day you're going to change and everything will change with you. That's not how it works. That's not life. It's more complicated than that.

Life is a tangled mess of other people's bullshit and other people's decisions. Even decisions they make on a whim.

Sometimes, you get to decide whether or not you care about them and their issues. If you do, you're fucked. Their problems become yours and sometimes that means you fall down a black hole and there's no easy escape. "Today I choose to be happy," is a joke. You can't be happy when there's a rope around your neck and another around your feet. You can't step forward, and even if you could, you'd just hang yourself.

Sometimes you don't get to decide a damn thing at all. There's not a choice you could have made that would have prevented what's to come. My sorry ass has been thinking about that all day. Whether I had a choice or not. And if what I choose is what I deserve.

Because right now it feels like that rope is pulled snug under my chin with another wrapped tight around my ankles, scratching against my skin with every step I take.

As I stare at the slip of paper I've kept in my wallet that says, *in a life where you can be anything, be kind,* I don't think twice about balling it up to toss the crumpled scrap in the trash can outside the restaurant.

I miss on the first try. *Figures.* It mocks me as it falls to the ground, daring me to pick it up and really discard it. Which I do, albeit spitefully.

A strong gust of wind blows the hair from out of my face, and without the scarf I left in my car, the chill sweeps down my collarbone and seeps into my jacket. The weather is just as bitter as I am.

I don't know how long I've been standing outside of Crescent Inn, one of the nicer restaurants in this town. I've always wanted to come here, but I could never justify it because of the price. Pulling my coat collar tighter around myself I peek in through the large floor-to-ceiling windows, past the wooden blinds that only cover the top third of the windows and search for Jase.

He's not hard to find. In the center of the room, filled with bright white tablecloths amid a sea of small cobalt blue vases, each housing an array of fresh flowers next to tea lights for ambience, he stands out.

Just seeing him does something to me. Even as a couple passes around me, giving me a disconcerted look for blocking the door and staring inside the place, I can't bring myself to go to him. I couldn't sleep without dreaming about him.

I can't think without wanting to know what *he* thinks about it all.

It's only when he brings his gaze to meet mine, as if he could feel my stare, that I dare consider taking the necessary steps toward him.

How did I get in this deep? How did I let the ropes of his life and my sister's death wrap so tightly around my every waking moment?

More importantly, *how the hell do I get out of this?*

I tell myself the only reason I came is because he said he found my things they stole when he called this morning. They were all thrown in a trash can a few blocks down from my place. There's no way it was a break-in. Jase is on my side; it was staged to disguise something else.

It's easier to enter though, knowing I'll get my book back.

"Good evening, Miss Fawn." The host greets me the moment I walk in. Without another word, he graciously takes my coat from me, ignoring the shock and apprehension that must show on my expression. With my jaw dropped, and the air absent from my lungs, I don't have a chance to ask him how he knew my name, as if the answer isn't obvious.

"Mr. Cross is right this way. Follow me, please." The skin around the man's light blue eyes crinkles when he offers me a gentle smile. His suit is perfectly fitted to his proportions; his shoes are shined so well the chandeliers in the foyer of the restaurant sparkle against the black leather.

He's professional and kind. Still, I don't move. I stay where I am, knowing with every step I take that Jase Cross tells me to take, those ropes get tighter and tighter. Holding me right where he wants me.

The only saving grace is that if I don't think about it, if I just surrender to him… it will feel weightless, easy and deliciously thrilling while it lasts. If only I could think of anything but the demise of what my life once was.

The polite smile falters on the gentleman's face, emphasizing the lines around his eyes even more. The chatter of the crowded restaurant is what breaks me in this moment. There are plenty of people here, witnesses if anything were to happen. And I do need The Coverless Book. I need to know what Jenny said.

With her in mind, one imaginary rope around my ankle loosens. I'm all too aware that it belongs to her.

With every step I take, I think back to what's led me here:

Jenny's disappearance and how I couldn't let it go.

Jase's bar and how I couldn't keep my mouth shut.

Jenny's death and how I need to have justice.

The gun Jenny gave me and how I shot at Jase rather than playing dumb.

The contract I signed giving away my time and body in exchange for a debt.

And the break-in I don't know enough about. The book and the message inside I have to obtain.

They may have left the ropes for me to take, but I damn sure slipped them into place myself.

The host pulls the chair out for me as Jase stands, buttoning his jacket and pinning his gaze on me. A gaze I return.

"Thank you." My words are soft and I'm not certain if the host heard me or not, but I'm well aware that my hand is trembling as I reach for the water. Even more certain when the ice clinks against the edge of the pristine goblet.

I can tremble as much as I need. I'm in this mess of tangled lies and secrets, the violence and the need for vengeance. Even if it ends up killing me, I would have taken every step just the same if I had to do it all over again.

"You didn't sleep." Jase speaks first and I shake my head, staring at the cold drops of water that drip down the goblet as I set it on the table.

When I lift my tired eyes to his dark gaze, I answer him, "Maybe an hour. I was in and out." I swallow and place my hands in my lap before continuing. "Just couldn't stop thinking about everything."

He nods once and doesn't speak; instead he searches my expression for answers. Or maybe for where my boundaries lie with him today.

"What you did yesterday is unacceptable."

The tremors inside of me tense with irritation. "Which part exactly?" I question and the defiance is clear in my tone.

"The part where you ran from me."

"Who are you to me where that is unacceptable?"

His fixed stare narrows. "Your lover."

"Do all of your lovers owe you thousands of dollars?" I dare to question him, feeling the anger simmer from his taut skin. It's so much easier to be angry. It's easier to yell than listen. Easier to hate what's happened, than to suffer through the aftermath.

The muscles in Jase's shoulders tighten, making him look all the more dominant and I don't stop pushing him. Maybe I have a death wish. "You're a man who coerced me, a man I fell for when we both know we shouldn't be together. And whatever's between us will end when the debt is paid. I will not listen to your every command because you happen to give one to me. If I don't want to be with you... I won't." His chest rises and falls quicker as his jaw clenches at my final words. "You'd be wise to remember I am not interested in being told what to do. This agreement was for information. That is all I want from you."

Thump, my heart wrenches inside of me knowing it's a lie. All I can do is remember CROSS in the hidden message of The Coverless Book and it stops its furious beating, but the beat it gives me in return is dulled and muted, slowing more and more by the second.

"I've already told you, I don't like it when you lie to me." He hardens his voice further as he adds, "Knock off your bullshit." Jase speaks through clenched teeth and before I can answer, a waitress appears with a bottle of wine draped with a white cloth napkin in an ice bucket and two glasses. It's a dark red with a silver label although I can't read what the label says.

I could use a glass of dark red wine. Then a long nap. One that lasts forever and takes me somewhere far away from the hell my life's become.

"Drink," he commands me when the waitress leaves and I smirk at him.

"If you thought I wasn't going to drink, you're just as much of a fool as I am." Some spiteful side of me wants to deny the wine, just because he told me to drink it. But fuck that. It's the only good thing I have going for me.

I take a sip and time passes with neither of us saying anything. The first breath is tense, but the next comes easier. With every second that passes, the hate and anger wane, leaving only raw ugly feelings to fester inside of me. When that happens, I don't want to think. That's my harsh reality. I'd rather get lost in him when I don't have the anger to hide behind anymore.

"What changed?" he asks casually, breaking the silence.

"I don't trust you," I reply, and my answer slips out just as easily. An anxiousness wells up inside of me. I didn't mean to say it out loud. He doesn't know about the message in the book. That's really what changed although without it, I can't even say for sure what it says. The table jostles as I plant my elbow and rest my forehead in my hand while I refuse to look at him. I can't look him in the eyes; I can't take this shit. A moment passes and another.

"Is there anything you do trust about me?" he asks, not bothering to question why it is I don't trust him. Maybe he has his own reasons.

Peeking past my hand and then lowering it altogether, I answer honestly again, only this time it's a conscious decision. "I don't think you'd hurt me. Not physically... which is truly ironic considering how we met."

Only after I answer do I look into his eyes. And I see turmoil raging within them.

"I would never hurt you. Not in any way if I can help it."

"And what if you can't?" I ask him with the sorrow that's buried its way into my every thought finally showing. "What if there's no way for me to come out of this undamaged?"

"That's what you're afraid of? That's what you don't trust?" he questions.

I hadn't expected to be so transparent with him. I don't even think I was cognizant of what I'd said until the words were spoken. I could blame it on the lack of sleep or the wine. But a part of me wants him to take it all away. A part of me thinks he can make me believe he'll fix my problems. I don't even care that he can't. I just want to believe that he can for a moment. Just a single moment of peace. That part of me is so tired of fighting. I hate that part of me.

"I'm scared in general, Mr. Cross." Emotions tickle up my throat, but with a short clearing of my throat, they're gone. "I've found myself deeper and deeper in a hole that I don't know I'll be able to get out of." My eyes feel heavy, as does the weight against my chest.

I don't know how I'm still sitting upright at this point. That's the truth.

"The debt? Is that what you mean by the hole?" he asks although the look in his eyes tells me he knows that's not what I'm talking about. I shake my head, no, confirming his assumption.

"It's because of the break-in?" he asks and I don't answer, swallowing down the half truth and hating that it's all I'm willing to give him. "Bethany?" he presses and I finally speak, "Yes."

It's a lie though. Things changed before it. "Do you have my book?" I ask him the second I think of The Coverless Book. Seeing the underlined words in my mind and needing to read the hidden message. Clearing my throat again, I ask, "Did they find it?"

I don't know where to go from here until I know what my sister left for me.

I don't know what to think of Jase until I see what my sister said. That's what hurts the most.

Leaning back into his chair, he lets out a long exhale, staring into my eyes and not answering. His thumb rubs circles over the pad of his pointer finger and he leaves me waiting.

"Jase, please," I plead with him, seeking sympathy and mercy. "I just want the book back."

He leaves me without an answer still, but only for a moment.

Wordlessly, he raises his hand and I expect the waitress to come, but instead Seth walks forward. I hadn't seen him before this, not since last night when he brought me a duffle bag of the things I asked him to bring. With my head buried in the hotel pillow, he opened the door and left my bags for me. I barely even got to see him before he left, muttering a thank you into the pillow as the door was already closing.

He's quiet and businesslike, but he gives me a soft smile every time. He's like a warden with sympathy for his prisoner. The thought makes a sarcastic huff of a laugh leave me, although it's barely heard.

I don't know where he was hiding or if he was seated, perhaps standing. I have no idea. But Seth nods at me with the same polite smile the host had for me in the foyer. As if no one in this world would dare admit what a shit-show my life is and how I look the part for it right now.

I can't hear Jase's murmur but I don't need to. Seth disappears for a moment, swiftly walking away when the waitress arrives with oysters Rockefeller and seared scallops. Setting the large plates in the center of our table, she then places two small plates equipped with tiny seafood forks as well in front of each of us.

She's courteous and polite, smiling at me but more so at Jase before asking if we need anything else. Jase shakes his head once and I do the same, not trusting myself to speak.

"I chose the courses while waiting for you," he explains.

"I'm not hungry," I tell Jase, spotting Seth making his way back to us with The Coverless Book in his right hand by his side.

"You haven't slept; you should at least eat."

The tight smile graces Seth's lips once again and then holding out the book for me to take, he tells me, "The rest is now in your car, Miss Fawn."

"Thank you," I say, and somehow the words are spoken; how? I don't know. My head feels dizzy as I hold the book tighter than I've held anything in my life. It could give me the answers to everything.

"That's all," Jase says lowly and Seth is gone before I can say anything else. Before I can even swallow down the ball of dread that's cutting off the oxygen in my throat.

I should ask him where he found it; I should say something or attempt to carry on conversation so it's not obvious that this book may change the way I think about him. He has no idea and he's given it over to me freely. I should try to keep my cover, but I'm an awful liar.

"I have to go to the restroom," I tell Jase as I stand up from the table and reach for my purse, setting the book inside before slinging the bag over my shoulder.

Jase only nods. I have to grip the back of my chair, taking him in for what could be the last time. The air changes around me, it moves around him, pulling me toward him, begging me to stay there... *just in case.*

I think if I ran, which I know very well I may do depending on what's in the book, I'd miss the way he looks at me the most. He doesn't just glance at me, he doesn't observe me the way others do, inconsequentially and only with little curiosity. He stares at me with a hunger and a need for more, to see more of me and what's inside of me. He looks at me like he never wants to stop seeing me.

Even knowing he's angry with me and how we're surrounded by prying eyes in a crowded restaurant, he only sees me. Yes, that's the way he looks at me. Like I'm the only one worth seeing. With my back turned to him, I know it might be the last time, and it hurts. I wasn't expecting that. I should stop expecting anything at all.

As I'm walking away, I feel the vibrations of my phone ringing silently, but I ignore it, quickening my pace to get away from Jase and from these thoughts.

The women's restroom door pushes open easily and I don't hesitate to lock myself inside of the stall farthest from the entrance, dropping my purse to the floor and quickly opening the book to where I was.

I check my phone just before opening the book, and it says Rockford called. For a second I hesitate, wondering what work wanted and why they called.

I drop it back into the inside pocket when I hear the door open and someone walking in. I can just barely make out a pair of red heels by the sink and I hear the telltale zip of a bag as she stands there. Maybe she's reapplying lipstick or checking her appearance. I have no idea, but either way, alone in the stall, I open the pages of the book, searching for the last page I read.

My eyes are tired and the black and white is more blurred than it should be. But the underlined words are still there and just beneath the lines, the first letter of the sentences are just as I remembered.

C starts the first sentence. R is next. Followed by O, S, S.

My fingertips slide against the indented lines. When Jenny left this message, I can only imagine the fear she must have felt, hiding it so deeply in this book.

With a deep, but staggering breath, I dig in my purse for a small Post-it note and a pen.

The next letter is an I. I write it down, then search for the next. M. M. I stop at the P for "Promise me you'll never leave." MMP makes no sense.

CROSSIMMP. Rubbing under my eyes and double-checking them, that's right. But it makes no sense. With my brows knit and the adrenaline pumping harder, I keep going. Q in "Quite the way to lead life." S for "Secrets always come out."

It makes no sense at all. There are no other words that can be made from the jumbled mess of letters. I search another chapter and another. Not reading at all, just gathering letters. And there's nothing else. No other words hidden.

My blood cools and I struggle not to cry.

There is no message.

Deep breath. Deep breath. Don't cry. Crying is useless.

A snide voice in the back of my head reminds me, so is searching for messages from the dead. They're gone. They don't come back. And they have nothing new to tell you.

I swear I can hear the crack that splits down my chest, through my heart and onward.

Hope is a long way of saying goodbye.

My own voice echoes in my head. Mocking some of the last words I ever spoke to my sister. And that's the moment I break down entirely. I suppose I can take the death, the coercion, the break-in, the fear of losing my life. But losing hope?

Even I can't live without hope.

So I read the lines again and again, although this time, they're blurry.

There is nothing here but false hope and lines from an old book with no title. Lines that for the life of me, my addict of a sister thought worthy of underlining, though I can't imagine why.

However gentle the knock at the stall door is, it still startles me.

Hiding my sniffling with the sound of pulling on the roll of toilet paper, I respond, "Just a minute."

"Are you all right?" The question comes out hesitantly. "I just... is there anything I can do?"

How sweet a stranger can be. Kind and caring for someone they don't know. If she knew, she'd stay far away from me. Everyone in my life dies tragically.

"Just allergies. I'll be fine."

She stands there a second longer until I add, "Thank you though. That's very sweet of you."

"I haven't heard someone use allergies before," the stranger in dark red heels replies, letting me know she's well aware of my lies. "Is there anyone you'd like me to get for you?"

Although I owe this woman no explanation, I answer her. "No, I promise I'm fine. Just a really rough... month." I say that without thinking, because my mind is riddled with thoughts of Jenny. And how I wish this stranger could simply go get her for me.

If only it were possible. That's what I really want and need, far more than I should.

The woman leaves and another enters. I sit there for longer than I'd planned, drying my eyes and rearranging my bag before heading to the sink. There isn't a lipstick in the world that could make me look better. But I try to hide my crying with the stick of concealer and powder in my bag. And then a coat of pale pink lipstick.

Letting it all sink in, the only relief I have is that there was no message about Jase or his brothers. There is no warning to stay away from him.

That knowledge releases the only inhibition I had for not losing myself in him. What a way to mourn. Grief is an aphrodisiac, or so I've been told. Although I've done damage the last twenty-four hours and I don't know where we stand.

With my purse on my shoulder and the book safely tucked inside, I head back to the table feeling flushed, overwhelmed and with no appetite at all.

"So you weren't tunneling an escape after all," Jase jokes weakly as I sit down across from him. He sets his hand palm up on the table, but I don't reach for it.

"I was... just realized it would take a little longer than I'd like," I joke back, just as weakly. "No appetite?" I question, noting that he hasn't touched the appetizers.

He shakes his head in response, his eyes ever searching, ever wondering what I'm thinking. "I need an answer first."

"An answer to what?" I ask.

"I need you to agree to stay with me."

"No." My answer is immediate and I question my sanity. He could protect me. Jase Cross could do that. At the cost of losing my only sanctuary and the place that houses the memories I have. Living in fear is the worst thing I could agree to. I refuse to do it. I refuse to choose staying with him because I'm scared.

Angling the small fork to ease the oyster from its hold on the shell, I struggle for an excuse and the only one I can offer him. Thinking eating will appease him, I lift the oyster up so he knows I'll do just that but first I tell him, "I'd like to stay with my friend for the time being."

With a salty bite left in my mouth, I swallow the heavenly oyster and set the empty shell back down on the bed of ice. The tension doesn't wane, not even when I eat another, refusing to look Jase in the eyes.

"Don't do this," he warns me.

My gaze flicks to his. "Do what?"

"Don't make this harder. I don't understand what's gotten into you. But you should consider your options carefully."

"Is that a threat, Mr. Cross?"

Exasperation grows in his expression as he tells me his patience is wearing thin.

"What changed?" he finally asks. "You treat me like I'm an enemy and I'm starting to think I am to you now."

Thump. My heart is a treacherous bastard, begging me to tell him about the book. Begging me not to lie. Telling me he'll understand.

He pushes the issue, asking, "Is there something you're not telling me?"

Thump.

"You wanted me, and I wanted you. I thought that's where we were."

"Did you forget the other night?" I ask meekly, remembering crying in the bedroom, remembering him walking away because I couldn't admit it out loud like he has just now. Raising my eyes to him and staring back with nothing but sincerity I remind him, "It's not like the two of us should be together."

"Do you want me?" he asks, not letting anything change in his expression.

With a single hard swallow, I answer him with raw truth, "Yes. More than anything else."

"Nothing else matters then."

"Not the debt? Not the fact that someone's after me?" I feel my expression fall, the kind of crumpling that comes with an ugly cry, but I don't give a shit, I let it out, I let it all out. "Not the fact that a part of me hates you because I hate what you do and that the life you lead is why my sister's dead?" I'll never be able to say those words without tears flooding my eyes. I don't blink and a few tears fall, but I won't cry after that. Crying does nothing.

As I'm angrily wiping my tears away, I note his lack of a response and continue the onslaught. I ask him, "How much is it that I owe you again?"

"I'm fucking tired of you asking me that. It'll be months before you've paid the debt."

"*The* debt..." I whisper, sniffling and looking away thinking about how it's *her* debt, not mine. But the thoughts vanish as I note how the restaurant is slowly thinning in attendance. It's sobering, the sight around us.

It's not just thinning, everyone is leaving. There are only two couples left. And both are preparing to exit. The young woman glances at me as she pushes her chair in, her eyes wide with worry.

"Jase." I can only whisper his name as my pulse races with concern.

"I was wondering how long it would take you to notice."

Thump. Thump. Thump. It's like a war drum. I whisper the question, "What did you do?"

Leaning forward, he places his forearms on the table. His eyes darken as they sear into me. "I've let you get away with too much."

I can't breathe, and I can't move; even when I hear the door click loudly behind me and bringing with it utter silence, I don't dare to do anything but stare into his eyes.

They contain a mix of hunger and depravity. His hard jawline tightens as he clenches his teeth and lets his eyes roam down the front of me then back to my apprehensive gaze.

"They couldn't stay here any longer, because I need to punish you. You've known this was coming. I should have done it sooner." Frustration and regret ring clear in his voice and guilt overrides my other emotions. "I take responsibility. You wouldn't behave this way if I'd punished you like I should have."

The way he says punish evokes a mix of reactions from me. I heat with desire and longing, wanting him to take control so I can stop thinking, stop doing, and just obey and receive what he's willing to give. The other reaction though comes from the knowledge of who this man is and how it will never change. Fear is ever present when he takes control.

"There are consequences. And like I've said, you've gotten away with too much."

CHAPTER
5

Jase

WITH THE DOOR SECURELY LOCKED, I CHECK TO MAKE SURE THE blinds have been lowered, and they have. Although the front door window is visible from this table, meaning someone could see if they dared to peek, but Seth is waiting outside and he'd take care of that problem before any prick would have the chance to see a damn thing.

"Jase, I'm sorry." Bethany's voice wavers as she speaks, showing her fear. I wondered which side of her would take over. I was hoping it wouldn't be this one. It makes everything more difficult, but she must be punished. This has to stop.

"You aren't. If you were sorry, you wouldn't continue to defy me." A deep inhale barely keeps me grounded as my temper flares. "You are the only one who has ever made me lose control like this. Do you know that?"

"Jase, I don't mean to," she nearly whimpers with more than a hint of fear and finally glances away from me, toward the door.

Her breathing is erratic and her fingers wrap around her silverware as if she'll use it against me. She may do just that, my fiery girl, if I give her a reason.

"Jase," she says and whispers my name.

"You're scared?" I ask her.

She hesitates to answer before closing her eyes and nodding. The fear is a constant. I'm not sure it'll ever leave her and I can't blame her.

"You just said you trusted that I would never hurt you." The pain inside of my chest is sharp like a knife, piercing and twisting, never stopping to offer a moment of relief. I'd bleed out here if I had to watch her paused in this moment, truly afraid that I'd hurt her. "I'm not going to hurt you, Bethany. This is a punishment that you can take. One that you obviously need."

"I'm scared," she whispers.

"Don't be. Parts of it you may even enjoy." That comment gets her attention. I keep her gaze to tell her, "I'm not going to let you get away with this shit any longer. You will be punished. Whether you're upset or scared or otherwise. I should have already punished you." At the word punish, she licks her lips. Her body will always betray her regardless of the brave front she puts on around me.

"You've run from me, lied to me, stolen from me, raised a knife to me... And you thought I'd do nothing?" I question her. "How much did you think I'd let you get away with, cailín tine?"

Using her nickname is what does it. I can feel the tension break, I can feel it warm and I notice how it melts around her. Her bottom lip drops, pouty and trembling, but her breathing has changed. No longer tense, but still quick with anticipation.

I give her a moment, letting everything settle for her.

"Still your cailín tine?" The Gaelic phrase sounds foreign on her tongue.

"Of course," I answer, reaching across the table to offer my hand and she still hesitates to reciprocate, but she does, setting her small hand in mine. Brushing my thumb across her wrist, I try to keep it soothing to calm her before the inevitable will happen. "I hate that it comes to this before you'll let me in. Do you know that?"

She exhales deeply before telling me, "I'm not exactly used to this. And I don't exactly like it either."

"You don't like what?"

"Having to be accountable to someone like..."

"To someone like me?" She only nods at my question until I

narrow my gaze and pause the motion of my thumb against her pulse. "Yes," she answers verbally.

"Well I enjoy your company, Miss Fawn, and from what I gather, you enjoy mine." Again she nods and this time whispers her yes along with it, nearly defiantly.

"When you're with someone, you have to make allowances for them. I have done my best to make allowances for you given this... situation."

"And I have not," Beth speaks before the judgment can fall from my lips. "I realize I am difficult and..." she pauses, swallowing thickly before adding, "I do appreciate some things... I am just very aware of others that..."

"That you will have to make certain allowances for," I say, finishing her sentence for her with the only outcome I'll allow. "Is that understood?"

She nods and speaks simultaneously, "Yes."

Pulling my hand away from her, I let the warmth of her words— that she appreciates me, no matter how small a part of me— flow through me, feeling my cock harden as I think about what I'm going to do to her. "This situation being new for you is no excuse. It's new for me too."

"What are you going to do?" she asks breathlessly.

"You're going to need the rest of your wine."

I'm careful and calm as I stand up, pulling the chair back and un-buttoning my jacket.

Her fingers linger on the glass but she doesn't pick it up until I pick up my own glass, downing the full-bodied red I know she loves. It's sweet and decadent, like her when she lets go and gives me control.

I set the empty glass on the table behind us. The aftertaste is smooth and I focus on that as I calmly remove everything from our table one by one. The candle, the vase, the small plates and then the large one still littered with hors d'oeuvres I thought she'd enjoy.

She doesn't just calm down; that wouldn't fit the woman she is. She's intense and wrought with emotion. She feels everything in exaggerated stages.

Every second that passes, the air gets hotter around us.

Each breath she takes picks up its pace.

After loosening my tie, I remove the last few pieces of silverware from the table, placing it easily on the table to our right.

"Sit here." My hand splays on the barren table in front of me. My palm is flat against the surface. "Right here," I say and pat the table again, closer to the edge this time and although she's slow, she obeys. Climbing onto the table, she's fully clothed. The blush that creeps up her cheeks is an indication that she knows damn well she won't be staying that way.

"Come closer," I command once she's on all fours on top of the table and when she's close enough, I position her body how I want it, feeling the race of adrenaline and desire run through my pulse.

"Jase." My name is merely lust wrapped in words that don't matter. "I really am sorry."

"I have a question for you," I say, and I don't bother accepting or denying her apology. "Are you terrified of me? Or of what I could do to you?" I ask her, placing my forearms on the table on either side of her. She's close to me, her luscious curves within reach. Her pouty lips near mine, ready to capture. But I don't kiss her. Not yet.

"Both," she admits and I don't blame her.

"I've done terrible things in my life. It makes sense you'd be afraid," I admit, feeling a crease in my forehead as her expression stays etched with concern. "But leading with fear is a bad move to make."

"I know," she whispers just beneath her breath. "I don't know what I'm doing. I don't know what I've gotten myself into. I'm angry, I'm lost and I'm terrified."

"I'll be angry alongside you. I'll find you a way. I'll make sure there's not a damn thing that will touch you. Nothing should scare you when you're with me." Reaching out, I cup her chin in my hand, feeling her smooth skin and continuing to caress her when she presses her cheek into my embrace. "Even me. I shouldn't scare you."

"Knowing how much I want to be around you is terrifying in itself. Which is ridiculous, all things considered." Her eyes open on her last point, her thick lashes barely revealing her eyes beneath them.

With one leg on either side of me, I press my fingers against her pussy, through the fabric that separates our skin and she keeps her eyes on mine, but her head falls back just slightly.

"Already hot," I comment. "Are you already wet for me too?"

She only nods and as I open my lips, moving closer to her to reprimand her for not answering verbally, she halts any inclination I have to do so.

She kisses me first. Without warning. Surprised, I moan into her mouth, feeling my rigid cock twitch with need to be inside of her. This greedy woman who takes from me when no one else would dare to do so.

"Even when you're in trouble, you still defy me and take from me."

She only answers with the hint of smile.

"You like to be the first to kiss, don't you?" I ask her.

"It's my call." I don't bother to hide the smirk that lurks on my lips.

I don't bother to hide the lust either as I answer her, "It was going to happen anyway."

"I could have run, I could bite you, or deny you."

"Why would you?" I ask her with genuine curiosity, my lips just barely away from hers.

"That's what people do when they're scared, Jase. You should know that by now."

Words catch in my throat, tightening it and warring with each other inside of me. "Strip" is the only one that manages to escape.

"Jase." I watch her swallow, I can even hear it before she tells me, "They'll see. Anyone could see from the door."

"I don't give a shit about anyone but you right now."

Words are lost to her as we stare into each other's eyes until I tell her, "Any man who dared to look through that door would die."

Her breath hitches and her thighs tighten at my words.

"Does that make you hot?" I ask her, feeling my own desire rising.

She nods as she whispers yes. I allow my gaze to wander down her body, although it stops too soon as I focus on her breasts when she pulls her sweater over her head. Through the tank top underneath, I see her pebbled nipples.

"Maybe he'd get a glimpse of you cumming with my lips between your legs."

Leaning in closer, I whisper in her ear as she pulls the straps of her tank top down, "What a way to die… for that to be the last thing he sees."

The exhale she releases is tempting, but I maintain control. I don't touch her again as she peels off every bit of clothing and lies bared to me, pushing her bra off the table for it to fall carelessly on the floor below with its companions.

Both of my hands grip her hips and I pull her closer to me. Keeping her gaze with mine, I lower my lips to her swollen nub and suck. With a single lick of her sweet cunt, I go back to her clit, sucking it until she's letting those sweet sounds flow into the air.

Her body rocks, her hands spear my hair. I love the way her nails scratch me as she gets closer and closer.

I have to remind myself that this is a punishment. I can't get lost in her.

The moment her back arches and her bottom lip drops with a deep moan, I pull away from her, smacking the inside of her thigh to take her away from the edge of her forbidden fall.

"No," I tell her. With flushed cheeks, she stares back at me breathlessly and wordlessly. "You don't get to cum tonight."

As she blinks away the haze of lust and confusion, my middle finger plays at her folds, spreading her arousal as I talk. "I will play with you, fuck you, and get myself off with the things I plan to do with you. But you will not cum."

All I can hear is her single breath before she nods.

"Verbally."

"I understand."

Rewarding how easily she accepts the punishment, I plant a kiss on the bright red patch of skin on her inner thigh. And then another, traveling up her body, over the curve of her waist and then higher. Standing up and dragging my open-mouth kisses up her neck, I unbutton my pants, letting them and my boxers drop to the floor so I can stroke myself.

"On your back," I command her and pull my shirt over my head. She positions herself with her heels on the edge of the table and her back flat against the tabletop.

She struggles not to lift her head and watch me as I undress entirely.

I can't resist toying with her breasts, plucking her nipples and pulling them back to bring those sweet sounds to leave her.

Her pussy clenches around nothing. I watch her, hot and flushed, ready to be fucked. The taste of her and red wine still remain on my tongue.

"You're taking this punishment well," I commend her and then pull her ass closer to me, nearly falling off the edge of the table.

She starts to answer, but I grip her hips in my hand and slam myself inside her. Fuck, she feels too fucking good. I can't close my eyes even though my body begs me to enjoy the rapture of pleasure fully and do so.

Her neck arches and her eyes scrunch as her heat clenches around me. The table jostles with the thrust of my hips and her breasts sway as I fuck her. I'm careful not to allow her to enjoy herself fully.

Her hands move to her breasts, her nipples barely peeking through her fingers as she gets close, inching her way toward her release.

I pull out fully, instantly missing her warmth.

She whimpers and struggles to stay still as I step back. It's hard to keep my breathing controlled, even harder to do it again, fucking her relentlessly on the table and stopping just before she reaches her climax.

The third time, I lower my body close to hers, feeling my skin heat and needing to be closer to her. She doesn't kiss me when I bring my lips close to hers this time.

She pushes her head back against the table, so I drag my teeth along her throat and up to the shell of her ear, loving how she moans even though she knows she'll be left wanting yet again.

"This is what a punishing fuck is," I hiss as I pound into her again and stay buried deep inside of her as I almost lose myself in the moment. "I take all my pleasure," I push the words through clenched teeth as I move myself slowly out of her and then slam all the way back in.

A strangled cry leaves her and she drags her nails down my back. The mix of pleasure and pain nearly has me finding my release too soon. I'm not ready for it to be over though, not by a mile.

"I get my pleasure, and you get nothing," I whisper in her ear as the intensity of the pleasure stirring inside of me subsides. Only then am I able to pull away from her enough to look her in the eye.

Daggers stare back at me, but not in anger. I can see the challenge clearly written on her face. My poor cailín tine has no idea how painful orgasm denial is. To be taken to the highest high each time, finding the edge of release so close, only to have it ripped away from you and the waves of pleasure yanked from you.

"I dream about the noises you make when you get off. I want to hear those sounds over and over again," I tell her and then recklessly fuck her, feeling the stir of my climax approaching in time with hers. Only to pull away at the last second.

"No," this time she whimpers and her body rolls to the side, wanting to get away. "Please," she begs me, her face pained.

"How can I reward either of us with that, when you don't listen to me? When you fight me every step of the way?"

She visibly swallows and tells me she's sorry again. I'm not interested in an apology.

I fuck her again, listening to the sound of me fucking her, of the table banging against the floor as my movements get stronger with my own needs taking over.

I suck in a deep breath as I pull away again. She can't resist touching herself, knowing it's only a small touch she'll need at this point and I grip her wrists, pulling them away and pinning them to the table.

The frustration, even the contempt, show in her expression. "Keep your hands here." My voice is deep and the threat is there. I can tell she's biting her tongue and I love it. I love taming my wild girl.

"Let me be very clear. I would have loved to get lost inside of you and give you every pleasure imaginable. But I will not be made a fool, Bethany. Do you understand?"

"I'm not a fucking idiot."

"You put a knife against my chest," I rebut. "That doesn't make you a smart woman, does it?"

"I'm sorry," she tells me again and her gaze falls to my chest, but I grip her chin, stealing her attention back to what matters.

"Do you think words are enough? Words are meaningless."

She shakes her head. "I can't go back. What more do you want from me?" She screams her question, the hoarse words ricocheting in the restaurant.

Even now she pushes me. She'll never stop. I know she won't. The fire inside of her will never die.

And I love it. I will live for the moments she defies me.

Knowing that to be the truth, I pin her hands above her head when I thrust inside of her this time and push my chest to hers. My muscles scream and a cold sweat breaks out along my back as I rut between her legs, hard and deep, listening to her strangled cries of pleasure.

I nearly don't stop. I nearly ruin the punishment, but fate would have me go through with it. The leg of the table that's closest to me, buckles and breaks. Forcing us to fall as the table crashes to the floor.

Silencing her scream with a desperate kiss, I pull her body on top of mine as my back falls against the broken wood. With an arm wrapped around her back, I roll over to lay her on the floor.

I only take a moment to make sure she's all right, and her response is to writhe under me, begging me to keep fucking her.

I slam myself as hard and deep as I can inside of her and stay right there. She claws at the floor, screaming and moaning with nothing to silence her cries.

Watching her gasp for air and struggling to contain herself, I push the question out with what little control I have left. "Tell me what you really think of me."

I shouldn't have asked and it shouldn't matter, but in this moment, being inside of her and having her at my mercy, I need to know. More than anything else, I need to know the truth.

She struggles not to thrash under me as I rub her clit, still buried inside of her. "Tell me the truth, cailín tine."

"I love you," she practically screams the repressed truth and I still. My body tenses, even as she continues to thrash beneath me, heaving in air and still pushing me away, although weakly.

I have to move. Before I lose myself inside her, and before she says anything else.

She loves me.

I fuck her with long strokes, each of them penetrating her as deeply as I can and pulling out until I'm barely inside of her.

Each time she lets out a moan of sudden pleasure and then her eyes seek mine, wanting more, needing me again and again.

I draw out her release, teasing her like this and nipping her lips. All the while hearing her say those words over and over in my head. *She loves me.*

She whispers it again, right when her pussy tightens and she cries out her orgasm.

When I finally feel my own release, I sink my teeth into her neck, not biting her, but needing to do something so I don't groan out words I'll regret.

The haze of desire fades slowly and then all at once when I sit up, pulling myself away from her, and she finally looks me in the eyes.

For a long time, the only thing I can hear is both of us breathing, both of us getting a grip on what just happened. She said she loves me.

As I clean between her legs, pressing the cloth napkin against her clit and forcing her head to fall back from the pressure, I'm all too aware that I didn't say the words back.

And I don't plan on it.

"You're not going to your friend's house to put her in danger and you're not going to a fucking hotel and leaving my men out there to watch over you. You're coming home with me."

Shock colors her expression at first when I stand up and leave her where she is. She reaches for her tank top before anything else and then finally looks up at me.

"I don't love you." The words rush out of her, the hurt written on her face. She tries to swallow up the evidence of her lie, but it doesn't work.

"Of course you don't," is all I answer her, burying the sensation that grows inside of me. I turn my back to her while putting my pants back on as she cleans herself up. "You're coming home with me," I repeat, focusing on what matters. A truth she can't deny, unlike what she's doing now.

The chair behind me groans against the floor as it's moved and I peek over my shoulder to see her nearly dressed and avoiding eye contact. "Did you hear me?" I ask her, feeling something stir inside my chest with restlessness.

Bethany kicks aside a scrap of wood to stand and nods her head while answering me, "Yes, and that's fine. I don't want to go back to my place anyway." Her voice is low, too low and devoid of any of the fight I'm used to from her.

The silence of the restaurant is uncanny as we wait there, with my eyes on her and her eyes anywhere else.

"Seth's waiting for us outside. You'll follow me and he'll be behind you."

She nods and audibly swallows but doesn't say anything else as she wraps her arms around one another. Not crossing her arms in front of her chest, but laying them atop each other. Her gaze lingers on the front door, but she doesn't move until I splay my hand on the small of her back.

That gets a reaction from her. She walks faster, fast enough for the pressure of my touch to be meaningless.

No one's out front of the restaurant, no one except Seth leaning against the hood of his black Audi and keeping watch. The light dusting of white on the ground outside is evidence that the snow must have come and gone already. Leaving behind it a thick white fog, and the curtain of white across every surface.

Bethany lets me open the front door for her and I'm granted a muted thank you. Same with her car door. She doesn't look toward Seth at all; she merely focuses her attention on each of her steps.

Seth's gaze turns questioning. Anyone with any common sense can see she's not well.

"Upset" is hardly a word I would use to describe Bethany. It's too weak. She's too volatile to simply be upset. But right now, it's the only word I can find. She's upset and I fucking hate it.

I love you.

She said it and then took it back. She's confused and upset. Confusion runs deep in my mind as well. For the first time since I've set eyes on her, I'm uncertain what to do with her.

I want to hear her tell me those words again, and to mean it. But I would never wish for a girl like her to fall for me, either.

"You can close the door, Mr. Cross," she tells me, staring at my shoes from where she sits in the driver's seat. The clinking of her keys is all I can hear as I stare down at her, waiting for her to look up at me. My hand is still firmly on her car door.

A gust of wind passes and I can hear Seth clear his throat in the distance. Still I don't look away, and neither does she.

"Bethany," I murmur her name and she hums back, a sweet sound, seemingly just fine, but still doesn't look at me.

"What's wrong?" My grip tightens on the door when the question leaves me. I already know and I feel like an asshole. She's a mess. That's all she's been since I've come into her life. A mess, but a beautiful masterpiece. She'll do more good in a week at the hospital than I'll do in my entire life. There's no questioning that.

"Nothing," she answers in a whisper, then peeks up at me, toying with her keys in her hand and offering a sad smile.

"You look like you're going to cry."

Her voice in response is stubborn, but it also cracks. "I'm not."

"Get out of the car, Bethany." I give her the command and step back although I keep my grip on the door, pulling it open wider and waiting on the vacant street. I can't help but notice our footprints on the sidewalk. Hers are so much smaller than mine, but the spacing is the same. They're in complete rhythm and time with mine.

She clears her throat as she steps out, moving over the curb and onto the sidewalk. Toe to toe with me, she stands there, both of her hands cradling the keys. Maybe to keep them from making noise, maybe to give her something to focus on other than me.

Either way she looks me in the eyes, daring me to accuse her of being on the verge of tears again. I can see it.

Instead I tell her, "I don't love you too." I don't think about it; I just say it. Feeling the restlessness sway inside of me, panicking and not knowing how she'll react.

Her large hazel eyes widen even more, for only a moment as her lips part just slightly and other than that, there's no response at all. No telling as to what she thinks. Until she tries to speak and the first word can't even make it out unbroken.

Instead of carrying on with the intention of speaking, she snags her bottom lip between her teeth to keep it from trembling and stares at the window of the car door rather than at me.

I add, leaning closer to her, close enough to feel her warmth and for her hair to kiss against me with the upcoming gust, "I lied to you and you lied to me. Now we're lying to each other."

I hate myself in this moment, for daring to lead her into this path. But the other path is away from me. I want her close, I need her as close to me as I can have her.

Her hazel eyes swirl with a mix of emotions. Complicated and in broken disarray, the amber colors bleeding into one another, but each still visible and adding to the beauty of her gaze.

"I don't love you." She shakes her head as the statement leaves her. Her body consciously denying the very words she speaks.

"I don't love you too," I repeat.

She's searching. Trying to figure out whether or not I'm lying to her and I don't know what she'll find. I don't know if I'm even capable of loving anymore. Not the way she needs. Not the way she deserves.

Before she can find whatever truth there is, I crash my lips against hers, letting go of the door to pull her into my arms. Her soft lips melt as I deepen the kiss. Her small hands reach up to push against my chest, but instead she quickly fists my coat and pulls me in even closer.

With a swift glide of my tongue against the seam of her lips, she parts them for me and lets me in. In the middle of the empty sidewalk, I pour everything into that kiss, holding her body against mine. Letting her feel what it is that I have. Maybe she can feel what I have for her. Maybe she'll know it better than I can.

I can feel her heart pound against her chest, maybe hating my own, maybe needing another to commiserate with.

CHAPTER
6

Bethany

THE QUIET IS UNCOMFORTABLE. OR MAYBE IT'S JUST MY THOUGHTS filling up the silence that are uncomfortable. Every second, I go through an entire day. Each day since Jenny's gone missing, even worse when she was found dead, and then each day that Jase tore through the shambles of my life.

That's what the mind does when placed in a quiet room.

His bedroom is a subdued masculinity. A calming presence that begs me to lie down and sink into the plush linens. But then... the thoughts come back. The memories. The what-ifs.

Sitting on the edge of his bed, I focus on the chaos that used to be. The Rockford Center kept me busy, kept me going. And I miss it.

I miss my patients. Marky Lindgren in particular. He always had a story to tell. Sometimes the patients are violent. Sometimes they're vile with what they say. Sometimes all they do is cry, and I keep reminding myself of what I'd tell them when they apologized.

"You're having a moment and you can have as many as you need."

People mourn differently. Funny how on this side of it all, I find my own advice something to ignore. I don't need moments; I need a way forward.

And that's why I miss Marky. Marky's a liar and he spins stories about the other patients to occupy his time. I remember one night he told me how the male patient at the end of the hall had slept with one of the patients that had just been admitted.

He said it so confidently, so seriously, I almost believed him.

And then he told me how she just had to break it off with her husband who was in room 3B. But the man in 3B wasn't going to let her go without a fight and that's what all the commotion was about. Why everyone was crying and yelling.

He said it was a love triangle and then he added... the man at the end of the hall would be fine with a threesome, but he'd never admit it to the woman. I shake my head remembering how he said it, baiting me and waiting for a response I didn't give him.

Each time someone would walk past his room, he'd create a dialogue on what they thought of the adulteress and the sordid affair that never took place. Some of his comments made me genuinely laugh.

The first time I let the smile show on my face, he laughed and then I with him.

He would break up the time with stories that didn't matter, stories you could get lost in. I let myself get lost in them too, because the man in 3B was always angry due to having Alzheimer's and not knowing why he was there. And the man at the end of the hall was violent because he wanted to end it all and we had to strap him down to keep him from doing just that. All over a job he'd lost. It was just a job and just an income. But the debt was too much for him to bear.

Real life didn't matter in Marky's stories though, and amid the chaos, the rounds of delivering pills and checking on patients, Marky's stories made some horrific days tolerable.

No matter how bad the days got though, going home I felt accomplished, needed, and like the chaos was worth it.

The man at the end of the hall found a way out of the hole he'd dug himself with bankruptcy. The man in 3B remembered some of the best times of his life when his family came and they'd just come two weeks ago before I was told to go on leave; it made all the difference for him.

I still don't know about the woman who just came in. She's not from around here and we were told to keep her "attendance"—as they called it—private.

226 | WINTERS

I wasn't even given her full name, only initials.

I miss the chaos, I miss Marky's stories, I even miss my boss and the bullshit rotating schedule. I miss my mind being occupied.

Right now, in the quietness of Jase's bedroom, I'd prefer to be in the halls of the Rockford Center, wondering what everyone else's story is and helping them with their tales, rather than having to face my own.

A creak in the hall catches my attention. A sputtering in my chest echoes to the pit of my stomach. "Jase?" I call out when the door doesn't open.

It's his own bedroom, so if he wanted to come in, surely he would.

But the door doesn't open and I'm left staring at a doorknob I haven't dared touch and wondering what the fuck I'm doing.

Neither of us spoke last night really. Which is for the best. I don't trust the words coming out of my mouth when he's near me.

So we didn't speak, apart from the necessary details.

Half a bottle of zinfandel, a full dish of chicken parmesan, and a soft pillow in a quiet house, with the firm chest at my back of a man who says he'll keep me safe... and I fell asleep. A deep sleep, one where you don't move and you don't dream, because your body sleeps just as heavily as your mind.

That's the kind of sleep I had and then I woke up to a note from Jase, letting me know that he'd be back later tonight and to "make myself comfortable."

I've been torn and now I'm breaking down. If I were at work right now, visitors might think I should be in one of the rooms, rather than in my scrubs holding a tray of medication to dish out.

Do I love Jase? I don't know. It's easy to want love when you're hurting. It's easy to hold on to anything that could fill the void pain has caused. I don't know what's real, and what's the product of coping.

Does Jase Cross love me? No. He doesn't. Not at all.

I think he feels bad for me. It's all sympathy. The way he looked at me tonight said it all. He feels sorry for me.

It's such bullshit. But at least I'm safe. All I need to be, right now, is safe.

And that's the dichotomy I'm supposed to *make myself comfortable* in.

He left me two rules on the slip of paper as well:

If the door is locked, stay out.

Your handprint opens the front door and the hall door behind the stair-well. Don't open the hall door at the moment and don't leave. I'm trusting you.

In other words, stay right where I left you. If I didn't feel so tired, I'd have my ass out of that front door, and walk in knee-deep snow to some shady hotel I could afford. Just to spite him.

But I'm tired. All the sleep in the world can't help the type of tired I am.

You may be tired, Bethany Ann Fawn, you may be sad and in a shit po-sition, but you are still a badass. You are not going to take any shit. And those rules Jase left you, those rules that sexy motherfucker thinks he can lay down while trapping you here, those rules can go fuck themselves.

My little pep talk kicks my lips up into a grin and the lyrics to a Pretty Reckless song play in my mind.

Tell them it's good. Tell them okay, but don't do a goddamn thing they say.

It's been my life's motto. Nothing's going to change that.

My first move is to push the curtains in the bedroom as far open as I can. They're heavy and the sky is full of white fog, not offering much light at all. I think it's the winter that's gotten me so down, at least it's part of the reason. The season can take some of this blame.

With a little more light in his too-dark-even-with-the-light-on bed-room, I go drawer by drawer. I don't find anything interesting. Socks, neatly folded in a row. Same with his ties. I let my fingers linger over them, feeling the silk and wondering how he could even choose a tie like this, given the patterns are hidden this way.

I finally find a drawer that's mostly empty; it only houses two pairs of jeans I'm able to put in his undershirt drawer, which is filled with white and black cotton undershirts… and now two pairs of jeans.

All of my things don't even fill the drawer: two pairs of PJs, a pair of sweats, a pair of jeans and a few tops. It's everything that was in my clean laundry basket. I have a closet full of clothes, but I wear these gar-ments over and over again. What can I say? I like what I like and I damn well like to be comfortable.

The toiletries are next, but there's not a space in the medicine cab-inet, nor under the sink. I'm able to clear room in the linen closet and shamelessly rearrange what was under the cabinet, putting most of it in the closet and finding a place for my own things there.

A tightness starts in my abdomen and works its way up every time I peek at the medicine cabinet. The pills are still at my house; the ones I stole from Jase. That's the only spot available to put anything in there, but I don't bother to touch anything else in that cabinet.

All in all, I waste about an hour. That's all the time I could fill. Then I'm back to staring at the doorknob, wondering when Jase will be back, wondering if I should leave, if I should go. All the wondering that drives me mad.

The clouds shift behind me, as does the faint light in the room. A band of white light shines across the room until it lands on my purse. It's only then that I realize my phone is probably dead since I haven't charged it.

As I'm rummaging for it, I take out The Coverless Book. I have no right to feel betrayed by it, but I do. Jase's charger on his nightstand works for my phone and once it comes to life, I stare at a blank screen. No missed calls and no missed texts.

I call the Center, keeping the phone plugged in and sitting on the edge of Jase's side of the bed. I'm given the voicemail before the second ring occurs. They shunted me there intentionally. If they were just going to ignore me, why bother calling yesterday?

I listen to the voicemail message far too long before hanging up. I have no one right now. No one.

The only people waiting for me, are the fictional characters in The Coverless Book.

CHAPTER
7

Jase

I COULD HARDLY FOCUS ON THE UPDATE FROM CARTER THIS MORNING.
Romano's planning something judging by how he's moving
storage units and Carter thinks he might take off, so we have to
strike now if we want a chance at getting him before he leaves. He
said Officer Walsh has members of the FBI in town, something about
them being involved with Romano's indictment. They're all over him
and watching his every move, which makes it impossible for us to do a
damn thing.

I couldn't focus on anything he was telling me in his office. All I
could think about was how Bethany had wrapped her arms around me
in the middle of her sleep. She clung to me without knowing, nestling
her head against my chest. I could live a thousand lives in that single
moment.

All I could picture was how serene she looked in her sleep. All
throughout the conversation with Carter and all throughout the drive
to the club.

If she knew her sister was still alive, she wouldn't sleep like that. If
she finds out I knew and I didn't tell her, she wouldn't cling to me like
she had last night.

I only have one lead that could change the course of where this is
all going. One chance, one moment, to hold on to Bethany like I want

to. One lead, who's waiting for me just beyond the glowing red lights of the sign ahead of me.

The Red Room isn't just a cover. It's not just for laundering and meetups. Just like the storage shed behind it isn't exactly what it looks like. It's inconspicuous, large and organized with wide open spaces. Everything clearly seen on first glance when you walk into the storage shed which measures forty feet on each side. I demand it be kept clean and tidy. So anyone looking for any hint of it being anything other than a place to keep the extra bottles of liquor and tables would know at first glance there's nothing else here.

Unless they opened the safe and found the secret door in the back of it. It leads to a winding iron staircase, down to a long hall in the basement with a vault door to a room.

The skinny hallway that leads to the room reminds me of the old warehouse I'd sneak off to when I was a boy. Back when I needed to be alone and get away. It was quiet, and offered the comfort of both safety and a place to simply be alone.

The room in that basement exists for one purpose. And one purpose only.

The men who find themselves here aren't feeling the security I did when I was younger and hiding in the warehouse.

No, the men who end up in this room are here to die, although they would say and do anything to believe that they'll get out of here still breathing.

The vault door opens with a slow, plaintive cry. It's heavy and made of thick steel. With Seth behind me, we enter the room comprised of four smooth concrete walls. It's soundproof and the floors are made of steel grids with a drain in the center of the room.

There's no furniture in the room, save an old iron chair bolted to the floor over the drain. I bring everything I need with me each time.

This time I've brought a pair of hedge clippers, the kind most people use for their gardens. They're in my back pocket, as is my pocket knife.

The muffled screams that come from behind the balled cloth in Luke Stevens's mouth fill the room as the two of us walk in.

His skin's paler and almost gray in this light than it was in the video we had of him and another man talking about where Marcus wanted

Jenny Parks delivered. That's the word that came out of his mouth. Delivered. As if she were only an object to be shipped off.

The steel cuffs leave bright red marks around his wrists and ankles, along with a trail of dried blood as he wrestles with his restraints, still screaming. Like it would do him any good to fight.

My nostrils flare with the stench of piss in the damp underground as I get a few feet from him and then look to my right to ask Seth, "How long?"

"Twelve hours now."

He stands closer to the prisoner than I do. We have a system that works. When something works, you don't fuck it up. He knows that and he stands where he always does, just behind the subject of our interrogation, where he can't be seen.

Crouching in front of Luke, a man who may know where Jenny is, I look into his dark eyes, taking in how dilated they are. Wondering what the hell he's on.

"You think twelve hours is enough?" I ask Seth and he shrugs. Luke struggles to look behind him, and his ass comes off the chair just slightly, but the chain wrapped around his waist keeps him down.

Standing up straighter, I pull the clippers from my back pocket and unlock them to look at the blade. "They're dull," I comment as if I didn't notice before.

"They'll still work," Seth says and this time he places a hand on either side of the back of the chair, close enough to Luke so our victim notices, but still not touching him.

I can imagine how Luke's heart races, how the adrenaline takes over. The fight or flight response failing him and every instinct in his body screaming for him to beg. Just like he's screaming now, behind the old shirt shoved in his mouth. Seth's silent and that's how he'll stay until I ask him if there's any reason not to kill the man in the chair.

"Take it out." On my command, Seth removes the shirt from Luke's mouth, ripping the duct tape across his skin in a swift motion. The bright pink skin left behind marks where the tape once laid.

"I didn't do it," Luke screams immediately. Even as the pain tears through him and he's forced to wince, he continues to plead. "Whatever it is, I didn't do it. I didn't fuck with you guys."

"Jenny Parks," I say quietly, and it's all I say. Realization dawns on the man that he did, in fact, do it. He fucked with us. And it shuts him up, although his bottom lip still quivers.

There's a knowing look of fear in his eyes. The lack of an exhale, the stale gaze he gives me. "You know her name."

His mouth closes before he speaks and he visibly swallows.

"Every time you hesitate, I take something from you," I tell him easily, crouched in front of him and waiting for him to acknowledge what I've said.

The second his mouth opens to speak, I grip his hand, choosing his pointer first. The clank of the cuffs and his protests mix in the damp air that still smells like piss. Seth does his part, shoving the shirt in the man's mouth as I clamp down on the clippers. My left hand keeps the other fingers bent, stopping them from interfering. My right hand closes the blades around his pointer. The flesh cuts easily; blood flows just as easily as he lets out a high-pitched muffled scream, but the bone I have to break away from the ligament first before it's cleanly gone.

I take a half step back, watching the blood pour from where his finger was moments ago. It streams out steadily and more blood creeps from under the metal cuffs that keep him held down as he struggles. Seth keeps his hand over the shirt, and watches Luke's face turn bright red, struggling to breathe, screaming with everything he has in him.

His chest heaves. But it never lasts long. The screaming is only temporary. Just like the hesitation and the lies.

"I've done this a few times, Mr. Stevens," I comment as I wipe the blade on his dark blue denim jeans. Although he's stopped screaming, the shirt stays where it is. Seth knows to only remove it once I'm ready for the man to speak.

I let out a heavy exhale and then crouch down in front of him again as I say, "I don't like to waste my time." My tone is easy, consoling even as I stare into his bloodshot eyes, noting the desperation that flows from his sweaty skin. I tell him, "I just want answers, and then all of this is over."

He tries to shriek through the shirt, his neck craning as he more than likely pleads with Seth to remove the gag. The tendons in his neck tense and he keeps it up, which only pisses me off.

"We don't have time for your comments or questions. Now answer mine. Do you know Jenny Parks?"

With the question asked, Seth removes the rag and the man in the chair stumbles over his words.

"She's the girl I took to the bridge." He does well with the first statement, but then he backtracks and barters. My irritation would show, if I weren't expecting it. After all, I have done this more than a few times. He started off strong, thinking it was a negotiation, but the tilt of my head changed his tone to one of a beggar.

"If I tell you everything… will you just let me go? Please! I'll tell you everything!"

I stare at the clippers and take in a breath. A single breath waiting for more information and then my gaze moves to Luke, my eyebrows raising in warning.

He looks to his left quickly, as if anything is there. He tries to get up as if the cuffs had disappeared. What he doesn't do, is give me the information I need.

The shirt is shoved back into his mouth and his ring finger goes next, leaving the middle finger on his left hand easily available for the next time I need to prove a point.

Tears leak from the man's eyes and his cries turn morbid as he mourns his mistake. I feel… I feel nothing but anger for him. Anger I don't show.

"Mr. Stevens, I read your file. You killed your mistress and then your wife. Or no," I feign a correction as I keep eye contact with Seth, not the man I'm determined to kill tonight. "Was it his wife first and then his mistress?"

"You've got it a little wrong, Boss," Seth tells me casually, the shirt still balled up in Luke's mouth, even though he's only crying, no longer screaming. "It was his sister and then his wife."

"No mistress then?"

Seth shakes his head in time with a sputtering of heaving coughs from Luke. "They stole his dope, or something like that." I stoop in front of the man and ask him, "Is that right?"

He's nodding his head even before the shirt's taken from him. As the damp cloth leaves his mouth, he nearly chokes trying to speak too soon. With a quick intake of air he explains himself. "They were going to take it all."

"Oh," I say and nod in understanding. "I see." Again I wipe the blades of the clippers on Luke's jeans. He glances down and then his head falls back as he tries desperately not to cry again.

"And you took Jenny Parks."

"I didn't take her!" He shakes his head as he denies what I said. And I wait a fraction of a second for him to explain. Which he does this time, the information flowing from his lips. "She wanted to go to Marcus. I was dropping her off! I was just supposed to drop her off at the bridge!"

"What bridge?"

"On Fifth and Park. The overpass." He nearly says more, but stops himself. With a knowing look I lean forward, but he continues. Just barely in time. "It's where I do all the drops for Marcus." His pale skin turns nearly white and his voice lowers. "Every three weeks or so, I have a pickup from out of state and a drop-off at the bridge. He gives an address. I go, pick up the unmarked package and drop it off at the bridge. A few weeks ago, he gave a name instead of an address. He told me to go to her, and to tell her Marcus was ready."

I can feel my brow pinch and a crease deepen in my forehead as I ask, "Do you know what he wanted with her?"

"No!" His head shakes violently with the answer. "I just had to pick her up and drop her off. That's all!"

"And what about the other drops?" I question him. "You ever take a peek at what's inside?"

Instead of answering, he swallows. Poor fucker.

His cry this time isn't at all like the last two. Seth covers his mouth as Luke's head falls back, and his middle finger drops to the grated floor alongside the other two severed extremities.

"Please, please." I know that's what he's saying behind the gag. *Please, stop.* I've heard it so many times in my life.

But in this world, there is no stopping.

I take a moment, wondering how he killed his wife. How he looked her in the eyes and stabbed her to death. Fourteen stab wounds. His sister was a gunshot to the back of the head. That one, that type of kill sounds like someone who stole from him. But fourteen stab wounds... that's anger. The twin sister of passion.

When Seth removes the shirt, Luke's head hangs heavy in front of him. He sucks in air like he's been going without it for too long. I could change that, but that's not in my favor.

"I want answers, Luke."

"Drugs. Lots of them. That's what the packages were."

"What kind of drugs?" I ask and for the first time, I grit my teeth, letting him hear the frustration.

He doesn't answer immediately and I stand up straighter, quickly gripping the hair at the back of his head and pulling it back so I can bring the clippers to his throat.

Seth takes a step back and I can feel his eyes on me, knowing this isn't the way it goes down. I couldn't give two shits about that right now.

"Heroin, coke, pot, you name it." Luke's answers are strained with his throat stretched out.

"And sweets?" I ask him.

The dumb fuck tries to nod and the blade slips across his skin. It's only a scratch, one he probably can't even feel with all the other pain rushing through him.

"Marcus doesn't need to deal. What's he doing with it?" I ask as I release him, turning my back to him and taking a few steps away to calm down.

"I don't know," is Luke's first answer but before I can even fully turn around the words rush out of him. "I think it's experiments and setups. He needs the drugs for planting them and I think a month or so ago, that deputy who OD'd? I think that was Marcus."

He insists he doesn't know after that, giving examples that he thinks Marcus may be responsible for, but not saying for sure that his guesses are true.

"You were in it for the money?" I question and to my surprise, the man shakes his head.

"At first... but then I wanted to be in with him. I wanted a place on his team."

The last sentence brings a chill to flow over my skin. "His team?"

Luke nods once. "I wanted to work with him."

"Marcus works alone," I tell him and he actually laughs. It's a sad, sick kind of laugh that graces his lips for only a fraction of a second, but then he shakes his head, looking me in the eyes. "That's not what Jenny said. She said he needed her. That she was going to make things right with Marcus."

"And what did you think that meant?" I ask him, feeling a frigid bite taking over my limbs. It grows colder and colder.

"That he was giving her an in to control it all."

"Control it all? You think that's what Marcus does?"

With hope fleeing Luke's eyes, he nods. "He has an army."

"And you think that's what Jenny was there for? To be in his army?" I ask him, getting closer to him.

He nods.

"Do you know anyone else in his army?"

He slowly shakes his head. "But she told me that's what she was doing. She said she was joining his army."

An army of men working under Marcus. I share a look with Seth and he shrugs but doesn't look so sure.

"I'm not convinced," I say offhandedly and Luke's body jolts up as his voice raises. He's adamant it's the truth. All the while he continues to spill his thoughts that mean nothing to me, I consider what he's saying. There's simply no way Marcus would trust anyone to be involved with his plans.

"So what's he doing with Jenny then?" I raise my gaze to the now silent Luke Stevens. "What is he going to do with her?"

"I don't know. All I know is that I dropped her off securely. I held up my end of the bargain."

"And what did you get in return?" I ask him. He hesitates, but I don't bother removing anything else from him.

"Money," he finally answers. "Four grand."

"Is there anything else we should ask him?" I direct my question to Seth, who merely shakes his head before suffocating the man with his shirt.

Luke fights to breathe, but it's useless. It takes a few minutes and still Seth keeps the shirt over his face when Luke's body is motionless for another minute longer.

"You think he'll keep her alive?" I ask Seth once the rustling and muted screams have settled to silence.

"To start an army?"

I shake my head and agree with the expression on his face. That it's unrealistic for Marcus to have an army. It may have been what he led her to believe, but there is no army.

"Any reason at all that he'd keep her alive," I answer him.

"Marcus doesn't do loose ends." Seth's answer causes a chill to travel down the back of my neck. The feeling of loss and failure intertwine and wrap around my throat as I ask him, "What am I going to tell Bethany?"

His answer is simple and I already know it's what I should do, even if it's not what she'd want. "Nothing. Don't bring her into this any more than she already is."

CHAPTER
8

Bethany

THE COVERLESS BOOK PLAYS TRICKS ON ME. I WAS CERTAIN EMMY'S mother would fire the caretaker for poisoning her daughter. But she says it's only medicine that was poured into the soup. With the bottle in her hand, the mother does nothing but reprimand Emmy. She doesn't look any deeper into it. She only tells Jake that he's out of line and that Miss Caroline did nothing wrong. Emmy begs her mother to hire someone else and fire Miss Caroline, all to no avail.

Hate consumes me. For the women who are supposed to protect and love Emmy. And for the situation the young girl is in.

I read about how Jake is no longer welcome on the property, but Emmy sneaks out to see him, refusing to go on with life as she has been.

She doesn't eat what Caroline cooks so Caroline stops cooking for her altogether, crying outside of the kitchen all while Emmy cries in her bedroom and her mother does God knows what.

It's only at night that anything seems right. Only when Emmy climbs out of her bedroom window to meet Jake. It's the two of them against the world.

There's a passage that makes me feel alive, a passage that warms everything in my body.

"Take my hand and trust me," he tells her. *"I promise to save you, because I love you."*

That's what you do when you love someone, he said. You save them.

And that's where I had to stop.

Three more sentences are underlined. I don't have my journal with me though to add them to the list. It's useless to add them anyway. I've accepted that there's no message buried in the lines. Maybe Jenny just wanted me to read the story. Maybe she fell in love with Emmy and Jake like I have. So many maybes and questions that will never be answered.

I lay the book on its pages, so I don't lose where I'm at. I have to rub my eyes, and take a break after reading the last line I underlined, the line Emmy's mother told Jake. *Hope is a long way of saying goodbye.* It's in the book.

The words I gave to her, she saw it here. I wonder when she read it. Which came first. Not that it matters. None of it matters anymore.

I don't know why I bother to keep reading when it only makes me sad inside. When I know there's no message buried beneath the black and white letters.

It makes no sense at all, either, that I reach out to the phone to text Miranda, Jenny's friend who gave me the book.

I want to text Jenny and I'm conscious of that. I nearly do. I nearly text her, *Why this book? What did you want me to get from it?*

I'm not that crazy yet, so I text Miranda instead. Or maybe that makes me crazier. I'm not sure anymore.

Thank you for giving me the book.

It takes a minute before my phone vibrates in my hand with a response. *Bethany?*

Of course she wouldn't know it's me. Feeling foolish, I answer her, *Yes, I'm sorry to message, I just wanted to make sure I'd thanked you.*

You should know, when I saw her with that book and she was underlining it…. She said you would understand better then. She said you'd be happy.

I'd be happy?

Miranda is no one to me. I'd have been just fine never seeing her again… until my sister died. That changed so many things. She's a person I would never confide in, yet here I am, not hesitating to bleed out my every thought and emotion without recourse into a stream of texts. *I'm anything but happy. Maybe if she was truly invincible, I'd be better.*

Feeling the need to explain, I follow up my messages. *Sorry, it's a line in the book. She keeps saying she's invincible.*

I stare at her next message, reading it over and over. *So that's where she got it... she was saying that for a while before she packed.*

Packed? I think to myself. Why would she have packed? Jenny didn't tell me that before.

I text her back, *Where did she go?*

Her answer is immediate. *I thought she went home to you. She didn't tell me where. I just assumed she was going back to you because she said she needed help.*

Jenny always said she wanted help, but she didn't really mean it. She only said it to get me off her back. It was always lies she told me.

But maybe that day, she was coming home. Maybe she finally wanted to get better. It's the sliding doors of life. If only one thing had changed, everything would be different. Maybe she was coming back home. Maybe that's when they got her. Maybe I was only minutes away from being back with her and they tore her from me.

I drop the phone onto the nightstand, not bothering to reply anymore.

Hating all the maybes, all the possibilities that could have, should have happened.

Everything stills for a moment, going out of focus. As if forcing me to embrace only one thing: She's gone. My sister is gone. My sister is gone, and I have nothing left. No one left but a man who I know is bad for me and one who will never love me.

The first tear that comes, I thought I could control. I can feel the telltale prickle, and how the back of my throat suddenly goes dry in that way that I know it's coming. I think I can keep it from slipping with a single long, deep breath. I think I can stop it and be just fine. I don't need a moment.

I thought so wrong. The first sob comes and in its wake and my failure to control it, heaving ugly sobs come bearing down on me. They're reckless, and unwarranted. Turning to my side, I bury my head in the pillow, wishing I could suffocate the sniveling wails that come from me without any consent at all.

I hate crying. I've always hated it.

The tears are hotter and larger as they slip down my heated face. Falling to my chin just below where my bottom lip quivers.

Jenny is gone. Such a simple thing, something I deal with constantly in work and have dealt with all my life. She's gone and there's nothing I can do about it.

The nightmares aren't real. She isn't hiding somewhere waiting for me to save her.

The book is only words; there's no deeper message within. It's only words, meaningless like Jase said they were.

It all means nothing.

I have nothing and I feel like nothing just the same. But why does nothing hurt so much? Why does it hurt this bad when you give up hope?

Something must find its way into hope's place in your heart. And that something feels like burning knives that keep stabbing me. I just want it all to stop. I want this chapter to end. Fuck, I need it to end. I can't live like this. I can't live in constant, all-consuming pain with nowhere to run.

Jenny, I hate you for leaving me. I hate you, but even hating you doesn't make the pain stop. I still love you and I don't think love can exist without hope.

It's funny how I cling to something that's not there. That I have faith that I'll see her again in another life. Or that if I somehow bring her justice, she'll know. That it will mean something to her, even if she's not here.

Settling back into the pillow, I lie there tired and feeling like I'm drowning. I start to think that it's okay to drown, that I shouldn't fight it anymore. I'm scared of what will happen when I stop fighting though. What happens when I sink lower and lower into the cold darkness?

That's the imagery that meets me in my sleep.

◌◦◯◦◌

Jenny

It's almost been a month. Every day drags, achingly slowly. Every second wanting me to suffer more and more. It's worse than what I thought it would be. The nausea and shaking. I can't get over how cold I am all the time here.

There's nothing but cinder block walls and a mattress on the floor. If I could think for a moment, I'd remember where I am, but I don't remember. I can barely stand up without vomiting.

My bare knees scrape on the floor as I brace myself. The floor feels damp at first, like it's wet, but the palms of my hands are dry. Rocking my body back and forth, I try to just breathe through the aching pain, the sweating, the constant moving thoughts that only stay still when I see her. That's the only time everything settles, but it falls into the darkness where I hate myself for what I've done and what I've become.

The rumbling happens again, the gentle shaking of the light above my head. I'm not crazy. It's real. The room shakes every so often.

He told me I could sleep through it. Weeks of sleeping while my body goes through withdrawal. He said he'd take care of me, that I had a purpose in this world.

He said he'd help me. Marcus can't help me through this though. No one can help me. No one can save me from where my mind goes when I lie down.

I can't sleep anymore. Bethany's there every time I close my eyes and I feel sicker and full of guilt. I can't sleep through this, knowing what I did to her. What I sacrificed to be here.

"It'll all be worth it."

My eyes whip up to his when I hear his voice. "It hurts," is all I can say and I feel pathetic. Hurts isn't adequate. "I feel like I'm dying." The sentence is pulled from me, slowly, as it drags too. Everything drags so slowly.

"A part of you is dying." His voice holds no emotion, no remorse, no sympathy. It's only matter of fact. "And that's a good thing."

My head nods although I don't know that I agree. Some moments I do. Some moments I just want it to end. I know what would make it all stop; I know a needle would make it go away. I nearly beg for it, but the last time I did, he left me alone in here. "I thought it would only be weeks," I tell him, gripping on to that thread of a thought.

"It has only been weeks."

Shaking my head violently and then hating the spinning that comes after, I grip the sides of my head and rock again, trying to settle.

His voice carries softly to me, as if it's rocking me as well, "It's been close to a month. It's almost over. Just sleep."

"I don't want to sleep!" I scream at him, the words clawing up my throat and scarring the tender flesh on their way out.

"Then don't." His answer is simple. In the dark corner of the room, he sits and watches. That's what he does. He observes. That's not what Beth would do. Licking the cracked skin on my bottom lip, I remember how she always had to be there, always involved, always telling me what I was doing wrong.

I wish I'd listened to her.

My rocking turns gentle just thinking about her.

"You said you'd tell her I was okay."

"I said I'll make sure she finds out." He corrects me sharply.

"Did she see it? The note Jeremy left for her?" His gaze meets mine when I say the name, we're not supposed to say each other's names. I know it's Jeremy though. He came in here to check on me the first few days. It had to be him because of the bandage on his chin.

Jeremy told me what Marcus did to his chin though. He said it was necessary and that's how I know it was him in the video Marcus showed me.

Jeremy's scar is not nearly as bad of a fate as what Luke would endure. Marcus said he deserved it. That it was meant to happen and to only tell him certain things. I listened; I was a good girl, but I regret it all right now. I want it all to stop. "Please," I whimper, "make it stop."

"It will stop in time and your sister will know in time." My sister. Bethany. I need her to know. "Things are going according to plan."

I comment, feeling hollow inside, "I just need her to know."

"Go to sleep, Jennifer." He knows the only person to call me Jennifer was my mother. I told him to stop, but all he says is that it's my name.

"I feel guilty," I confess to him as shivers run down my arms. I don't know why. Maybe because there is no judgment from him, only truth and facts no matter how cold and callous they are.

"You should," is his only answer.

"When will she know that I'm okay?" My eyes burn searching for him in the dark corner.

"That depends on something I can no longer predict."

"On what?" I ask him, feeling a new pain run down the seam of my chest.

"Jase Cross."

CHAPTER
9

Jase

SOME DAYS, BAD SHIT HAPPENS.

Some days you take a loss.

Other days, like today, the puzzle pieces to the overall bigger picture form and you can feel the bad shit and losses preparing to come. It's like watching it all tumble around you.

It's all I can think on the drive back home. That's it falling, everything is going to fall and I'm not sure how to stop it.

As I turn right onto the long gravel road, I feel the vibrations in the car and remember the footage played for Seth and me in the back room after we took care of Luke Stevens.

Declan finally got hold of video from a coffee shop's security feed of their parking lot that showed a section of the graveyard.

A young prick with a bandage covering half of his face snuck up on us and we had no fucking clue. He was right there, hiding behind the car and then at the windshield when the cop car came into view and I was focusing on that, rather than on him tucking a note in the wipers. He hid, crouched down by the wheel, but I should've seen his hand, I should have seen him walking up in the rearview by the tree line. I should have seen, but I didn't.

Marcus may truly be building an army; an army of faceless men like this prick. An army I don't have names for.

Seth's taking care of the surveillance at the bridge Luke mentioned. We have eyes everywhere, watching and waiting. But in order to see what's going on, something has to happen. Something has to fall. And I need names and faces to recognize.

The only one I have right now is Jenny Parks.

"Shit." The curse falls from my mouth as I pull up to my driveway to the estate, seeing the cop car in plain view. Officer Walsh is standing off to the right of the yard, looking out into the woods.

Just what I fucking need.

It's one thing after another. With the rise of adrenaline, my gaze instinctively goes to the second story window on the right, the curtains wide open, but Bethany nowhere to be found.

As I park the car and the faint music I wasn't listening to shuts off, a thought passes through me: *She wouldn't have called him.* There's no way he's here because of her.

With the car door opening, the bitter air hits me and it only makes the sweat on my skin feel hotter.

"Officer Walsh," I call out, and my voice carries through the cold air. That's all I say to greet him, walking steadily past the cars to the yard where he stays put. He rocks on his heels as I slip my keys into my pocket. "Anything I can help you with?" I ask when I'm close enough to him.

"Beautiful view," he comments, taking his gaze back to the forest.

With the thin layer of snow and the white fog along the tree line, it's eerily beautiful.

I don't bother to comment, or to play with his niceties. If she called him, if she wanted to break me like that, get it over with. So I can deal with her and fix this shit.

She wouldn't do that, I think as I swallow, shoving both my hands in my pockets. The moment I glance at the trees, Officer Walsh finally looks back at me.

"I thought maybe if I told you something, you could tell me something," he says, and then clears his throat. A look crosses his face like he doesn't know if he's making the right move. Curiosity sneaks up on me and I give him a small nod as I say, "You first."

"My last case in New York... I failed to save a girl. She's all right now… but I didn't protect her like I should've. It's why I asked for reassignment. I failed her."

He doesn't look at me when he talks, so I take in every bit of his expression. Noting the sincerity in his voice. But wondering how good of a liar this prick is.

"She moved back here. Close to here, anyway."

"That why you're here?" I ask him. "Are you looking for her?"

"No, not looking," he answers me but still doesn't look at me. "I know where she is."

A breeze rushes by, causing his coat to slip open for a moment. His badge shows, just as the gun in his holster is on display for the moment. He shifts and buttons up his coat as he talks.

"I'm looking for someone else. A man named Marcus. He's the one who *saved* her." He rolls his shoulder back as he says "saved" and a grimace mars his face. "He's the one who got her out of that mess." His gaze finally meets mine when he adds, "He got her into it though. He used her, and then claims to have saved her."

His jaw clenches and an anger I haven't seen from him is left unchecked. It's evident in the way his shoulders tense, plus the way he breathes out heavily. And in his voice when he says, "Marcus put her through a hell that I can't even imagine surviving."

Emotion drenches his confession and I can feel the vendetta that wages war in his eyes.

"What is it you want from me?"

"I want Marcus." His answer is immediate. "Anything you have on him."

I swallow, hesitating and Officer Walsh shakes his head with disgust. "You know him. I know you do. I've read the files and all the paperwork. For a decade or more, you and your brothers' names have been right there along with his."

"Sure," I tell him, "Names on paperwork. But Marcus doesn't have a face, he doesn't have a number to call, he doesn't have a location. There's not a damn thing I can give you on Marcus." I'm surprised by the resentment that laces itself around every sentence that's spoken.

"If I could hand over Marcus to you, I would. Because I don't know what he's thinking or why he does the shit he does," I say with finality, and then question my own statement.

Officer Walsh considers me for a long moment, maybe waiting for more.

"I don't have anything for you, Officer."

"If you're not with me, you're against me," he responds lowly. "You know that?"

"Words to live by," I comment with a nod and this time I'm the one staring off into the woods.

"If you do find something, would you even consider telling me?" he asks and I can feel his eyes burning into me.

"I wish you all the luck in the world," I tell him and then breathe in deep, debating on answering his question truthfully, lying or simply not answering at all. I settle for the last option and ask him, "Is there anything else I can help you with?"

(꩜)(꩜)

"What's that?" That's the first thing Bethany says to me as I set the large cardboard box down in the middle of the bedroom. She didn't respond when I walked in; she remained under the covers, in the same position she was in when I left.

Her brunette hair tumbles down her body as she raises herself off the bed. Off my bed. That knowledge does something to me, as does the white light from the open curtains kissing her skin.

"Did I wake you?" I ask her rather than answering her question. The look of sleep plays on her face, making me eager to get in bed with her. As she sits up, crossing her legs in bed and pulling the covers into her lap, her baggy sleepshirt falls off her shoulder and she has to readjust it.

"Only for a minute I think. It's been hard getting to sleep," she answers as I climb into bed, and it groans with her words.

"Just a single minute?" I tease her, wanting to put a smile on her face. She gives me a small one, accompanied with the roll of her eyes. It's my cue to lean forward, taking a single kiss from her. She's still guarded, still giving me questioning gazes and still stiff when I reach out and place my hand on her thigh.

Tucking her hands into her lap she doesn't answer me, she only shrugs and then those hazel eyes look up at me, peeking through her thick lashes.

"I went to your place," I say to change the subject, getting off the bed to go to the box and needing to get away from the look in her eyes.

I grab the pills out of the box. They're years old; we don't even make sweets in the pill form anymore. But I would never throw this bottle away. "I thought you may want some more of your things. Grabbed some mugs, your throw blanket, stuff like that."

She says thank you softly and then clears her throat to say it again louder.

"You brought my mugs?" she questions me with her brow furrowed and it only makes her look cuter. Her legs are bare as she makes her way to the box, the t-shirt stopping just past her ass.

"You have a lot of them on the counter with that box of tea." I shrug as I sit on the bed, watching her go through the box and staring at her ass as she does. "Thought you'd like them."

She takes a few things out of the box, setting them on my dresser behind her and lining up her computer, charger and a few other things in a row.

"Why are you like this?"

Her question catches me off guard. "Like what?"

"Why are you trying to make me happy… I don't understand what you want from me."

I would be frustrated if she wasn't genuinely curious. "Did you expect me to keep you here with nothing of your own?"

"I don't know what to expect," she says, and the honesty in her voice is raw and transparent.

"Right now, I want you to stop fighting me."

She smiles wide for the first time since I've walked in, staring down at an owl mug in her hand. It's a sad, soft smile. "Fighting is what I do best though. Came into the world fighting, I'll leave it that way."

I can't help but return the smile to her. "That's fine with me, cailín tine. Just don't fight with me."

"You okay?" she asks me, setting down the mug and stalking over to me. I lean forward and pull her petite body between my legs, resting my hands on the small of her back before I answer her.

"I had a long day."

I lower my head to rest in the crook of her neck and she does the same. Her lips leave a small kiss that rouses desire from me.

Just as I'm ready to take her, to lay her on the bed and fuck away my problems, she stops me, pulling away to tell me, "I did nothing today."

"Some days that's good to do, to just heal and let the world move around you."

"That's one way to put it."

Every ounce of lust dampens, seeing her lack of life. Fire dies when it's closed off and not allowed to breathe.

I want her to breathe, but she's suffocating herself.

"Did you go to the kitchenette?" I ask her and she shakes her head. "I didn't leave the bedroom."

"I need to show you around," I comment, noting that she's been like this for a few days. Listless. Depressed. "You can't just lie around and expect to get better."

"Get better?" she bites back, her eyes flashing with indignation. "There is no 'getting better,' Mr. Cross. I'm simply trying to adapt to my new reality and I don't have a damn thing to distract me."

She stands up straighter, squaring her shoulders and leaning closer to me. "I may be taking up residence in your bed. I may do all sorts of shit with you I'd never tell a soul I craved so badly, but you," she points her finger to my chest and then licks her lower lip. The act distracts me and instantly I want to take her, punish her for tempting me. "You can tell me how you want me in bed. You can boss me around while I crawl on all fours for you, I don't give a fuck." She shrugs halfheartedly and her shirt slips off her shoulder. She knows what she's doing to me. The little smirk on her lips dims though when she looks me in the eyes and tells me, "You don't get to tell me how to live my life."

"I wasn't," I respond and I'm surprised by the sudden change. The hot and cold between us.

"I want you, I'm not afraid to admit that. Even now, when I'm not able to do what I love, I can't go into work. I'm afraid to go back to my own home," she admits and swallows, looking anywhere but at me and crosses her arms. "And I'm coming to terms with the fact that everyone in my family has died tragically and there wasn't a damn thing I could do about it." She shakes her head.

"Even now, I want you and I love the distraction of you." Her fingers linger on my chest and she steals a quick kiss before whispering down my neck as she pulls herself away from me. "But you don't get to tell me what to do or how to mourn. You'd be wise to remember that, Jase."

That's my cailín tine. Not hidden deep down, just failing to find a reason to come out. I'll give her a reason. I can give her that.

"Tell me something," she says and takes a seat on the black velvet chair next to the dresser. She lays her head back against the wall and pulls her legs into her chest.

"What do you want to know?"

"Who is Angie? What happened to her?"

Surprise lights inside of me, along with dread. "Why are you asking?"

"One time you said I reminded you of someone. Do I remind you of her?"

"She's not the one you remind me of." As I answer her, every muscle in my body tightens.

"Is that where you learned to do those things? The fire? With Angie?"

"No," I answer her again, feeling my throat go dry.

"Well then who the hell is she?" she questions flatly, shaking her head.

"She's someone who died a while back."

"I'm sorry," she whispers and I tell her it's okay although the tension grows between us.

"Do you want to talk about it?" she asks and I shake my head no.

"Everyone dies, Jase, that doesn't define her as to who she was." I don't think Bethany's aware of the magnitude that her words have. "Who was she?"

"A girl who died because of my mistakes."

"And I don't remind you of her?" she questions again, a dullness taking over her gaze.

"No."

As she goes through the things I brought her, I go to the bathroom, placing the pills where they belong. In the same spot Angie left them. The pills were hers and they've been there since the day she died. Not this same medicine cabinet, but the same location. Bottom shelf on the right. That's where she put them.

The irony isn't lost on me that Bethany took them. I stare back at myself in the mirror after I close the medicine cabinet and wonder if I should've left Beth alone. If I never should have tainted her by knocking on her door almost two weeks ago.

"Well," she says, sitting up straighter and making her way to the bed behind me. "Since it's already uncomfortable I might as well tell you, I did some math."

"Go on," I tell her when she breathes in deep, pulling the comforter all the way up. I suppose she got cold.

"One hundred dollars every ten minutes. That's fourteen thousand, four hundred every day. Which would mean the debt is paid in twenty-one days. Not months."

The semblance of a grunt leaves me and I run my thumb along my bottom lip. The only sweet distraction from this conversation is that her eyes lower, lingering on my lips and her own lips part.

"So if you're wanting me to stay here," she starts, staring at my lips as she speaks. Standing up, I walk as she talks, so I can stand across from her. "I want it in writing that the debt won't exist after twenty more days."

Leaning against the dresser, I cross my arms and gaze down at her. "You think you earned fourteen thousand dollars yesterday?"

Indignation flashes in her eyes. "The deal was time, nothing else. And I gave you all my time and listened to you." Her throat tightens as she swallows and my gaze falls to her collarbone and then lower.

"You stay with me for twenty days, which I'm doing to protect you-"

"Which I didn't ask for." She's quick to cut me off. "In fact, I think we can both agree I was resistant but did it because it's what you wanted."

"No good deed goes unpunished, huh?"

"It was never my debt," she rebuts.

Time passes with each of us staring at the other, waiting for the other one to give.

"You listen to everything I say for forty days—"

Again she cuts me off. "Twenty."

"No fucking way," I answer her, keeping my voice low. "Sleep doesn't count as listening to me."

"Thirty max, including yesterday, so twenty-nine days." Her voice is strong as she negotiates. I have to focus not to glance down at her breasts and the way they peek up from her crossed arms.

"Twenty-nine days of you doing whatever it is that I want?" I ask her, feeling my cock go rigid. I unzip my pants and let them drop to the floor so she can see.

Color rises from her chest to her cheeks. She swallows, watching me stroke myself as she answers. "Twenty-nine days," she agrees.

"Get over here and get on your knees." I barely get the words out before she's moving, kicking the sheets away so they don't trip her up.

She takes me into her mouth and I shove my cock in deeper, gripping her hair so I can control it.

Before she can choke, I pull her back and listen to her heave in a breath. She stares up at me with eagerness, her hands grabbing the back of my thighs.

"I'm going to use you and get my money's worth, cailín tine."

(୬)(୬)

Sleep's dragging her under. I can admit I'm exhausted as well. Not in the same way, but I can't go to sleep. I don't want tonight to end.

"I can still feel you," she whimpers. The sheets rustle between her legs as she moans softly, pushing her head into the pillow and letting the pleasure ring in her blood.

Her eyes are half lidded as she peeks up at me. "Does it feel the same for you?" she asks.

I let the tip of my nose play along her cheek and then nip her earlobe. "Does it feel drawn out to you? Like wave after wave and a single touch would make the next crash on the shore?"

Her eyes close as she breathes in deep and steady.

"Sex certainly changes things, doesn't it?" I ask her, remembering how only hours ago I worried about where her mind was headed. She hums in agreement.

I pull the sheet down from her chest slowly, exposing her all the way down to her waist. A shudder rolls through her and with a single tug on her nipples, they harden for me.

"Jase," she murmurs my name.

"I'm not done with you yet," I tell her and her hazel eyes widen.

"I stored the lighter and alcohol pads in the nightstand yesterday, hoping to play with you this morning, but you were asleep."

She huffs a small playful laugh as I open the drawer, still lying in bed. "Is that why you said sleeping doesn't count?"

Keeping one small pad folded, I run it along her closest breast and then pluck the other one, letting the moisture cool on her skin and sparking her nerve endings.

Sweet sounds of rapture slip through her lips as her hands make their way between her legs. She doesn't touch herself though, not until I tell her, "It's all right to play with yourself, but be still."

The fire blanket is in the drawer, I remind myself of that as I flick the lighter, staring at the flame and then gently bringing it to where the ethanol is still lingering on her skin. The flame grows along her skin, licking and turning a brighter yellow, but it's gone just as quickly as it came. By the time her mouth has parted, the evidence of it is all gone.

"Again," I tell her, sucking the other nipple into my mouth and running my teeth along her tender flesh before moving back to her right side, wiping the alcohol pad around her areola and then lighting it aflame again.

This time she moans louder, her knees pulling up the sheet that's puddled around her waist.

"Do you know why I enjoy fire?" I ask her, massaging and pinching her left breast once again.

"Because it's dangerous," she answers me softly and I shake my head no.

"Because it's wild," I correct her and then do it again, a larger portion this time.

Once the fire's gone, I grip both her breasts in my hands and run my thumbs over both nipples.

"Which one makes you feel more alive, cailín tine?"

CHAPTER
10

Bethany

I SUPPOSE I WAS NEVER UNDER THE ILLUSION THAT IT WAS A TIT FOR TAT OF information. So long as he answers my questions and keeps searching for answers I'll never be able to find, I'll willingly warm his bed.

In fact, I have little to no objection to it at all.

It's obvious I'm a fool, that I have no grip on reality, let alone my own mind. I feel like I'm losing it to be honest. What's the point in trying to stay afloat in the middle of the deep dark ocean when there's no land in sight? I could fight it, and I feel like I have, like I'm exhausted from fighting to stay above water. Or I can fall into Jase's arms, and let him hold me for a moment.

Fear plays a small part, but it's shocking how small a part it is.

Someone is after me, and this arrangement prevents them from getting whatever it is they want from me—which can't be good—and could lead me to information. Although that piece... that last piece about information. I'm starting to lose hope for that to happen.

I'm starting to accept it never happening.

If I think about it like I'm an undercover cop, suddenly it's all okay in my mind.

That's what I tell myself anyway. It's all pretend. My life is turning into a tall tale like Marky used to feed me. And that makes the jagged pill easier to swallow.

These are the thoughts that lead me to biting my thumbnail as I lie in Jase's bed. The clock on his nightstand, a beautiful contemporary clock with a minimalistic face of sleek marble and only hands to tell the time, must be lying to me because it reads that it's after noon already.

I sink back under the covers, pulling them up easily since I'm in bed alone and listen to the ticking. My hand splays under the sheets onto the side of the mattress where Jase lay last night. The thought of last night brings a faint kiss of a smile to my lips, but it falls just as quickly as it came, finding the bedsheet cold to the touch.

I called work again when I first woke up, ready to leave a message this time. Half of me wanted to be professional and ask what the phone call regarded, the other half wanted to call my boss an asshole, assuming it was him. Instead of leaving a message, I found myself talking to the lead nurse on Michelle's case.

"I'm so sorry," she started and then immediately dove into discussing the restraints they had to use on her arms. "She was eating the gauze, Beth. I have no idea what to do with her other than restrain her. I've never had a patient with pica and I don't know what to do."

"She loves pickles. So make pickle ice." I rattled off what I'd been doing with Michelle. She's a new patient, pregnant and newly diagnosed with pica. It's a psychological disorder where patients have an appetite for non-nutritive foods, or even harmful objects. "It'll most likely diminish after the pregnancy."

"I know, but what am I supposed to do?" The stress and frustration were all too relatable. "She can't stay restrained for six months."

"Listen to me," I said as I gripped the phone tighter. "Mix half pickle juice and half water, add in a soluble supplement, freeze into ice chips and then give them to her throughout the day, constantly."

"That can't be it."

"I'm telling you, you keep that by her bedside and she eats it slowly. Something about the cold makes her pace herself."

"Okay... okay," Marilyn sounded hopeful and I felt it too, until I heard someone ask who she was talking to and then the line went dead. When I get back to work, I'm going to kill my boss. I can hear his excuse now, that I'm a workaholic and I wouldn't be able to help myself, but that they should know better.

That was the only distraction I had.

I'm slow to sit up, forcing myself to rise although I have no plans, no control, nothing at all I want to do... but read I suppose. Thank all that's holy for books.

The small piece of me that anticipated—and looked forward to a note from Jase—is disappointed when I find his nightstand empty of any slip of paper.

I shouldn't feel so hollow in my chest. I shouldn't feel this kind of loss.

Bringing my knees up to my chest, I rest my cheek on my right knee and wonder what happened to me. What the fuck happened to the woman I was? Without work... I'm no one. My life is utterly empty and the one thing that's filling it shouldn't be in my life at all.

One breath, and the screaming thoughts quiet. Two breaths and I find it hard to care. This will all be over soon. It's temporary and nothing more. I'll be back to work, unraveled or not.

Until then... I'll read and let Jase fuck me. Maybe one day, I'll even get out of bed.

The Coverless Book
Three quarters through the book

Emmy

I remember all the times Miss Caroline took me to the appointments. Mother always met me there. It was Miss Caroline who took me on long drives and told me stories the whole way. No matter how many hours it was. That's all I can remember as we sit outside of the shed. It's a large shed, with running water and an outhouse with plumbing around the back.

Jake said it's his cousin's place, so it's okay that we stay here.

I can remember the trips to the hospitals. The long drives we took to get to them. The hotels we stayed in. Miss Caroline always stopped for ice cream on the way to and back. And she let me eat all sorts of things I never had at home.

I remember all those trips... but those are the only trips I've ever taken.

Until this one.

"What's wrong?" Jake's voice breaks my thoughts. His hand cradles my chin. "You look like you regret this." I hate how his voice sounds like he really believes that.

My hair tickles my shoulders when I shake my head and tell him, *"You're crazy to think that. I love you, Jake."* He needs to know that. *"I was just hoping to go inside. It's been a few days since we've slept on a bed."* I want to give myself to him. But not like this.

His lips part and instead of words coming out, he closes them again, kicking the rubble under his shoes. *"We can't go inside, Em."* He stares off at the large farmhouse. *"Your mom filed a report and the sheriff called. We can't go inside."*

Feeling a wave of nausea, I lower my head to my hands. *"Your family doesn't know we're here?"*

"My cousin does, and he's bringing us blankets. I've got money once we get out of this town. But, for tonight... Our parents are looking for us."

The crickets from the cornfield get louder as the sun sets deeper behind the crimson sky. It's nearly dusk already.

"I'm sorry I can't give you more right now, but soon I can."

I find his hand in mine, and tell him, *"It's why running away is so scary. The unknown."*

His eyes stare deep into mine as he says, *"The only known in my life I need, is you beside me. As long as I have you, nothing else matters."*

He tells me he loves me and I feel that drop in my stomach again, but I make sure I tell him I love him too and that I can't wait for all of the unknowns I'll face with him.

That's just before I go around the back of the shed to where the faucet is to wash my face. It's just before I get sick in the field. It's just before I look down at my hands as I'm cleaning myself up and see nothing but blood.

Three more times, I cough up blood and my eyes water. My face heats and then all at once, it stops. It's not a lot, it's not a lot of blood. It's because of whatever Miss Caroline put in the soup for all that time. I know it is. She made me sick. I'll get better now; Jake knows that too. I'm not sick, I'm recovering from what she did to me.

I hide what happened from Jake, though, all the blood I just coughed up. I don't want him to see.

I just want to be loved and to love him. Isn't love enough?

"Are you okay?"

Hearing Jase before I see him startles me. I hadn't noticed how erratic my breathing was until he came in. I set the book down on the nightstand.

"Yeah, why?" I ask him as I rub my eyes, and try to come back to reality. I catch a glimpse of the clock and realize nearly two hours slipped by. The uneasiness and shock that the book left me in won't shake off when I look back up to Jase.

"You look horrified."

I answer him, "It's just a book."

"What happened?" he asks me like he really cares as he takes off a black cotton shirt, damp with sweat. His body glistens, his muscles flex with every movement and with the increase of lust, the problems of my fictional world fall away.

"She might really be sick," I tell him, although my eyes stay glued to his chest.

"Who?" He stands still, a new shirt in his hand as he waits for my answer.

"Don't worry about it," I tell him. "She's invincible." Hearing those words come from me with confidence makes my stomach drop.

Jase has a different reaction. His lips pull up into an asymmetric smile at my remark and the way his eyes shine with humor is infectious. I feel lighter, but still, the sickness of the unknown churns in my stomach.

"I can't stay here," I tell him, knowing I need to do something and just as aware that there's nothing for me to do here. He removes the space between us, climbing up onto the bed to sit cross-legged in front of me. He doesn't love me like... like I feel for him. That's the truth that sinks me further into the bed.

Being around him, knowing what I feel for him and coming to terms with that, but not feeling the same from him... it's killing me. It makes me want to run. It's scary when you realize you love someone and that they may never feel the same for you. Not in the same way. Nothing like what I feel for him.

It doesn't stop me from breathing him in though.

The sweet smell of his sweat is surprising... and heady. The way he looks at me, it's all the more intoxicating.

"You agreed to twenty-nine days," he reminds me.

"Twenty-eight now," I correct him in return.

"Twenty-eight then."

"I can't stay here like this. Doing nothing day in, day out."

"I don't expect you to."

"What am I supposed to do?" I ask him, truly needing an answer.

He considers me for a moment. "I really don't know what to do," I tell him when he hesitates to answer me. It's harder for me to admit that than I thought it would be.

"I don't have any answers for you," he tells me beneath his breath, quietly, like he's sorry.

"I love work. I want to go back to work."

"I don't know that you're in the right mindset to do that."

My voice rises as I ask, "How am I supposed to get better when I have nothing to do to make me better?"

"Time." He answers me with a single word, joining me on the bed. "You could start with putting your mugs in the kitchen." Looking at the box still where he left it yesterday, he tells me, "You could do whatever you like."

"I can't leave," I answer him boldly, letting him know it pisses me off.

"Yesterday I didn't want you to, no. But that doesn't mean you can't leave. I'm not trapping you here, you're locking yourself in this room."

I hate him for his answer, although I don't know why.

"Where would you go after you're done with work to let loose?" he asks me.

"A bar."

"I like that," he says and scoots closer to me, pulling me into his lap. I settle against him, resting my back to his front.

"You order wine or mixed drinks at the bar?"

"Mixed. Vodka and whatever the bartender wants." The rough chuckle makes his chest shake gently and I love the feeling of it. His stubble brushes my neck as he asks, "And then?"

"Grocery store if I need to, although I really only keep K-cups and cardboard pizza in the fridge."

"Cardboard pizza?"

"You know, the kind that come in a box and you put in the toaster oven?"

That makes him laugh too. The sound of him laughing eases everything.

"You have a pretty smile," he tells me and his voice is calming.

"You have a pretty smile too," I tell him back and he makes a face.

He changes the subject quicker than I expect. "We don't know who broke in."

My own smile falters and I stare at my fingers, picking absently under my nails at nothing.

"I know that's not what you wanted to hear and it's not what I was hoping to tell you. But there are no fingerprints, no cameras anywhere."

With his hand on my chin, he forces me to look at him as he explains, "We looked into everyone's surveillance cameras, Beth. It's not quite legal, but they'll never know. Whoever it was left no trace at all."

"So I'll never know and they could come back." I'm surprised how much pain accompanies that knowledge. My chest feels like it's been hollowed out and bricks put in the place of whatever it is I need to survive.

"No. That's not true. We have a lead on your sister," he tells me with hope and authority.

"A man named Luke Stevens. He's no one around here, but he was seen with your sister before she went missing."

He hands me a picture of a man I've never laid eyes on. He's got to be in his forties, with a clean-cut look to him and I could only imagine what the hell Jenny would have been doing with someone like this.

"You think he did it?" I dare to ask Jase.

"I'm not sure, but I'm going to find him and get as much information as I can from him, cailín tine."

"Miranda told me she packed her bags," I say and swallow thickly, needing to calm the adrenaline racing in my blood. "She said Jenny packed before she went missing." The image of my sister doing just that and then leaving with this man plays in my mind. "Maybe she was in love with him," I surmise.

"I don't think—" Jase bites down to stop himself from saying something else.

"What?"

His inhale is uneven and he looks past me before saying, "I just wanted you to know that I'm working on it. But don't do this. Don't let your mind play tricks on you. All we know is that he was seen with her."

"Seen doing what?"

"Getting into a truck around the time she went missing but they aren't positive of the date."

I have no words as the theory in my mind unravels.

"It could be nothing, but we have a name and I'm working on it," he tells me and takes my hand in his, stopping me from my mindless habit.

"So now there are two names?" I ask, remembering the last time we talked about information.

He nods once, but doesn't give me the other name. The one he promised wouldn't help me.

"Which do you think broke into my house?" I ask him and instead of answering, he tells me, "I'm having Seth install a top-of-the-line security system. Everything will be repaired, and all the locks will be changed."

The information sparks a reaction I don't expect and I have to pull my hand away, but he doesn't let me so I blurt out the question, "You want me to go back... to my place?"

"No," he says and his quick answer alleviates some of the unwanted stress. "I'd prefer you here by my side and for the next twenty-eight days, I want you here at my place. But you need to be able to go home and feel safe. I get that and I wanted to make sure it was safe."

I can only nod, feeling overwhelmed and not knowing what to do. When he squeezes my hand, I squeeze back and tell him, "Thank you."

"I have to go. Late-night meeting."

Late meeting. My lips stay closed although I don't have to say anything at all. My gaze drops just as my lightheartedness does. I can never forget the life Jase leads. I need to remember.

"Don't look at me like that." His voice is low and a threat lays behind the words.

"Like what?" I ask him as if I don't know what he's referring to.

"Like I'm less than you for what I do."

"I don't," I protest, hating that it's obvious.

"You do."

Biting back my pride, I apologize, "I'm sorry."

"It's never going to change, Bethany. This isn't something I can run away from."

He stares at me like he's repentant. Like he'd change it if he could, although I don't believe him. All I can tell him back is, "I didn't ask you to."

CHAPTER
11

Jase

I'M THE LAST TO ENTER THE KITCHEN AND AS I MAKE MY WAY TO THE counter, Carter pushes a tumbler with ice and whiskey my way.

"You want to meet her, huh?" I ask Carter, looking him in his eyes as I bring the glass to my lips and let the liquor settle on my tongue to burn.

Carter only lets a smirk show, filling the empty tumbler in front of him and then asking Declan if he wants a glass too.

"I'll have beer," Declan announces and Daniel looks over his shoulder at Declan, a grin on his face too before reaching into the fridge. The bottles clink together and the telltale sound of the beer fizzing fills up the silence as I wait for my answer.

"You told her not to come in here, didn't you?" he asks, the smile only widening.

"You're a prick," I tell my oldest brother and when they all chuckle, I finally let myself smile and pull out the barstool. I'm a prick for lying to her too, but they don't need to know that.

"If she met us, if she knew what was going on, maybe she'd feel a little differently," Sebastian says as he enters the room, touching his elbow to Carter's in greeting and taking the last tumbler of whiskey.

"Maybe," I agree although I'm quick to take another swig of the whiskey.

"What's the update on Addison?" Sebastian asks Daniel. His response is to share a look with Carter first. They're going through the next stage of life together. All three of the men although Sebastian's wife is furthest along. Daniel and Carter just found out about the pregnancies.

Daniel picks at the label on his beer bottle as he answers, "They said it's just high blood pressure. She just needs to take it easy."

A moment passes where no one knows what to say. Addison never thought she could get pregnant and for good reason. She went through a rough life as a child.

"Aria's happy that she gets to pick out everything with a friend," Carter says to break up the tension.

Sebastian contributes to the easy feeling by remarking, "Chloe's happy she won't be the only fat one." He adds quickly, "Or so she said," which gets a good laugh and a clink of beers and glass tumblers.

"It feels good having all five of us in here, doesn't it? Like old times," Declan comments.

All four of my brothers and the one man, Sebastian, who sticks out because he's older.

"We do have a real reason to meet," Carter says and glances at the closed door behind me. She can place her hand to the panel and enter, or simply try to listen from the other side of the door.

"Romano." Daniel and I say our enemy's name at once.

Carter nods. "He's scattered. There's no doubt."

"What made him run?" Sebastian asks.

"He's outnumbered. It's not just Talvery men looking to settle a vendetta, but us too. It's quiet with Officer Walsh and the FBI leaning hard on the local cops," Daniel answers and Carter nods along with him. "If he was ever going to leave, now is the time to do so."

"If he comes back, which he has to in order to get everything out of his warehouses, all of his supply and the stashed guns are on Fourth. If he comes back, there are only two roads he can use to come into town," I comment, knowing if he comes back, I don't want to give him another chance to leave.

"You think he'll come back for it?" Sebastian asks.

"He's got money hidden away in the warehouse on Fourth, we've staked out that street and he knows, but he doesn't know that we're aware his money's there. Maybe he thinks with him gone, we'll forget about him," Carter answers him.

"Forget about him?" There's a tension in Daniel's voice, akin to outrage. "We aren't going to let him run."

Daniel's comment goes unanswered.

"I say we blow up his estate and the warehouse too. Destroy everything."

"He left men behind." Carter's quick to rebut my suggestion.

"Not enough," I answer him, staring into his eyes.

"With the FBI and former agent on our asses, do we really want to risk it?" Declan asks, wanting to be safe.

"Yes. We do. We can't let what he did go unanswered. We can't let anyone think they can run from us," Daniel says, his body tense and the beer he has in his hand tapping against the granite.

"Calm down," Carter tells our brother, but I'm with Daniel.

"He's right," I say to voice my opinion.

"Destroy everything in his name and send Nikolai after him," Daniel suggests.

"Nikolai?" A tension coils in my stomach. "He tried to kill me; he tried to take Addison, your soon-to-be wife." I can't help that my voice rises, the same outrage Daniel had a moment ago slipping into my cadence.

"Do you plan to chase him, Jase? You going to risk your... what's her name? Bethany? Are you going to risk her to chase after him?" he questions me.

"Sending Nikolai is smart," Declan adds and Sebastian nods in agreement. I crack my neck, not looking at my brothers, knowing they're not on my side. All while questioning if they're right. If I could really risk leaving Bethany behind.

"With Marcus still here... you're right. We should send Nikolai."

"Aria will never forgive me if something happens," Carter admits and stares into the swirling whiskey in his glass.

"She doesn't have to know," Declan says which brings all of our eyes to him.

"It's easy to say that, but they always find out. The truth always rises to the surface." Sebastian's sentiment sends a chill down my spine. I warm it with the remainder of the whiskey in my glass.

The empty tumbler hits the granite in time with the door opening behind us. All five of us turn to see Bethany, standing in the now open doorway with her hand still in the air.

The sight of her is enough to ease the tension in the room.

"You look like a deer in headlights," Daniel comments and then waves her in.

"I'm sorry," she says immediately, not moving an inch. "I didn't mean to interrupt."

"Were you planning on just sneaking around then?" Carter asks and grins at her. "We can pretend we didn't see you if that's the case." The ice in his tumbler clinks as he brings it up to his smile and takes a sip.

The long sweater hangs loosely on her, but when she wraps her arms around herself, I can just barely make out the dip in her waist. With keys jingling in her hand, and seeing as how she's slipped on leggings and boots, it's obvious she's heading out.

Doubt sinks its claws into me. Holding me in place as she stands there. Bethany's wide eyes meet mine and she nearly turns around when I don't say anything.

"Come meet my brothers," I say loud enough to stop her in her tracks before she can run off completely.

She hesitates a moment and then walks to my side, her insecurity showing. The moment she's beside me, I wrap my arm around her waist.

"I'm sorry," she whispers although it's not low enough that the rest of the guys wouldn't hear.

"Guys, meet Bethany. Sebastian, Carter, Daniel and Declan." I point at each of them one by one and she gives them a small, embarrassed wave. "Sebastian's not blood, but still family," Carter comments and then fills his glass and mine again. "Want a drink?" he offers her.

"That's actually why I came in here," she says and Daniel interrupts her by saying, "I like her already," which gets agreeable laughter from the rest of the guys.

Her nerves are still high, no matter how much I run soothing circles along her back. Her voice is strained when she looks up at me and says, "I forgot I told a friend I was seeing her tonight. It's the weekend. I was just going to head out."

It's more than obvious to not just me, but to all of the men standing here that she's searching for permission.

It's not like her, I wish they could see her. Really see her. I tell myself she just needs time.

"Have fun." With that I smile down on her, not giving her any restraints. Seth and his men will watch her and inform me.

Blinking, she holds back the obvious questions that beg to be spoken. Instead she only nods and nearly says thank you, but those words turn into an, "Okay, I'll see you tonight?"

My brothers and Sebastian say nothing, only observing and drinking. I know they're judging, and I hate them for it.

I can see her need to run and before she can turn and leave me, I capture her lips with mine. Her lips are hard at first, and she utters a small protest of shock, right before she melts into me. Her lips soften and her hands move to my back when I deepen the kiss just slightly.

It doesn't last long, but it lasts long enough to bring color to her cheeks. With her teeth sinking into her bottom lip, she smiles sweetly and barely glances at my brothers, giving them a wave before quickly walking away.

I leave the door open, watching her walk out of sight.

"She seemed nervous."

"No shit," Carter says and laughs off Declan's comment at the same time Sebastian asks for another beer.

"What are you doing with her?" Carter asks me and everyone goes quiet. "It seems different from what you mentioned." All eyes are on me as I stand alone.

I can feel all of their eyes on me, the questions piling on one after the other in their gazes. With my forearms on the cold, hard counter, my shoulders tense. I lower my gaze to my folded hands firmly placed on the granite.

"That's a damn good question."

CHAPTER
12

Bethany

I
T FEELS LIKE THERE WAS A HEAVY BELL THAT RANG TOO CLOSE TO ME.
That's the only way I can describe how I'm feeling. The sound left a
ringing sensation on my skin, maybe even deeper.

Every minute on my drive home I thought it would go away, but it
didn't.

It tingles, and refuses to go unnoticed. Even now as I sit with
Laura in the parking lot outside of a strip mall with a bottle of
cabernet half gone and tempting me to take another swig... the
ringing doesn't stop. I'm trapped in the moment when it happened.
When the world shifted and made it impossible for me to get away
from the giant bell.

The moment Jase kissed me like a lover in front of his brothers.

I've heard of Sebastian Black; my sister went to school with him.
I've heard of the Cross Brothers. I've seen Carter from afar at The Red
Room once. To be in a room with such men, with intimidating, dangerous men, I couldn't think or breathe. It was a mix of fear and something else. Something sinful.

Even with them talking, joking, acting as if it was just an ordinary
day and ordinary people in an ordinary kitchen, I couldn't shake all the
stories I'd heard of these men.

But then Jase kissed me.

Every part of my body has woken up, and it refuses to let the memory become that, a memory. It's holding on to it instead, trying to stay there. Going out with Laura has definitely dampened the ringing, but not so much though that I can't feel it still, even hours later.

"What's wrong with you? You love this song." Laura cuts through my hazy thoughts and my gaze moves from the yellow streetlights and lit signs of the chain stores to focus on her instead.

I hadn't even noticed music was playing.

"Hey," Laura says and pats my arm as she leans forward with a hint of something devious in her voice. "You know how..." she shifts uneasily and restarts. "You remember how you helped me interview for the position at the center?"

"Of course," I answer her and wonder where she's going with this.

"Aiden didn't like me during the interview."

I cut her off and say, "He was a grade-A dick for no reason." I still remember how shocked I was at his unprofessionalism.

"I hit his car a week before," she blurts out.

"What?"

She can't stop grinning. "I was so embarrassed. It was a rough day. Like really bad and he backed up out of nowhere in the parking lot and I just tapped him." Her thumb and her pointer are parallel as she holds them up and whispers, "Just a teeny tap."

"You hit his car?"

"And then I might have... you know," she stops and laughs again. "I called him a dickhead when he was yelling at me. Like he was screaming in my face and it wasn't like it was helping anything and like I said, it was a rough day and I just snapped." Her shoulders shake with another giggle. "And then I showed up for the interview the next week."

"Oh my God! And you never told me?" I can't help laughing either. I can absolutely see Aiden and her screaming at each other in a parking lot over a scratch on a car. They both have a habit of taking out their aggression on the least suspecting.

"I was so embarrassed I couldn't tell you."

"Well no wonder he didn't want to hire you," I comment.

"I know. I had to go back in and apologize. I'd already sent him insurance information that he didn't even need, but still. I felt awful. It was so awkward and... unfortunate."

"But he still hired you," I say and hold up my finger to make that point clear.

"Because of you. He never would have if you weren't there backing me up."

"Knowing about the car... I'm going to have to agree with you now. I just thought he was an uncalled for asshole at your interview."

"I never told you and I want to thank you again, Beth. Thank you."

"Of course, I love you." I almost add how she was by my side through everything with Jenny before she died, and that getting her a job is insignificant in comparison, but I leave that out. I'm not wanting to drag the mood down.

"I love you too."

She spears her hand through her golden locks, moving all her hair to her left shoulder and glancing at her split ends. "You're off, like even more than you have been. And don't tell me *you're fine,*" she says, mocking the words I've been giving her all night.

Reaching out for the bottle of wine, she gives me a pointed look. The swish of the liquid is followed by the sound of a car riding down the half-empty lot and I look at it instead of her.

Again not answering her. It's only about the dozenth time she's asked me what's going on.

"A cop came to your house today." Her voice is clearer and when I look back, this time she isn't looking at me. I wouldn't call her expression a frown, it's something else, something etched with worry.

"When I was waiting for you to get home, which—by the way, where the fuck were you?" She pauses and sucks in a breath before relaxing into the seat and then taking another swig. She offers it back to me and then repeats, "I was waiting and a cop came by. I told him you weren't home and he said he'd come back later."

"Officer Walsh?" I question her and she nods, then takes the wine back before I can take another sip.

"I was going to tell you at dinner, but you seem really not with it. So like... I don't know."

This time I grab the bottle and take a drink before it's all gone.

Laura looks at me with a slight pout, although I'm not sure it's quite that. It's genuine and sullen, but there's a sadness I can't place.

I watch her look out to the shoe store we just left before she exhales with frustration. "You always tell me everything," she starts. "I know this is hard and you're not a 'speak your feelings' type of girl, which is ironic since you tell everyone else to do just that."

The wine flows easily until the bottle is empty, but I don't let it go.

"It just seems like this isn't mourning, it's something else and I don't know what to do or how to help you."

Laura's voice cracks as she raises her hands into the air, trying to prove a point but needing to wipe under her eyes instead.

"No, no, don't cry." My reaction is instant, reaching out to clutch her shoulder. The leather of her seats groans as I sit up and reposition myself on my knees to face her in the small car. "Everything's fine," I tell her but she only shakes her head.

With her eyes wide open and staring at the ceiling of the car, she responds, "It's not though. You're not okay."

"Seriously," I start to tell her and then catch sight of a car I recognize, and a prick I know too. Seth raises his hands in surrender at the wheel of his car, although his wrists stay planted on it, and my throat tightens. I can't hold on to my train of thought and I have to sit back in my seat, taking a steadying breath.

Jase sent Seth to follow me.

Maybe I should have guessed it. Maybe I should have known I'd be followed.

It's a strange thing, to feel safe, to feel wanted and protected by someone I know I fear and hate on a level that's unattainable to my conscious.

I rest my head against the cold window and close my eyes.

"We were having a good time," I tell her softly. Feeling the tingle of the bell, and falling back into old habits with Laura, I felt like I escaped for a moment. I'm nothing but foolish.

"Shit, no, don't you cry too." Laura presses a hand to her forehead and then over her eyes.

"I swear, I'm fine," I tell her although I can't help but to look past her and at Seth instead. "I..." I trail off and have to swallow before I lie again, "It's just hard to stop thinking about Jenny."

Fuck, that hurts to say. To use her as an excuse. To bring her up in conversation at all.

"And now we're both crying," I tell her with a huff and pull my sweater to the corner of my eyes. "I don't want to cry. It's just my eyes glossing over. It's not crying... I'm not crying."

"You're an awful liar." Laura's voice is soft and I'm pulled to her, to tell her everything. To lean on her like a friend would do.

How selfish is that?

"Tell me about work. I miss it. What kind of person misses work?"

Laura works in Human Resources at the center, but they get all the gossip just the same as the nurses who do the rounds like me.

"Well there's a cute guy who came in last week," she starts to tell me with feigned interest. Then her head falls to the side to look at me as she says, "But his name is Adam and we both know Adams are dicks."

Her comment forces a small laugh from me and then she reaches for the bottle.

"I don't know what's funnier, your taste in men or your pout when the wine's gone."

Instead of commenting, she pushes her hair back and tells me about a few new patients, all of which piss her off for good reason. A man who was drunk at the wheel and killed two people. She thinks he's faking insanity because ever since he was admitted all he can talk about is how totaled his truck is and he hasn't shown a damn bit of remorse for the couple he killed even though he knows he's being charged with their murder. We get those kinds of people sometimes. Assholes who fake mental illnesses to get out of legal trouble. Or even to get out of work for a week.

"Oh, I do love this one old woman who came in though. She said it's actually the 1800s and she's talking to dead people. I like Sue a lot. She's so sweet."

"I wish I were at work."

"I wish you were too," she adds and pats my thigh. "You'd love Sue."

"I'm sure I would." It's never a boring day at the Rockford Center. That's a truth no one can deny.

"I can't drive us home." Laura's statement makes me look at her and then at Seth. "You want to Uber?" she asks me and I shake my head no, getting out without thinking.

"What are you doing?" she calls out as I step out onto the asphalt and make my way to Seth's car. I ignore her calls for me to *get my ass back there*. I'd smile at the way she whispers it and tries to keep me from knocking on Seth's window if it weren't for the anxiousness creeping up on me from what I'm about to do.

I don't have to knock though; he rolls down his window but doesn't say a word.

"Oh my God, I'm so sorry," Laura says and tries to pull me away again. "My friend is a little bit more drunk than I thought." She tugs at my wrist and again I ignore her efforts.

"Will you give us a ride home?" I push out the question. Seth lets out a smile, a handsome smile with perfect teeth, all the while staring at Laura and her wide eyes.

"We don't need a ride," Laura's quick to tell him. "I'm so sor-"

"I don't mind," Seth cuts her off and asks, "Where are you going?" I'm still staring at Laura and the way she's looking at Seth that I don't notice he asked me.

"Home," is all I answer him and he nods once, the playfulness gone from his expression and tells us to get in the back.

I don't know what came over me or why. Maybe it's the piece of me that wants Seth to pay for watching me like a hawk. I can't explain it, but it feels like a step forward. Not the literal step forward I take to get in the back of the car, but a step out of whatever place I was in just hours ago.

Laura snatches me when I open the door, and she immediately slams it shut instead. The thud is loud and nearly violent.

"What the fuck?" she hisses. "Do you even know him? Do you want to get us killed?"

"Yeah, I've met him a couple of times," I tell her and shrug, feeling like the worst liar in the world. A heavy weight presses against my chest as I escape the harsh wind, opening the door again and scooting over to the other side so Laura will get in too.

She takes a little too long to decide so I tell her, "Hurry up, it's cold out there and you're letting all that cold in here!" My admonishment works.

"Let me get my bag."

As she turns to walk away, Seth asks me all the while watching her, "Whose home?"

Whatever's settled into my stomach feels thicker. "Can you drop her off first?"

"You think she'd be okay with that?" He finally turns in his seat to look at me. "Because I don't."

I watch her texting on her phone a few spaces over with her driver's door open although she still stands on the street.

"I want to tell her," I admit to him. "You can stop me if I say something I shouldn't."

"You shouldn't say anything, Bethany."

"Well, I'm going to say something. I have to tell her." We both hear her car door shut and he says lowly, "You really shouldn't." The way his shoulders tense and he grips the wheel makes my chest feel hollow and I almost reconsider, but I have to tell her something.

She's my best friend and she deserves to know. I can't not tell her. I can't let her cry for me like she's doing.

Her car beeps from the alarm and then she's seated beside me, thanking Seth and referring to him as the "handsome savior" of our night although I can still hear the hesitation and worry in her tone.

She gives Seth a tight smile and then he asks again, "Where are you guys headed?"

"Can you take me to Jase's?" I dare to ask Seth, knowing Laura's going to ask me about Jase, paving the way for it to happen.

Seth's returning smile is tight, but he nods.

"Who's Jase?"

Ignoring Laura's question and her stare of confusion, I ask Seth, "Can you take Laura home first?"

"No fucking way are you staying in this car, drunk and with a guy you don't know." She glances at Seth who puts the car in reverse to leave as she adds, "No offense."

"He works for Jase," I answer her, finally looking her in the eyes.

"Who the hell is Jase?"

"Jase Cross," I tell her, gauging her expression when I mention "Cross." Everyone knows about the brothers and I can see the exact moment when it sinks in.

"You're with Jase?" she questions me softly and then swallows so loud, looking between me and Seth, that I'm sure even he can hear it. I only nod.

"With him? Like what does that even mean?"

My hands turn clammy and I have to wring my fingers around one another in my lap. "I can't even look you in the eyes," I tell her and then cover my face with my hands as my head sinks back into the seat.

"No, Bethy, no. Don't cry."

"I'm not going to cry," I protest, forcing my hands down and staring straight ahead at the back of the black leather seat in front of me. "I'm just..." I can't finish. "I don't even know what I feel. Ashamed, I think."

"Ashamed because you're with him? Or ashamed at what you've done?" she asks cautiously. She whispers, "Did he make you do anything? I will fuck him up. I don't care who he is."

"No, stop. No, he didn't make me do anything." Although I tell her that, the first time we met flashes in my memory. I think I'll leave that out of this conversation.

I have to shake out my hands, feeling them turn numb and having a wave of anxiousness hit me. "I'm ashamed because of both... neither. I don't know. I'm confused."

"Okay." Laura's patient with me although she keeps looking at Seth like he's not to be trusted.

The way she looks at Seth, questioning him and his intentions gives me an uncomfortable feeling. More than that, I feel like I should be defending them. Which is outrageous, yet it's exactly how I feel in this moment.

"He's a good guy," I tell her to ease her worries. "Jase treats me really, really good." Emotions tickle up my throat and I have to swallow them before I tell her, "Seth watches out for me for him."

She asks the obvious question. "Watches out for what?"

With Seth as my witness, I tell her everything.

I don't even leave out the part where I almost shot Jase. I tell her literally everything that I can remember. Including the part where I think I love him. Fuck my life.

CHAPTER
13

Jase

I T'S NOT EVERY DAY THAT I FEEL LIKE A PRICK.

Taking advantage of someone's weakness is how I survived, how my brothers and I rose to the top.

There's not a single doubt that I'm taking advantage of Bethany. It's easy when you're hurting to fall for someone, to trust them, to want there to be a way out of the pain.

Listening in on her conversation in the car, listening to her recount the events with Laura Devin, makes me feel like the worst fucking prick alive.

I made her love me. I made sure she had no other option. And worse than that, I don't know that I will ever say the words back to her.

"Boss." Seth nods when I see him and I nod back although my gaze travels to Bethany. Watching her climb the steps as I open the door for her.

Her cheeks are tearstained but there's a sense of lightness around her. Even more than that, her small body brushes against my chest as she walks in. She did it on purpose. She wanted to touch me and I fucking love it. Prick or not.

"Have a good night," I tell him and he smirks at me as he replies, "You too."

Bethany rocks from one foot to the other, watching me as I close to the door to the cold and then turn to her fully.

"Let me help you," I tell her and then act like a gentleman, helping her out of her coat.

With my fingertips lingering on her bare skin, I lower my lips to the shell of her ear and whisper, "Seth put you on speaker from the moment you knocked on his window."

She shudders from my touch and lets her head fall back into my chest. "Are you angry?" she asks with her eyes still open, staring past me at the now closed door.

"No, I'm not."

"I had to tell her." Her words slur slightly and I can smell the hint of alcohol on her.

"Of course you did."

"And you heard everything?" she asks and that's when her expression falls. No doubt she's questioning where my opinions lie. When I nod in response, she doesn't voice her question.

She takes a different approach, changing the subject altogether.

"What were you talking to Seth about before I went to him?" she asks me, her own curiosity showing.

"Maybe about you?" I give her a flirtatious response that's only a half lie, rather than telling her about Marcus.

"Oh… and what about me?" she asks although the flirtation isn't quite there.

"I wouldn't tell you, you like to gossip too much," I tease her, giving her a kiss on the crook of her neck. She rewards me by wrapping her arms around my shoulders, and planting one of her own on my neck.

The knowledge of what I'm going to do tonight keeps me from pushing for more. It keeps me from wanting more, it keeps me from lifting her ass up and pinning her against the wall.

"Are you okay?" I ask her, holding her close and not letting her go just yet.

"Me?" she questions and I nod against her, feeling her hair tickling along my stubble as I reply, "Yes, you."

"I feel better in a way," she confides in me and stands upright so I let her go. "It feels good to say it all out loud and still be able to stand afterward."

Staring into her gaze I admit to her, "You don't strike me as a girl who would ever not land on her feet, cailín tine."

"You know, I forgot to tell Laura that," she murmurs and sways slightly. Enough that she feels the need to take a step back and steady herself.

"How much did you drink?"

She shrugs and then says, "The normal amount when we go drunk shopping."

"No bags though?"

"Oh, well there's this thing where I owe this guy some money so I'm on a tight budget at the moment," she jokes with me and her smile is infectious. "Really, I just wasn't interested tonight in shopping."

"Only gossiping?"

"Yeah," she answers and then says again, "I can't believe I forgot to tell her."

Walking her to the bedroom, I ask her what she forgot to tell Laura.

"The nickname." Her answer stops me just outside the door although she continues, "I think she'd understand better, if she knew."

CHAPTER
14

Bethany

I T'S DIFFERENT HERE. MAYBE BECAUSE IT'S HIS ROOM. HIS HOUSE. HIS place.

He's different here. He's more transparent. Less hidden with his emotions. Other than anger and dominance... and lust, he hasn't shown me more than that beyond these walls.

Or maybe it's just tonight. Maybe it's just the wine talking or the relief that I finally told Laura what's going on.

I don't know, but when I look at Jase, he's different.

And he's not okay. Pain riddles every move he makes. Not the physical kind, the kind that wears away at your mind.

His head hangs lower as he asks me what we did. As if he doesn't already know. His voice is duller, his grip less tight on my waist as he pulls me into the bedroom.

With every step my heart beats slower, wanting to take the agony away from his. The answers I give him are spoken without thinking. I'm more concerned with watching him than I am with making small talk.

With his back to me, he pulls the covers back and tells me to strip and get into bed, which I do.

My mind starts toying with me. Insecurity whispers in my ear, *"Maybe it's you."*

"Are you okay?" I ask him, letting a tinge of my insecurity show.

"Fine," he answers shortly, but he gets into bed with me.

"You're still dressed," I comment, listening to my heart which is quiet. I think it's waiting for him to say something too. For him to tell us what's wrong.

"I know," is all he gives me as an answer and the high I was on, all that relief I felt, vanishes.

I feel sick. Not hungover or drank too much sick, but the sickness that comes when you know something's wrong. The awful kind where you can guess what it is, but you don't want to just in case it'll go away if you never voice it.

I know what I need, but I don't ask him for it. Instead I pull the covers up close around my chin and lie there. My pride is a horrid thing.

I'm aware of that.

If I could simply let it go, I could communicate better. I know that. I've known it all my life. But still, I don't ask him to hold me.

I don't have to though. I don't have to tell him what I need to feel better.

The bed groans as he moves closer to me, wrapping a strong arm around my waist and pulling me closer to him. It's a natural reaction for me to close my eyes and let out an easy breath when I take in his masculine scent. It engulfs me just as his warmth does, just as his touch does.

"You promise we're okay?" I ask him and then my eyes open wide, realizing the mistake I made. The Freudian slip.

Kissing the crook of my neck, he murmurs a yes.

He gives so much and I feel so undeserving. The ringing on my skin comes back, the bell of what happened earlier reminding me that it's okay. That it's better than okay.

My hand lays over his and he twines his fingers with mine before planting a kiss on my cheek.

Before he can pull away, I kiss him again. Putting everything I have into it, trying to give him what I can in what's a very unbalanced relationship.

That's what this is. A relationship. Fuck me, when did it happen?

The second I pause, pressing my forehead to his and pulling my lips away, he does what I just did to him, kissing me and giving me more.

With a warmth flowing through my chest, I settle into his embrace.

"I want to ask you something." His whispered question tickles my neck and makes a trail of goosebumps travel down my shoulder.

"Yeah?"

"How are you feeling about your sister? Are you okay? You didn't mention her to Laura. Or how you were handling it. And the last few days you seem…"

"Seem what?"

"A little more than sad today before you went out and yesterday," he answers honestly, and I want to pull my hand from his, but he doesn't let me. He holds me tighter and closer as my composure cracks.

"Tell me, cailín tine," he whispers at the back of my neck, running the tip of his nose along my skin. I love it when he does that. I love the soft, slow touches. I love how he takes his time with me.

It takes me a long moment to answer him. "I feel like I've slowed down, which makes sense because I'm not working anymore. I am crying when I hate it and I can't stop myself, but that damn book is sad too, so it could be the book's fault right? I don't know."

"You can't hide behind a sad book," is all he says and then he looks at me like he wants more.

Staring at the still curtains and listening to the heater turn on with a click, I let it all out; I don't think, I just speak. "Everything is moving so fast. That's what it feels like. Like the world didn't just refuse to slow down with me while I mourn but it sped up too."

Kind eyes look down on me when I peek over my shoulder to see his response. He's propped up on his elbow, his hard, warm chest still pressed against my back. I roll over to face him and look him in the eyes as I say, "It became chaotic and unpredictable and I'm a person who likes consistency and schedules and predictability and it's all gone. In one second everything changed, and now I can't be anything but slow and everything is going so fast." He's silent, so I continue.

"Except when I'm with you. Everything slows down then. It stops and waits for me when you show up."

I don't expect to say the words I've been thinking out loud. I say them all to my folded hands in my lap rather than to Jase. I need to see what he thinks though. If he understands or if I'm just crazy.

He leans down to give me a small kiss. It's quick and gentle. I want more but I don't take it. Even when the tip of his nose nudges mine, I don't do anything but wait for him to say something.

"That's a good thing, right?"

"Yeah… but I think the world is going so fast because of you too. Because of lots of things. And here I am stuck with a rope around my feet."

"I could see that," he comments, brushing the stray hairs away from my face and his touch brings back that tingling full force.

"You make it easy to talk," I murmur.

He doesn't say anything at all, he merely touches his fingers to my lips and gives me a small smile.

"I do that with my patients. I put on a smile all day long and they trust me, they open up to me. Jase, don't treat me like a patient."

"Well, first off all, you're not a patient. Second, you better not touch your patients like I touch you."

"You're awful," I tell him halfheartedly, but still feeling a hollowness in my chest that I can't place.

"I smile at you because sometimes you smile back, and that's all I want. I want to see you smile."

Breathe in, I remind myself. *Breathe out*. I have to, or else I think I'd forget in this moment. It's not often you can feel yourself falling, but I'd be damned if I didn't feel like that right now. Even knowing who he is and what he does.

"Why are you so sweet and charming… yet the very opposite too?"

He shakes his head gently, not taking it like I thought he would. Then he answers with another question of his own. "Why are you so strong and confident, yet… feeling like this?"

I don't have an answer. The old me would though. The me from only two months ago before Jenny went missing, would know why. I work in a psych center, for fuck's sake. I would have known. I could have answered. Being in it though… I've lost my voice. I have nothing to say, because I don't want this reality to be justified.

"Because that's life, cailín tine. We aren't just one thing. Life isn't one story. It's a mix of many and they cross paths sometimes."

I swallow thickly, understanding what he's saying and hating it. Some parts of life are simply awful. When I close my eyes and focus on one more deep breath, Jase's strong hand cups my chin and my eyes lift to his.

I nearly apologize for being the way I am. But it's not some stranger I've lost it in front of. Or my boss. Or my fucking family from New York. It's Jase.

I expect him to say something, but he only pulls me closer to him, letting time pass and the wretched feelings that have welled up, slowly go away.

Mourning is like the tide of the ocean. It comes and it goes. It's gentle and it's harsh.

Slowly, the tide always subsides. But it always comes back too. It never goes away for long.

"The world stops when you see me, huh?" he questions softly after a moment, teasing me and letting the sad bits wash away like they're meant to. I love the teasing tone he takes. I love this side of him. I love many sides of him.

"I didn't say that," I'm quick to protest.

"You practically did," he teases, although the smile on his handsome face tugs down slightly as his eyes search mine.

"I don't love you," I murmur the words, feeling the hot tension thicken between the two of us. He leans closer to me, nearly brushing his lips against mine. All the while, I keep my eyes open, waiting for what he has to say.

"I don't love you too," he says and I can practically feel the last bit of armor fall as I lean into his lips. His hand brushes my shoulder, my collarbone and then lower, barely touching me and feeling like fire as he caresses my skin.

The covers swish around us as I lean back, giving him more room and urging him closer. I've never wanted a man like I want him. I've never memorized the rough groan a man gives as he kisses me like Jase does, with reverence and hunger.

I let him take me as he wants. What he wants is exactly what I want.

Time doesn't pause for us though. It doesn't go by slowly either.

It's all over far too soon. Maybe because I never want this one moment to end.

"I have to go," he tells me after glancing at the clock on his night-stand. He makes no effort to move though, other than to run his thumb along my bottom lip.

"Okay," I whisper, not wanting to chance that he'll stop touching me. All I want is for him to keep touching me and for my world to stay still and in pace with me, not wanting to take the next step forward.

"Don't follow me, Bethany," he warns, his voice sterner, but the lust still there.

"Okay," I repeat and my eyes finally close as he leans down, press-ing his lips against mine once again. He tries to move away before I'm ready for him to go, but I reach up, pulling him back to me with my hands on the back of his neck. I hold him there, deepening the kiss and listening to his groan of satisfaction as I do. Kissing this man changes ev-erything. I can't think about anything other than wanting him with me. I'm highly aware of it and I know it's dangerous, but still... I want it.

It's wild and dangerous, and I love it just as much as I love the fire.

When he finally leaves me, I hold on to the warmth he left in the covers, and I bury my head in the pillow he slept on, rather than the one he gave me. I stare at the clock, watching the hands move slowly. Trying to keep it moving slowly with me.

I don't follow him. Not because of a debt or an agreement. But be-cause he asked me not to. Because it means something to him.

I would have stayed like that longer than I'd care to admit, really I would have, but that's when my phone chimed with a message from Laura.

CHAPTER
15

Jase

I KNOW HE'S HERE BUT HE HASN'T SHOWN HIMSELF YET. I SAY ALOUD TO NO one, "When I was a kid, I hated the dark."

The playground is quiet tonight. With its broken swing that creaks as a gust of wind blows, and the full moon's faint blue light that shines down and covers every inch of the fallen snow, it's the perfect setting for Marcus. The kind of setting that's eerily familiar. The place where you don't go and you walk as quick as you can to get far away.

The backyard playground of the abandoned school is where no one goes unless they're up to no good. Like I am tonight.

"Most kids do," a voice answers from somewhere to my right, under the old, ten-foot rusty slide. I can just barely make out the brown broken bits through the veil of snow.

"I figured you'd be there. In the dark, just watching." I make my way to where he is, but stop short. I stay by the swing set, close enough to hear, but not bothering to look at him.

I'll play by his rules. He has what I want, Jenny Parks. We both know that I know.

I can hear the faint laugh carry in the night, but he makes no other comment and instead there's nothing but the bitter cold between us.

"What about now?" he asks me and I resist the urge to turn my head to face where he is. Instead I stare at the graffiti on the back of the brick building.

"What about now?" I question.

"Are you still afraid of the dark?"

His question makes me smirk. "I never said afraid... I said I hated it."

"You didn't have to say you were afraid, Jase. Every child is afraid of the dark."

A moment passes and I stalk forward to lean against the metal bar of the jungle gym.

"You wanted something?" I ask him, knowing that my back is to him and knowing he could sneak up on me if he wanted. I'll risk it.

"You wanted something," he answers me as if it's a correction. His voice a bit louder this time, followed by the sound of footsteps. "Don't turn around just yet."

"Understood," I respond quickly, knowing in my gut I'm walking away from this. He wants me to know something. And I want to know what it is.

I can hear him stop just a few feet behind me and I stay where I am although the need to turn rings in my blood. I've never crossed Marcus and from what I know, he's never crossed me. But he isn't on our side either, and that makes me question where his intentions lie.

"You're looking for information and I came with... a gift."

My pulse quickens as I hear more movement behind me. Gripping the bar tighter until my knuckles have turned white, I ignore every need to turn, making my muscles tense.

"A gift?" I press him for more information.

"Yes," is all he gives me.

"Is it Jenny Parks?" I dare to ask, giving up information, but in the hopes of cooperation.

"Jenny is fine."

A beat passes and the muscles in my arms coil, my grip too tight, the adrenaline in my blood racing to get somewhere, or to do something. To simply react.

It's a puzzle with Marcus, attempting to ask the right questions, because he has all the answers.

"What are you doing with her?"

"I'm helping her." His voice is faint this time, as if he's farther away now. The crunch of the snow beneath his feet makes me realize he's pacing. Maybe considering telling me something.

"You know I want answers… I want her sister to have a life with her. She wants her back." There's only the soft call of a midnight wind that whistles in the lack of his answer. "What do you want me to know?" I ask him, acknowledging to both of us that's all he'll tell me anyway.

"Did you have a nice conversation with Mr. Stevens?"

An exhale of frustration slips through my lips at the change in subject. I answer him, "It went well."

"What did he tell you?" he asks.

"He said you were building an army," I say and raise my voice to make sure he can hear me. He does the same and takes steps to come closer, but still stops far enough behind me that I can't see his shadow yet against the pure white snow.

"Building one?" The tone of his voice lingers in the air, and his answer leaves a chill to run down my spine. "Did you think I did all of this on my own? There's always someone looking for salvation, for redemption, for something to believe in."

"You're their savior?"

"I'm no savior and the things they do… it's no redemption."

"So you're using them?" I ask him and rein in the simmering anger as Jenny's face from the pictures in Bethany's house flickers in front of me. Back when things were different.

"I'm giving them what they want," he answers.

"And then?" I ask him. "What are you going to do with Jenny when she's done doing your bidding and you have no use for her?"

Silence.

My head falls forward, heavy as I struggle with the need to force an answer from the man I used to fear. I focus on staying still. On not facing him so I can gather more information. I need an answer. I need to know where Jenny is. I have to know if she'll ever come home.

"Did you know wolves used to live here? Back in the day, so to speak."

My eyes open slowly and I stare straight ahead as my shoulders tighten. "You love your stories. Don't you?" My voice is menacing, not hiding my disappointment and outrage.

"Oh I could tell you a story, but the truth will hurt the most."

My teeth grind together, my patience wearing thinner and thinner as all the pictures I've seen of Jenny from when she was a girl hugging her sister, to only a few years ago when she was in school, play in my mind.

"They'd run in packs and terrorize the people." He paces again, I can hear him doing it and a part of me wants to turn around; I want to look him in the eyes and see the man who plays with fire like he has. The only reason I don't is because he has the upper hand. He has Jenny. He has the answers.

"They attacked people, but farms mostly, leaving the families little food for themselves..." He pauses and lets out a soft sound, nearly a chuckle although I'm not certain it's humorous; it sounds sickening.

"They ruled and there was not much to be done. Much like you and your brothers," he says and the S hisses in the air. "They don't run wild here anymore though, because hunters found a way. Well, there were two ways." I remain silent, biding my time, struggling to stay patient with him.

"The first, I'm not a fan of," he says and steps closer to me, but still I don't react. "They'd find the female mates and put them in cages for the males to see. When the males would inevitably come to find their mates, they'd try to release them, to no avail. And then they'd wait there for the men to come, with their tails tucked under them, begging in whimpers for their mates to be freed." Every hair stands on end as he tells his tale. All I can think about is Bethany. "I've been told you didn't even need a gun to kill them when they did this. When they came to get their mates, they were so willing to do anything and accept anything in order to free their mates, you could turn your gun around and beat them to death with the end of a rifle."

My skin pricks with the imagery that floods my mind. The fog of my breath in front of my face paints the picture of a wolf, bloodied and dead and next to it a caged mate, with bullet wounds ending her life.

"Are you implying something, Marcus?" I dare to ask him, feeling the anger rising. "If you're threatening-"

"Bethany is safe," he answers before I can finish and the simple confirmation is more relief than I thought imaginable, given my current position.

"The other way though... I... I find it more fitting," Marcus says, and continues his story. "The farmers would dip a knife into bloodied water. Wolves love the taste of blood. They knew that, so they'd tempt them. They'd dip it and freeze it over and over. Practically making a popsicle, made just for wolves."

The swing blows and creaks again as he tells me, "They'd leave the knife for the wolves, and the wild animals would lick and lick, enjoying their treat and numbing their own tongues with the ice. They'd continuing licking, even after they'd sliced their own tongues. After all, they love the taste of blood and they couldn't feel it."

"The wolves would bleed out?" I surmise.

"They would. They would lick the knives even after the ice was long melted, and bleed themselves to death."

"Now, if only I'd heard that at bedtime, maybe I would have had better dreams," I lay the flat joke out for him, downplaying the threatening tone he chooses, and keeping my voice casual.

"Humor is your preference, isn't it?"

I don't bother answering.

"What's the point to your story, Marcus?" I ask him bluntly.

"I brought you a gift," he answers. "I brought you a bloody knife."

My jaw clenches as I wait for more from him.

"Trust me, you're going to want this one, Jase. I think you've been waiting for it for a long, long time."

"What is my bloody knife?" I ask him, gritting my teeth and praying it's not the body of Jenny Parks. That's all I can think right now. *Please, don't let it be her.*

"Inside the trunk of the lone car across the street is your package. I sent you a video, you should watch. He's had a high dose of your sweets. I'd think it'll wear off by tomorrow... Good luck, Jase."

CHAPTER
16

Bethany

"T HIS IS COMPLETELY AND TOTALLY SHADY," I MUTTER UNDER MY breath and then look over my shoulder to make sure no one saw me walk into the alley behind the drugstore. It's nearly 3:00 a.m. so the store is closed, as is everything else around here. "Could you freak me out any more?"

Meet me behind Calla Pharmacy. I have something for you.

That's the text Laura sent. And the messages afterward were a series of me asking why the fuck we were meeting there and her not answering my question, but insisting that I come.

"You have no idea the shit I was imagining on the way down here," I scold her although it's only concern that binds to the statement. The buzz from earlier has worn off completely, as if the current situation isn't sobering enough.

"Sorry." Laura's hushed voice is barely heard as she grips my arm and pulls me farther down the alley to where she parked her car.

"We can do shady shit at my house," I say, biting out the words.

"What if it's bugged or something?"

All I can hear is the wind as her words sink in.

Concern is etched in her expression as she looks back at me and then nearly opens her trunk, but she stops too soon and places both of her palms on the slick metal.

The streetlight from nearby barely illuminates us.

"It's dark and cold and you're freaking me out," I finally speak and ignore the way it hurts just to breathe in air this cold. I lift my scarf up to cover my nose before shoving my hands in my pockets and asking, "What the hell are we doing here?"

Every second it seems scarier back here. It's a vacant small lot, no longer asphalt as the grass has grown through patches of it. It's all cracked and ruined. Even though it's abandoned, there are still ambient noises. The small sounds are what spike my unease.

Like the cat that jumped onto the dumpster and the cars that speed by every so often out front. I should have told Jase. I should have messaged him, but I didn't.

"Why did we have to come down here? And why couldn't I tell Jase?"

"We just had to, okay." Laura's fear is barely concealed by irritation. "And he doesn't need to know about this. I did something," she quickly adds before I can get in another word. Her soft blue eyes are wide with worry and she looks like she can barely breathe. Her gaze turns back to the trunk and chills run down my arms.

"There better not be a body in there," I tell her more to lighten the mood, but also out of the sheer fear that she fucking killed someone. At this point, I don't know what to predict next.

"Jesus," she hisses. "I didn't kill anyone." She searches behind me and then over her shoulders like someone might be watching. "I'm not one of the crazies in your nut hut."

There's a small voice in the back of my mind telling me that Seth is somewhere. Seth is watching and Jase will know everything she says and does right now. But only if Jase knew I left, only if Seth is watching me nonstop. The thought is comforting for a split second, and then I regret not telling Jase.

"You promise you didn't say anything?" she asks and I nod.

I remind myself, this is Laura, Laura the friend I met in college, the girl who I ran to when I got dumped and needed to consume my weight in ice cream and fall asleep in front of romcoms. My Laura. My best, and really, my only friend.

There isn't a damn thing she could do that would be problematic.

292 | WINTERS

With that thought lingering, I get to the bottom of it. "Why are we here?"

"Look… first…" It's a heavy sigh that leaves her when she stares at me. The look she's giving me is begging for forgiveness and acceptance.

"You're freaking me out," I admit and grip her hands in mine. They're cold, just like the air, like my lungs, like everything back here on the cold winter night. "Just tell me; I won't be mad."

Laura's never done anything like this and I don't know what to expect. I always know what she's going to do and say. She's the voice of reason more times than not. But this… "I have no idea what you did, but it's okay. Whatever you have to tell me or show me, it's okay." I hope my words comfort her like they do me. Even if they are only words.

"You have to accept it," she tells me and her voice is sharp. The worry is gone in her cadence, replaced by strength.

"Accept what?" The question I ask goes unanswered. Instead a breeze blows, forcing Laura's blonde hair to blow in front of her face although she makes no move to stop it. Bits of soft snow fall between us and all she does is stare at me and then make me promise.

"Promise you'll take it. Promise you'll never mention it again." She inhales too quickly and finally moves, shifting on her feet to look behind me before adding, "Promise it leaves with you and you forget where you got it."

My stomach coils and I nearly back away from her, but she grips my hand instead. "What the fuck is it, Laura?"

"Promise," she demands.

"Whatever it is, I promise." The pit in my stomach grows heavier as the trunk creaks open, darkness flooding it and hiding what's inside at first glance.

It's only when she pulls it out and shoves it into my chest that I see it's a black duffle bag.

The trunk shuts and the thud of it closing is all I can hear as I hold the bag. It can't be more than fifteen pounds, but until the hood is shut I have to hold it with both hands and then rest it against the flat back of the car.

"Don't open it. Just take it."

I look Laura dead in the eyes as I answer her, "You've lost your fucking mind if you think I'm not looking at what's in here."

"Don't. In case someone's watching."

"What is it, Laura?" I ask her again, my voice even but somehow sounding eerie in the bitter air.

"Your way out of the debt," is all she tells me until I grip her wrist, forcing her to look at me instead of walking back to her driver's seat like she intended.

She glances at my hand on her wrist, and then back up to me before turning to face me toe to toe.

I don't expect the words she says next. The casualness of her statement, yet how matter of fact it is.

"If you want to be with him, this is the world you live in. There's a risk of people going after you. If you don't... I think you're still in that world, regardless. It has a way of not letting go."

A silent shrill scream rings in my ears from the need to run, the need to do something. It comes from anxiety, from the need to fight or flee. I choose fight. I was born to fight.

She finishes, "But at least this gets rid of the debt."

It takes a second and then another for me to comprehend what she's saying.

"The debt? I owe him-"

"Three hundred grand." She nods as she speaks. "And now you have it to pay off."

"No fucking way." I'm adamant as I shove the duffle bag into her chest but she doesn't take it, she doesn't reach out for it and the bag falls to the icy cracked ground. "Where did you get it?" I hiss the question, with a wild fear brewing inside of me. "Take it back," I beg her before she even answers.

Her baby blue eyes search mine for a moment and I'm left with disbelief and confusion.

I tell her with a furious terror taking over, "You don't have that kind of money."

"I didn't and then I did," she answers simply.

Emotions well in my throat. "Take it back, Laura. However you got it, give it back."

"No," she says first and then adds, "I can't anyway."

"No, Laura, fuck! No." I have to cover my face as it heats. "Please tell me-"

"I'm more than fine," she cuts me off. "I wanted to do something for a long time. An offer I had and wasn't sure if I wanted to take or not."

It's only the ease of her confession that settles me slightly.

"You can always go back."

"No," she answers me, "I can't and I don't want to. I'm not taking the bag back either and I have to go, I have the night shift and you promised me. You promised you'd take the bag."

"What did you do?"

"I can't tell you," she murmurs. There's no fear or desperation when she speaks to me and my head spins with the denial that this is even happening.

"You can, you can tell me anything." I feel crazed as I reach out to her, stepping forward as she steps back and kicking the bag at my feet.

"I can't tell you," she says, stressing every word and pulling herself away from my grasp. "That bag is yours. And I have to go."

She leaves me there with the duffle bag at my feet, the snow clinging to my hair and the cold of the night settling in to wrap its arms around me, the same way I wrap my hand around the strap to the duffle bag.

CHAPTER
17

Jase
Years ago…

I KNEW SOMETHING WAS OFF BEFORE I EVEN OPENED THE DOOR. I SPENT the hour before coming here arguing with Carter about even bringing Angie here.

I didn't trust her at The Red Room though. Not with the shit I have going on and the people that come and go. I tried to help her before and she took off, coming back worse. And the last three nights she destroyed the place, searching for anything to numb the pain she was in. She was fucking skin and bones. Her cheeks were so hollow. Addiction will do a lot of things to a person. It turns their curious smirks into glowers of pain, their bright eyes into dull gazes to nowhere.

It wasn't just the addiction though. She couldn't be sober because then she remembered what she'd done.

Fuck, the memory of it makes me sick.

"She's not with me, but that doesn't mean I can't help her."

"You can't help everyone, Jase." Carter's hardened voice is clear in my mind. He looked me in the eyes and told me, "You can't help her. You can't and shouldn't. You shouldn't have brought her here."

"I don't want to help everyone." I bit back the answer, feeling the anger rise inside of me. It was the first disagreement we'd ever had. I had to do it, though. "I want to help her. Just one person."

"Why? She's not yours."

He didn't get it. For the first time, he showed his confusion. He didn't understand that I didn't want her, I just wanted her to be okay. Even if she was nearly a stranger, even if I'd never want her to walk through the doors of the bar again once she left.

I needed to feel like I could make it right. We all make mistakes, but it's okay if you can make it right. I just needed to make it right.

"You shouldn't have brought her here." That was the last thing he said to me as I made my way back to the guest bedroom, questioning everything I'd done. I'd like to think that was why I thought things were off when I got to the door. But it was something deeper than that.

With my hand on the doorknob, I remember how I told her to just sleep before I left. Get some fucking sleep to help her with the withdrawal. Her eyes were so sunken in and dark as she screamed at me. It could have been the cocaine or the heroin. She looked nothing like the woman I'd known before.

I had to empty the room out to keep her from throwing things. She liked comic books, so I went out to get her some. It would only be weeks. Only weeks of helping her get back on her feet, then she was someone else's problem. Then she'd be able to think clearly and choose whatever she wanted to do next. But as it stood, the addiction made every choice and it was leading her to an early grave.

I remember the way my scar shined on my hand, the light brighter there than on the metal knob as I pushed the door open.

It was quiet, too quiet for her not to be sleeping in the empty bed.

The bathroom door was closed and I glanced at the clock. 3:04 a.m. Someone once told me the Devil gets a minute every day. 3:07 to come and do his darkest deeds. I stared at the clock, knowing the Devil's deeds were done all day long, whether he was here or not.

Every second I sat on the chair in the room, I thought about what to tell her. I didn't know her well enough to know what to say. All I could think of telling her was that it would be better tomorrow. That she just had to take it day by day. It takes weeks to get through the worst of it, sometimes longer.

She didn't listen the first time, or the second, but maybe she'd listen now. Maybe tomorrow. Back then, I had hope.

The next time I looked at my watch, nearly forty minutes had passed. It was then that I realized it was still too quiet. Far too quiet.

I knocked at the door, but she didn't respond. "Angie?" I called her name, and still nothing.

I knocked harder, feeling that gut instinct that something was wrong. I remember the way her name felt as I screamed it and hammered my fist against the door, all the while, it was far too quiet.

Testing the knob, it wasn't locked, so I pushed it open. I knew then though, the Devil had come and gone. And that I was too late.

She'd shut the shower curtain, but even through it I could see the slash of red on the tiled wall. I'll never forget that first sound I heard that night when I went to check on her. It was the sound of the shower curtain opening.

The blood was all over her hands and arms. The first thought I had, was that she must've regretted it and tried to stop the blood from the cut at her throat.

She tried to take it back.

I didn't cry for her in that moment, but I leaned back against the wall, taking in her red hair and how it matted to her bloodied skin. Her eyes were still open, so once I could move, I closed them for her, even though my hand shook.

I failed her. I did this to her. It was all I could think.

Falling to my knees next to the tub, I prayed for the first time since my mama died. I asked God to take over for me. To help her and forgive her and forgive her sins.

I didn't ask him to forgive mine though. I'd be more careful about mine, but I knew I'd keep doing it.

I couldn't take back the years of what we'd already done. I couldn't take any of it back.

Carter was right, I never should have brought her there.

"I remember the first time I met Angie. I thought she was a sweet girl although a little too loud when she was drunk. She was older than me, and didn't want a damn thing to do with me other than to score drugs for a party. Which was fine, because the feeling was mutual." I talk easily, like I'm only telling a story.

"Coke or pot for the weekend. Whatever the flavor of the week was, she wanted it. It was easy to sell it to her. With her long red hair and wild green eyes, she wasn't my type, but I couldn't deny she was kind and polite. She used to stand on her tiptoes to turn around after getting her stash, doing a little curtsy of thanks that would at least get a chuckle from me.

"You remember Angie, Seth?" I speak clear enough that both Seth and Hal can hear me. The basement room today feels hotter than ever. More suffocating than it's ever been before.

"Of course." Seth answers calmly as I roll up the sleeves to my shirt. I'm careful and meticulous, but even so, I know I'm on edge. I'm on the verge of losing it and I haven't even touched the surface yet. He adds, "One of our first regulars," when I don't respond.

I made the mistake of watching the video Marcus sent me the second I got out of the park. I brought Hal here and waited. I didn't sleep, I didn't go home. I just waited until Seth said Hal was alert enough to go through with this.

Like always, he's standing behind Mr. Hal, who's in the interrogation chair. Although there's no interrogation today.

There are no questions for him. No need for a shirt to smother his screams. I want to hear them. I want the memories of tonight to somehow mask the memories I have of Angie's last day.

"You remember her?" I question Hal, feeling that crease deepen in the center of my forehead as I pick up the hammer. It's an ordinary hammer.

The tool of choice is fitting. Angie's dad worked as a carpenter. When he died, she went off the rails, that's what she told me once when she was struggling with her sobriety. It was easier than dealing with reality and the party drugs she bought for weekends became necessary every day. And then a few times every day. And then harder drugs. Just so she didn't have to think about her dead father.

So it made sense to me to choose a hammer.

"I don't know who you're talking about," the man answers. Confidently, stubbornly, like somehow he's got the upper hand here. Maybe he thinks I actually have questions, but I don't. All I have for him is a story.

I watch the light shine off the flat iron head of the hammer as I walk closer to him. There are no cuts on his wrists from trying to escape, nothing that shows any fear. And that's fine by me. I don't want him scared, I want him in pain. In fucking agony the way Angie was.

In the same agony Bethany's stuck in. The thought strikes me hard, and I hate it. I want it to go away. More than anything, I want her pain to stop.

My arm whips in front of me, the metal crashing against the man's jaw and morphing his scream into a cry of agony in a single blow.

The left side of his jaw hangs a little lower and the man fights against his restraints as he screams from the impact.

Glancing at the splatter of blood across my dress shirt, a huff of a breath leaves me, trying to calm the rage, trying to calm the need to not stop.

But Bethany's pain never stops. It never fucking ends.

"Marcus showed me a video. Only one. You knew her," I say and shrug, like it's not a big deal. Like he wasn't forcing himself down her throat while she was high and crying on a dirty floor.

"You knew her better than me," I comment. Thinking back to who she was before it all went downhill and trying to get the loathsome video out of my mind. If I could bleach it away, I would.

"She came in a lot, but only to get what she needed," Seth speaks from behind the fucker. He's reading me, his eyes never leaving me as I pace in front of the chair, waiting for Hal to stop his bitching and moaning.

"I want him to hear this," I tell Seth, raising my voice just enough for him to know not to console me like he's trying to do. I don't need that shit. I don't need to be told I couldn't have helped her or I couldn't have stopped it. I could have. I know I could have if I wasn't so fucking high on power and young and stupid. It's more controlled now. But back then, there was no protocol, and we sold to anyone and as much as they wanted.

"She was young, I had the drugs, I couldn't tell her no at first. She was the first person I told no. The first one where I realized I ruined her life." I'm staring at this asshole, and he's not looking at me. He's whimpering, looking down at his bare feet that are planted on the steel grid beneath him. He's not paying attention, so I swing the hammer again. Down onto his right foot. Crack! And then the left. The clang of the metal and the crack of small bones ricochets in the room. The black and blue on his skin is instant.

He screams and cries, but all it does is make me angry. He didn't care that Angie cried. He didn't care about what he did to her. He can mourn for his own pain all he wants, but it's not enough.

I have to walk away, seeing Bethany's face and knowing she wouldn't approve of this. What alternative is there though? To let this world turn with no consequence?

It's the fact that we feel pain when others feel nothing. This man feels nothing. The regret is hard enough and the guilt too, but walking around in a world where it isn't acknowledged, where those feelings travel alone… it's a hell that hides in every corner.

Hal cusses at me, spitting at my feet and sneering an expression of hate. He can't hold it long though. I slowly draw the sharp edge of the hammer across his throat as I speak.

"It was my fault, Hal. My fault that she got hooked and when she did, I sent her away. We'd only just begun in this game. We were bound to make mistakes. And Angie Davis was one of them."

Fuck, the guilt comes back full force just saying her name.

"I told her no, only a few months after I met her. I gave her the sweets, I told her to get better and then she could come back. Instead, she found you."

If she hadn't come to me, if Angie had gone to Bethany instead… My fiery woman, she would have known what to do. "Angie wanted help, she really did." I equate her to Jenny in this moment. Wondering if it really would have been different. If she really wanted help and if Bethany could have fixed her. I wish I could go back.

I can smash this hammer into his head, but I can't take her pain away. There's not a damn thing I can do to take Bethany's pain away

I think the words Hal's trying to say are, "Please, don't," as he spits up blood. It only reminds me of the way Angie said it in the video I saw hours ago. *Please, don't.*

"It's fine to party and have a good time, but she was slipping. She wasn't herself. Addiction grabbed hold of her and wasn't letting go. Anyone and everyone could see it."

"Yeah, I remember," Seth comments, nodding his head even as looks at me like he has nothing but sympathy for me. Fuck that. I don't need sympathy. I don't deserve sympathy.

"I remember. She was clinging to you crying, begging you for more." Seth still hasn't accepted what I have. Every word he says sounds like an excuse. "You sent her away with a way to help her."

Fuck, I should have known better. I wasn't in it like Carter was. I'd only just started and I didn't realize the ripple effect and the tidal wave it was capable of creating.

"I was young and I was stupid. I gave her whatever she wanted and however much she said she needed. Even when I knew it was getting bad. It took a long time before I sent her away…"

"Jase," Seth's tone is warning, cautioning me in where my mind is going, but I cut him off.

"No." My response echoes in the room even though it's pushed through gritted teeth while I tap the hammer in my hand, blood and all, as I add, "I take that blame. It's my fault. All of it."

Lifting the hammer up, I point it at Hal. "But you," I start to speak. I can't get the rest out though. I can't voice where this story inevitably turns.

Instead I crash the hammer onto his knees. Bashing them relentlessly. Then his thighs. His arms. Every bone I can break.

Screams and hot blood surround me. The man's cries get louder and louder. Does he cry in front of me at the memory? Or at the realization that there's no way he's getting out of this room alive?

It's what I've wanted for so long, some kind of justice for Angie, but I thought it would feel different. I thought it would feel better than this.

Instead the pain seeps into my blood, where it runs rampant in my body. The memories refuse to stop.

With a deep inhale I back away, letting the screams dull as I think about how sunken in her face was when she came to me after a month of being gone. I didn't know. I didn't take responsibility for what I'd done, and I let her walk out, thinking she'd be fine.

Because that was the story I wanted to hear.

"She told me things you had her do, but you didn't have a name then. How you took advantage of her. You had others come in while she was tied down on the table. She told me how she didn't even care when you tossed the heroin at her. That she remembers how badly she needed the hit. Even as you and the other men laughed at her and what you'd done."

Seth isn't expecting the next blow I give to the guy, straight across his jaw. He lets out a shout of surprise as the blood sprays from the gushing wound, down Seth's jeans and onto his shoes.

The once clean, bright white sneakers with a red streak are now doused in blood.

He takes a step back, getting out of my way and keeping his hands up in the air. He's acting like I'm the one who's gone crazy. But how could I be sane if the very thought of what happened didn't turn me mad?

"Seth, she ever tell you the things she did when we sent her away?" I ask him. Feeling a pain rip my insides open.

He shakes his head. His dark eyes are shining with unwanted remorse.

"She said she did shit she was so ashamed of, she couldn't tell me. She said she didn't deserve to live."

I smash the hammer down onto Hal's shoulder. But he doesn't scream this time and that only makes me hit him harder. Still, he's silent. His head's fallen to one side and I don't care. Maybe his ghost will hear me.

"All the money and all the power in the world, and I couldn't save her," I scream at the man. "You know why?" I keep talking to him. To the dead man. Feeling my sanity slip. "Why I couldn't save her?" I ask him, knowing Seth's eyes are on me, hearing his attempts to calm me down but ignoring him.

"Because she couldn't live with the things she'd done when she wasn't sober. She remembered it all. And she couldn't deal with it."

There is never true justice in tragedy.

You have to live with yourself after what's done is done.

"Angie couldn't do it," I tell him. "She couldn't live with the memories and she couldn't forgive herself."

I locked her in a room to help her get over the withdrawal. I gave her the pills and I gave her a safe place.

She killed herself.

"She had a sister. She had a mother who needed her. I couldn't even get out of the car at the funeral because of how they were crying."

It's the endings that don't have an honest goodbye that hurt the most. They linger forever because the words were never spoken.

I don't know who I'm talking to at this point. Seth or a man who didn't feel remorse for what he'd done, only for himself. I should have made him suffer longer. I should have controlled myself.

I hate that I ever sold her anything. I hate that the beautiful red-head at the bar would never smile again. All because of a dime bag of powder that took her far away from the world she wanted to leave. All because I sold it to her.

Every blow, I would take too. I deserve it.

Bethany should do to me what I've just done to this man. I led Jenny down that path. We sold her drugs, we bribed her with them for information. Even if it wasn't her first or her last, I know we sold her something and then let her walk away.

The thought only makes me slam the iron of the hammer down harder and more recklessly. Crashing into his face, his shoulders and arms. Every part of him. Over and over again, feeling all the anger, the pain, the sadness run through me, urging me to do it again and again.

When my body gives out and I fall to the floor on my knees, heaving in air, I finally stop. Letting my head fall back, and closing my eyes.

I could never tell Bethany. She deserves to hate me. I don't deserve her love, let alone her forgiveness. Not any of it.

CHAPTER
18

Bethany

T HE VERY IDEA OF LEAVING THREE HUNDRED THOUSAND DOLLARS IN the back of a car makes me want to throw up. People kill for this kind of money.

I can hardly even believe I actually have that amount. I didn't count it and I don't intend to. I don't want to touch it. All I did was unzip the bag once and then close my eyes again, pretending like I didn't see it.

Three hundred thousand dollars. I don't know what Laura did to get this money, but maybe I can give it right back to her. I don't think Jase gives a shit about the debt. A very large part of me believes it's more than that.

I won't know until I do this. Although sickness churns inside of me at the possibilities, I focus on the one thing I want to happen. I hand it to him, telling him honestly where it came from. He hands it back, telling me it's not my money and he doesn't want it.

"That's what will happen," I say for the dozenth time under my breath to no one. Maybe the dozenth is the trick, because I'm starting to believe it.

He wasn't home when I got back last night and he wasn't home when I woke up after only sleeping a handful of hours. He didn't answer my texts. He's nowhere to be found. The money was in the car while I paced inside waiting and waiting. I finally had to come out and make sure it was still there. I ended up getting in, just to kill time rather than pacing and pacing. I drove past the graveyard a few times, but I never got out of the car.

Pulling out the keys from the ignition, I stare up at the large estate, going over the dialogue in my head one more time.

The debt is paid. The time we had together was time I spent with you and nothing more and nothing less. That's what I'm going to say to him. I can do it.

I'm burning up in the car, the sweat along my skin won't quit. I know part of it is from the duffle bag in the back. I look over my shoulder once again, just like I have the entire drive down here last night and even an hour ago to make sure it didn't magically disappear.

Part of this anxiousness though is because I don't know what Jase will say or what he'll do with me once the money's handed over.

It's not just a debt. I know that. It can't be just a debt to him.

Opening the car door lets the cool air hit me and I relish in it. Calming down and shaking out my hands.

This world Jenny brought me into… I'm not fighting it anymore. I'm walking into it, ready for what it will bring me. It's another step forward. I can feel it. Just like telling Laura everything. Maybe it's a small step, but it's one I'm taking.

My heels click on the paved path to his door. The door that I open on my own.

He could take that away, but why would he? The doubts swirl and mix with the fear that what we have is only about the debt. Maybe he likes holding it over my head; maybe he thinks he won't have the upper hand if I pay it off.

That thought actually eases the tension in me. He's never going to have the upper hand when it comes to me. He should know that by now.

Calm, confident and collected I walk into the foyer and then past the hall, listening to my heels click in the empty space. The clicks, the thumps, they all only add to the urgency to tell him. To get it off my chest and to get that cash out of the back of my car.

"Jase," I call out his name, seeing the bedroom door open, but he doesn't answer.

A chill follows me, bombarding me even as I stand in the threshold of the dark bedroom and see only the light from the bathroom.

There are moments in time when you know instinctively everything is wrong. You know you're going to see something that you don't
want to see. It's like there's a piece of our soul that's been here before.
A piece that's preparing you for what's to come. Warning you even. And
maybe if I was smarter, I'd take the warning and I wouldn't step foot
into his bedroom.

I'm not smart enough though.

With the sound of running water getting louder as I approach, I
creep quietly to his master bath.

The water's so loud I'm sure he couldn't hear me. That's what I tell
myself.

Thump, my heart doesn't want to be here. *Thump*, it wants me to
stop. I test the doorknob, and it's not locked. Something inside of me
screams not to take this step. Not to go forward. *It's the wrong time, I'm
not ready for it.* I can feel it trying to pull me away.

But I'm already turning the knob and with a creak, I push the door
open.

I catch sight of his clothes on the floor first; he's still hidden from
view from where I'm standing. The mix of bright and dark red splotches
and smears wraps a vise around my lungs.

I can't breathe, but I still move forward.

Blood. There's blood on his shirt. That's blood, isn't it? Fear wrig-
gles its way deeper inside of me, like a parasite taking over.

"Jase," I barely speak his name while taking a small step forward.
My gaze moves from the blood on his clothes piled on the tile floor, to
his naked body seated on the edge of the tub. He's covered with the way
he's sitting, and his head's lowered, hanging heavy in front of him. I'm
not sure he heard me the way he's sitting there. Like he's stunned, like
his mind is elsewhere, lost in another place or another time.

Despair is crippling and I swallow hard. My trembling fingers reach
out to pick up his shirt, wanting to believe it's not blood. There's not a
mark on his skin, no cuts or bruises that are fresh. The cut I gave him is
scabbed over.

The warmth of the air flows around me as I step closer and lift the
shirt off the floor. It can't be blood, Jase isn't injured. Jase is fine.

But it looks like it. I don't understand. There's so much blood, in different patterns. Smeared and stained into the undershirt. I still don't want to believe it. I wish it would be anything else. My head spins as I grip the shirt tighter, staring at it as if it'll change, it'll go back to being clean if only I look at it the right way. But it's blood. There's so much blood, my hands are wet with it.

"Bethany." Jase's voice catches me off guard and I scream, pulling the shirt into my chest out of instinct before shoving it away when I realize I've pressed the bloody clothes to my own.

I could throw up with the revolting disgust and fear that sink into my bones. The blood is on me.

"Whose blood is that?" The question tumbles from me as I take a step backward and Jase stands up tall. My hands grip the doorway and my fingers leave a trail of blood.

There's a look in his eyes I will never forget when my gaze finally reaches his.

A darkness I haven't seen before and the fear that accompanies it is all-consuming.

In sharp spikes, the chills take over and I take another step back. Out of the bathroom and away from him.

That piece of my soul that was warning me before… it wasn't about the blood, it was about Jase. I know it to be true when he takes another step forward, so much larger than mine with his hands raised and he tells me to calm down.

If I could speak, I'd tell him he's crazy to think I should calm down. If I could speak, I'd scream at him, demanding he tell me what he's done.

But I can't. Every syllable catches in the back of my throat in a way that feels like I'm choking.

"Let me get a shower and we can talk," Jase states calmly, the savage look in his eyes just barely dimming.

My head shakes, all on its lonesome and I turn and run. As fast as I can, I run away from him.

"Fuck," I hear him mutter as I bolt to the door, sweeping myself around it and crashing into the hall wall. I don't stop running, even though I don't hear him behind me.

Thump, thump, thump, thump. My heart pounds faster than my heels, ushering me away.

As I reach the door, I hear him call out. With my hand on the scanner, I turn around to see him with a pair of sweats, walking toward me, not running.

Maybe he thought that would keep me from leaving. Maybe he thought I wouldn't be threatened or I wouldn't be scared.

But he was wrong.

So fucking wrong. The second I swing the door open, I hear him scream my name and start running. I slam the door closed knowing he'll have to use the scanner too. It's another second I have ahead of him. Only seconds.

Run!

I scramble to my car and to find my keys. With terror raging through me at Jase getting his hands on me and forcing me back inside, at not knowing what he'll do to me or what he's capable of, I shove the gear into drive and reverse out of the driveway. I'm senselessly speeding away with the sight of him swinging the door open the moment my car hits the gate. Crashing it open and denting the hood of my car.

Even as I scream, I keep my foot on the gas, not caring about the damage, just needing to leave as quickly as possible.

I need to run and never stop.

Run far away and not look back.

The car jostles as I go over a curb and then another, my tires screaming as I race out of the long drive and backroads to get to the busy streets.

My gaze spends too long in the rearview, waiting for his car to show. It doesn't, but that doesn't keep me from tearing down the road.

My grip is hot, my pulse fast. I need to get the fuck out of here.

It's only once I've gotten onto the main road and I'm minutes away from my home that I let myself think of anything other than the need to go faster.

How could I love him? How could I want to love him?

Thoughts run wild in my mind, fighting with each other to be heard. There's a pounding in my temple and I don't even realize when I've run the red light until a car beeps their horn at me.

Fuck! I have to veer to the right to miss hitting the SUV. A wave of heat flows over my skin, far too hot as my tires squeal and I barely keep my car on the road.

That doesn't stop me. I keep going. I don't stop. I can't stop. I need to go faster. I need to get away.

With my chest heaving, I catch sight of the blood. Oh my God, the blood.

I need to get it off. I need to get this off. Bile climbs up my throat and I have to swallow it as I pull into my driveway. It's a reckless turn but I don't care. I need to get inside and get this off.

Get this blood off of me. Get Jase Cross off of me.

It's all I can think about as I slam the door shut to my car and run to the porch. The gust of cold air brings with it the white mist of an incoming storm tonight.

My hands are still shaking as I search for my key and that's what I'm staring at when I hear Officer Walsh's voice. "Bethany?"

The surprise and shock make me scream and drop my keys. They bang as they hit the ground and I stay perfectly still.

"Fuck." The word is spoken faintly as I stare back at him on the other end of my porch as he gets up from the chair. Like he was waiting for me.

I know my expression is one of fear and guilt, a doe-eyed woman caught in the act of something awful and I can't change it as our gazes lock.

"Is that blood?" he asks, standing straighter, but with his hand behind him as my feet turn to stone and refuse to move.

"No," I lie and his head tilts as his hand pushes his coat back and his fingers rest on his gun.

"I didn't do anything," I spill the words out, pleading with him to understand. My pulse rages and I can barely stand up straight. Fuck, no. How did this happen?

"Tell me everything. I can help you," he urges, but it doesn't sound sincere.

"You have to believe me. It's not me. I didn't do anything."

"Tell me whose blood that is."

"I don't know," I practically shriek.

"It is blood then?" he questions. Immediately, I feel caught. I feel trapped. The bite of the air creeps in, cracking the heat that's consumed me.

My lips part, but instead of giving him words, all I can do is swallow as my vision becomes dizzy.

"Tell me everything, Bethany; what happened?" His question comes out harder this time and he takes a step forward. I instinctively take a step back and my back hits the wall of the house.

With a trembling voice I whisper, begging him to let me go. "I can't," I tell him. "I don't know."

My inhale is ragged as he takes another step closer and I have nowhere to go.

"I wish I didn't have to do this." Pulling out the cuffs from behind his back, he tells me, "Bethany Fawn, you're under arrest."

A
SINGLE
TOUCH

From *USA Today* bestselling author W. Winters comes the conclusion to the breathtaking, heart-wrenching romantic suspense trilogy, Irresistible Attraction.

Sometimes you meet someone, although maybe *meet* isn't quite the right word. You don't even have to say hello for this to happen. You simply pass by them and everything in your world changes forever. Chills flow from where you imagine he'd kiss you in the crook of your neck, moving all the way down with only a single glance.

I know you know what I'm referring to. The moment when something inside of you ignites to life, recognizing the other half that's been gone for far too long.

It burns hot, destroying any hope that it's only a coincidence, and that life will go back to what it was. These moments are never forgotten.

That's only with a single glance.

I can tell you what a single touch will do. It will consume you and everything you thought you knew.

I felt all of this with Jase Cross, with every flicker of the flames that roared inside of me.

I knew he'd be my downfall, and I was determined to be his just the same.

A Single Touch is **the third and final** book of the Irresistible Attraction trilogy.

A Single Glance and *A Single Kiss* must be read first.

"Past is a nice place to visit,
but certainly not a good place to stay."
—Anonymous

PROLOGUE

Bethany

MY CALCULUS GRADES ARE SLIPPING. THE LARGE RED D SCRIBBLED IN *Miss Talbot's handwriting stares back at me. One look at it shoves the knot in the back of my throat even deeper down my windpipe. My bookbag falls to the floor in the nursing home with a dull thud as I whisper the word, "fuck." With my hand rubbing under my tired eyes, I let out a heavy sigh and stare at the ceiling in the hallway.*

There's no way I'm going to be able to stay in college if I don't pass. There's no coming back from this. My grades didn't slip like this last year when Jenny was here with me every day at four o'clock on the dot. I only have one more year to go, but this class is a core requirement. I'll never need to know how the hell derivatives work in order to be a nurse, but I can't fail this class. I can't fucking fail.

"Bethany?" The soft voice belongs to Nurse Judy. She told me exactly how she got her degree and that I could do it just like she did. She's the reason I changed my major sophomore year to pursue a nursing degree. Just as she creeps into the long hall, I shove the test into a notebook while stuffing it into my worn leather backpack, listening to the sound of the zipper rather than what she's saying.

I'll fail calculus, lose the scholarship that's paid for more than half of my college education, and be left with even more debt and no degree to show for it. Perfect. I don't know what I'm going to do. Other than work a nine-to-five at whatever minimum wage job I can get. If they'll even hire me.

"Did you hear me?" Nurse Judy coaxes me out of my downward spiral and

it's then that I see the worried look in her dark brown eyes. "Your mother had a relapse."

"A relapse?" The confusion leaves a deep crease on my forehead.

"We don't know what caused it, but she's with us, Bethany. Mentally aware."

"Aware?" All the air leaves me with the single word.

"She woke up, not knowing what happened during the last three or so years. But she knows time has passed. She knows you and your sister have been on your own and that she has Alzheimer's."

"I don't understand how that's possible." Fear is something I never expected to feel in this moment. I've had so many dreams come to me in the middle of the night where my mother would be lucid. Where she'd tell me it was okay, that she was back now. Back for good and that she remembers everything. They were only dreams though. It's only ever a dream.

I can barely swallow as I stare past Nurse Judy and walk forward without conscious awareness. "Is she okay?" It's the only thing I can ask. I can't imagine what it's like to wake up one day to have lost years of time. To wake up and find your children look different and everything's changed.

The oddest thing in this moment is that I hope she still loves me. I just want her to love me still.

Even if I'm failing. Even if I'm no longer her little girl. It's been years since she's been lucid and this is what I want most of all.

"She'll be better when she sees you," is the answer Nurse Judy gives me. With each step, I know I'll always remember this moment. It's like something flipped a switch in my head and a voice gives me reassurance. This moment will never leave you. This moment will define you.

"Are they here?" my mother's voice calls out. Echoed in her voice, I can hear the strain of past tears. "Did they get your messages?"

My answer drowns out Nurse Judy's as I round the corner to the living room in the home, my steps picking up pace just as my throat tightens. "Mom," I croak.

She's frail and thin, as she was yesterday and the day before. Somehow I thought when she came into view, she'd look like she did the last time I held her hand and she asked me again who my sister was.

She had her makeup done perfectly although she didn't need it. Mom used to say she'd never grow old. Even joked about it that day as she brushed her *blush up to her temples. That was the day we took her to the hospital. She'd forgotten who my sister was and it took me a long time to realize she'd forgotten who I was too. She thought I was her best friend from high school, the girl she named me after. A girl who had long since died.*

My mother squeezes me harder today than she did back then and the tickle in the back of my throat grows impatient as I hold my breath and squeeze her back just as tight.

I don't cry until her body wracks with sobs against mine. "Sorry," she tells me. "I'm so sorry," is all she can say over and over.

As if she chose this. As if she wanted to forget the life she had and let the memories fade and die. That's what forgetting is, it's the death of the life you had. It doesn't just kill you though. It kills everyone else as well.

I only pull away from her for a moment, just to tell her there's nothing to be sorry for, but the words are lost when she looks into my eyes. Her own are gray and clouded with a gaze of sorrow.

"Mom?"

Her expression changes in an instant. Confusion clouds her face, where just minutes ago there was clarity.

My mother is in there, or she was, but the moment is gone.

"Who are you?"

"Mom, come back," I beg her, feeling my chest hollow and then fill with agony. "Where'd you go?" I ask her, not giving into the fear this time, only the loss. "Mom!" Hope is undeniable. "I'm here, Mom; I'm here!"

Her hand tightens on my forearm, too tight.

"Mom," I gasp, trying to pry her hands off of me as she refuses to look away, refuses to react to anything at all. She's merely a statue and the realization frightens me. I turn to look over my shoulder just as I hear the front door shut from the hall. My heartbeat races. Where'd Nurse Judy go?

"Mom," I protest, writhing out of her grasp. "Help!" I finally call out, the fear winning.

"Everyone I loved has died," my mother says, and her voice is ragged. Despair and loss morph her features into one of pain and her grip on me loosens.

Staring into my eyes with sincerity, she tells me, "Everyone you love will die before you do." As if she's talking to a stranger she only intends to bring pain, they're the last words she speaks before her slender body relaxes into the chair. Her gaze wanders aimlessly as I stand there breathless from both fear and despair, knowing I was too late. That's when I hear the quickened footsteps of my sister running into the room.

Running to see her mother. Who's already gone.

Seconds pass, and I can't look at Jenny. I brush the tears away as Nurse Judy pushes past us both, aiding my mother, whose consciousness has drifted to another place and another time.

"Mom," my sister cries. And I don't blame her.

That was the last time my sister cried for our mother. She didn't even cry at her funeral nearly a year later. Jenny always held it against her that our mother didn't wait for her. She held it against me too, knowing I at least got to hear Mom tell me she was sorry.

I never told her what else our mother said. I tried to forget it. I did everything I could to kill that memory.

It's come back though. It refuses to die, unlike other things in my life.

CHAPTER
1

Bethany

T HE CLOCK DOESN'T STOP TICKING.

It's one of those simple round clocks. There's nothing special about the white backing and thick black frame. *Tick, tick, tick.* It's loud and unforgiving. The torture of it is all I can focus on to bring me sanity as the last hours of my life fall like dominoes in my memory.

The money in the trunk.

"You still haven't explained where you got the three hundred thousand dollars." Officer Walsh's voice is hard.

The blood on Jase's clothes and the look in his eyes when I came into his bathroom.

"Or why you were covered in blood. Whose blood is it, Miss Fawn? You need to tell us."

Fear is what motivated me to run from him. Fear is the cause of all of this. It's left me now, though. In its place is something more resigned.

One long, deep breath falls from me as I stare at the painted white bricks of the interrogation room's walls and listen to the *tick, tick, tick.*

My piss-poor decisions have led to this point in my life.

The point of waiting. I've fucked it up enough; I may as well just let it all fall. When Alice fell, she landed in Wonderland. I'm thinking that's not where I'll land, but I'm ready to feel the weightlessness of what's to come. I'm simply tired of fighting it.

There's another officer in the room. He's younger. When I first listened to their demands for me to answer their questions, I sat here hours ago with my shoulders tense and feeling the need to curl up into a ball and hide. The young cop sat across from me, his arms crossed and his gaze never wandering from me.

I don't like him or the way he looks at me.

"We're doing a DNA test now. You think it's going to hit, Walsh?" The other officer, Linders, finally speaks to Walsh, even if his eyes are still pinned on me. There's a certain level of disdain that seeps into my skin every time I meet his gaze.

"I'll tell you what I think," Officer Walsh answers. He's staring at me too, even as he taps the stack of papers in his hand and continues, "I think she was in the wrong place at the wrong time and that she has names."

Tick, tick, the clock goes on. It's been like this for hours in this cold interrogation room. An ache in my back reminds me how uncomfortable this metal chair is.

"I don't think so. I think she was hired for a hit or was hiring someone else and it went wrong." Officer Linders speaks clearly, although his voice is low and rough. "A hit or drugs. There's no other explanation. Who'd you get the cash from?" he asks me. It has to be the hundredth time they've asked about the cash. "Where did it all go wrong?"

"I already told you," I start to say but don't recognize my tired voice anymore as I lift my gaze to Officer Walsh's and then to Linders's. "I don't have anything to say."

Officer Walsh leans forward, exasperated. The metal legs grind against the floor as he repositions in his chair. "I saw how scared you were," he says. Compassion wraps itself around every word and his gaze pleads with me to give him something. "I can help you."

A second passes and then another.

I could let it all out. I could tell them the truth. I know I could. Maybe they'd give me a new name and send me off to some place where bad men can't find me. Somewhere free of all these memories. A place where I didn't have to think of my sister or my fucked up life.

Where I wouldn't feel the presence of Jase Cross on every inch of surface I can see, smell, touch.

As I swallow, the click of the the heat switching on is all that can be heard in the room.

I don't want to live in that world. In a world where Jase Cross doesn't hover over me. Even if he scared the hell out of me. Recalling the sight of him sitting there on the edge of the tub, tilting his head to look me in the eyes, makes me close mine tight. I don't know what happened, but I can't leave him.

More than anything, the incessant ticking of the clock reminds me that every second that passes, I'm not with him. He's not okay and I'm not with him.

Let me fall to whatever may await me, and I'll crawl my way back up to Jase. I'll find him or he'll find me. And when that happens, he better fucking confess. I deserve to know what happened.

Strands of my hair wind around my finger as I ignore Officer Walsh. He hasn't charged me yet, but I know he will. I'll be charged with obstruction of justice for not giving them information about the blood on my shirt when it comes back confirmed from a human... or maybe with a name. God forbid it comes back as from a missing person. And who knows what I'll be charged with because of the cash in the back of my car. I don't even know what the offenses will be, since so many have been listed off in their speculation of what I've done.

But I'll never say a word. And that's how I know I care more for Jase than I should. And why he needs to tell me *everything*.

"There's no helping anything. Whatever she says will be a lie." The dark stare of Officer Linders makes my stomach curl.

Good cop, bad cop, I suppose. I manage to offer him a hint of a smile. My mouth moves on its own and I didn't mean for it to do that. It just happens. As if I need to tempt fate any further.

"Let me make you an offer," Officer Walsh starts and Linders huffs in disdain, rocking back in the chair and for the first time his gaze shifts from me. He's young, very Italian in appearance although he doesn't have an accent. He scratches at his coarse dark stubble as Officer Walsh draws my attention.

"I used to work for the FBI and I have some friends in town, looking into things." There's a sense of compassion and empathy in Cody Walsh's voice that's hypnotizing, like a lullaby that draws you in. "What

I'm trying to tell you is that I have connections. I know what happened to your sister. I know Jase Cross has been seen at your residence."

His light blue eyes sharpen every time he says, 'Cross.' "What I know is that you can have a happy life. You can start over, Bethany. All you have to do is tell me what happened."

It's like he read my mind. A way out. This is the bottom of the barrel, isn't it? When you need witness protection to find a way out of the hole you've dug for yourself.

Officer Linders clears his throat and the spell from Walsh is broken for only a moment as my eyes flick between the two of them. A man with hate for me, and another who I've felt from the first day I saw him, that he wanted to help me.

"All you have to do is tell me what happened." His hand gestures an inch above the table as he adds, "No matter how guilty you may feel; no matter what you've done."

Everything seems to slow as a part of my conscience begs me to consider. The part that remembers how dark Jase's eyes were when I last saw him. The part that's fear's companion. The part that questions if I'm strong enough for all this. Even if Jase tells me what he did and why he was sitting there like that, like he was someone else. Even if I pretend as though what happened earlier today will never happen again.

And yet another part of me is like a signal amid all the noise. A part that's fading away. A small part that remembers this all started because I wanted a single thing from Jase Cross.

A name. The murderer who made the one person I had left in my life disappear. Justice for my sister.

A name Jase has yet to deliver.

I have to blink away the thoughts, and Officer Walsh seems to take it as me considering his offer.

Say nothing, do nothing. Say nothing, do nothing. Fall down the rabbit hole; they can even throw me in that pit if they want. When I finally land, I'll do what I've always done. I'll stand up on my own and keep moving. With Jase or without.

Three knocks at the door startle me, causing the chair I'm firmly seated in to jump back. Officer Walsh is the one to stand and rise, leaving Linders staring at me, relishing in the hint of fear I've shown. I can barely hear someone outside the slightly ajar door speaking to Officer Walsh over the sound of my heart racing.

All my life, I've lived by elementary rules. *Do what is right and not what is wrong.* It's the simplest way to break down the laws of life. And yet here I sit, not knowing my judgment and wondering when the black and white of right and wrong turned so gray for me. Especially since I can't even list all the wrong things I've done recently. There are too many to count, yet I'd defend them all.

"Be right back." Officer Walsh is tense as he grips the door, locks eyes with me, then leaves the room. With only Linders across from me, a new tension rises inside of me.

I don't like the way he looks at me. Fear and anger curl my fingers into a fist in my lap.

Say nothing, do nothing.

He stares at me and I him, neither of us saying a word until a small red light goes off to my left. It's oddly placed in between the painted bricks. If it had never come on, I would've never known of its existence. And the little red light changes everything.

"It's clear for the moment, but I don't know how long we'll have, so I'll be fast," Linders says quickly with a new tone I haven't heard from him. Leaning forward, the distaste vanishes, and the hate I felt he had for me is nowhere to be found.

"It's all being scrubbed; every shred of evidence on you is going to vanish. Or it already has. Officer Walsh won't have anything to hold you on and no charges will be pressed."

"What?" Disbelief takes the form of a whisper.

"He already knows someone here at the station is in their back pocket. It'll be all right," he assures me when my expression doesn't change. "If you want to go to a cell, tell me. If you'd rather stay here, we'll have to keep this up when Walsh comes back, but I'll make sure he doesn't cross the line. There are others too who are loyal to Walsh, but I'll stay with you the entire time. Unless you want to be alone."

"I don't understand." I don't know why that's my reply.

Because I do understand. The pieces line up with one another perfectly. The Cross brothers control the police department. I knew that. I know that now, even. But to be a part of it, to see it happening…

"Mr. Cross told me to protect you and get you out of here." His eyes search mine, although there isn't a bit of judgment to be found.

"Thank you," is all I can say although I wrap my arms around myself and contemplate what would have happened if I was in a different mindset. If I was ready to spill my guts. If I was wanting that new life Walsh sold me so well.

I should feel relief, which I do. The more nagging thoughts are of how powerful Jase is. How much damage a single man could do. And how little I know about him. Yet how willing I was to fall for him.

What if I had said something? What then?

"The shirt's been destroyed and that's really the only damaging piece he had on you," Linders tells me, clearing his throat.

The money.

"What about the money?" The question leaves me with haste just as the red light vanishes, blending in with the wall once again.

"Are you going to sit there and deny everything? Maybe I should put you behind bars and see how you like that," Linders sneers, forcing my body to turn ice cold. I can feel the blood drain from my face, even if I'm consciously aware this time that it's all an act.

"What's it going to be, Miss Fawn? Are you going to talk? Or do you want us to stick you in a cell like the criminal you are?" Those are the options he offers me as the door opens and Walsh returns. Walsh's demeanor is defeated as he motions for Linders to follow him out of the interrogation room.

Linders doesn't though. He doesn't obey the command from his superior. He waits for me, wanting to know an answer.

Words get stuck in my throat and I try to swallow them, I try to speak.

Nothing comes. Not a word is spoken as I stare into Linders' gaze, knowing he's one of so many men who do Jase's bidding.

Jase is still here, still in this room, protecting me even when I didn't know it.

CHAPTER
2

Jase

"I T'S RISKY WITH THE FBI ALREADY INVOLVED," SETH SPEAKS FROM the driver's seat as we're parked out front of the police station. His eyes seek mine out in the rearview mirror and I meet them, but I only nod, not bothering to speak. "Four men now, active agents, coming all the way down here from New York." He sucks his front teeth in the absence of a response from me.

It's all my fault. It's my fault she's in there. I know it is. What I don't know is what the fuck came over me.

A voice in the back of my head answers instantly. *She did.* Bethany Fawn came over me.

"We should prepare for someone to take the fall," Seth continues and a grunt of acknowledgment comes from my chest.

I've already been thinking about it. How best to handle this particular fuckup of mine. It involves a dead former FBI agent by the name of Cody Walsh and one of my men in a jail cell taking the fall. Judge Martin will give the minimum sentence. All because I fucked up at a time when fucking up isn't a possibility.

"Someone who needs the money for their family. Someone who'd go away for a year and be all right with that." Seth rattles on.

"Chris Mowers," I finally answer him and then clear my throat although my eyes stay glued to the double doors at the front entrance.

"He's new to the crew, young and seemingly naïve. His dad isn't doing well. Medical costs and looking out for his mother while he's serving time should do it. Besides, we've primed him for this." Chris wanted to work for me. I told him to go through the police academy, to earn a position we could use to our advantage. "He's not going to like it. But we can make it worth it."

My answer receives a single nod from Seth followed by the impatient tapping of his foot in the front seat.

"You're too nervous," I comment. I'm well aware of the consequences and everything at stake in this moment. The nerves he feels are nothing compared to the turmoil rattling inside of me. "Knock it the fuck off."

With his hand running over his chin he takes in a deep breath, but doesn't speak. Instead he releases a long sigh.

"You have something on your mind?" I push him.

I start to think he's going to keep it from me, whatever it is he's thinking, and then he finally says, "She's different."

Bethany. Every muscle in my body tenses at the mere mention of her.

"Yes," I answer him, feeling a pressure inside of my chest that makes me grit my teeth.

"She's in your head." He swallows after speaking.

Narrowing my eyes, I answer him with an acknowledging yes.

"I don't know how to help that," Seth admits, breaking eye contact in the small rectangular mirror for the first time. I hear him readjust in the seat in front of me as he adds, "I don't know what I should have done differently." When I don't immediately respond to that, he doesn't say anything else.

The sound of a car driving past us intrudes on the silence and I watch the tires leave tracks on the asphalt after driving through a small puddle. The brutal cold hasn't stopped the early spring flowers from pushing through the dirt out front of the police station.

Staring at the double doors that hold my cailín tine behind them, I finally answer him, "This is all on me. I know where I fucked up and you did everything right."

"What if it happens again?" he questions and a coil of anger tightens inside of me. He adds, "What do you want me to do? When you took off, I knew I should have stopped you."

I don't have time to answer him. Instead my attention is drawn to the doors being held open by Curt Linders while Bethany walks through them. With her arms crossed, she stands at the top of the concrete stairs, looking smaller than she ever has to me. Her hair is wild as the wind blows from her left and it's then that her gaze lands on our car.

"You don't have to worry about it," I say without taking my eyes off of her. "The next time I'll be the one taking the fall," I answer him and push my door open, not hesitating to go to her. Curt's shock doesn't go unnoticed. Neither does Seth's protest to simply wait for her and for me to remain inside the vehicle.

Neither of them understand. At this point, all I want is to be seen with her.

Let them all see. They need to know she's mine.

I'm drawing the line here, hoping it keeps her beside me regardless of what happens.

Bethany manages to take two steps by the time I've closed the distance between us. She's hesitant even as I wrap my arm around the small of her back.

A sharp hammering in my chest beats faster than my shoes thud on the pavement to get her in my car and away from this situation.

The feeling of failing her, of her knowing and seeing who I truly am grips me and in turn, I hold her closer. I'll never forget the way she looked at me before running off.

"It was a mistake," I mutter beneath my breath, but the tension in her body doesn't lessen and she doesn't look up at me in the least.

Seth's quick to get out and open the door for us. I'm only grateful she doesn't pause before slipping inside.

The door shuts with a resounding click as another gust of wind blows.

"You all right?" Seth asks me and I look him dead in the eyes to answer him. "No more fucking questions."

I don't have the answers to give him. None that I'm willing to give, anyway.

The bitter cold from outside doesn't carry into the back of the car.

The warmth is lacking nonetheless as we leave the police department behind in silence.

The dull hum of the car doesn't last long. "Nothing will happen to you. I promise you." My words are quiet, but I know she hears them.

Her hands stay in her lap and she answers while still looking out of her window, "Thank you."

I didn't expect this distance between us. I didn't expect the damage to be so obvious. Regret urges me closer to her, leaning across the leather seat to grip her chin between my thumb and forefinger and forcing her to look at me.

She doesn't resist, but uncertainty lingers in the depths of her hazel eyes and her breathing becomes unsteady.

"I'm sorry," I whisper. "I should never have let you see that."

She only swallows, the sound so loud in the quiet space between us.

"No, you shouldn't have. But I shouldn't have run."

"It would have been better if you hadn't." There's no fire, no fight, nothing except hurt. "I know it scared you."

It's the way she hesitates before answering. The strained way she breathes in when she looks into my eyes. *She doesn't trust me.*

"I don't know what to think right now. I'm going back and forth."

"Back and forth?"

"Whether or not I'm capable of standing beside you. Of demanding you tell me what the fuck happened." Her voice drops as she adds, "And whether or not I can stomach the truth."

It's been a long damn time since I've felt the sense of losing someone. Of feeling them slip through my fingers. I can feel it; I can fucking *see* it. I just don't know how to change it.

"Marry me." I let the idea slip out, but keep my composure. I can't lose her. I fucked up, but everyone fucks up at some point. She'll get over it. I just need time. "They can't make you testify if you're legally married to me." The excuse comes out easily enough.

Her eyes widen as I lean back in my seat. I thought about it every second we sat outside the department. She needs to be my wife.

"You're fucking crazy to think I'd take that proposal seriously."

"If something happens--"

"I'd go to jail," she cuts me off, her fire blazing as the irritation grows in her eyes. "I'd rather go to jail than marry someone because I accidentally saw something I shouldn't have." She eyes me as if I've lost it, and maybe I have. "I'll stick to my story that I don't know how any of it happened and I don't have anything else to say. Thank you very much," she says, and her final quip comes with the crossing of her legs away from me. She stares out the window again and it's then I realize where the term 'cold shoulder' comes from.

"I had a moment, Bethany. Don't hold this against me." My voice is calm and like a balm it visibly soothes her prickly demeanor.

She's slow to look over her shoulder, peeking at me before saying, "Everyone has moments, but it scared the fuck out of me, Jase."

"I'll apologize again, I'm sorry-"

"I don't want an apology." Her entire tone changes, and a different side of her I've never seen presents itself. She's calm, receptive, concerned even. "What the hell happened?"

I've never spoken about Angie to anyone so openly. Not even my brothers know all the details. Not Seth. No one.

I repeat forcefully, "I had a moment."

She pauses, considering me, but returns to the cold condition she had moments ago as she says, "I want to go home."

"No." I answer her with more force than I intended.

"Yes," she snaps back. "You can have your moment. But if you aren't going to tell me what the hell happened, I'm not going back to your place right now so I can have my own damn moment."

I shouldn't be so turned on by her anger.

"You still owe me twenty-seven days." I remind her of the only card I have to play, leaning closer and daring her to fight me. The tension in the car thickens and heats.

"Fuck you," she retorts far too casually, pulling the sleeves of the large white sweater she was given in the department down her arms. It's a simple plain sweatshirt material, and it does nothing to show off her figure. I had Linders offer it to her since her own shirt was confiscated… and now incinerated back at The Red Room like it should have been initially. Before she ran.

"Did you forget about our deal?"

She ignores my question and replies, "I had three hundred thousand in cash in the back of my car."

"They destroyed it."

The question's there, lingering in her gaze. "I'm well aware of that," she says, then swallows loud enough to hear. "Is it really about a debt for you?"

"Would I ask you to marry me if I only cared about a debt?" I question her unspoken thoughts.

Time pauses and it feels like I have her back, like she's close enough to hold on to forever so long as I don't slip up.

"The suggestion wasn't asked, it was told. In order to save me from having to testify... It's not the same."

When she speaks, she's careful with every word. "I don't want to be under your thumb, Jase," she admits. "That's all this is. I'm playing into your hands over and over. I think I have control in situations when I don't."

I'm just as careful with my reply. "I know I fucked up. I shouldn't have let you see me like that--"

"Why?" she cuts me off. "Why wait there for me to see? You had to know I would."

And just like that, she's slipping away again.

I can't fucking breathe. This damn shirt feels like a noose around my neck; I clutch at it, unbuttoning my collar.

"I need you right now." The words fall from me and I'm not even aware that they have until she threads her fingers between mine and squeezes.

"You can tell me," she whispers.

How do I tell her the truth: I killed a man who hurt a woman I barely knew and it doesn't feel like it was enough? How do I tell her I can't get what happened years ago out of my head and the sight from that night will never leave me? How do I share that burden with anyone?

Let alone with her, a woman I can't lose? I'm barely conscious of it myself.

"Jase, I deserve to know."

My gaze drifts from hers and finds Seth's in the rearview mirror.

"I don't have answers right now."

"That's becoming a theme for you, isn't it?" she bites back, pulling her warm hand away from mine. Leaning forward she places her hand on the leather seat in front of her. "Seth, please take me home."

There's no room for negotiation in my tone. "You're coming home with me."

"The hell I am--"

"You belong with me!" The scream tears from me before I can stop it. Chaos erupts from hating the blur of failure around me and the uncertainty.

I feel insane. The stress of everything that's happened is driving me mad and I'm losing the only person who can keep me grounded. I can't look her in the eyes, knowing how badly I've failed her but she makes me, her fingers brushing the underside of my jaw until my gaze lifts to hers.

"I didn't say that I wasn't still with you. I didn't say I don't belong to you." She pauses, halting her words and seemingly questioning her last statement.

I won't allow it. She can't question that. Above all else, she needs to believe with every fiber in her that she belongs to me.

My fingers splay through her hair as I kiss her. With authority and demanding she feel what I can't say. She meets every swift stroke of my tongue with her own demands.

Reveling in it, I remind her of what we have.

This won't come around again. I can feel it in my bones. What we have is something we can't let go of. I've never been surer of anything in my life as I am of this.

It takes her a moment to push me away, with both hands on my chest. It's a weak gesture, but I give it to her and love how breathless I've left her.

Barely breathing, she alternates her stare between my lips and my eyes before nipping my lower lip.

The small action makes me feel like everything will be okay. I'm all too aware that's exactly what it's intended to do.

"Come home with me." It's not a command; I'm practically begging her.

She doesn't say no, but she doesn't say yes either. "You scare me. *This*," she says and gestures between the two of us, "scares me."

"Do you think it doesn't scare me too? That fear doesn't have a grip on me sometimes?"

"I didn't ask for this," she answers and when she does, her voice cracks, the emotion seeping in.

"I didn't either, but I'm not afraid to make known what I want. I won't let fear do that to me."

"I'm not saying this isn't what I want. I'm saying I need to breathe for a minute. You need to take me home."

It's then that I realize the car has stopped at the fork that determines which way we'll go.

"Take me home." Bethany whispers the statement like it's a plea. Seth waits for my order and when I nod, the car goes right, heading toward her house.

"I'm giving you space, Bethany. But it's temporary."

She doesn't let me off so easily. "Are you willing to tell me whose blood was on my shirt?"

I shake my head, but offer her a question in its place. "Are you willing to seriously consider my offer?"

"Offer?" The fact that she's forgotten so easily hurts more than I'll ever admit.

"Marry me."

"Tell me what happened."

"Say yes." Neither of us budge, neither of us give anything more than the gentle touch of our fingers meeting on the leather seats.

"When I marry someone, it will be because I never want to be away from them. Not because I involved myself with someone who doesn't trust me, who keeps secrets from me. Someone I know I shouldn't be with and who's giving me every reason to run."

I can't come up with an answer. I have nothing. Words never fail me like this.

"Everyone's entitled to a moment. But if you're going to keep it to yourself, prepare to be by yourself."

All I can give her is a singular truth as the car slows to a stop in front of her house. "I won't be by myself for long, Bethany."

"You will if you don't figure out how to answer my questions, Jase. I'm not in the habit of helping those who don't want to help themselves."

CHAPTER
3

Bethany

The Coverless Book

Twentieth Chapter

Jake's perspective

"SHE'S A HEALER. SHE'LL HELP YOU GET BETTER."

"I'm fine, Jake," Emmy pleads with me. I know she's scared to be in the woods searching out a woman some call a witch, but I won't let her die.

Staring at the dried herbs that hang from a line outside the leather tent, Emmy hesitates. "It's nearly twice a week," I tell her and my fingers slip through hers. She's lost weight and she looks so much paler than she did nearly a month ago when we ran away.

"The farmer's sister is nice, they're all nice, but she's not helping you."

We've been staying in a small cabin on the back of a farm in exchange for labor. It would be perfect this way... if Emmy didn't get sick and spit up blood so often.

"Please. Do it for me."

Her eyes are what draw me to her. She can't hide a single thought or feeling. They all flicker and brighten within her gaze. Her lips part just slightly *but before she can kiss me or I can kiss her, a feminine voice calls out to our right, "Are you ready?"*

Emmy immediately grabs me and hides just behind my left side. She doesn't take her eyes from the woman though. Shrouded in a black cloak, it's harder to see her among the shrubbery, but as she unveils her hood and walks toward the fire, the light shows her to be nothing more than human.

"Jake…" Emmy protests.

"For me," I remind her, squeezing her hand after prying it from my hip and following the woman under the various tanned hides that protect her potions and remedies.

"I know what ails you, but tell me what you think, my dear?" The healer doesn't look at me; she doesn't speak to me at all. Emmy's quiet, assessing at first, but quickly she speaks up.

I only watch the two of them taking a place in the corner, quietly praying to whatever gods may be listening, to help Emmy. I can't lose her.

"When I'm with him, I'm invincible."

The healer's smile wanes as she places her hand just above Emmy's but quickly takes it away, snatching a bag of something dried…flowers maybe? "Take these," she says as she hands the bag to Emmy. "You like soup, don't you?" The chill of the night spreads under the tent, the wind rustling everything inside. "It'll take the pain away."

"When I'm with him, I'm invincible."

I keep dragging my eyes back to that underlined line. She's changed. Emmy's changed. When did she need Jake to be invincible? And more importantly, why did he let that happen?

I have to remind myself that it's fiction. With that thought, I put down the book and force myself to face my own reality. I'm sure as hell not invincible. Not with Jase Cross and not without him either.

Laura's never going to believe me.

It's funny how I keep thinking about telling her what happened as if it's the worst hurdle to overcome at this point.

Telling your friend you lost hundreds of thousands of dollars they loaned to you… or gave to you, whichever… the thought of telling her that makes me feel sick to my stomach.

I have to rub my eyes as I get up off the sofa, The Coverless Book sitting right in front of me, opened and waiting on the coffee table. I couldn't close my eyes last night without seeing Officer Walsh, the blood on the floor, or Jase's intense gaze and the demons beneath that darkness.

Rest didn't come for me last night, no matter how badly I prayed for it.

Beep, beep, beep. Gathering my mug of hot-for-the-third-time coffee, I promise myself I'll remember to drink it this time as I test the temperature and find it acceptable to drink.

The last time I burned the tip of my tongue.

My cell phone stares back at me. The book stares back at me. The door calls to me to go back to Jase.

And yet all I can do is sit back on my sofa, stretching in the worn groove and staring across the room at a photo of my sister in her high school graduation cap with her arm wrapped around a younger, happier version of me.

Life wasn't supposed to turn out this way.

She was never supposed to go down that path and leave me here all alone.

"I still hate you for leaving me," I speak into the empty room even though I don't believe my own words. "But damn do I miss you." Those words are different. Those I believe with everything in me.

I wish I could tell her about Jase and the shit I've gotten myself into.

If only I had my sister back.

There are multiple stages of grief. I had at least three courses that told me all the stages in detail. I had to take all three to work at the center. If you're going to work with patients who are struggling with loss, and a lot of our patients are, you have to know the stages inside and out.

Acceptance comes after depression. It's the final stage and I've heard people tell me that they can feel it when it happens.

I used to think it was like a weight off their shoulders, but a woman told me once it was more like the weight just shifted somewhere else. Somewhere deeper inside of you, in that place where the void will always be.

Denial.

Anger.

Bargaining.

Depression.

Acceptance.

The five stages in all their glory. I've read plenty about them and at the time I associated each one with how I felt when my mother died, but maybe every death is different. Because this feels nothing like what I felt with her.

There are so many reasons to explain the differences. But one thing I can't make sense of is how I feel, with complete certainty, that I've accepted Jenny's death too soon. A month since she's been missing, weeks since her death.

I'm not ready to accept I'll never see her again, but I have. How fair is that?

"Do you hate me for it?" I ask the smiling, teenage version of my sister, with her red cap in her hand. "Can you forgive me for accepting you're gone forever so soon?"

Wiping harshly under my eyes, I let the exasperated air leave me in a sharp exhale. "And now I'm going crazy, talking to no one." I swallow and sniff away the evidence of my slight breakdown before confessing. "Not the person you were in the end, but the real you. Could the real you forgive me?"

As if answering or interrupting me, or maybe hating my confession—I'm not sure which—the old floor creaks. It does that when the seasons change. When the weather moves from bitter cold to warm. The old wood stretches and creaks in the early mornings.

Still, I can't breathe for the longest time, feeling like someone's with me.

Any sense of safety has vanished.

I wish Jase were here. It's my first thought.

Even when he hides from me, I still wish he were here. I'm choosing to stay away and yet, I wish he were here. How ironic is that?

The back and forth is maddening. Be with him, simply because I want to. Or hold my ground because he can't give me what I've given him. Truth and honesty in their rawest form. He makes me feel lower than him, weaker and abandoned. It's hard to turn a blind eye to that simply because I want his protection and his touch.

It hurts more knowing I went through my darkest times naked in his bed. Bared to him, not hiding this weakness that took me over. He couldn't even tell me what happened that landed my pathetic ass in jail.

Without a second thought, I snatch my phone off the table and dial a number. Not the one I've been thinking about. It's not the conversation I've been having in my head and obsessing about for the last hour.

No. I'm calling someone to get my life back. My life. My rules. My decisions. My happiness.

The phone rings one more time in my ear before I hear a familiar voice.

"There's only one thing I've ever had control over in my entire life, and it's been taken away from me."

"Jesus Christ, Bethany. Could you be any more dramatic?" My boss sounds exasperated, annoyed even and that only pisses me off further.

Leaning forward on the couch, I settle my heels into the deep carpet and prepare to say and do anything necessary to get my job back.

"I need this, Aiden," I say and hate that my throat goes dry. "I can't sit around thinking about every little detail anymore."

"Did you take a vacation?" he asks me.

"No."

"You need to get out of town and relax." The way he says 'relax' feels like a slap in the face. Is that what people do when they're on leave for bereavement?

"I don't want to relax; I just want to get back to normalcy."

"You need to adapt and change. That takes a new perspective."

Adapt and change. It's what we tell our patients when they're struggling. When they no longer fit in with whatever life they had before. When they can't cope.

"Knock it off," I say, and my voice is hard. "I'm doing fine. Better than fine," I lie. It sounds like the truth though. "I need to feel like me, though. You know me, Aiden. You know work is my life."

"Go take a vacation and I'll think about it while you're soaking in the sun."

"I can't." I didn't realize how much I needed to go back to work until the feeling of loss settles into my chest like cement.

"Well, you can't come back."

"Why the hell not? Why can't I go back to what was?"

"Why can't things go back? Do you hear yourself, Bethany?"

"Stop it," I say and the request sounds like a plea. "I'm not your patient."

"Your leave is mandatory. You aren't welcome back until the leave is over."

"My patients are my life."

"That's the problem. They shouldn't be. You need something more."

"I don't want something more." The cement settles in deeper, drying and climbing up to the back of my mouth. It keeps more lies from trickling out.

"I'm looking out for you. Go find it." The click at the other end of the line makes me fall back onto the sofa, not as angry as I wish I was.

Fuck Aiden. I'll be back at work soon. I just have to survive until then. I hope I remember this moment for those long nights when I can't wait for my shift to end.

Swallowing thickly, I consider what he said.

I need something else.

Something more.

A memory forms an answer to the question: what is my "something more?"

Marry me.

My palm feels sweaty as I grip the phone tighter, then let it fall to the cushion next to me.

Marry me. His voice says it differently in my head. Different from the memory where he told me to do so because then I wouldn't have to testify against him.

I can't see straight or think straight. I'm caught in the whirlwind that is Jase Cross.

Knock, knock, knock.

Startled by the first knock, feeling as if I've been spared by the second, I stop my thoughts in their track. Someone at the front door saves me from my hurried thoughts, but the moment I stand to go to the door, I hesitate.

I shouldn't be scared to answer the door. I shouldn't feel the claws of fear wrapping around my ankles and making me second-guess taking another step.

I will not live in fear. The singular thought propels me further, but it doesn't stop me from grabbing the baseball bat I put in the corner of the foyer last night. The smooth wood slips in my palm until I grip it tighter and then quietly peek through the peephole.

Thump. Thump.

My heart stops racing the second I let out a breath, then put the baseball bat back to unlock the door and pull it open. "What the fuck is wrong with me," I mutter to myself.

"Mrs. Walker," I say and then shut the door only an inch more as the harsh wind blows in. "I wasn't expecting you."

The older woman purses her thin lips in a way that lets me know she's uncomfortable. She has the same look every time she stands to speak at the HOA meetings. Which she's done every time I've been there. I glance behind her to check my lawn, but the grass hasn't even started to grow yet.

"Is there something I can help you with?"

Her hazel eyes reach past me, glancing inside my house and I close the door that much more until it's open just enough for my frame, and nothing more.

"Is your grandson doing all right?" I ask her, reminding her about the last time we spoke. When she needed help and I came to her aid. Technically to her grandson's aid, who'd been struggling with his parents' divorce and needed someone to talk to.

"I was wondering if you were all right?" she clips back.

"Me?"

"There's been some activity... some men around your house lately." Her eyes narrow at me, assessing and I'm not sure what she'll find. I close the door behind me to step outside on the porch.

"Men?" I question.

"A number of them. In cars that seem... expensive. Same with the clothes."

"Are you suggesting I'm some sort of escort, Mrs. Walker?" I throw in a bit more contempt than I should, in an attempt to get her to back off.

"No. I think they're drug dealers." Her answer isn't judgmental. Just matter of fact.

The tiny hairs on the back of my neck stand on end and I have to cross my arms a bit tighter.

"This is what happened to your sister. Isn't it?"

Words escape me. The memory of my sister on the steps right in front of me causes the cold to seep into my skin, and then deeper within. I can see her there still. I can't tear my eyes away from her. God help me, I'm losing it. She looks just as I saw her last. Except for her hair, she's wearing it like our mom used to. Memories flood my thoughts. None of them good.

"Are you all right? You're as white as the snow," Mrs. Walker says as she grips my shoulder and I snap, pulling myself away from her.

"Please leave me alone," I tell her and refuse to look back at my sister. I can feel Jenny's gaze on me. It's like she's sitting right there on the porch steps. Watching us now, but not saying anything.

I don't move until Mrs. Walker does, leaving in silence. It's only when she's walking down the stairs that I dare look at them.

My sister's not there. Of course she's not. She's gone. My sister's gone.

Whipping my door open, I pace in the hall.

What the fuck is wrong with me? I need to get the fuck out of here.

My keys jingle as I lift them from the hook in my foyer. I nearly leave just as I am: unshowered and in pajamas. I haven't even brushed my hair yet today. With my hand on the doorknob, I settle my nerves.

Just take one breath at a time. One day at a time.

Shower. Dress. And then I'm heading to Laura's.

She'll help me. She has to know a way out.

If Jase loves me, he'll give me space. I just need to breathe. He'll understand if I go away for just a little while. I'll do what Aiden said. I'll go away. Somewhere no one knows. I have to get away from here. Somewhere in the back of my mind, my inner bitch is laughing at me for thinking Jase would ever let me leave. He doesn't know what my mother told me though. I can't fall for him. I can't risk it and knowing that makes me want to run faster than I've ever run in my life.

CHAPTER
4

Jase

I T'S ALWAYS QUIET OUT HERE. ALTHOUGH IT WAS QUIET LAST TIME AS WELL, and that's when everything fell apart.

Rows and rows of stones. Centuries have passed and nothing's changed. I think that's why I come here. It doesn't matter what happened before or after, the stones stay in familiar rows like silent sentinels.

I've lived with many regrets and many failures. It's not often that I can see them the moment they happen. I shouldn't have told her to marry me. Now that it's done though, I can't stop from wanting to tell her again and again until she agrees.

I can make that right.

Unlike so many other things I can't fix. The gust of breeze blows dried flower petals across the gravestone before me. With the petals clear of it, it's easy to read my brother's name etched in stone.

I'll make it right with her. There's only so much I can make right, and she deserves it. Not many do.

If I had to pinpoint a time when everything changed, a single moment when everything went wrong, I'd be forced to choose between two.

The first is the moment Romano hired a hit on me that went awry and resulted in a funeral for my closest brother. An old soul at such a young age, he never did anything to anyone. Tragedy changes a man forever.

If fate had ended its interference there, I don't think my brothers and I would have a normal life, but it wouldn't be one so cruel. Maybe one more empty though.

"I figured I'd find you here," Seth calls out from a distance. Shoving his hands into his black windbreaker he makes his way to me. I'm not ready to leave though.

The second moment is when Carter was taken by Nicholas Talvery, beaten, and changed into a broken boy hell-bent on fighting the men who lived to destroy us. He blazed the path for us, viciously and mercilessly. Because of him we stayed. We didn't have to run; we were more than capable of fighting together.

Two old men, men who ruled ruthlessly, they're the ones so easy to blame.

Since then, everyone has left us and no one could be trusted. Pillars of life crumbled to insignificant dust in favor of simply surviving and adapting to be more like them. To dedicate our lives to destroying them before they could do the same to us.

I hate what we've become, but I can't let go of how it all started and what still needs to be done.

Talvery is dead; Romano is close to gone, but Marcus is still here. Still giving orders, still deciding everyone's fate as if it's his right. They may be the root cause of it all, but Marcus planted the seeds, Marcus knew.

"I'll make them all pay." The promise to my brother drifts away in the bitter wind.

"What's that?" Seth asks and then braces against the harsh chill, zipping his jacket before glancing at the stone on the ground. I can see the question written on his face, but he doesn't voice it. Instead he tells me, "I didn't hear what you said."

He's taller than me, just barely. But on the hill of the grave he looks taller still.

"You found me," I comment and huff a sarcastic laugh. "Should have gone somewhere else."

"I have good news and bad. I didn't think you'd want to wait for either," Seth tells me, and the way he lowers his voice suggests an apologetic tone.

"Let's have the good news first," I tell him, staring off into the distance past the rows of gravestones to the green grass, waiting to be filled.

"There are patterns in the movements of the men we've been watching." Seth takes a half step closer and adds, "Marcus's men."

I focus all my attention back to Seth. "Patterns?" He nods and says, "Between the ferry and the trains. They're transporting something."

The smell of fresh dirt and sod blow by us as he adds, "They're spending a lot of time at each location. Declan thinks there are holding points."

"And what about Marcus? Where is he?"

"We don't know yet."

"Find him." My answer is clipped, but easy enough. It's progress in this slow game of chess and we're carefully moving pieces on the board.

"Bethany still doesn't know about Jenny?"

"No. I'm not telling her until I know where she is and that she's alive still."

"Right," he says. The single word brings defeat to the air and I can't place my finger as to why. "I don't know that we'd be able to sneak up on him or set something up without him knowing. He has eyes everywhere. The more people we follow, the more are involved--"

I cut him off, knowing the risk involved, knowing Marcus will more than likely know when we come for him. "Just find him."

"Of course. I'm on it."

"And the bad news?"

CHAPTER
5

Bethany

"WHY DON'T WE TAKE IT FROM THE TOP?" LAURA ASKS ME IN her living room as I pace in front of the floor-to-ceiling windows that look out over the park. Although, from up here on the twentieth floor, it's merely a square of green.

"Which top?" I ask her. "The one that involves Jase or the one that's easier to swallow?"

"I get the easy one, you're on leave and need to go on vacation before Aiden will quit being an ass. That one I've got. How about the one where you went to jail?"

"I don't think I was technically in jail since I never saw a cell." I don't stop my pacing.

"So the money is gone, but Jase doesn't care. All the evidence is gone and he wants you to marry him just in case this happens again?"

I only nod.

"See, it's the marriage thing that I may be hung up on..." she trails off as she lowers herself to a dusty rose velvet chair and takes a sip from her tall wine glass. She settled on prosecco when I said I didn't want any coffee and word-vomited up everything—including seeing my sister on my front porch steps. I'm surprised she didn't go straight for the vodka.

"The 'marry me' part? Not seeing my dead sister and feeling her there?"

She shrugs. "Sometimes we see what we want to see. You feel alone and need someone to talk to. You didn't want to tell me about the money. She was your rock for a long time..."

Was. Past tense. My steps slow to a stop as I pull my still-damp-from-the-shower hair away from my face and look back down at the park.

"I'm sorry about the money," I say and have to clear my throat after speaking. I'd say anything for her not to bring up Jenny again. She's gone. Truly gone.

Fuck. It shouldn't hurt like this still, should it?

"Don't worry about the money--"

Cutting her off, I ask, "Will you hide me?" Shock flashes in her eyes. Swallowing thickly, I continue, "I don't know how you got the money, but there's obviously a lot I don't know. If there's any way to hide me—please do it. I just need to get away for a while."

"Away from Jase, you mean?" She barely says the words and I nod.

"I need to cope and think on my own and he's just..."

"All consuming," she finishes my statement for me, but somehow the words seem to be meant for someone else as she looks past me, staring at the white and blush striped curtains instead.

"Yes."

She nods once, downing her glass and then standing up, all the while not looking at me. As she rounds the corner to her kitchen, no doubt to fill her glass, she tells me, "I have someone I can call. I can ask him for a favor."

Hope is nowhere in her cadence; her tone is resigned.

I can feel some hope though. A tiny bit at the idea of being away for just a little while. Enough to get out of the chaos. Enough to breathe. Taking out my phone, I contemplate telling Jase just that. To give me space and time. That I'll be back.

I slip my phone back into my jeans. Not yet. He's not going to like it. He needs to get over it, though. There are plenty of things I don't like about this arrangement either, and I've rolled with the punches as best as I can. I return to gazing at the park and brush my fingers against the cool glass. I've never felt like this before. I've never been so... so helpless.

I hear Laura before I see her and I'm quick to turn my back on my reflection as she lets out a long breath.

"Did you call?" I ask her and she doesn't answer immediately. Instead she stares through me, looking to the park outside.

She snaps out of it as I bite out her name.

"What?"

"Did you call?" I ask her again and an eerie feeling crawls over my skin at the way she swallows before answering me, although she only nods.

"What's wrong?" I question her and she shakes her head, then returns to her seat.

"It's just work. Not you."

Relief isn't so forthcoming, but I don't think Laura's lying to me. Especially not when she offers me a tight smile.

"Is it Michelle? Is she okay? I heard dealing with the pica condition has been difficult."

Her hair swishes as she shakes her head. "She's doing fine. All your patients are fine," she says as she leans back, moving her hair to one side and braiding it. "Don't worry about them, you workaholic, you."

"What is it then?" I ask her. "Anything I can do to help?"

"Did I tell you about the patient with no name?" she says and her features turn serious. A haunting memory reveals itself in her eyes.

"Just initials?"

"Right. The woman with only initials…" She pauses before telling me the rest. "Somehow… someway, she got hold of a bottle of antifreeze."

"What the hell?"

"She tried to kill herself. She drank the entire thing and needed an emergency transfusion. Every ounce of her blood had to be drained for her not to die."

"How could that have even happened? That's impossible." She shakes her head only ever so slightly, but her expression holds a different answer. My hands tremble as I walk toward her. I can't believe it. "When did this happen?"

"Three days ago."

"How the hell did it happen?" I walk closer to her, unable to contain the horror and shock that a patient in our facility was able to obtain a means to end it.

"That's the thing," she says and looks me dead in the eyes. "There is no investigation."

Chills flow down my arms. All my concerns seem so meaningless in comparison. I've never been so grateful for a tragedy.

"She had to have dialysis, the antifreeze did so much damage. We were waiting to hear what kind of inquiries would be made. What paperwork and interviews we needed to prepare for... but Aiden told us that it never happened. To act like there was no incident and not to speak a word of it. So you... you better not tell him I told you."

"How can there be no investigation?" The question leaves me slowly, barely able to form itself.

"Whoever is paying for her to be there paid for the antidote, the dialysis... all of it with cash and they don't want any attention brought to it."

I drop into the seat next to her, processing it all and unable to shake the cold sensation that's taken over.

"Whoever it is, they want her there and they don't want anyone to know about it."

"Did they give her the antifreeze?" I dare to question.

"No. Aiden's the only one on her charts. After he told us, I followed him to his office." She swallows thickly. "I think it was an accident. He's on her charts, bringing her items she asked for. I think he made a mistake. But I don't understand why he's not fired. He should have checked it."

"Aiden? No." I can't believe that. Aiden's better at his job than that.

"I think he fucked up. She's smart and wants to die. Really wants to die." She licks her lower lip and then tells me, "But whoever's paying for all of this? They want her alive."

A cheerful series of dings in different octaves fills the room, forcing her knuckles to turn white as she grips the chair and then cusses beneath her breath.

"Your doorbell is going to give you a heart attack," I comment and then look to the large cobalt door. "Who is that?"

She doesn't look back at me as she stands and tells me, "The person I called."

There are little moments when you know someone's screwed you over before they show their cards.

It's in the way they talk; the way they look at you. Even the way Laura walks right now. Unlocking the deadbolt and opening the door without speaking, without checking to see who it is.

All the while I sit there, denying this feeling of betrayal as if it's not really happening.

Even when Seth walks through the door, tall, handsome and demanding Seth, I still want to deny it.

"I'm tired of being the last to know," is all I can mutter, leaning back and hating that the last person I had in my corner denied me a chance to get out of this mess. "I suppose it's my problem to deal with, isn't it?"

I can hear her apologies, her pleas for me to understand all the while Seth is saying something, but it's all white noise. I'm not interested in hearing what her excuse is. She of all people should know I need to get away. She lives in solace. She preaches it to me constantly.

"So, Seth?" I finally speak up although my ass is still firm in the chair. "Seth's who you called? Or did you go straight to Jase?"

They both speak at the same time.

"You have to forgive me, Bethany—I didn't have a choice."

"Jase doesn't have to know you were thinking about leaving him."

The chair pushes back against the wall; it would have tipped over if the wall hadn't been there to block its path because I stood so quickly.

"First off, you always have a choice," I push the words through clenched teeth at Laura and then turn to Seth. "Secondly, I wasn't leaving him. I wasn't running, so fucking tell him for all I care!" I don't mean to scream.

I don't mean to lose control. *Who the fuck am I kidding? What control did I ever have?*

"Beth, please," Laura says as she reaches out for me and I snatch my arm away.

"How could you?" I can't look at her. Not because of anger. Because of the hurt that rests across my chest.

"One day I'll tell you why. Just forgive me," she pleads with me.

"I love you," I tell her. "But right now, I really hate you."

She covers her mouth with one hand and watches me walk to Seth, who hasn't moved from the threshold.

"Seth."

"Bethany." He says my name sweeter than I say his. He even affords me a smile. "Are you ready?"

"No. No, I'm not. I wasn't expecting you. When I asked my *good* friend," I pause to look at her from the corner of my eyes, only to see her leaning against the wall. Her arms are crossed over her chest and her focus is straight ahead at the window rather than at us. "When I asked her to call someone, I wanted to leave. Not go back to Jase." Before he can respond I add, "Not right now. I just need to breathe."

"No, you don't," he tells me as if he knows what I need. As if he knows what I'm going through.

"I hear things. I see things. I don't feel okay." I don't expect my voice to crack or the admission to stir up so much emotion, but it does.

"Hey," he says then reaches out to brush my shoulder, and I notice how that gets Laura's attention, how she watches him touch me.

He squeezes my shoulder gently when he tells me, "It's going to be all right." His voice is soothing, his dark eyes calming. "Come on, come with me." Seth holds out his hand for me to take once he's released his grip, as if he's some sort of savior. "Jase doesn't know, but you should tell him what you're feeling."

Guilt isn't something I expected to feel.

"If she wants to, she will." Laura speaks up for me, and when I look back at her over my shoulder, I can see her swallow and it's not until I nod that she nods too.

I already forgive the two-timing bitch. I don't understand, though. I'll never understand why she sold me out.

Seth's eyes stay on Laura's a moment longer as he speaks, right before he looks back down to me, letting his hand fall to his side. "He's going through something right now. He's making mistakes and focusing all his time and energy on you. It's causing problems."

"He shouldn't." I refuse to be used as an excuse for someone else.

"I know that. He knows that too."

He starts to say something else but I cut him off. "I'll drive home myself."

"I wanted to show you something."

"I don't want to see anything, talk about anything, or do anything at all but have a moment to just be away from all of this," I practically hiss. "What can't you understand about that?" Anger and desperation twine together. "I'm not okay, but I'm trying to be."

"I wanted to show you something. But it can wait. We have time. Plenty of time. If you want to go home, know that I have to keep an eye on you."

"How's it feel to be a babysitter?" I can't help the snide comment although I immediately apologize. "I'm not usually such a bitch," I comment after he accepts.

"You could tell me whatever it is. I could go there myself."

He only shakes his head.

"If you could be a non-problem… he has enough of them."

"Wouldn't me leaving be exactly that?" I already know the answer before it's fully spoken.

"The fuck it is." His quick response and even scorn at the thought throw me off. "He needs you by his side." His statement strikes me at my core. The emotional crack destroys what little resolve I have left.

"I just don't know if I'm the woman that can be by his side." I almost tell him I don't know if I can be by anyone's side. Especially not now, with every day passing and the warning my mother gave me sounding louder and louder in my mind.

"Well, he chose you. And between the two of us, I know you are."

CHAPTER
6

Jase

"HOW COULD YOU BE SO FUCKING RECKLESS?"

I don't answer my brother. The silence is deafening as my shoulders tense and I lean against his desk with both my fists planted on the edge of it. He refused to wait for this meeting and demanded it happen right now; that's how I knew he was aware of my fuckup.

Neither of us say anything. I can feel his eyes on me as he turns from the windows in his office and slowly takes his seat. The smell of polished leather and old books invades my senses as I do the same, sitting across from him and feeling the disappointment flow through me.

The need to check on Bethany rides me hard as I sit there. All I can think about is Bethany and how I hurt her.

Seth's watching her though. *She's fine.* I've been telling myself that repeatedly since I left her. That, and that she'll forgive me. That she just needs space.

She loves me. I remember that she told me she did once. The reminder doesn't feel so truthful anymore.

"It's unacceptable." I say the words so he doesn't have to. "What I did could have cost us everything." All I can think about is Bethany, and all he can think about is the mistake I made. The first one in a long damn time.

"The fucking FBI is breathing down our necks and you do that?" Carter doesn't hide the rage as he slams his fist down.

I don't react. This is how he is and how I knew he'd be. He can scream all he wants. What's done is done and his display of anger won't change that.

I don't say anything for the longest time, until finally, "I know," is somehow spoken from my lips.

"What the fuck were you thinking, leaving like that? You drove in public while covered in blood. It would have taken a single phone call. We don't flaunt this shit. It's one fucking rule none of us has ever broken." His chaotic breathing has lessened. The cords in his neck are no longer as tense.

In this moment, he reminds me so much of our father. Maybe because he's focusing his rage at me for the first time that I can ever remember. "Everything we do is with reason and intention. Careful. Meticulous. We don't leave evidence." Every word is spoken calmer and more relaxed. He even sits back in his seat before running a hand down his face.

"What were you thinking?" he asks again.

"I don't know."

My answer is quick, as is his rebuttal. "Bullshit."

"Bull-fucking-shit," he repeats and with his words, the sky darkens behind him. The night is settling in, as is his disbelief. My knuckles rap in synchrony on the wooden armrests of my chair as he looks at me, and I look at him.

"You always know what you're doing. You're always in control, yet you did it anyway." His voice is calm, his composure returned. Tilting his chin up, he asks me, "Why? You had to have known she'd see and that you were risking everyone else seeing just so she could see."

"I shouldn't have-"

"But you did. You wanted her to see you, Jase. There's no other explanation. You don't fuck up like this. None of us fuck up like this."

My brother's words hang heavy in the air. Waiting for me to accept them.

"She doesn't need to see what I do. What I'm capable of."

"You wanted her to, though."

"I won't do it again," is all I answer him, still not wanting to accept I'd do something so stupid and reckless. "I was emotional. I was caught up in the past."

"You wanted her to see," he repeats and I lift my gaze to his dark eyes.

"It doesn't matter. It'll never happen again."

He looks like he wants to say something else. Like the words are just there, right on the tip of his tongue, toying with the idea of falling off.

The room is silent though. For a moment and then another.

"She doesn't need to see that," I tell him, content with that truth and then I crack my knuckles one at a time. "I won't do it again."

"She already knew, Jase." I pin my gaze to my brother's. "Even if she doesn't admit it. She already knew."

"Knew what?"

"What you were capable of. She knows what you do. She already knows. You're right that you don't need to show her. But you're wrong to think she didn't already know."

With an open palm, my hand moves to the harsh stubble surrounding my mouth and then to my jaw.

"Some part of you wanted to know what she really thought of it all. Is that it?"

I ignore his question. "I scared her."

"She should fear what you're capable of. It's new to her." Carter leans forward on his desk, resting his elbows on the hard wood and it gets my attention as what he says registers.

"What do I do now?"

A flicker of a grin shows on Carter's face. "Because I should know what to do when the woman I love fears me?"

"I didn't say that."

"What are you saying then?"

"I'm saying I fucked up, she's scared, and I don't want her to run." My voice lowers of its own accord and a confession escapes as I say, "I can't let her run." With my head lowering, I think back to the way she looked at me before closing her front door. She looked back at me the way she did in the restaurant. Like it may be the last time.

"She's not the only one afraid then, is she?"

"I'm asking for advice, Carter. It's not something I care to do often," I comment, hating the way something in my chest twists with agony.

"She's not like us; she didn't grow up in this world."

"She fixes the ones we break though. Addiction and loss... she stares that in the face every day."

"You think because she works at the Rockford Center that she could handle seeing you covered in blood?"

"I wasn't covered in it," I say. My rebuttal is useless.

"Not to her. She doesn't see *this*. This is different. It's not something she can control with a bed, pills and a conversation."

"Neither is loss. Loss isn't controlled." The need to defend her overrides my sensibility.

Carter's gaze is assessing. Running my hands through my hair, I question my own sanity.

"She's under your skin." Carter's tone verges on discouragement.

"Which is right where I want her to be," I admit freely, correcting him. "I'm not letting her go."

"Then don't allow her to see what frightens her without first giving her a way to handle it. You blinded her to what's going on, then showed Bethany her own worst fears without warning. What did you think would happen?"

"I wasn't thinking," I mutter, staring at the dark red in the carpet beneath our feet.

"Start using your head again. How's that for advice?"

It's hard to hold back from rolling my eyes. "Any other advice you want to offer?"

"Promise her she doesn't have to be a part of this world if she doesn't want to. You should have never come back like that... She's seen already, she knows and she hasn't walked away."

"What if I can't hide it all from her? What if I don't want to hide it?" The truth is buried in the questions, something that loosens the tension. Something that makes me feel like I can breathe again.

"She knew before, Jase," he repeats himself again. "You're fooling yourself if you think she didn't know who you were and the world you inhabit before."

"Knowing isn't the same as seeing," I comment and regret what I did. I regret losing it and putting her in a place to be shocked and frightened. "I'll do better." I make the promise to her, although Carter's the one who hears it and the one who gives a single nod.

"Do you know how I knew I should fight for Aria, rather than let her go?" Carter asks me and I wait for his answer. "Without her, I just can't go back to being without her. There is no version of my life where I'd be okay knowing she wasn't with me and not knowing if she was okay. I needed to make sure she was loved. I couldn't move forward not knowing if she would be loved if I weren't there."

There's that word again... *love*.

"If you want her, make her see that. She knew what she was getting into. She'll be exposed to more of our world over time and she'll learn to deal with it in a way she can. She didn't run, though. She's not going to leave you, Jase."

"Is that why you called me in here?" I ask him, watching the wind blow the trees in the distance behind him. "To give me advice and watch me sit here with my tail between my legs?"

The leather groans as Carter sits deeper in the wingback chair. "Romano's been indicted."

"Indicted?"

"The FBI agents that have set up camp aren't going to be leaving anytime soon. They're fucking everywhere."

"Did they find the explosives on the east side?"

"No, we got there first. Any evidence of an association with him has been wiped. But they're digging. So we need to be careful." I don't miss the way Carter looks at me when he says the word *careful*.

"You think he'll pay them off?" I ask.

"I think he'll try. I would."

His phone vibrates on the desk, halting the conversation momentarily. With a glance he sits up, and messages back. It must be Aria. "I've got to go; do you have anything else?"

"I want her to marry me." I say the words out loud. Freeing them. He's the one who brought up love. I've never considered him helping me, but he has Aria and if he can have her, I should be allowed to have Bethany.

"Then tell her." Carter's response is easy enough.

"I did."

"Was that before or after she was arrested?" I look past him, letting out a frustrated sigh. "You've never waited for anything. Why would a marriage proposal be any different?"

"Timing may not have been the best."

"Best?" Carter actually laughs. He has the balls to let out a deep, rough chuckle that fills the room and forces me to crack a smile.

"I told her she wouldn't be able to testify if we were married."

"You're a fucking dumbass, Jase. I'm a goddamn bull in a china shop and even I'm more graceful than that."

"It felt right." I drag my hand down my face remembering how her eyes widened.

"Like I said, you're a dumbass. You like shocking her," my brother comments. "I'm not sure that's exactly what she wants or needs from you at the moment."

"What does she want?" I say out loud and Carter answers as if he's known Beth her entire life.

"Someone to help her with the things that matter most to her. Someone to love her."

His phone vibrates again and that's when I check mine and my stomach drops. "She needs someone to kick her ass. That's what she needs," I murmur under my breath.

CHAPTER
7

Bethany

"SETH TOLD ME."

The heat in Jase's car is stifling. For the first time, he's driving and Seth is nowhere to be seen. It's just us.

"What did he tell you?" I ask.

"You said you wouldn't run," he says and his tone is accusatory.

A small and insignificant sigh falls from my lips as I stare at the passing trees, small buds forming on the branches and lean my head against the passenger side window. "I wasn't running."

The steady clicking of the blinker is the only sound until we turn at the end of the street. "What would you call it?" he asks me and I answer.

"Following my boss's orders to take a vacation while getting away from the chaos for a moment."

"You really think you would have come back?" I can tell from the huff that leaves him that he doesn't believe I would have.

"I would have missed you, worried about you and thought about you every second I was gone. You're a fool to think otherwise." I second-guess my harsh manner and turn to look at him. He only gives me his profile; he's still staring at the road. His stubble is longer than it's ever been, but I love the masculinity of it, along with his dominating features. "I'm sorry. I shouldn't have called you that."

Quiet. It's quiet and that's how I know he doesn't believe me. I suppose it works both ways. The mistrust between us runs deep with not just everything that's happened, but the way we've handled it all.

Laying a hand between us, palm up, I offer a truce. "I thought you'd come last night. I was waiting for you."

"You didn't message me."

"Neither did you." I give him back the same accusatory tone.

"Seth suggested that I give you space. Carter agreed with him. I thought I could use some as well, given that you made plans to leave."

"You scared me--"

"I apologized." His words cut me off and I steady myself, pulling my hand back to my lap.

"Do you want me to apologize? I'm sorry. I'm sorry I made you think I'd run." Transparency is what I'm aiming for, so I let the words spill out. Every bit honest. "I could've handled it differently. I didn't trust you'd let me go."

"You're damn right, I wouldn't have and I won't now." Anger simmers inside of me until vulnerability stretches his next words. "You knew before."

My heart does a silly thing. It beats out of rhythm, making sure I'm listening to it. "Knew what?"

"You knew who I was."

"I still know. I'm still here, aren't I?"

He finally glances at me as the expensive car drives over gravel for a short moment, jostling the smooth ride.

"I would do anything for you. Name it, I'll do it. Whatever you need to make you want to stay."

"What?" I say and the word is as exasperated as I am. "What are you talking about?"

"If you want to leave, you come straight to me. In exchange," he says as he taps his thumb rapidly on the leather steering wheel. "Name it. Whatever you need in exchange for *me* being the person you run to."

I don't hesitate to take away the card he's been playing to keep me under his thumb as I say, "Drop the debt."

"It's dropped."

He says it too easily, too quickly. The words were waiting to be spoken. It didn't matter what I said. The long drive is winding as we approach the Cross estate. The dent in the fence is already fixed, but my mind replays the images of when I sped away as we drive by it.

"I don't believe you. The moment I do something you don't like or the second I make you think I'm leaving you, you'll say I owe you."

"I'll write it down in fucking blood, Bethany." There's no menace in his words, only desperation and he adds, "I'm trying," while staring into my eyes. I can feel it deep inside of me, his need to hold me.

I barely whisper, "Why do you want me?"

"Because you make it okay. You make it all right."

"I don't know what I'm making okay, Jase. Can't you understand how *that's* my problem?"

The car comes to a halt on the paved driveway and he lets out a long exhale, staring at the bricked exterior rather than at me before he tells me again, "I'm trying."

"I'll try too," I answer quickly, remembering the tit for tat our relationship started as and may always be. "Let's go back to the beginning. There's no debt this time, but I still have questions. I don't want to forget what happened to my sister. I want to know who. I want to know why."

Jase merely stares at his front door as he turns off the car. Not speaking, not acknowledging what I've said for so long that I eventually move closer to him and almost repeat my suggestions until he takes my hand in his and squeezes lightly.

Hope moves between us, drawing us closer.

"Can you give me a name?" I ask him, praying he'll trust me this time. It's a futile prayer.

"I'd rather not."

"Do you have anything new?"

"No."

I have to swallow to keep from telling him that there's no point if all he'll ever be is a sea of dark secrets to me. I nearly breathe out, *what's the point?* and storm off. I can already hear the car door slamming. Instead, I stay in the parked car with him, letting him hold my hand.

Our relationship is uneven; it may always be. Jase needs this. I think he needs it more than I do.

That's the point. This is for him. I can take what's mine another time. "I don't know that I can live with all the secrets," I admit quietly.

"Ask me something else," Jase says, the slow stroke of his rough thumb pausing on my knuckles as the crisp chill enters the car in place of the heat.

"Whose blood was it?" I dare to ask. There's a pitter-patter in my chest that keeps me from inhaling when he hesitates.

Clearing his throat, he answers, "A man's. Someone who hurt a lot of people."

I push for more, staring at him, willing him to look at me, but he still doesn't.

"Name," I demand. "I deserve to know whose blood was on me."

"Hal."

Settling back into my seat, I note that he doesn't give me more, but he's given me something. "I don't think I like that name anymore."

My off-handed comment is rewarded with a slight huff of a laugh from Jase before he looks at me, really looks at me. The kind of look I'll remember forever. Not at all like the way he was in the bathroom this past weekend.

"Are you okay?" he asks me, and I don't know what prompted it.

"You really do scare me… sometimes."

"I don't want to."

I squeeze his hand when he stops squeezing mine and say, "I know you don't."

"Ask me something else," he says, looking out of the window.

"Are you okay?" It's all I can think to ask.

He nods once but doesn't say anything else and I get the feeling he's keeping something from me. Enough so that I open the car door and head inside. It takes a moment for him to follow. The wind is un-kind, ushering us inside as quickly as possible.

It seems like this is temporary. That we're pretending it's okay when it's not. There's something unsettling in the air between us as we walk to the bedroom quietly, our steps even and echoing in the empty hall.

"Do you have a 'something?'" I ask him as his hand grips the door-knob. He twists and pulls it before looking down at me questioningly.

"Something other than work?" I ask him and his answer strikes me hard. "Family. I have my brothers."

The pain of loss is a horrid thing. It comes and goes; it sneaks up on you but it also punches you in the face at times.

It feels like it's done all of those things to me in this moment. All at once.

Leaving Jase standing in the doorway, I drop my purse on the bed while kicking my shoes off without looking at him and try not to let it eat at me, but it is. Obviously so. Jase's keys clink on the dresser, then his watch before he takes off his jacket.

"I shouldn't have said that," he admits with his back to me before facing me. "I wasn't thinking."

The comfort of regret is what lifts my eyes to his.

"Yes, you should have. It's what I needed to hear."

Maybe he's my something.

There's no other logical explanation for why I'm so drawn to him. He's talking as he walks to me, saying something but I don't hear a word. Just the soothing cadence of his voice as I stare at his lips, his broad chest.

Just love me.

Pushing myself off the bed, I press my body to his, surprising him as I kiss him. It's needy, it's raw. His response is just as primitive. He tears the clothes from my body, but I don't move to remove his; I don't trust myself to loosen my hold on him. My fingers are braced at the back of his neck, keeping his lips to mine and urging him to devour me. To take from me, to use me. To make me feel alive and worthy of life.

I love you. The words are trapped inside of me. Maybe he can feel them when I kiss him. Maybe his lungs are filled with the knowledge when he breaks our kiss for only a moment to suck in air before tossing me onto the bed and then covering my body with his.

His fingers press on my inner thigh as his tongue delves into my mouth. Each stroke against my clit is sensual but demanding, just as Jase is. Every second I feel hotter. And with his palm pressing against my most sensitive area, a sweat breaks out along my skin so suddenly, I moan into the air and throw my head back to breathe.

He rocks his palm against my heat, and presses his hardened cock into my thigh. His stubble scratches along my neck and the sensation pushes me closer and closer until the all-consuming need throws me off the edge of my release.

"Spread your legs wider," he commands, pulling my thighs farther apart and I obey.

Breathless still with the waves of pleasure rocking through me, my nails dig into the bedsheets as I wait for him to settle between my hips.

There isn't an ounce of hesitation at having him between my legs after touching me like that.

The warmth of the high is still wrapped around me, making the small touches he gives me trace pleasure on my skin. "Are you expecting your period?" His question quickly changes that.

My lungs lurch and I'm quick to push him off of me.

"Fuck." Embarrassment rages in my heated cheeks and I climb off the bed as I snag my clothes, keeping my legs closed tight.

I can't look at him as I scatter to the bathroom, flicking on the light and digging through the basket in the cabinet under the sink. *Damn it. Damn it, damn it, damn it.*

I haven't had many sexual partners and it's been years since I've had a boyfriend, but the last time something like this happened, I stained the sofa cushion of my high school fling. The hollowness that comes with a dry throat and embarrassing memories takes over as I find a thin liner that will have to do for this moment.

I'm sitting there taking care of it all, feeling foolish and wondering if my period is why I've been so emotional and tired and down and unable to think right.

"Are you all right?" Jase's voice comes from outside the bathroom and I prepare to face him.

Opening the door to see him standing there, a small trail of hair leading down and drawing my eyes to the edge of the boxer briefs he slipped on, makes me that much more self-conscious. "I'm sorry."

"It's fine." His expression is easy, but the way he bites the edge of his lip and lets his gaze linger makes me feel anything but. "It's good you got it. We've been reckless."

I hesitate to respond when I look over his shoulder and see he's changed the sheets.

"Thank you for…" Closing my eyes and swallowing tightly, I fail to say the rest out loud.

"It's fine. Do you need anything?"

He leans against the doorjamb, not taking his eyes off of me. When he crosses his arms, his muscles become taut and I find myself feeling hot all over again.

I need my something. I need it more than anything.

A hint of worry crosses his expression when I don't answer him.

"I don't want to lose what we're building, Bethany. I don't want to lose you."

"Then don't."

⟨♡⟩⟨♡⟩

Jase

I couldn't give two shits about her period.

I couldn't give two shits about her wanting to leave yesterday.

All I care about right now is pressing my body against hers, ravaging her, hearing those soft sounds slip from her lips. I'm still hard for her, still needing to feel her, to remind her how good it is.

"Strip down… all the way." With the simple command she stares up at me, her chest rising and falling heavily. Her hair is a messy halo and her hazel eyes are in disarray.

Leaning forward and bending down enough to whisper at the shell of her ear I say, "Don't make me tell you twice, my fiery girl."

Her eyes close and her head falls back instinctively. Like the good girl she is, her hands move to the button on her pants just as I unhook her bra through her shirt.

"You make me weak," she whispers.

"You do the same to me." No confession has ever felt so sinful to be spoken.

"You want to know why I want you?" I ask her, watching her undress and then stepping out of my boxer briefs to stroke my cock. "I can't get those little sounds you make out of my mind. They're addictive."

Her pale skin turns a bright red, flushing from her chest up to the temples of her hairline.

"You're beautiful, you're innocent in ways I find challenging, and a fighter in ways I respect." I've never thought about it like this before. I've never considered the specifics, and the statement forms itself as I take her nipple between my fingers and pull gently to direct her to the shower.

With a twist of the faucet and then the splash of hot water, steam billows toward us.

"You want to know why I want you?" she questions me as I grip her ass, one cheek in each hand and pull her up to me before stepping into the shower with her.

She gasps from the contrast of the hot water and the cold tile as I press her against the wall, but still keep us under the stream.

The warm water flows over my skin and it feels like heaven. Being cleansed and still having her in my grasp must be what heaven is like.

"Why?" I groan the word in the crook of her neck and then let my teeth drag down her skin, just to feel her squirm.

"Because you make me feel alive. You make me feel like everything matters and yet, nothing but you does."

I have to pull away to look down at her. Her hair's darker and wet, slick against her flushed skin.

Looking up at me through her thick lashes, I bring my lips just millimeters from hers and tell her, "You're damn right, nothing but us matters." Then I slam myself inside of her, letting her scream in pleasure in the hot stream. Her nails dig into my skin as I thrust inside of her, loving the feel of her tightening around my cock as she gets closer and closer.

Steadying her in my grasp, I keep my pace ruthless and deep as she bites into my shoulder to muffle her screams. I'd admonish her, forcing her to let me hear all the sweet noises she makes, but the hint of pain makes the pleasure that much more intense.

So I fuck her harder, silently begging her to bring me more of both the pleasure and the pain.

CHAPTER
8

Bethany

"ANYTHING YOU WANT, IS YOURS."

"You make big promises," I tell Jase as I follow him down the end of the hall. He keeps calling it a "wing" though. He says it's his wing of the estate.

Makeup sex is a real thing. There must be something special that happens to your brain when you have makeup sex. I'm convinced of it. I bet a decade of research could prove a thing or two to support that thought.

The kind of makeup sex that leaves you sore the day after. The kind of sore I am now.

"Anything within reason. Does that make you feel better?" he asks with a grin growing on his face. I can't help but to reach up and brush my thumb against his jaw.

He tells me lowly, "I need to shave," before I can sneak a small kiss that makes me rise up onto my tiptoes. A deep groan of satisfaction comes from his chest when I kiss him again.

"I like the stubble," I comment softly as we stop at the entrance to what looks like a library, one that's worthy of a museum. The antique weapons housed on a bookshelf full of creased leather spines and unique coverings draw me in.

Wow doesn't do it justice.

"The fireplace is real. It's from a castle in Ireland," he says as he walks to it on the other side of the room while my fingers trail down a set of old books with red covers. "Not like the glass one in the other room."

"Fireplaces seem to be your thing," I speak without really thinking about the words as my gaze drifts from one shelf to the next. "You like to read?" He nods. "And collect weapons?" I tilt my head at the knives on display. The bottoms of the blades have rust that extends to the handles.

"Yes," he answers and reaches out to gently caress my hip as I lean against him. The more I touch him, the more he touches me. Tit for tat, like all things with us.

"Where's your desk?" I ask, noting how it looks like a combination of a sitting room and office. "There should be a desk in here." The room has a primitive air to it, dark and cavernous with a large rug on the floor and walls covered with shelves.

"My office is at the bar. Not here. This is just for me." I lift my fingers from the books at his last comment until he adds, "And you, if you like it. You can come in here whenever you'd like."

I can imagine listening to the crackles of the fire as I turn the pages of The Coverless Book. "I think I'd enjoy that."

"Good, let me show you the rest."

Today is apparently the day Jase forces me to go on a tour. Between the gym, the cigar room and the billiard room, all three of which look entirely unused and are outfitted with as much dark polished wood as they are wealth, I'm not sure what Jase does as a hobby.

The only room he truly seems to enjoy is the office that's not an office… and the fire room. Which I've already explored with him.

"I love that you call it a fire room," I comment as we pass it, feeling my cheeks heat.

"What would you call it?" he questions and I change the subject before I find myself wanting to go inside of it—the wooden bench room—rather than hear him tell me more stories. It's the intellectual side of him I need to feel safe. Although his touch is just as addictive.

"You said you didn't used to use this gym," I comment, nodding my head toward the last door we passed on the left. The equipment looks virtually brand new.

"I didn't, but lately the other gym has... The women seem to like the main gym."

"The women?" My eyebrow raises on its own.

"Chloe, Addison, Aria, they live in the estate with us. You'll meet them soon, I think."

I don't anticipate the pressure that overwhelms me at the thought. As we walk down the hall toward the foyer which leads to the door separating this wing from the rest of the estate, I drag my fingertips along the wall. All the while thinking how close he must be to his brothers since they live together. Only a hall away.

"So they... they get how it is?" I ask him, watching my feet and wondering if they feel the same way as I do. "Chloe, Addison and..."

"And Aria. Yes. They grew up in this life. They aren't like you." I can't explain why it hurts so much to hear him say it like that. *Not like me.*

"They're your brothers' girlfriends?" I'm quick to keep up the conversation and not let on how I'm feeling.

"No. Declan is single. He's happy being on his own."

"No one's really happy being on their own." I didn't mean to say that out loud.

"You were alone for a long time," he notes.

"I had my work."

"That's still alone."

"I didn't say I was happy." My rebuttal is quick and unfortunate. I'd rather talk about his brothers.

"So one of the three women is..."

It only takes two more steps and a side-eye for Jase to tell me that Chloe is Sebastian's wife and remind me that I met him in the kitchen the other day.

"Right." I nod and try to picture his face again, but I can't. It seems like most of Jase's family has their own little family. I like that. I don't know why I do, but it makes me feel safer still. "What about Seth?"

"He doesn't have a girl... that I know of. I think he has other things in mind," he answers cryptically.

"What do you mean?"

"He's been off."

With a cocked brow, I motion for him to continue.

"He's seeing someone, that's obvious enough. I just don't know who."

"You could ask him."

"That's not the way I go about things."

"Aren't you friends?" Of everyone I've met, Seth's the only person I had mentally filed as a friend of Jase.

"I trust him to the point where it would be hard to think…" He doesn't finish his thought but before I can pry he speaks again. "I don't really have friends, but I'm friendly with him."

"How did you guys meet?"

"Push came to shove a few years back, and he was there, in a spot where he could have done a lot of things. Seth could have ended us— me and my brothers—before we really got started… all because I fucked up." He scratches the back of his neck and even though he's speaking so casually, his expression is hard and unforgiving.

"What did you do?"

"It was at The Red Room. We'd just opened and I let someone in who I shouldn't have. I showed him something that no one's supposed to see." An ominous tone tinges his last statement.

I whisper, "Are you going to tell me what?"

"A basement where I bring people to…"

"To kill." I finish the sentence so he doesn't have to.

"Yes, let's go with kill."

"And what happened?"

"The doors were open, the man saw and took off. None of us were armed as a show of faith, which was fucking stupid. Seth was out there in the parking lot, and he saw us running after him."

"Seth just happened to be there?" I question, not understanding.

"He'd stopped by The Red Room that night, wanting to work with us. We told him no. He came back at just the right time."

"Why couldn't you work with him?"

"He was too… he was too big, too set in his ways. He came from a town where he was the person everyone went to. I don't need someone looking over my shoulder, someone wanting to take command."

"Too many chefs, so to speak."

"Something like that. Anyway, that night he saw, and he could have let the fucker take off. He didn't."

I've been to The Red Room enough to imagine someone bolting from the doors. The forest is close; the highway is even closer. It wouldn't take much to get away if only you got past the parking lot.

"After helping us take care of the body, he told me, *'If you change your mind, I'm good at taking direction,'* or something like that."

"And that convinced you?" I ask him.

"We would have been done if that asshole had gotten out and told the feds what he saw; it turned out that he was undercover. We didn't have the police back then on our payroll. We didn't have much protection. Things were harder then and we needed the help. That's really what it comes down to."

"So you aren't friends then. Simply coworkers who rely on each other?"

"He's more of a friend to Declan. They're closer than we are."

It's quiet as we come to the stairwell and he tells me the upstairs is mostly unfinished. He's never had a reason to complete it.

Taking my hand, he lets his middle finger trail down the lines in my palm. There's a hint of charm and flirtation I'm not expecting. One that breaks the tension, scattering it in any and all directions until it's gone.

"I like touching you," he says faintly.

Something about the ease he feels around me makes me want to stay by him forever. I'm so aware of it in this moment.

So aware, that it's frightening. With every breadcrumb of information Jase gives me, I fall deeper in love with him. Even if the pieces are perverse and disturbing... maybe more so because of it. Even if I wake up tonight like I have the past few nights, breathless and covered with a cold sweat, dreaming about the darkness I know is inside of him... even then. The fear is still there, but love is stronger. Which is why I'd fall back asleep next to him, willing my eyelids to shut and show me something sweeter.

"Ask me something," Jase offers.

The memories of everything that's happened flicker through my mind as I search for a question, and one is most apparent. A detail I've yet to tell him.

"Do you know anyone who wears white sneakers with a red stripe down the sides?"

His brow pulls together as he turns to look at me. "Why?" he asks.

I have to pull my hand away, feeling too hot, yet cold at the same time to tell him.

"When my house was broken into, that's all I saw from where I was hiding in the cabinet."

"White sneakers with a red stripe?" he clarifies.

"Right down the center, from front to back on the sides."

"Why haven't you told me this sooner? Is it all you saw? You're sure?" The questions hold an edge to them. Not anger, not resentment, more like an edge of failure and I hate it.

"I'm sorry… I just didn't know."

"You didn't know if you could trust me." He completes the statement for me and I nod. "I'm sorry," is all I can say, feeling like I've failed him.

With his hand brushing against my jaw, I lean into his touch and close my eyes, reveling in it.

"If I could start our story over and start it differently, I would. I want you to know that."

There's so much I'd change if I could. But then I wonder what our story would look like if it hadn't started so intensely.

"How many women have you done this to?"

"Done what?" he asks.

"Brought back here. Showed off this place to… told your deepest, darkest secrets?"

"None. You're the only one, cailín tine." His nickname for me still makes my stomach do little flips in a way that excites me.

"You've never called anyone else that?" I tease him and he nips my neck in admonishment while wrapping his hands around my waist and letting them slip lower.

"Never. You're my only fiery girl."

He's so consumed with lust in the moment, but there's something nagging at me, something that feels off.

"Why don't I believe you?" My question pulls him out of the moment.

"Because you see my sins, however many of them, and you've

judged me guilty of them all." The honesty of it stares back at me from the depths of his dark eyes. "If you'll lie, you'll cheat... if you'll cheat..." He doesn't continue and I bring my lips to his even though pain etches its way between us. "Even a saint has to start somewhere... I'll never be a saint though. If I could change for you, change this life, this world, our pasts, I would. But it's not going to happen. I can't start our story over."

I kiss him again, feeling the heat between us, feeling his hard lips soften as I press mine against his. I finally answer him, "I know." And then remind him, "I'm not asking you to."

When Jase tries to take me back to his bedroom, I tell him no. Instead I lead him to the plush rug in his office that's not an office. I ask him to light the fire and I slowly undress, watching both hunger and flames in his eyes once the fire's ignited.

I pick the knife I want him to use on me and I lie down without a weighted blanket at my feet, without cuffs, without rope this time, although I tell him I miss the rough feeling when it's all over.

We're both moths to each other's flames, ignited by our touch. We're drawn together, destroyed together. It used to scare me, but there's no fighting it. *Isn't that what love is?*

You can say chemistry was never our problem. Take away the drugs, his brothers, the feeling of loss and betrayal, and all that's left is the simple truth that's he's mine and I'm his. In the most primitive way, we make perfect sense. We're drawn to one another in a way where nothing else matters. It all fades to a blur when I stare into his eyes.

But that's where the problem truly lies. He wasn't meant for my world and I wasn't meant for his. Everything else matters with him in a world where every step is dangerous, and we should have accounted for that. I'll never be able to escape Jase Cross or his merciless world.

This attraction will never allow it.

❦

Jase

The light of the fire dances across her skin in the darkness, and the shadows from the flame beckon me to touch her. The sight of the dip in her waist is an image that would start wars. Her breathing is steady in her deep sleep and part of me wants to leave her here, resting on her side on the luxurious rug with the only covers being the warmth of the raging fire. The other part wants to have her again in my bed.

The low hum of a vibration steals my attention. My muscles stretch with a beautiful pain as I pull myself away from Bethany and get my phone. Still naked and still hungry for more of her and the promise of keeping her here, I check my messages.

It's a text from Seth, just the person I need to speak with.

Anger has a way of destroying the calm, even when Bethany stirs with a feminine sigh in her sleep. Her hand reaches right where I just was and it seals her fate.

I text Seth back. *Meet me first thing tomorrow. We have things to discuss.*

CHAPTER
9

Bethany

I T ONLY TAKES ONE DEEP BREATH IN THE MASSIVE KITCHEN AND A LONG stretch of my back to release the tension from last night. Things are better. It feels like a huge step forward, but something's still holding me back. The nightmares haven't stopped; they've only changed.

Last night, my mother reminded me that everyone I loved would die before me and that it was okay. It's not the first time I've dreamed about being back at the home, with my mother looking me directly in the eyes and telling me what felt like a message from death. The terror gripped me the same way she did all those years ago. It was like I was back there, but not really. We were on my porch and I couldn't move. I couldn't speak either. My sister came to help me, ripping our mother away and yelling at her, screaming at her. It was so unlike her, but somehow I believed it.

When they were done fighting with each other, my sister turned to me and looked me in the eyes. She said my mother was right. They would all die before me.

That's when I woke up. At 5:00 a.m. in the morning, in an empty bed that held the faint, masculine scent of Jase Cross.

I can walk around pretending I'm not uneasy, but I've never been good with pretending.

As my gaze falls to the slick counters and I hear the thump of footsteps getting louder, cuing someone's incoming arrival, I put away my thoughts of my family, or what used to be family.

Carter's deep voice reverberates in the expansive space. "Bethany."

His gaze is narrowed and even harsh. Even the air around him warns me not to mess with the man. Some men are just like that; the feel of danger comes with their strong posture and chiseled jaw.

"Cross," I answer him tersely with a cocked brow.

I find myself comparing him to Jase, but even though they look alike, Jase is nothing like him. He's charming and approachable in a way I don't think I'll ever find Carter to be.

An asymmetric grin pulls at his lips. "Funny you should call me Cross when you're with my brother and he's also a Cross."

"Suits you though."

He huffs a short chuckle and lets the smile grow as I pull the fridge door open, searching for a can of Coke or something with caffeine in it. "Something funny?" I ask him.

There's a case of Dr. Pepper and the hint of a smile appears on my face too. It's been a while since I've had one of these and they're in glass bottles… that makes it even better.

"You aren't the only one who thinks that."

"Thinks what?" I ask him genuinely, already forgetting what I'd said before as I'm too distracted by my beverage.

"Nothing." He shrugs it off and goes to the cabinet, pulling out a box of tea bags and a pretty mug with owls on it. I nearly tease him, taunt him for the girly mug, even though I know it must be for his wife. I bite my tongue and stifle the playful thoughts as I prepare to go somewhere else and stay out of Carter's way. This isn't my house and he isn't my family. I'm more than aware of that.

I only get one step away though before Carter speaks with his back to me, putting a mug of water in the microwave. "Spring will be here soon," he tells me.

Stopping in my tracks, I turn rather than look over my shoulder and wait for him to turn as well. He does slowly, awkwardly even with his broad shoulders.

"Why does your face look like that?" he asks me when he takes in what must be a confused expression.

"Is that your attempt at small talk?"

"People like to talk about the weather, Miss Fawn."

It's my turn to let out a huff of a laugh, small and insignificant, but it breaks the tension, one chisel at a time.

"Spring's my favorite season."

"It's Aria's too. Well," he continues talking as he retrieves the mug from the now beeping microwave and sets a bag of tea into the cup. "Spring and fall. She said she can't pick just one."

It doesn't pass my notice that his expression softens when he talks about Aria. The recollection softens something inside of me too.

"How long have you and Aria been together?"

"Just a little while." His answer is… less than informative. Maybe it's a Cross brothers thing.

"I heard she's expecting?"

"That's right." His grin turns cocky and I half expect him to brag about how it happened on the first try or how his swimmers are so strong. Some macho bullshit like that, but it doesn't come.

"Congratulations."

"Thank you."

"Well, I'll let you get to it," I tell him, but he doesn't let the conversation end.

"Jase really likes you." The statement surprises me, holding me where I am.

Warmth flows through me, from my chest all the way to my cheeks. I don't know what to say other than, "I really like him too."

"He's turning back to his emotional… hotheaded younger self."

"Hotheaded?" I pry. Carter doesn't seem to take the bait though.

"When we were younger, he used to be a real troublemaker," Carter says as he leans against the counter, staring into the cup of tea and lifting the bag of leaves. We both watch the steam billow into a swirl of dissipating clouds although I'm across the room.

"Really?" The shock is evident.

"Not because he was… like me. Not that kind of trouble."

If Carter's going to talk, I'm damn well going to listen. Taking a step closer to the counter, I ask him, "What kind of trouble?"

He peers at me, but not for long. "He just couldn't keep his mouth shut. It should have gotten him into more trouble than it did really. I know if I'd done it... My father never hit Jase. I can't remember a single time. He liked the belt and took it out on us mostly, me and Daniel."

A sadness creeps inside of me at the ease with which Carter speaks of his father beating him and his brother. He was the oldest. I'm the youngest, but I remember the way my mother used to yell at my sister for things that I didn't even think were wrong. With parted lips, I grip the edge of the counter, cold and unmoving as he continues. "I remember so many times my father would say to Jase, *your mouth is going to get you in trouble.*"

"Parents sometimes take it out on the eldest."

"If I'd talked like Jase did when we were younger, I'd have been punched in the mouth." Carter's statement doesn't come with emotion. It's merely the way things were for them back then.

"He used to say it like it was. He never had a filter, and couldn't just be quiet. There were so many times he said shit to my father that made my back arch expecting to be hit there. He had the balls to call everyone out on their shit and never stopped for a moment to question what he was saying."

"Honesty without compassion is brutality." I say the quote and then add when Carter looks back at me, "I don't know who said it. It's just a saying."

Standing up straighter, he holds the tea with both hands and tells me, "He was compassionate, too much. That's why he never let a moment pass him where he thought he could change what was happening if he only made people aware of how wrong it was."

It's hard to keep my expression straight. I can only imagine Jase as a young boy, watching everything that happened and speaking up, expecting it to help, when there was never any help coming.

"He used to have hope." My first statement is quiet and I think it goes unheard so I raise my voice. "It sounds like he was a good kid," I comment and Carter's forehead wrinkles with amusement.

"Sure, as good as the Cross boys could ever be."

"You know," I start to say, and that stops him from walking off while I tap the glass base of my Dr. Pepper on the counter. "My sister was like that. When I was growing up and she was in high school and even part of college, she was a lot like that."

"Is that right?" he asks, leaning against one of the stools and listening to my story.

"When our mom got sick, she had Alzheimer's." I have to take a quick sip as the visions of my sister, a younger, healthier version, flood into my mind. Jenny would stand outside the university before every football game and every council meeting with flyers she'd printed from the library. "My sister wanted to educate people. She said it might help them because if you can diagnose it early, it can lessen the symptoms."

I'll never forget how often Jenny stood there after mom was diagnosed. I met her outside the stadium one chilly October night. She had a handful of flyers and tearstained cheeks. She'd been there every night that week, and I wanted her to come home. I needed help. *Mom* needed help.

When I told her to come home, she broke down and cried. She didn't want to go home to a mother who didn't know who she was. She said she blamed herself, because she knew something was wrong and she hadn't said anything. She did nothing when she could have at least spoken up like she would have before she was busy with classes.

All the while she spent her nights standing there, I did what was practical. I listened to Nurse Judy, I figured out the bills and how to pay them all with what we had. I took care of the house and learned how to help any way I could.

My sister looked backward, while I tried to look forward. I think that's where the difference really lay.

"That doesn't sound like mouthing off," Carter comments.

"Maybe that wasn't the best example," I answer under my breath, not seeing the similarity so clearly like I did a moment ago. I find myself lacking, not unlike the way I felt back then. The visions of her that night she cried on the broken sidewalk don't leave me.

"She blames herself then?" Carter asks and I have to blink away the memories.

"Yeah, she did. Blamed," I correct him. "She passed away this past month."

Something strange happens then. The air in the room turns cold and distant as Carter looks away from me.

Some people deal with death differently, but it's odd the way he reacts. He doesn't look back at me. He stares off down the hall and past the kitchen toward his wing of the estate, avoiding my prying gaze.

"I'm sorry," he finally speaks, although he pays close attention to the mug in his hand. His lips part but only to inhale slightly; I think he's going to say more but he doesn't. And then it's silent again.

I don't like it. The little hairs on the back of my neck stand to attention and the uneasiness I felt when I walked into the kitchen greets me again.

"When she died, I inherited her debt and met your brother, so if nothing else…" My voice trails off. *What the fuck am I even saying?*

It's hard to swallow, but I force down a sip of the cold drink and let the taste settle on the back of my tongue where the words all hide. *At least her death led me to Jase.*

Was I really thinking that?

Was I really drawing a positive out of my sister's murder?

"A debt? Did Jase help you out of something?" Carter's dark eyes seek mine and I reach them instantly. Suddenly he's interested.

"The debt my sister owed," I state, feeling a line draw across my forehead as I read his expression. No memory is worn there of the money she owed the Cross brothers. Money Jenny owed to Carter.

Jase blamed Carter, didn't he? He said Carter wouldn't let it go even if Jase wanted to.

"Who did she owe money to?" Carter asks and the wind leaves my lungs in a heavy pull. Drawn from me so violently, that I drop the bottle to the counter with a hard clink.

Jase lied. Staring into Carter's clueless eyes, I see it so clearly now.

He lied to me about the debt.

About my sister owing it.

I thought so poorly of her. That she would owe so much money to men like him.

And he put that on her.

With a sudden twist, my gut wrenches with sickness and I have to focus on breathing just to keep from losing it.

He lied to me. It was all a lie.

How can I believe anything that comes out of his mouth? How many lies has he told me? How many things has he kept from me?

"Where are you going?" Carter's voice carries down the hall, chasing after me and I ignore him. I don't trust myself to speak.

Every step hurts more and more. I've fallen for him. That's the only explanation for the way my face crumples as I storm off. The way my eyes feel hot although there's no fucking way I'll cry. I won't cry for a man who lies to my face over and over again.

I let him touch me. I let him use me. Because he lied about a debt.

I'm foolish. I'm a stupid little girl in his man's world.

"I hate him." The words tumble out in a single breath as my hands form fists. I hate that I believed him. That I fell for him.

No... no I don't. My throat dries at the realization.

I hate that I wanted him to treat me like he loves me. I hate that I believed he did.

You don't lie to the ones you care for. You don't use them.

You don't coerce them and blackmail them.

I thought he loved me though.

Maybe he still does... the small voice whispers. The voice that's gotten me deeper and deeper into bed with a man who tells me lies. A voice I wish would speak louder, because I desperately want it to be speaking the truth. But the rest of me knows it's a childish wish, that I need to grow the fuck up and slap the shit out of Jase's lying mouth.

CHAPTER
10

Jase

"WHAT DID HE SAY SPECIFICALLY?" I QUESTION SETH, comparing notes.

"To meet… to come alone… and that he has evidence he doesn't want to use against us."

Our pace is even as I walk with him from the foyer to the office. I waited for him outside after taking Bethany to bed last night. Watching the late dusk turn to fog in the early morning and preparing for what has to happen today.

I respond, "Officer Walsh is my new favorite person to hate."

"Do you think it has to do with Jenny?" he asks.

"I doubt it. If he has something on us and if he's going to use it to blackmail us…" My teeth clench hard as I release an agitated exhale.

"Do you think you should tell Bethany? In case this leads to something?"

"No." Shaking my head, I think about the way Bethany's going to react when she finds out about her sister being alive and the fact that I knew this whole time. "I want to know I'll be able to bring her back before I tell her anything."

"Marcus will know when we find her. I don't see how he won't know when we approach. Unless it's only a few of us, but that would be suicide."

"We'll all go. He can know. I would think he already knows we've been watching."

He stops walking and the sound of two men walking down a long hall turns to one and then none as I turn to him, waiting for him to speak.

"You think Marcus would go against us?"

"I don't know," I answer him honestly and feel a chill run up my spine. The silver glimmer of the scar on my knuckles shines in the dim hall lighting. "We've never openly been against him, but he's never taken from us either. He has her. He knows we want her back. It was his call to decide that and ours to decide the consequence."

"We don't know that. We don't know how it happened and what she's doing with him."

"There's too much we don't know, but we don't have time to wait. If we find their lookout point or storage centers, or anything at all, we go in." My words are final and Seth's slight nod is in agreement.

With a tilt of his chin, we continue back to the office. Every step I take grows heavier, and the anxiousness of getting down to what we have to discuss stifles the air and coils every muscle in my body.

I force myself to stay calm with my hand on the doorknob to my office, careful not to say anything until he walks in first.

"Did you get it?" I ask him as I flick on the light. It's still early morning and the sky's a dark gray. Pulling back the curtains, the harsh sound of them opening is the only thing to be heard as Seth walks to the row of books on the other side of the room.

Clouds cover the sky, hanging thick and with varied shades of gray. Rain's coming and with it, a darkness that will cover the day.

"I did," he tells me, leaving a book he's eyeing to come to stand where I am and hand me the box.

"What do you think?" I ask him.

"I agree with you," he says simply. "It's why I like working for you."

As I'm inspecting it, he delivers news I didn't think would come so soon. "There may be a room, or tunnel, or shelter of some kind."

He leans his back against the leather chaise, crossing his arms in front of his chest. "The blueprints for the bridge don't show anything. So what's under the bridge is… we don't know."

"You're sure of it?"

He bows his head in acknowledgment. "We've kept an eye on the people associated with Jenny being taken. They're out there, making these rounds and going to the same spots. Last night, one disappeared. Nik was watching him, and then he was gone. There has to be some hideout there we haven't yet found."

Slipping the box into my pocket, I ask him, "Did he do surveillance?"

"Not yet." Uncrossing his arms, he slips his hands into his pants pockets and glances at the unlit fireplace before turning back to me. "I wasn't sure how you wanted to proceed."

"You seem distracted," I tell him, rather than giving orders. It could be a setup. It could be suicide. Carter should know before we decide anything.

"Me?" he questions.

"You didn't think I'd noticed?"

His answer is to tilt his head. With a cluck of his tongue, he pushes off the chaise and walks to the bookshelf before confiding in me. "We're distracted for the same reasons, I think."

Every hair stands on end at the thought of him being distracted by Bethany. The skin across my knuckles stretches and turns white as I crack them with my thumb, one by one and consciously resist forming a fist.

"What reason is that?" I ask and my voice is low.

"A girl."

"Bethany?" I question and now my tone is threatening.

"She's yours and I have mine."

"So you are seeing someone?" I ask him and the edge of jealousy seeps away, although not as easily as it came.

Instead of answering, he suggests, "You should take Bethany to the graveyard. I think it'd be good for you two."

"You're good at distraction," I comment as I eye him moving down the rows of books he's seen before.

"You go there often..." he pauses before continuing, seeming to struggle with how he wants to say what's on his mind. Choosing a new book, one I recognize by the distinctive spine, he tells me, "I almost took her there when I picked her up a few days ago. Thought you could meet her there, but then I got your message."

"Why would she want to go there?"

"She's empathetic. She reacts to emotion. If she saw the end result of what you've been through... it makes things more real. To see loss."

"She knows what a graveyard looks like. She's been there herself a time or two."

"She hasn't though. She didn't go to her sister's funeral. I don't know about her mother's either. She was working a lot back then."

The fact that Seth knows this and I don't makes me feel a certain way; I hate him for it, but I'm grateful for the message. We work differently, we see things differently. I could have never imagined it'd work so well for so long.

"I have to tell you something before I forget." Tapping my fingers along the hard walnut shelves, I let my gaze stray down the shelves. "You need to get rid of your shoes."

"What?" His surprise is met with a huff of humor. "Now you're going with the distraction method," he jokes although he's still waiting for me to explain what the hell I'm talking about.

"The ones you wore when you went to check on Bethany. When she thought there was a break-in."

"I don't even know what shoes they were."

"White with red stripes on the sides," I answer him and finally make my way to take a seat. "She saw them, so it's best to get rid of them." As I sit down, I focus on the box, thinking about it rather than Seth and the fact that Bethany saw his shoes.

"Fuck." Seth closes the book in his hand with a thwack, lowering his head and shaking it. "That could have ended badly."

"If she didn't tell me, I imagine it would have if she'd seen you in them."

"Are you going to tell her it was Marcus or Romano or some random burglars or what?"

"She's too smart to think it was random." Leaning my head back, I close my eyes and hate the way all this started. "I don't know," I answer him. "One fucking lie after the next with her."

A creaking sound snaps my eyes to the open door of the office.

The dim light behind her places a shadow of contempt across her hurt gaze and pouty lips. Her small hands are balled into fists gripping the hem of her gray sweater. Even enraged, she's in pain. It's etched into every detail of her. *Fuck.*

"Bethany." Her name tumbles from my mouth as I stand up, feeling the thrum of disaster in my blood.

CHAPTER
11

Bethany

"I CAN EXPLAIN," JASE REPEATS AS HE ROUNDS THE WORN LEATHER chair. Through my blurry vision I can barely make out Seth backing away from both of us as I stalk into the room.

I'm shaking, trembling, on the verge of a rage I didn't know was possible.

"I hate you," I sneer and how my words come out so clearly, I'll never know. They strike him, visibly, across the face as he stops with both hands up a foot away from me.

"What did you hear?" he asks me calmly and I want to spit at him. I can already see him spinning a new lie in his head, just waiting to know what I heard so he can manipulate it. Betrayal is a nasty thing, twisting a knife deeper into my rib cage.

All I can remember is how I felt standing in the threshold of my kitchen, too afraid to speak or move, and knowing I had nowhere to run. "It was Seth? It was your men all along?"

My vision blurs with the present and the past.

"I sent him to check on you. I was with Carter and Aria; I couldn't come so I sent Seth."

"Seth crept into my house. It was Seth." I repeat it and I still can't believe it. I can't believe it's true.

"He was only going to stay with you because I thought someone was threatening you--"

"Someone?" I question, feeling raging tremors run through me. Even now, he hides from me.

"It doesn't matter--"

"The fuck it doesn't!" I scream out of nowhere, shocking both of us.

"It's all right." I can hear Seth but I don't dare rip my eyes away from Jase.

"Get out," Jase gives his partner in crime the command and I listen to his heavy footsteps as he leaves. I can't even look him in the face. He didn't come just to stay with me, that's bullshit. It's all bullshit.

"Who?" I demand.

"Marcus." Jase's chest rises higher and falls deeper, moving slower as he tries to stay calm and collected. I take a step to my right, and he takes a step to his left.

"So you sent your men?"

"Seth said you weren't there, that you took off or something happened. So I sent every man I had."

"He didn't knock. He didn't try calling me or saying my name when he walked in." Shaking my head, I deny the innocence that he's trying to portray.

"He thought he may have frightened you into hiding."

I complete the series of events for him. "You thought that would be good. Scare me into your arms." My glare lifts to the specks of gold in his dark eyes. "You thought it would be easier to convince me, didn't you?"

I can hear the deep inhale he takes as he sucks in a breath. "I made a mistake."

"*One fucking lie after the next with her.*" I repeat the words he used before he knew I was outside the door with a taunting flourish. "How many lies, Jase?"

He doesn't answer me; he merely steps closer. "Can you even remember how many you told?" My voice gets louder with each question. Still, he doesn't answer.

"How about the debt? I just found out Carter never knew about it."

Jase doesn't react, he doesn't falter, still hiding behind a hard façade.

"Are you going to say there was truth to that? That my sister did what? What do you want to say she did, what did she do to rack up that debt? Tell me all the horrible things she did."

I can't explain how the pain flows; the best way to describe it is to say it's like a river flowing over jagged rocks. "You'll never know how much it hurt me to think she'd done something horrible to have a debt like that." I can't even speak the sentence clearly as I brace myself on the furniture.

"I'm sorry."

"So it was a lie too?"

"Yes."

"And the break-in? It was all you all along?"

"Yes."

With heated cheeks and a prick at the back of my eyes, I remember how I fell out of the cabinet that night and called for him. I remember how awful I felt the next day for ever thinking poorly of him.

How stupid I was. All I am with him is a step behind and foolish.

"You held me after. You *knew* and you held me after." I feel sick. My body leans to the left as my head spins and the bastard dares to reach for me.

"Get the fuck off," I say as I shove him away with every ounce of strength I have. It does nothing but push me backward, hitting the chaise and brushing my elbow against the leather. "Stay the fuck away from me," I grit out with disdain, pointing a finger at his chest.

He walks right into it. My finger is now touching his chest.

It's the lack of respect for my boundaries. This is the last fucking time I let him disrespect me.

His chest is like a brick wall, hard and unmoving, even after I slam my fist into it. My throat feels raw as I scream and the sides of my hands spasm with agony as I beat them against his chest over and over. "Get away from me!" Tears stream down my face in an oh-so-familiar path.

I hate it. I hate it all.

I hate the way it hurts. I hate that he did it.

I hate that I know he'd do it again, no matter how much he insists that he'd start the story over if he could. He'd do it the same way each and every time, because he doesn't trust me to love him.

"I hate you," I scream at him and his idiocy. "Stay away from me!"

Jase doesn't try to hold me back or stop me. He simply watches me lose it. The look on his face is one I recognize and it only makes my heart hurt more.

When our patients don't want to admit they're not okay but they're struggling to do anything at all we tell them, sometimes you have to break. You have to let it out, you have to feel it, you have to move through it even if you're a sobbing mess the entire time.

Sometimes a good cry or screaming session to let the anger and sorrow out is unavoidable.

Sometimes you have to break, even if you know you won't be put back together when you get to the other side of it all.

My body feels heavy as I drop to the floor on my knees. Struggling with the weight of it all. I can feel his hands on me, his grip to stay close to him, but I ignore it.

How many times have I held on to someone just as Jase is and told them to do it, to let it all out? To break apart. Not because you want to, not even to make anything better. Simply because you have to.

"You're a monster." The statement swells as it leaves me, strangling me as it goes.

Still, Jase holds on to my wrists.

The smooth wood is cold and I just want to lay my heated face against it. To let it all out, but Jase is there, not leaving me alone.

"I had to," he says and the statement is stretched with desperation.

I can barely swallow at this point, let alone speak.

There's no use fighting his grip on me; he's stronger. There's no use trying to wipe my eyes, since the tears keep coming.

"I didn't mean to hurt you," he whispers once I've stopped altogether, just feeling every piece of me shatter.

He didn't mean to, but he did it anyway.

"I didn't want to lie to you," he says and his voice is calming as he brings me into his lap.

He didn't want to, yet he did.

A heave of sorrow erupts from inside of me as I realize I didn't want to love him, but I did. I didn't want to trust him, but I did.

"There are very few things that a person has to do," I whisper against his shirt, staring at the crack of light under the door. "You *chose* to do that to me. You *chose* to lie and scare me to get me to do what you wanted. You *chose* to manipulate me."

The gentle rocking is paused and it's then that I realize how hot I am, leaning against him and I try to pull away. This time he lets me.

The irony is that all he had to do was ask or even tell me. I was so desperate for someone and something. Him scaring me had nothing to do with it. "You didn't have to do it."

"I told you, I told you if I could start it over, I would." His voice is low, but has an edge of anguish.

"You didn't tell me why though," I say and lift my head to look him in the eyes, finding my own reflection staring back at me. Crumpled and weak, just how he sees me. "You didn't tell me it's because you lied to me every step of the way."

"There are reasons."

"There's no reason good enough."

"I couldn't let you go."

"It's not your decision to make." Every response from me turns colder and more absolute. Inside I'm on fire, the blaze of hate destroying everything that made me feel alive with Jase Cross. It rages in my mind, changing the memories, making me feel like they weren't real.

It was all a lie.

"You wanted me to marry you and weeks ago you fed me one lie after another so I'd do what you want."

"Bethany," he pleads with me.

"I told you I loved you and you made me feel like you loved me too." My brow pinches together as I wipe violently under my eyes. "How could you when you knew it was all a lie?"

"Bethany, don't. It's not like that--"

"But it is! That's exactly what it's like!"

Placing both of his hands on my shoulder, he tries to console me as if he's the man who should be doing that. "It's over with now, it's better now."

"I never want to see you again." As I speak the words, my heart splits in two. I feel it slice cleanly, seemingly fine, then bleeding out in a single beat. "I have to protect myself and you keep hurting me. You won't stop." I hate that my bottom lip wobbles. I hate that I believe what I'm saying.

I hate that it's the truth. "If you need me to behave some type of way, you'll lie to me. You'll pull strings and make me do what you say."

My head shakes at the idea, hating what he's done and wanting to deny it; Jase's shakes on its own, but for different reasons I imagine, because he knows I'm telling the truth. I'm not the one who's lied. Feeling my resolve, I push myself up off the floor, ready to leave him. Preparing to piece myself back together and lick my wounds, but he stops me with one statement.

"Marcus has Jenny." Jase's voice is low, the words coming from deep in his chest.

Jenny?

"How dare you." I have no air in my lungs. No will to do anything but slap him. Hard and fast, leaving a red mark and forcing his head to whip to the side. "You don't get to use her against me. You don't get to manipulate me with her *ever again!*" I scream in his face and then clench my teeth together when he grabs my wrists as he pins me to him, restraining my elbows so I can't hit him, so I can't move. All I can do is look in his eyes.

"She's still alive, Bethany," he whispers and it's so compelling.

I want nothing more than to believe him. To believe the liar who's already brought shame to her memory.

"She's dead." A fresh flood of tears threatens to fall, but I won't let him see them. He doesn't get to be there for me. Not again. I pull away from his grasp, ripping my arm away so I can free myself.

The bright red handprint against his cheek is still there. "She's alive. We have a video of her with a man after the funeral. After the trunk was discovered."

"With Marcus?" I can barely remain upright. She's alive. I'm so cold. A freezing wave flows over my skin. *She's alive.*

Hope makes my body tremble.

"A different man. He's dead, but we have an idea where he's keeping her."

"Where who is keeping her?"

"Marcus."

I'm so confused, so consumed by questions, but one begs to be answered. "How long have you known?"

Silence. The silence is my answer.

"I have never hated you more," I speak when he doesn't. Swallowing thickly and feeling a spiked ball form in my throat, I continue. "You saw what that did to me. How could you watch me mourn her death…" I have to stop and breathe in deep.

"Because I love you… I didn't want to tell you if I couldn't save her."

"So you can save her now?" I question him, focused on my sister before realizing what he said.

I love you.

"You're telling me all this now because we've fallen apart." I speak the unforgiving truth. "Not because you can save her." *And not because you truly love me.* I keep that bit to myself.

"I'm trying. We have a plan. I didn't want to tell you until I knew for sure."

"You're sure she's alive?" Jenny. My sister's face plays in my mind and I have to cover my own. *Please, God. Let her be alive.*

"As of two weeks ago, yes."

Two weeks. Two weeks is so long. Too long. Please, God.

"Will you save her for me?" I beg him, looking up at him and praying for him to do just that. Even if he doesn't love me. Even if he lies to me a million times more until the day I can see her again. "I'll do anything," I confess and my voice cracks.

"I'm doing my best. It's the first time we've ever tracked anything that has to do with Marcus."

I have never felt more at his mercy and more alone than in this moment. I don't know what to believe or what to do. It's too much.

"I'm breaking, Jase. I can feel myself slowly breaking down and I can't stop it. Don't take advantage of me. Don't do this to me. I'm not okay."

"I'm not taking advantage of you."

"Then don't say you love me if you really don't. It's not fair. Because I do love you. I hate you right now and we're not okay, but I love you." I don't know how I'm even able to speak, since the sudden rush of emotions are warring with each other at the back of my throat.

Jase struggles to hide his as well. "I don't love you, is that what you want to hear?"

"Don't do that. Don't use what we used to have." My finger raises as I yell at him, my voice cracking. *He loves me.*

Heaving in a breath with the intensity growing in his eyes his own voice trembles as he says, "Whether you believe it or not, I love you and you're staying here."

With an exhale and then another, a calmer one, his expression softens as he waits for me. He's waiting for me to say it again and I know he is. "Everything I've done is for you. I love you, cailín tine."

"I don't want you to call me that right now." I stop him with the statement, not knowing what to believe. Adrenaline is coursing through my body. Fight or flight taking over. He won't let me leave and he's the only one left to fight. "Of everything I learned today, the only thing that I can focus on right now is that my sister is still alive."

"I know. And I'm here for you." He tries again to appeal to the side of me that's still holding on to hope for us. I'm ashamed to admit that side still exists.

"How could you watch me cry for her and accept her death when you knew she was alive? I can't even stomach the thought."

"I'm sorry."

"Do you expect to say you're sorry and I simply forgive you?" I throw his own words back in his face. "Words are meaningless."

"You can't leave me when we fight." He says the words like they're a truth that's undeniable. Like nothing else matters.

"Lying to me isn't the same as fighting. And what you lied about… I'm not okay." Pulling away from him, I feel the chill in the air. "Nothing about this is okay."

My legs feel weak when I stand and he tries to right me, but I do it myself.

"I'm going to the guest room." I give him my final words. The only ones I have for him in this moment. "Don't lock me in and don't trap me. But leave me the hell alone for right now."

Loneliness is a horrible companion, but it's the one I need right now. I think about messaging Laura, but I'm still pissed at her. Instead, I sit on the bed and look out of the window. Just to think. Just to break down again. All alone.

Does he know the nightmares he's given me? The hate I feel for myself knowing I'd said goodbye to my sister, even though I still felt her presence. I knew I shouldn't have, that it was too soon.

Shame is what comes for me when the loneliness no longer matters.

I don't hear the door open and I don't hear Seth walk in until he speaks from across the room. "Are you all right?"

Lifting my head from my folded arms, I glance over my shoulder. I'm certain I look like a wreck, with my knees pulled into my chest so I'm merely a ball of limbs staring out a window.

"What do you think?" I ask him.

"I know you hate me--"

"I don't hate you."

"Well, I know you're mad at me, and I'm sorry."

"Okay." The petty answer leaves me instantly. I'll be damned if I'm simply going to forgive him in this moment.

The bed dips and I turn back to Seth, warning him to get the hell out. "I'd like to be alone."

"Just one thing." Although it's a statement, he says it like it's a question.

With a nod, I agree to hear him out.

"He lied to you, he does that," Seth tells me easily, like there's nothing wrong at all with it. "He made mistakes he's not used to. He decided to do things he shouldn't have." There's a rhythm to his voice that's calming. I fall for it, listening to every word he says. "He's not the only person I've ever met that lies to make other people feel better."

"He could say he's sorry," I counter as if a simple "sorry" would make much of a difference. Then I remember... he did. He said he was sorry. I don't remember for which part. Maybe all of it. He was right though, words are meaningless.

"He's not. He'd do it again if he had to." I'd be pissed off if Seth wasn't so matter of fact and if I wasn't so convinced already that what he's saying is the absolute truth.

"Then why should I ever trust him again?" That's really what it comes down to. I don't know that I can believe him or trust him ever again.

"Because he's trying to be a better man... for you. He's done all of this, *for you*."

I try to respond, to disagree. But I can't. Intention matters and be-hind all of this, he wanted to keep me safe. He tells me one last thing as he makes his way out.

"You know he loves you." Seth sounds so sure of it. "Just love him back." With that he shuts the door, not waiting for a response.

CHAPTER
12

Jase

"I'D SAY SHE'S PISSED," I COMMENT IN THE DARK NIGHT AS I SHUT MY car door. I fucking hate that I'm not there now, just in case she wants to talk or yell… even if she wants to hit me again.

"I'd say she has a right to be." Glaring at Seth's profile, I note that he doesn't look back at me until he adds, "She loves you, though." When his eyes reach mine, I look ahead instead.

He changes the subject to ask, "You ready for this?"

It's bitter cold as the clear, glassy surface of the puddle beneath my boot is shattered. I don't hesitate to take another step and another. Moving quickly through the harsh wind to the warehouse.

"No one's ever ready for this shit."

"I don't like not knowing what to expect," Seth comments, and it's only then that I notice how tense he seems.

"Whatever happens in there, we'll figure it out," I assure him. "Follow my lead."

"I'm not sure I'm the best at that, Boss."

"You've always been the best."

"Not at following… I like lists and control and knowing what to do. If you're telling me that you don't know, I'm telling you I might not follow."

There's always been direction. Always been a sense of right and wrong and a certain way to do things. Recently though, everything has been like walking through fog.

"Whatever you do," I finally answer him, "don't point your gun at me. Aim it at the prick who brought us here."

With a huff of a laugh he tells me, "I'll try to remember that."

Pushing open the double doors, I feel every muscle in my body coil, ready to act. Bright light greets us instantly, blinding me momentarily. It only makes the adrenaline in my blood pump harder and faster.

"We've been waiting for you." Officer Cody Walsh's voice reverberates in the large empty space. Blood rushes in my ears as I take in the man who's been like a dog with a bone ever since he arrived in town.

There's no back room or secret entrances in the empty warehouse. The ceilings have to be twenty feet high and the room itself is vacant, all 1200 square feet of it. With the exception of a steel shelf on the back wall and several stacks of old metal chairs behind Officer Walsh and another man I've never seen before, there's nothing here. Nowhere for anyone else to hide. That doesn't mean there aren't cameras.

"Good to see you again, Officer," I speak and other than my voice, the only sounds are the large fans spinning above us as we walk to them, slowly closing the distance. Seth stays back slightly, letting me lead the way.

Officer Walsh is in jeans and a black leather jacket, nothing like his typical attire, save the expression on his face.

"Undercover tonight?" Seth mutters beneath his breath, although it's a joke—there's a serious hint of a smirk there—and I share a quick glance with him. All of the FBI cases we could find on Walsh are sealed, except for one case. The one that has information on Marcus as well. His files were squeaky clean, with numerous medals and honors, referrals. But not a damn thing about undercover work. Anyone could spot him as a cop. He'd die in a week out here if he pulled that shit.

Our boots smack off the cement floor as my eyes adjust to the fluorescent lighting and we get closer to the two of them.

The other man is younger. Maybe in his thirties, or late twenties. In dark gray sweats and a long-sleeve black Henley, he would come off as relaxed if he didn't keep looking between Cody Walsh and the two of us.

"I don't think we've met," I address the other man, and the moment he opens his mouth to greet me, Officer Walsh whips up his gun to the side of the man's head and fires.

The racing of my heart isn't quite as fast as I am to pull my gun from its holster. With both hands on the steel in my hands, I stare at Walsh pointing the barrel at the unsuspecting man beside him. If Walsh sees my gun and Seth's aimed at him, he doesn't react, he only watches the man to his left. The dead man falls to his knees, his eyes dead and vacant with a rough bullet hole leaking blood down his face. Walsh continues to focus on him until finally, the man falls face-first onto the floor with a dull thud.

"I was wondering when you were going to get here so I could kill him," Walsh admits, his eyes watching the bright red blood pool around the nameless man's face.

Our pistols are still on him and he only seems to notice now.

"I wouldn't if I were you. If I don't make it back to the office and pull the tapes out of the mail room, all the evidence will be dispersed."

Seth's gaze sears into me. I can hear the soles of his shoes scrape against the ground as he shuffles his feet although his gun is still up.

Keeping myself calm, I lower the gun and shrug as if I'm unaffected. "I didn't take you for a man who liked the dramatic."

Officer Walsh is a man who's strictly by the book. That's everything we found on him. Clean record and a man who believes in black and white with no grays in between. This… this is to throw us off. It can't be his normal.

"I didn't take you for a man who liked being late."

"You killed him because we were late?" Seth questions. He lets a hint of humor ease into his tone, but his gun still sits at his side.

It's only then that Officer Walsh takes his gaze from me and focuses on Seth.

"No. I shot him because I don't need him and he knows too much."

"Good to know that's how you do business." Seth's criticism is rewarded with a tilt of Walsh's head.

"What's his name?" I question.

"It doesn't matter." Walsh looks between the two of us, making me second-guess his plan of action.

"It does to us," Seth speaks for me, and I don't mind in the least, since the same words were going to come out of my mouth. I want to know everything about the dead man lying on the floor. What he did, who he worked for, and most importantly: why he was standing beside Walsh in the first place?

"Joey Esposito."

"Anything else we should know about him?" Seth asks and Walsh simply stares at him. I didn't come here for a pissing contest.

"What do you want?" I speak loud and clearly, breaking up whatever's starting between the two of them.

"To share two things with you. Both of them are pieces of information I think you'll find valuable," he says and then nudges the leg of the dead man on the floor. It's a dull prod with no emotion behind it, just enough to be noticed. "He worked for Romano."

Just hearing the name *Romano* raises the small hairs on the back of my neck. I feel my eyes narrow but other than that, I keep my composure. Seth does the same. Remaining still, unmoving. Unbothered.

That's more like him.

"I'll hand over the whereabouts of Romano freely. I'd prefer for you…" he pauses to glance at Seth before adding, "the two of you, to know that I'm willing to negotiate."

"Handing something over for free isn't a part of negotiations. Negotiations require something in return." Seth corrects him and I have to fight the grin that plays at my lips.

The irritation in Walsh's demeanor is something I didn't know I'd enjoy so much. Maybe because it's obvious he wanted the upper hand by killing this poor fuck the second we got here. Maybe it's because Seth isn't making it easy for Walsh. Either way, I make a mental note to tell him I like his style when he's not following.

Before Walsh can respond, I comment, "How'd you get the information regarding Romano's whereabouts? Esposito just gave it to you? Or did he think you had a deal?" I let the implication hang in the air, that his deals aren't to be trusted as I take a step forward.

"He came to me, wanting something I couldn't offer. He decided to rat, I decided to skip the judicial system and deliver his sentence to save some financial burdens. How's that sound? Reasonable, *Mr. Cross*? Besides, I already knew where Romano was. That's not the information Joey was giving me. Romano's in protective custody."

The way he says my name makes my skin crawl. He ignores the silent snarl and continues talking, grabbing the back of a simple metal chair, letting it drag across the floor with a shrill sound.

"What's more important is that the indictment was dropped." He leaves the chair in front of Seth, then grabs another. There's a stack of them, and he delivers one to each of us before taking a seat himself.

Seth hesitates, so I sit down first. Both of us, across from Walsh. All of us holding our guns, but settled in our laps.

"Dropped?" I question, feeling my curiosity, my disbelief even, show on my face.

"It's confidential."

"So he gave something up?" Seth surmises and Walsh shrugs but wears a slight grin. "Fucking rat."

"Jail or death. He didn't have many options, did he?" Walsh comments.

"He made a mistake coming back," Seth responds and then sits back in his seat when I give him a look.

"What's the other thing?" I ask Walsh, squaring my shoulders and moving away from the subject of Romano. "You said you had two things to say. The first is that you have Romano's whereabouts. What's the second? I'm guessing it's these recordings you say you have? Negotiation and blackmail in the same conversation?"

Walsh tosses a small notebook into my lap. It's small and something easily tucked away, like something that would fit inside of a wallet. "The hotel Romano's been placed in and his room number. He's got three police offers posted next door. If they hear banging around and screaming, they've been told to let it happen."

"And you're fine with that?" I question, feeling my shoulders tighten. "It's got 'setup' written all over it."

"I'm not letting Romano walk away. He's the reason Marcus came back here." Walsh leans forward, his elbows resting on his knees so he's closer to me as he tells us, "I want him dead but it can't be on our hands.

Too many people are involved. Take him. I've read the files on Aria Talvery. I saw what happened with your brother."

"You saw what happened to Tyler?" I question him, not understanding how he knew.

"Tyler?" he responds with a shake of his head. "Carter. Carter is with Aria, unless I'm mistaken." It's silent for a long moment.

"What happened with Tyler?" he asks when the quiet air lingers for too long.

"Nothing of your concern." I shift my weight in my chair as Walsh leans back further. "I want Romano for an entirely different reason."

"Then take him. I'm giving him to you, both to start off with a good rapport."

"Seconds before blackmailing us?" Seth interrupts him and Officer Walsh shrugs. "Both to have a good rapport. And to show Marcus I'm here and I'm not going anywhere."

"Marcus came back... here? For Romano?" I question, thinking back nearly a decade ago when I first learned about the bogeyman that is Marcus. "How long have you been after him?"

"Six years now," Officer Walsh tells me and it doesn't add up. Marcus never left. Marcus couldn't have been in New York fucking with Walsh while keeping up his reputation down here and pulling strings. The cogs turn slowly as I assess Walsh, wondering where it went wrong, needing to know what piece is missing.

The reality of what Walsh is willing to do in order to get to Marcus coming into focus.

Seth readjusts in the seat, shifting his gun from hand to hand and then he stands, pushing the metal chair back as he does and stating, "I'd rather stand if you two don't mind."

I don't move my gaze from Walsh, who merely watches.

His pale blue eyes raise to mine and then to Seth's as he says, "My only request is that you don't kill him at the hotel. Make it look like he took off and skipped town. Do that and he's yours."

"In exchange for?" I wait for the other shoe to drop. Seth stands still to my left. His wrists are crossed in front of him and one hand still holds the gun.

"What do you think I want?" he asks lowly.

He's slow to pull a recorder out of his pocket, and with the click of a button, Seth's voice is heard and then the sound of something creaking. I recognize it immediately.

"*Who's this fuck?*" *he asks and I answer,* "*Hal. The second he wakes up, bring him to the cellar.*"

"*You have questions for him?*" *Seth asks.*

"*No. No questions.*"

Officer Walsh stops the recording, although the visual memory of opening the trunk and showing Seth in the parking lot behind The Red Room continues playing out in my mind.

"What was bugged?" I ask Walsh, running my thumb along the rim of the barrel. Motherfucker. Anger courses through me uncontained inside, although I don't let it show.

"I'm guessing a gift from Marcus?" Walsh speculates with a glimmer in his eye. "The recording has enough evidence for me to piece together how you got hold of Mr. Hal Brooks, that he was alive when you took him… and what you did to him after."

"What exactly are you implying?" A trace of anger can be heard in the hiss of my question.

"That you're fucked… unless you've got information for me. It was in his clothes and found on Mr. Brooks body."

It sinks in slowly. Marcus bugged Hal. He set me up. Between Marcus, Walsh and Romano, the list of men to kill keeps getting longer.

"What information are you looking for?" I ask, looking him dead in the eyes.

Walsh merely stands, glancing at the dead man on the floor and the dark pool of red that's staining his face as he looks off to the front double doors in the distance.

"I'll contact you when I have specifics." With that he stands, leaving me to calculate every possible way we can kill him. He's a man hell-bent on vengeance and willing to burn everything that lies between him and it.

As the two of us stand up slowly, watching his hands and how he places the gun back in his holster, Walsh adds, "Go tonight for Romano. Tomorrow the teams change. I mean it when I say I intend to have a good rapport with you two."

Turning his back to us, he places the chair he'd taken on top of the

404 | W WINTERS

stack. "Unless you want to help me clean up, I think you'd better getting going."

The metal of the gun is warm when I slip it behind my back in the holster, taking in everything I can about Officer Cody Walsh. It's silent, save for the, "Until next time," Walsh gives us on our way out.

Neither of us speaks until we're far enough out in the distance.

Still seething, we both climb into the car and listen to the *thunk* of the doors closing as the sound of crickets off in the distance fades to silence.

"We're screwed if he mails the recordings or hands them out to the fucking FBI." Seth says the fucking obvious, tapping his foot in the car.

We should have incinerated him. That dead fuck and all the evidence along with it. Instead, I had to freak the fuck out over shit that happened years ago.

Seth keeps up with the tapping. Tap, tap, tapping as my frustration grows.

"Knock it the fuck off."

"I'm thinking," he retorts and then lets out a "fuck" and punches the side of the door.

"Feel better?" I ask him when he lifts his fist to examine his hand.

"Much," he answers dryly.

The keys jingle in the ignition as the engine turns over, humming to life. Seth rolls his window down, breathing in the cold air until he comes up with a solution

"I'll find out where the info is and get rid of it then get rid of him," he speaks.

"That easy?"

"If we put him in the cellar, yeah. That easy."

"You think he'll tell us where it is?" I glance at him and let out an uneasy exhale, shaking my head as the wind blows by. "I don't think he will. I think he'd die before quitting."

"Then how?"

"Declan has to find something."

"Declan's looking into something?"

"I asked him to look into something before I know whether or not it's a dead end. I don't know yet; it may be useless."

He's reluctant to nod, but he does. "And what about Romano?"

"Go tonight and take three men with you. Two for lookouts." The order comes out as easy as the plan should be. "If he's in their custody, he's unarmed and it should be in and out."

"We'll hit him with chloroform. Keep it quiet."

"Just make sure you take out any cameras first. And stay silent, wear masks. Don't trust it not to be recorded."

"Got it. Want me to send a report to Carter first?" he asks and I stare off to the right side as the car comes to a stop. Just happens to be the graveyard. "No, I can do it. I'll tell him."

I'll tell my brother just how badly I've fucked up. With all of this.

Then I'll deal with Bethany.

And then Romano.

CHAPTER
13

Bethany

MY EYES FEEL SO DRY BUT I CAN'T KEEP THEM CLOSED. EVERY TIME they shut, I see Jenny, in the hands of a villain. She's out there and I'm lying in a comfortable bed, protected and doing nothing.

The thin slit of light from the hallway that lays across the bedroom floor and hits the dresser widens as a soft creak fills the quiet room. Jase's footsteps are cautious and muted.

"You don't have to be quiet," I let him know although I have to clear my throat after. It's raw and in need of a hot cup of tea. A luxury I can afford, as I'm not *missing and presumed dead*.

"You're not sleeping?"

"How could I?" I answer Jase with the question as he walks to the bed and lowers himself to sit by my side, making the mattress dip where my legs lay.

He tells me, "I didn't expect you in here."

For a moment, I reconsider every thought that brought me back to his bedroom and ask, "Do you want me to leave?" If he does, I will. If he doesn't, I'll stay. Simply because I want to be here. I still want to be next to him when I do fall asleep. I want him to hold me, but I'm too prideful to ask. More than that, I'm ashamed that after all the lies, I still feel like I need him.

His answer is quick. "Never."

"I don't want to give you an ultimatum." I spit out the words that I've been saying over and over in my head the last hour or so. "I hate them and I think they're awful."

Jase is deadly silent, listening to what I have to say. I can feel his eyes on me although I don't look up at him. Resting his head on my thigh that's covered by the blanket, he waits for me to continue.

"It hurts to even say it. I can't deal with lies. I don't want to be a woman who lets a man lie to her."

"I won't."

"I don't know that I believe you." Finally looking into his eyes, I suck in a deep inhale to calm my words. "I can't stay if I find out you've lied to me about something. I can't be with you if that's all there is between us."

"There's nothing else and there will never be anything else."

My mother used to warn us about 'always' and 'nevers.' Especially about the people who speak them with certainty.

With the window cracked, a gust of cool air blows in trailing along my skin and with it, the ends of my hair tickle down my bare arm as I prop myself up. "You sound so sure."

"I am." His hard jaw seems sharper in the faint light with the shadows from the moon. There's an intensity that swirls in his eyes, but it seems different now. Not so much riddled with fear as it is with loss and regret.

Or maybe it's a reflection of myself, maybe it's just what I want to see. He may be certain, but I'm not so sure of anything anymore.

I can only nod, and lie back down. Back to his bed although I'm on my side and I intend to sleep all night with my back to him. I'll do it every night until the hurt goes away. That deep pain that's settled into my chest like fucking cancer.

"Is there anything else I can…" Jase pauses and I hear him readjust as the bed jostles.

"Anything else you can say or do?" I finish the question for him, my eyes open and staring straight ahead at nothing in particular.

"Is there?" he asks when I don't answer the question I raised.

"We just move on, don't we?" I tell him, feeling that pain spread like a web, tiny and sticking to everything inside of me as it spins. "That's what happens."

"Why do you sound so defeated?"

"Because it hurts, it all hurts and I don't know how to fix it other than to believe you. Even that hurts right now."

The mattress groans as he leans forward, rubbing my back as I lie there, refusing to give in to anger. "What matters is that Jenny's alive." My bottom lip trembles and my throat goes tight as I ask, "You're going to save her, right? You're going to bring her home?"

"I'm doing everything I can," Jase whispers as he lies down next to me although he's not under the covers. He pulls me in closer to him and as much as I'd love to shove him away for everything he's done, I need to be held by this man for the very same reasons.

"When we were little, she was my hero," I admit to Jase, still staring ahead at the blank wall that's been a photo album to me all night, flicking through memory after memory. "I was thinking about the time when I'd just reached high school and how she helped me with my English homework. She loved poetry. She was so good at it."

It sounds like Jase is going to say something, but instead he stays quiet. He kisses me on my shoulder though, through the sleepshirt and then on my jaw by my ear. The kind of kiss where I'm forced to close my eyes. When he lays my arm in the dip at my side and then rests his forearm in front of me, I twine my fingers with his.

His touch means more to me right now than I think he'll ever know.

The second I part my lips to thank him, he speaks first. "Tell me more about her."

"I don't know what to tell you. She was my big sister, the one who looked out for me, helping me with everything... until it all went wrong."

"What went wrong?"

"Our mom did. That's when everything changed." The hollowness in my chest seems to grow thinking about it all, so I stay quiet. The silence doesn't stretch for long.

"Do you still hate me?"

For lying about my sister while I was mourning her?

For lying about scaring me into staying with you?

For lying about the debt and taking advantage of me?

The questions line themselves up in my head, but stay unspoken.

"No," I answer him. "I hate what you did, but I don't hate you."

"Why do I feel like things aren't okay?" he questions and that gets a reaction from me. Fighting the covers with my legs, I turn around to face him, propping myself up with my elbow and feeling the comforter fall down my shoulder.

"Because I'm still upset," I say and frustration comes out in my tone. "What would you have me do, Jase?" The exasperated question escapes easily from my lips. "I don't know if you've lied about something else… or if you will."

"There are no other lies." Anger colors his statement and reflects in his gaze.

"I don't believe you." There's no emotion in my words, only facts. "There are only so many times you can lie to a person. Only so many. But what am I really going to do? That's why I'm hurt. I don't want to leave you." Fuck, saying the words makes me feel weak, down to my core. I don't want to leave him. Not just for my sister's sake, either. "I feel *pathetic*." I practically spit the word out.

"Do you forgive me?"

"You said you were sorry." That's all I can say.

"That doesn't answer my question."

"It doesn't matter," I tell him.

"It does."

"I forgave you without you even apologizing. It's about trusting you and trusting myself after falling for you. The trust isn't there anymore," I admit.

"I can give you reasons to trust me--"

"Time will," I cut him off. "Even when I hate you, you're still what I need. You don't understand how much I feel that I need you."

"I do. I know what that's like," he confides in me and I feel like it's the truth. Why else would he want me here? Why else would a man like him deal with me, in this state, right now?

When I don't respond, he asks me, "How can I make it right?"

"You can start with finding Jenny and bringing her home."

"I can't guarantee--" he starts to say, but I don't want to hear it.

"I finally let go… I let go and she was still out there." My voice cracks. If I had kept looking, if I'd kept asking around and demanding answers… Maybe she would be home now.

"I can't make that promise to you, Bethany."

Letting go of the regret, I focus on what we can do now when I tell him, "I know you can't promise, but I wish you could."

Instead of lying down like I think he's going to do, he sits up and walks his way around the bed to stand in front of me. "I have to go," he tells me and I nod into the pillow, keeping my hands down on the bed, although I question if I should reach up and wrap them around his neck to pull him down for a kiss. Is it so bad that I want to be kissed when I'm hurting? Even if it's by the one who caused the pain?

"Where are you going?" I ask him, not hiding the surprise or the slight worry in my cadence as I glance at the clock. "It's late." I say the excuse as I sit up and wrap my arms around myself.

I expect him to hesitate, to lie or to give some vague response. "I'm going to kill the man who murdered my brother," he answers and my heart lurches inside of me. All the pain I've been going through and turmoil, he may have had a hand in it, but I forgot he suffers through it too.

"Jase, are you okay?" I don't think I've ever pushed myself up quicker in bed as I get onto my knees and move toward him.

"I'm fine, anxious though," he answers me as I sit in front of him, neither of us touching each other in the dark night. It's all shadows and cool gusts of air between us and I wish it would go away; I wish I could change everything.

"I'm sorry," I whisper, and do exactly what I wanted to do a moment ago for myself, but right now it's for him. Sitting up taller, I press my lips to his for a tender kiss, my fingers brushing against his stubble and then laying across the back of his neck. Jase tilts his head down and cupping the back of my head, keeps me there for a second longer. Just one more beat.

"Are you going to be all right?" I ask him in a whisper, my lips close to his, not wanting to let go.

"I'll be fine," he answers me and I don't think he's lying. I think that *he* thinks he really will be fine, in a situation where nothing at all is fine.

"Do you care that I'm going to kill him?" He doesn't let me go as he asks the question.

"Only in the sense that I care about what it does to you." The answer is immediate and true to the core. Maybe it's wrong, but there's so much that's not right that I simply don't care about being wrong anymore.

"I want you with me. You can know, or you can guess, you can ignore it all. I don't care so long as you're with me."

"I want to know," I tell him even though a tremor of fear runs through me.

"All I care about is you being here when I get back. Tell me you'll be here."

"I'll be here."

I wish I'd told him I loved him, but he kisses me and then leaves me breathless on the bed. I can feel it in his kiss and when he leaves, when the door is closed and he's long gone, I ask as though he's still here with me, *why won't you tell me you love me?*

I refuse to believe it's not love. It's fucked up a million ways and then some, but this is love.

CHAPTER
14

Jase

"I N SOME CULTURES, PEOPLE BURY THE MEN THEY MURDER FACE DOWN so they can't come back to haunt them."

Four stories up in the vacant and grand estate, the large windows are open and the rooms are all bare. The empty old office is bigger than the entire house I grew up in. The ceilings are tall; the light wood floors shine with polish. When Romano left his place weeks ago, he took off and got rid of everything. One day he was here, the next he was gone. The worst decision he made was coming back.

"Face down? Like in their grave?" Seth asks from across the large room. There aren't any lights in the room; the full moon and the streetlights give us everything we need. He's still dressed in jeans and a shirt, both black. His men are downstairs sweeping the place and preparing for what's to come, while we're up here with our guest of honor.

I nod, listening to the muffled noises that come from behind the balled-up rag in Romano's mouth. Hysteria is setting in for the old man as his face turns red and Carter, Declan and Daniel join us. He's never looked so old to me. So close to a fucking heart attack and then death. Wouldn't that be ironic? If the fucker had a heart attack while tied down in that desk chair and we didn't even get a chance to kill him.

"They thought if they buried the men they killed face down, when their spirits woke up, they'd be disoriented," I explain to Seth and to whoever else is listening.

Seth lets out a rough chuckle, playing with a knife as he sits in a wingback chair in the corner. The leather is old and cracked. I guess that's why Romano left it behind. Everything left in the room was meant to be thrown away. Now Romano's been added to that category.

"I've heard of feeding the dead to pigs. They'll eat anything," Seth answers.

"Can't bury a man if he dies with dynamite in his lap, can you? Or feed what's left of him to the pigs?" Carter questions and then pats my shoulder as he enters the room. He only glances at Romano, not paying him much mind as he walks around the room. This estate has to be a hundred years old. It was a family legacy. One that's ending tonight.

Although the conversation borders on lighthearted in tone, tension is thick in the room.

"This used to be your office?" Carter asks Romano as he leans forward, placing a hand on the soon-to-be dead man's shoulder. From behind the rag comes nothing but rage and the muted sounds of what I assume are curse words.

I wonder what it's like to be him right now. I'd rather have a heart attack than to be him right now.

Carter only smirks at him, standing up and pushing off of his shoulder, sending Romano rolling away in the wheeled desk chair. Gagged and tied down, this is how he'll die. In the room where he made all of his decisions. Decisions to murder and decisions that require consequences.

"Any situations tonight?" Carter asks Seth who shakes his head. "In and out, he was sleeping so the chloroform was easy. Overall it was," he says as he looks Carter in the eyes, "uneventful."

"And the detail in the next room? Did they try to interfere?"

Seth answers, "Didn't see them, didn't hear them. It was all over in under ten minutes. Even if it was filmed, we were masked and didn't talk. There's no way to ID us."

"Good work," I chime in and my brother agrees.

"Explosives are planted everywhere but the main room where we hid the cash in the safe. It'll look like he came back to hide evidence, but mistakenly set it off too soon," Carter explains.

"What a tragedy." Daniel's comment drips with sarcasm. Out of all of us he's been the most quiet, the most still. Leaning against the back wall and staring at Romano all night.

Romano says something. It could be his last words for all I care, they won't be heard.

Declan adds, "It keeps the feds off our back, they go away. I want them the fuck out of here. And we take over the upper east side."

"All our problems solved." Triumph comes darkly from Carter's voice.

Almost all. Marcus and Walsh are becoming more difficult problems by the day, but I keep that opinion to myself.

"I wish they all knew," Daniel speaks up. As he kicks off the wall and walks closer to the far edge of the room to look down at the tied-up man, the light sends shadows over the harsh expression on his face. "It's too quick and not public enough for what you deserve," he tells Romano. His voice is hoarse, and anger and mourning both linger there.

The memory of Tyler dead in the street plays tricks on my mind as I look out the large window feeling the cool breeze against my face. The cast iron fence separates the estate from the road and it's just beneath us. The road ahead is a backroad; many don't travel on it and it's not the road Tyler where died, but any black road slick with rain will carry that memory forever.

"Justice is a funny thing, isn't it?" I murmur as I tap my blunt nails along the windowsill, opening the window even more, as much as I can to feel the cold air blow in. "It never feels like enough."

"What?" Daniel asks from behind me, so I turn around to face him.

"It's never going to feel like enough… because it's never going to be all right." With the singular truth exposed, a raw pain grows from my empty lungs and radiates upward.

"I'm grateful he didn't get away and the feds didn't fuck this up for us. We'll spread it around, that we didn't like him talking to the cops," Carter says and looks pointedly at Seth, who nods. Rumors travel fast in this town and everyone needs to know it was us. Romano fucked with us. Now he's dead. That'll make a lot of other pricks question whether or not they're willing to do the same.

"What about Tyler?" Daniel asks. His forehead creases as he

continues, "They should know Romano killed him and that's what gave him a death sentence."

"We'd be admitting we didn't know the truth until recently," Carter speaks up, shaking his head. "It's easier to keep it a secret."

A *lie*, hisses in my ear, and I have to turn away from my brothers, once again looking out into the empty street only to see the ghost of memories there.

"I don't like it." Daniel disagrees with Carter. Seth and Declan are quiet, simply observing the two of them.

"Tyler deserves justice," I speak up before being conscious of it. "It shouldn't be kept a secret."

"Romano dies tonight." Carter's harsh words whip through the air. "What more do you want?"

I'm surprised by Daniel's words as he says, "Humiliation, pain... I want it to be a spectacle." He's still filled with hate over Tyler's death. He's still angry. He's still grieving. I'm convinced the five stages of grieving aren't like steps where you take one after the other. I think they're waves that constantly crash onto the shore and you never know which one will hit you.

"That's not going to help our FBI situation," Declan answers, peeking up from the corner of the room where he's standing behind Seth. I can feel all their eyes on me, but I don't look back yet. All I can look at are the spikes that line the top of his iron fence. All I can think about is how awful it would be to die like that, to fall onto the spiked fence beneath us and be impaled next to an asphalt road. It'd be the last thing he ever looked at.

"We decided this was how it would be... now you want to wait?" Carter questions, his voice tight with incredulity.

"No, we don't have to wait." I turn to finish my thought, looking at Daniel as I suggest, "We can throw him out this window. That would be a *spectacle*, as you called it."

Daniel smirks while Declan lets out a chuckle and then asks, "Wait, are you serious?"

"He can die committing suicide by jumping onto a spiked fence," Daniel says and smiles over Romano's muffled pleas. The man's fighting in his chair now, causing it to roll slightly across the floor. I kick the back of it gently, just to push him away from me and torture him some more.

"Who would kill themselves that way?" Declan asks. "Who commits suicide by spearing himself onto a fence?"

"No one," I answer him and Daniel adds, "That's the point."

"That would send a message," Seth comments although it's not meant to agree or disagree. He stays neutral in all of this.

Carter's voice is low as he says, "It would send a message to the feds too. That we don't care they're here and that we're still running this town. Is that the message you want to send?"

"That's the message we *need* to send," Daniel presses. "What are they going to do? We don't leave evidence. They'll know, but they can't do anything about it."

"Just like they can't do anything about Tyler," I say and my statement is the nail in the coffin for me. Romano murdered our brother and left him on the street to die. "This is justice."

He'll do the same.

"No one knew about Tyler; how could they have done anything?" That's the problem, isn't it? With so many lies and secrets, no one could do anything for Tyler. It was just a tragedy.

Just like Jenny. I think about how many times Bethany went to the cops and filed a missing persons report for her sister. How they told her they were sorry, and they didn't know what happened when the trunk was found.

"We need to do this, Carter," I say and look him dead in the eyes, feeling a numbing prick flow over my skin. "No accident, no dynamite. We give him the death he earned."

Time ticks slowly, with Seth shifting behind me and Declan staring at Daniel, who's waiting for Carter's final decision. *Tick, tick, tick.* It's too slow.

"Take the cash, leave the safe empty and open. Wipe for prints." Carter gives the order and I walk from the open window to Daniel, feeling the cold gust of wind at my back carrying Romano's muffled screams.

"You all right?" I ask him lowly so it's just between the two of us, and he nods although he can't look me in the eyes, he can't look away from Romano.

"Who gets to do it?" he asks me although his voice is coarse and he has to clear it. "Who gets to do the honors?"

"You can if you want." I give it to him. I'll suffer the rest of my life, hating that Tyler died in my place. Whether Romano breathes again, whether I kill him, none of it will change that. But at least now everyone will know. And that's something.

"It was supposed to be you," he reminds me, as if there's any way I could forget.

"I know, but doing this isn't going to bring Tyler back." Daniel's expression wavers, the hardness falls for a moment and he nods again. I watch as the cords in his neck tense.

"If we're doing this, it has to be done clean," Declan speaks up. I'm not sure if he disagrees and thinks we should go the safe route, or if he's simply covering our bases.

"We're always clean," Seth answers him.

"Let the feds see," I tell Declan. "Let everyone know." I pat Daniel on the back and then look Carter in the eyes as I say, "No one takes from us and gets away with it."

"It's settled then," Carter agrees. "And the men that came back with him? What about them?"

"Make it clean," Declan repeats to Carter, the undertone of his voice harsh. Romano's cries can still be heard and I kick the chair just slightly, sending him rolling backward again.

"There's no deal to offer any of Romano's men, no loose ends," Seth says and nods.

I wait until Seth lifts his eyes to mine. "Go through every part of this town. Every asshole who ever got a paycheck from him. Find them in their homes, at the bar. I don't care if they're balls deep in the back room of a strip joint. Find them, kill them."

"They die tonight," Carter talks as he walks to where I was, no doubt judging what it'll take to make sure Romano's impaled. It won't take much at all. It's just outside the window. "There aren't many left. We already have locations on most of them."

"They'll scatter like roaches if we wait until tomorrow and the FBI doesn't know yet, but the moment they find Romano, they'll be everywhere. So we end it tonight," Daniel agrees, walking to Romano and turning the chair. He has to crouch down to be at his eye level. "Wipe them all out."

"Start with him," I speak to Daniel, and he looks over his shoulder at me. His lips are pressed in a straight line, with a grim look covering his face.

"End it," I tell him. Carter steps to the side, and we all wait.

Pushing the gagged, screaming man with a bright red face to the window, Daniel looks out onto the road—a backroad that will be empty until the morning.

The gag comes off first, bringing a stream of Italian profanity from the dried throat of this dead fuck. Romano pulls on the ropes, fighting as best he can against them. It's foolish really, he should wait until we untie him for his best chance, but he doesn't, knowing his end is coming.

Seth's the one to cut the rope at his feet; one quick swipe and the nylon threads are released. Romano attempts to run, still bound to the back of the heavy leather chair and he falls hard on his side, seething in pain. The crack of his skull hitting the floor ricochets in the room.

With Carter holding his left side and me holding his right, Seth cuts the binds and helps us hold him up, holding him steady and restraining him as he tries to run and fight. I can't breathe. My muscles are too coiled as Romano struggles with the last bit of strength he has left in him.

Backing him up to the window, I stare at Daniel's face. I expect anger, I expect hate, but agony is all that's on his face. It's still not enough; being the one to end Romano... it's not enough. It won't bring Tyler back.

We release our hold as Romano falls backward from the force of the shove Daniel gives him in his chest. Romano's arms whip out to grab onto whatever he can, but there's nothing there, nothing that can keep him upright. His scream dulls as he falls the four stories and then it's silenced.

Staring down at him and the scene, I no longer see Tyler. The street's empty. All I see is a man who killed all his life, a man impaled with the life draining from him slowly.

Turning to Seth, I tell him, "Check that he's dead, then find the rest."

CHAPTER
15

Bethany

I T'S BEEN QUIET THE LAST FEW DAYS. TOO QUIET.

The ominous feeling that settles in when you know things won't last... that's in the air. I've been breathing it in and suffocating from it. Jase is being careful with me and both of us are feeling bad for the other one.

It's easy to give someone sympathy, it's easy to love them. Accepting their love though, accepting it in the way they're able to give... that's the difficult part, because that's where you get hurt.

I forgive him, but I'm waiting for the next bad thing to happen.

Jase is just waiting, on edge and waiting for something... I don't know what.

The other end of the line goes to voicemail. So I dial the number again, stretching at the end of the sofa. Jase's non-office is now my hideaway. The smell of old books and leather is too much to resist.

Ring. Ring.

On the second ring, it picks up and I recognize the voice instantly.

"Laura," I say and my gut falls. I wasn't expecting her to answer. "I didn't know you were working day shifts this week."

Animosity and betrayal stir in my stomach. More than that though, I miss her.

"Bethany?" She sounds surprised to hear my voice.

"I just wanted to call about Michelle, the pregnant patient with pica on floor two, and maybe talk to Aiden…" I trail off, waiting for Laura to tell me she'll get him. After a few seconds of silence and then the way she says my name, I know that's not going to happen.

"Bethany," she says but I can already tell there's too much sympathy in her tone. "Michelle died two days ago. I'm sorry. I thought Aiden called."

The leather turns hot under my tight grip. I can barely breathe. When I worked in pediatrics before this for my internship, death was common. It was so common I'd check the paper for the obituaries before coming into work so I'd be prepared. It's also why I left. At the center, it rarely happens, but now it feels like death's following me everywhere.

"Beth? Are you there?"

"I'm here," I answer her although my body's still tense and it hurts to swallow.

"You weren't answering my texts and I know you're mad, but I thought you knew. I swear. I'm so sorry."

"How did it happen?"

"Magnets. They obstructed her bowels," Laura answers.

"If I'd been working--"

"Don't think like that."

"I had a rapport with her." I can't even say her name as tears prick my eyes. She was young and beautiful. Before getting pregnant, she was healthy. If only, if only. I think it too much now. Every day I wonder 'what if' in all aspects of my life. It's not a healthy way to live.

"She wasn't well and…" Laura stops when she hears my quick inhale. I'm not crying, but I'm damn close to it.

"There was nothing any of us could have done. The behavioral approach was working and she was released. Her husband checked her out… it happened in her home."

With a hand over my heated face, I focus on calming down, but it takes a long moment. Struggling not to lose it, I debate on simply hanging up.

"I'm sorry," Laura tells me again and I don't know what to reply. It's not okay, but that's the answer we're supposed to give, isn't it? That or thank you, but there's nothing to be thankful for right now.

"You need to come back to work," Laura tells me when the silence stretches.

"Everything's changed."

My voice is tight when I answer her. "I want to come back." Focusing on breathing, I try to calm down. "I can't believe she's dead. It feels like I was just with her."

"Tragedy happens." Seconds pass as I try to accept it, staring at the unlit fireplace.

"You should come back." I'm grateful for Laura's distraction as she adds, "Aiden's gone for three days and he told me to schedule you for next week. So you're on."

My eyes lift to the bookshelves, feeling wider, more alert. "I can come back to work?"

"We need you. There's so much that's happened."

The way she says it makes my heart still and I can feel a deep crease settle between my brow as I ask, "What? What happened?"

"I can't tell you over the phone; just start back on Monday."

A cold prick flows over my skin, knowing something's wrong, but not knowing what. "Okay." I take a moment, which feels awkward and tense, but I make sure Laura knows I'm genuine when I tell her, "Thank you."

"Are we okay?" she asks me softly. I can practically see her nervously wrapping her finger around the phone cord in the office like she does. It's a habit I picked up from her.

I answer her honestly, "I don't understand why you did it. Why you called him and didn't tell me."

"There's a lot you don't know."

"You could tell me," I offer her. "Really, if you'd told me no, or if you told me you called him before he showed up…"

"I… I can't tell you right now, but soon? I can tell you soon, if you want."

"I want to know. I do."

"And then we'll be okay?" she asks me as if that's all she wants.

"Yeah," I answer her even though I don't know if it's truthful. I don't know why so many people are hiding secrets. Or why each one hurts more than the last.

When I hang up the phone with her, I hear the front door close from all the way down the long hall. Jase is home and it surprises me how much I want to go to him, how much I want him to hold me like he does every time he gets back and just before he leaves.

I wait for him, holding my breath at first, but I can't hear where he's going or what he's doing. Leaving my phone on the glass table, I pick my book back up, although my gaze flicks to the open door.

CHAPTER
16

Bethany

H E'S BEEN QUIET, BUT THERE'S A LOOK IN HIS EYES THAT'S ANYTHING but. I can feel the tension crackle and it promises that if I follow him, I'll be given everything I could possibly want in this moment. And so I do. The second he looks at me, I close my book and leave it there to go to him.

"Come on," he commands but it's soft and low, pleading almost. My heart yearns to follow him quickly; to show him I accept his demands.

"I don't want this distance between us anymore." Jase's voice is calming and deep.

"I don't either," I admit to him and reach out to take his hand when he offers it. There's something about the roughness along his knuckles and the warmth of his skin that's soothing. His touch consoles a part of me that's desperate to heal.

"Trust works both ways," Jase tells me as I gauge the changes in the fire room. Everything's been moved out, most notably the chaise and the wooden bench. In place of the plush white rug is a black blanket, large and heavy. The room's barren, but still beautiful, with the crystal fireplace and lit chandeliers.

"Both ways," I repeat, registering his words and wondering what he has planned.

He said he found a solution to our problem. Funny how a man's solution involves sex... or so I assume. To be honest though, I need this.

I need *him* like this. I close my eyes knowing *we* need this.

"Strip here." He gives me orders as he places a handful of things in the middle of the blanket.

A candle, a lighter, a bottle of ethanol, some sort of white cloth, and the weighted blanket. Tremors of pleasure send a warmth flowing through me, meeting at my core and heating instantly.

By the time I've stripped to nothing, he's done the same. The light from the fire emphasizes every etched muscle in his taut skin. His cock is already rigid and my bottom lip drops at the thought of being at this man's mercy.

A deep, rough chuckle whips my eyes from his length to his gaze. "Ever needy and greedy, aren't you?" he teases me and that's when I see the glimmer of light that reflects off the blade. The tension rises, stifling me, wrapping its way around me... and I love it. I crave it. It does nothing but ignite a fire inside of me.

My feet patter on the slick black blanket beneath us as I make my way to him, tucking my hair behind my ear as I prepare to drop to my knees in front of him. I want to please him, to prove to him that I still desire him, that there's still a roaring fire between us. I don't get a chance to though.

Catching my elbow, Jase stops me and instead puts his hand on mine, pulling my fingers back and making me hold my hand out flat. He's silent as he gives me the knife.

"It's heavy," I comment weakly as he sits cross-legged and I do the same in front of him. The heat from the fire is the only thing that keeps the chills of the cool air away. My heart races as I glance at the small silvery scar still on his chest.

"I want us both to play," he tells me, wrapping my hand around the handle of the blade and then bringing it to his chest. "First you need to shave me."

The command is simple although my gaze shifts from the small smattering of hair on his chest to his eyes. Scooting closer to him, I watch the way his throat dips, the way the cords tighten as I prepare for the first stroke.

Before I can press the blade to his skin, he lays a hand on each of my hips, holding me steady. The warmth of the fire is nothing compared to his touch. With every small exhale, I drag the blade down carefully, feeling it nick each hair along his chest. Breathing in, I then drag the blade over his skin, blowing softly across it as I go and gently bring the back of my fingers across his body to check on the smoothness of it.

"Don't leave any behind," he tells me, sitting upright and still not moving.

"Does it hurt at all?" I ask him, running my fingers over what I've just done and then moving the blade to a patch of fuzz on his upper pec by his shoulder.

"You're only shaving me," he answers with a handsome grin, mocking me.

"I mean the scar. Where I cut you before," I whisper, not looking into his eyes and then grabbing the cloth next to Jase to wipe the blade clean.

"No," he answers and then takes the knife from me. "It feels like a memory that fate made happen."

He does the same to me, shaving away the little bits of hair, making sure there's nothing between us that the fire would catch.

"You first," he tells me and he tips the bottle of ethanol, the cloth pressed against the opening. The smell of alcohol hits me as he wets the rag. "Where you put it, the fire will catch, but do it quickly." Before relaxing his shoulders and sitting back, he lights the candle. "Use this for the flame but hold it upright to keep the wax from dripping."

I've paid attention and I've seen what he does. Nodding, I know exactly what he's said and why it works, but still I hesitate, holding the rag in my hand and staring at his chest.

"What if I hurt you?"

"The blanket's fireproof and I can lie down, Bethany. I'm here, and you're more than capable."

I remember what it's like, the memory of the fire tickling then blazing. Heating my skin before vanishing and leaving me breathless and hungry for more. I can give that to him. The very idea of it makes me eager to do it.

Reaching out, I wipe the damp cloth against his skin in a small motion, not covering much area at all. My pulse is fast and my hand trembles slightly. I can't help it; the only thing that keeps me composed is the intimacy of the moment and his touch steadying me.

"A cross?" he questions and I let my lips kick up as I pick up the candle. "Over your heart," I answer him in a whisper as I lift the flame. It catches quicker than I anticipate, blazing in a short burst and vanishing as my heart races.

Releasing my shock in a single breath I look to Jase whose eyes are wide with desire as his chest rises higher. "Again," he commands in a deep groan. This time when I get closer to him, he grips my wrist holding the cloth out and tells me, "Use more and in a different spot. When it lights, press your body against mine and feel the aftershocks of the fire."

He takes his time, moving my hair behind me and telling me to braid it and be careful. Playing with fire is something we've always been warned not to do, and maybe that's why it's so exciting.

I do as he says, wondering what type of pleasure or pain it'll bring. I'm too slow the first time, too slow to feel anything but the heat of his chest where the reddened skin felt the kiss of fire. Still, with my body pressed against his and feeling the rumble of desire against his chest, it's erotic, it's forbidden and I want more of it.

"Fire needs fuel to stay alive. It has to breathe, but you can smother it. It needs to move, but you can deny it." His words are mesmerizing, and the feel of dulled flames extinguished as I press my body against his is unlike anything I've felt before. It's gone too fast.

Taking my hand, he runs the rag over my breasts before I can run it down his body. I light him first and as I lean, the fire catches against my skin. As my head falls back, Jase presses his body to mine, gripping the hair at the base of my skull and pulling it back as his teeth scrape against my neck.

He takes control then, laying me down and playing with me, toying with the fire between us.

It's a dangerous game to play with fire, but I feel like he's made the rules. I feel invincible with him, like nothing matters except for what he tells me in that moment.

The light flicks between us, burning hot and roaring until it extinguishes. It happens so fast, but each moment seems more and more intense. Hotter, heavier and upping the stakes of how much of our skin is sensitized.

Until the lights have gone out and the heat dissipates, leaving me yearning for more.

More than the fire this time. I need *him*. The pieces of him that fire can't give me. I breathe into Jase's kiss, "I want you."

He devours me, pushing me to the floor and bracing himself above me, settling between my spread legs before tilting my hips how he wants them. Jase isn't gentle when he enters me. He teases me at first, pressing the head of his cock against my folds and sliding it up to my clit, rubbing me and taunting me before slamming inside of me to the hilt and making me scream. I watch him hold his breath as he does it, and he watches me just the same.

I'm lost in the lust of his gaze, lost in the gentle touches of his hands on my breasts where the fire just was as he pistons his hips, deliberately and with a steady pace that drives me to near insanity. He's controlled and measured, even through the intense pleasure. I feel him hit my back wall, the ridges of his cock pressing against every sensitive bundle of nerves as he fucks me like this. Deep and ruthlessly, but making every thrust push me higher.

I barely notice when he raises his body from mine. The heat from the fireplace blazes, but it doesn't compare to what it feels like to have his body on top of mine. I lift my shoulders off the ground, reaching up to hold on to his, but he shoves himself deep inside of me, making my back bow. Throwing my head back with pleasure, I see the lit candle, I see him tilt it to its side where it rolls away, the flame still lit, the fire growing, catching in a crevice of the hard wood floors.

Lighting ablaze.

"Jase!" I scream, pausing my body, but he doesn't stop, he crashes his lips to mine, hushing me as the fire roars behind us. Pressing my palms against him, I try to push him away so he can see, but he resists.

He ignores me to the point where I feel as though I've imagined it.

"Fire." I breathe out the word in a ragged whisper as he fucks me while the pleasure mounts and stirs in my belly; it overrides the fear. Jase tells me at the shell of my ear, "I know."

My heart races chaotically as I look into his eyes and he speaks with his lips close to mine, "Trust me." The fire behind us echoes in his eyes.

It takes me a moment to realize he's still. He's stopped. And the fire is real.

With the flames reflecting in his dark gaze, I reach up and pull him toward me, urging him on before kissing him.

The flames grow brighter and I can't stop watching them. Even as he ruts between my legs, bringing my pleasure higher and higher, my body getting hotter and the intensity of everything mixing with the fear and pain and utter rapture.

"It's on fire," I say and the fear creeps into my voice. "The room's on fire." Even so, Jase doesn't stop. He's savage as he fucks me into the ground, kissing his way down my neck. My nails dig into his skin as I hear and feel the fire grow. My heart pounds against his. "Trust me," he whispers.

The flames rise higher and higher, igniting against everything around us, even though it doesn't travel across the black blanket. "Kiss me," Jase commands, gripping my chin and pulling me back to him.

"Jase," I gasp his name, the fear and heat of the fire stealing me from him. His lips crash against mine and with a hand on my back and another on my ass, he moves me to the floor, pinning me there with his weight.

Thrusting himself inside of me, my back arches, my head falls back and I stare at the flickers of red and yellow flames as they engulf the room surrounding us.

And then, just in the moment when I'm breathless with fear, water rains down upon us. It comes down heavily. No sirens, no noises at all. Only water, leaving a chill from the cold droplets to bring goosebumps along my heated skin.

"There's always something to calm the fire," he groans in the crook of my neck and then drags his teeth along my throat as the deluge descends around us, extinguishing the flames. Every thrust is that much deeper as I lift my hips and dig my heels into his ass.

Even knowing it's safe, knowing the fire's gone, my heart still pounds with a primal instinct to run. I can't though, pinned beneath Jase and wanting more of him.

The light goes out around us, the flames diminished to nothing. The warmth of the room vanishes as the water washes us of the fear from being consumed by the fire.

Lifting his head up to look down at me, I stare into Jase's eyes as he presses himself deeper inside of me and then pulls out slowly, just to do it all again. Every agonizingly slow movement draws out my pleasure, raising the threshold and I whimper each time.

That's how I fall. Staring into his eyes longingly, praying for mercy to end it just as I whimper and beg him for more. Clinging to him as he hovers over me and loving this man. Loving him for all he is and knowing what I do. Knowing I never want to stop.

CHAPTER
17

Jase

"I LOVE THE SMELL AFTERWARD," I COMMENT, LISTENING TO THE crackling of the flames in the fireplace. I lit it for the heat and the light both as Bethany lays against me, still on the floor.

Although I used the thick blanket to dry her off, her hair's still damp and the light from the fire casts shadows against her features, making me want to kiss along every vulnerable curve she has.

"The char?" she asks weakly, sleep pulling her in. The adrenaline should be waning now. Sleep will come for her soon and I hope it comes for me too.

"The water. It has a smell to it, when it puts out the fire."

"It does," she agrees and then lifts her head, placing a small hand on my chest as I stay on my back. "Will you tell me something?"

"What?"

"Anything," she requests in a single breath and lies against my chest. Spearing my fingers through her hair, I think of the worst of times in this room. I think of the fire, the way it feels like everything will end, the intensity and the simplicity of it all being washed away.

"Do you know how many men I've killed?" I ask her as the question rocks in my mind. "Because I don't."

Although I keep running my fingers along her back and then up to her neck, noting the way the fire warms her skin with a gorgeous glow, her own hand has stilled, and her breathing has stopped.

"Are you scared?" I ask her and she shakes her head, letting her hair tickle up my side. "I just don't want to do anything to stop you from saying more. I want to know."

"I used to keep count and memorize their names," I admit to her and remember when I first built this room. Its purpose was different then and the memory causes my throat to tighten.

"I'd sit here, and let the fire go. I'd let it burn whatever I'd brought, I'd let it spread and surround me. All the while, spouting off each person's name. Every person I murdered with intent or for survival. Every one of them. And there were many.

"At first, I'd give both first and last names. Then it became only first names because I'd run out of time otherwise. I thought if I could say them all before the fire went out, it'd be some kind of redemption. In the beginning I could do it. I could say them all before the water would come down. It never made me feel any better, but I did it anyway.

"Then I started forgetting," I confess. "Too many to remember, and the names all ran together. Some names I didn't want to say out loud. Names of men who I'll see in hell and smile knowing I put them there."

"Don't talk like that," Bethany admonishes me. She whispers, "I don't like you talking like that."

"Like what?"

"Like you're going to die and go to hell. Don't say that." The seriousness of her tone makes me smirk at her with disbelief.

"Of everything I've done and said, that's why you're scolding me?"

"I'm serious. I don't like it." She settles herself back down and nestles into me, seeming more awake now than before and with tears in her eyes.

"Why are you crying?"

"I'm not," she tells me. "And you're not a bad man. You just do bad things and there's a difference. God knows there's a difference, and I do too."

"Don't cry for me." I offer her a weak smile and brush under her eyes. Her soft skin begs me to keep touching her, to keep soothing her and never stop.

"I'm not," she repeats although she wipes her eyes and tries to hide it. "Don't talk about you dying... and we have a deal."

She doesn't look me in the eyes until I tilt her chin up, lifting my shoulders off the ground to kiss her gently and whisper, "deal," against her lips. I can feel her heart beat against mine. This is the moment I want to keep forever. If ever given a choice, I'll choose this one.

"Tell me something else." She states it like it's a command, but I can hear the plea in her voice.

"Something nicer to hear?" I let a chuckle leave me with the question in an attempt to ease her.

"No, doesn't have to be nice. Just something more about you." The fire sparks beside us as I look down at her. Her bare chest presses against mine and I drink her in. The goodness of her, the softness of her expression.

"Hal, the man I killed... he hurt Angie. You heard me mention her before."

The mention of another woman's name makes her pause and I remind her, "She wasn't mine and I didn't want her like that, but I've always felt responsible for what happened."

"What happened to her?" She doesn't blink as she whispers her question staring into the fire.

"She came and went when we first... opened the club... she was one of our regulars on the weekends. Buying whatever she wanted to party with her friends."

"Drugs?" Bethany asks and I nod, waiting for judgment but none comes.

"One day she came to the bar on a weekday. I thought it was odd. She was dressed all in black and her makeup was smudged around her eyes. She wanted something hard. That's what she asked for, 'something hard.'" The memory plays itself in the fire and brings with it a hollowness in my chest.

"I told her to get a drink, but she demanded something else. So I told her no. I sent her away."

"Why?"

"I thought she would have regretted it. She'd just come from her father's funeral. There was nothing I had that would take that pain away and I knew she'd chase it with something stronger when it didn't work. She went to someone else. And I regret sending her away. I wish I could take it back. I wish I could take a lot of it back. By the time I saw her again, she'd changed and done things she didn't want to live with any-more. She was so far gone... and I'm the one who watched her walk away and sent her to someone else. Someone who didn't care and didn't mind if she became a shell of a person who regretted everything."

"You tried to help her. You can't be sorry about that." Bethany's adamant although sorrow lingers in her cadence.

"I can still be sorry about it, cailín tine," I whisper the truth as I brush her hair back. "And I am. I'm sorry about a lot of things. Mistakes in this world are costly. I've made more than my share of them."

"That doesn't make you a bad man," she whispers against my skin, rubbing soothing strokes down my arm, desperate to console me.

"You remind me a little of her in a way," I admit to her. "She was a good person. Angie was good, what I knew of her. She was good but sometimes dabbled in the bad and was able to walk away. I needed her to be able to walk away. To go back to everything and be just fine. To still be good. It made me feel like it was fine. I thought what we were doing was fine; that it was a necessary evil. It's simply something that's inevitable and something we'd rather control than give to someone else. But it's not fine and it never will be."

Bethany asks, "You think I'm a good person, dabbling in the bad?" Her voice chokes and she refuses to look at me even when I cup her chin.

"It's the same with you. I'm not comparing you to her. She's noth-ing compared to you but the good. You have so much good in you. Even if you cuss up a storm when you're mad and try to shoot strangers."

The small joke at least makes her laugh a small feminine sound be-tween her sniffling.

"I'm not willing to let you go though—I'm afraid you'll never come back to me. Or worse, that you won't be able to go back to the good."

"You are not bad," she says and her words come out hard which is at odds with the tears in her eyes.

"I'm not good, Bethany. We both know it."

"And I'm not all good either. In fact, there are a lot of people out there who would tell you I'm a bitter bitch and they hate me," she at-tempts to joke, but it comes out with too much emotion. "You don't have to know if I'll still be good if I walk away, Jase. I don't want to walk away. And we can be each other's goods and bads. People are supposed to be a mix of both, I think. You need that in the world, don't you? You are needed," she emphasizes, not waiting for my answer. "And I need you," she whispers with desperation.

"I'm right here," I comfort her and she lets me hold her, clinging to me as if I'm going to leave her.

It's quiet as she calms herself down and I think she's gone to sleep after a while, but then she asks, "Is this... is this cards or bricks for you?"

"I don't understand."

"I'm insecure and I need to know. It's one of the bad parts of me. I'm insecure."

"You need to know... cards or bricks?" I ask, still not understanding.

"There are two kinds of relationships. The first is like a house built of cards; it's fun, but you know it's going to fall down eventually. Or you can have a house made of bricks. Bricks don't fall. Sometimes they're a little rough and it takes time to get them right, but they don't fall down. They're not supposed to anyway--"

"Bricks." I stop her rambling with the single word. "I'm not interested in cards. I don't have time for games."

"Then why lie to me?" She whispers the question with a pained expression. With her hand on my chest, she looks into my eyes. "I don't want to fight; I just want to understand."

"I kept you a few steps behind me. That's how I saw it. Not because I didn't trust you—I didn't trust that the information I had wouldn't hurt you. I didn't want to give you false hope."

She's quiet, and I don't know if she believes me. "Please. Trust me."

"I do. I trust you." At the same time she answers me, my phone pings from where I left it in the pile of clothes.

Bethany doesn't object to me leaving her to answer it. Although she watches intently, waiting for me to come back to her.

Reading the message Carter sent, I try to keep my expression neutral and tell her, "I have to go."

"You do that a lot," she comments before I bend down to give her a goodbye kiss.

"I'm sorry."

"Don't be. I'm right here. I'll always be here." A warmth settles through me with her whispered words.

"Is it going to be okay?" she asks, not hiding her worry.

"As okay as it ever is," I answer her truthfully. "We may know where Jenny is," I tell her and watch as she braces herself from the statement. "We're going to find her tonight."

"Jase, I love you," she whispers. "Make sure you come back to me. I'm not done fighting with you yet." A sad smile attempts to show, masking her worry, although it only makes her look that much more beautiful.

"I look forward to coming back here so you can yell at me some more," I say to play along with her, leaving a gentle kiss against her lips. When I pull back her eyes are still closed, her fist gripping my shirt like she doesn't want to let go.

"I'll come back." I swallow thickly and promise her, "I'll come back."

CHAPTER
18

Jase

T HERE'S A BRIDGE THAT LOOKS OVER THE FERRY. IT LEADS TO THE DOCKS where our shipments come in. With my brothers behind me and Seth next to me, we stare at the worn door that lies beneath the bridge.

It's made of steel and looks like it's been here as long as the bridge has; the shrubbery simply obscured it.

"We still don't know what's inside," Sebastian comments.

"Jenny," I answer. "I know she's in there." I can feel it in my bones that we're closer to where we're supposed to be. Even in the pitch-black night, with the cold settling into every crevice, we're close. I know we are.

"Let's hope so." Carter's deep voice is spoken lowly as he steps next to me, facing the bridge and considering the possibilities.

"Ten men?" I ask Carter, looking over my shoulder at the rows of black SUVs parked in a line. "Do they know?"

"They know we need them here and that's all. They're waiting for orders."

"Ten of them?" Seth repeats my question.

"Do you think that's overkill?" Carter questions in return. It's just the four of us, me and Seth and him and Sebastian, along with our ten men. Daniel and Declan are home with guards of their own. Just in case anyone sees us leaving as an opening to hit us where it hurts. In this life, there is never a moment for weakness and having someone you love at home is exactly that, a weakness waiting to be exploited.

"I don't know if it'll be enough," Sebastian answers. His hand hasn't left his gun since we got out of the car. He's ready for war and prepared for the worst. He knows what it's like to be given an order by Marcus better than any of us. By the way he's acting it looks like he expects each of our names to be on a hit list given to Marcus's army.

"It wasn't supposed to turn into this. It should have been low key." Seth looks concerned as he searches the edge of the bridge for signs of anyone watching or waiting. "He has eyes everywhere."

"If Marcus wants to kill us, I imagine he could do it with no men," I tell the group who have gathered around us.

"We're walking underground with no concept of what's there."

"Explosives would do it," I say, completing the thought that lingers in the back of my mind.

"You think he knows?" Carter asks.

"I think we should assume he does," Seth answers.

"If he didn't before we got here, he does now." The realization hits me hard. "All of us can't go in there. This was a mistake."

"What the hell are you talking about?" Carter snaps.

"There are too many questions unanswered. If we all go in, he could see it as either us declaring war or an opportunity... We can't give him the opportunity. He can know war is coming though."

"We go in together," Carter insists as I grip my gun tighter, feeling my palm get hot with the need to do something.

"Think about Aria." I try to persuade him to go back home.

"I am. I'm thinking about my family and about bringing them home. Open up the fucking door."

"Don't leave her a widow," I warn him. "Not for me."

"She knows what I'm doing. She knows the risk." I can only nod, thinking that Bethany knows the same. Carter adds, "She told me not to come home without Bethany's sister. She knows and she wants Jenny home too. Open it." With the command and the four of us moving forward, the men gather behind us, all of us walking to the small door.

With a gun trained on the lock, Sebastian fires and a flash of light

438 | WINTERS

and red sparks from the gun being shot leads to the groan of the heavy door being opened. Sebastian steps aside and only nods as we move forward. His eyes are focused straight ahead as he orders the men around us, keeping a lookout and moving forward to clear the way.

"I'll go in first," I tell him, stepping in front and preparing myself for what we'll find.

The steel floors grate as I step forward, letting my eyes adjust and not daring to breathe. The musk of the water's edge is heavier when the door opens. A steel rail keeps me from stepping forward and it's then I notice the door leads to a spiral staircase down. It reminds me of the shed at The Red Room. The place men go to die but unlike them, we're walking down there willingly. A cold prick flows down my skin like needles.

"We don't have a choice." Carter pushes the words through clenched teeth before I can urge him to turn around.

"This is my fight," I tell him one last time.

"We fight together." The weight against me feels more significant than it ever has before. "Bastian," I call before taking another step forward. "Don't let a single man here die."

He tells me simply and then motioning with his chin for me to continue, "I wasn't planning on it. In and out. No casualties."

With a nod and a look back at Carter and Seth, I take the stairs one at a time, noting how many there are and how far down it goes. Maybe two stories, if that. It's got to be twenty feet down and the steady drip from leaking pipes is all that makes a noise down here.

Four men stay at the top and just outside the door as lookouts. The rest join us, making it ten men in a tight space, eight of them waiting on the stairs for the door at the bottom to be opened.

Bang!

It takes a second shot to shatter the lock and I toss it to the floor before slowly pushing open the door. Seth's behind me, his gun raised and ready. Steadying my breathing, focusing on my racing pulse, I take in every inch that I can see.

There's no sign of anyone. No sign of anything at all down here. Anxiousness makes me doubt myself. Maybe she's not here at all. With that thought, unexpectedly the lights turn on, one after the next, quickly illuminating the place.

The sound of guns cocking and raising fills the tight space, but no one fires. The lights are newer than everything else. They're placed into sconces bracketed against the walls which are a mix of thin plaster and tightly packed dirt.

"Electric," Seth notes. "Someone was hired to install these," he says and I can already see the wheels spinning.

"Look for a paper trail when we get back," I tell him, leading the way further into the unknown territory. "If Marcus hired someone, they may have seen him or someone who has."

"Already noted."

I have to stop before I get more than five feet in; there are so many rooms, so many branching paths. "It's almost like a mine the way it's built with a maze of halls."

"Where do we start?" Seth asks. His expression appears over-whelmed as he moves his gaze from one hall to the next. All open doors, and all could lead to armed men or worse.

My brother comes up behind us, considering everything carefully. All the while I hear the tick of a clock in my head.

"It could take hours." The second the words slip out of my mouth, I hear a skittering in the dirt.

A scraggly boy, thin but tall with lean muscle watches from the shadows to the left. The second I spot him, he takes off. My gun lifts first, instinctively ready, but he's unarmed and I can hear his footsteps getting farther away.

"Left," I yell out and chase after him. He's the build of the kid who left the note on Carter's windshield. "He works for Marcus." My lungs scream as I chase after the kid, rounding a hall and barely spotting him through another. Seth's right at my heels and the men behind him spread out, watching each door. Careful and meticulous, not reckless like the man in front has to be.

The need to find this kid, to stop him rages hard inside as I race through the underground, chasing after the sound of him running. He may know where she is. He'll know what this place is at least.

I can hear them all behind me as Seth and I take the hall carefully, checking doors as we go.

My lungs squeeze and I struggle to breathe in the damp air as I lose the sound of him first. Then I lose sight of him with the sconces slowly flickering off and on.

It's my worst nightmare. Trapped in a small space with everything riding on this moment and yet I have no answers and it's all slipping away.

I don't stop running, searching every corner with Seth and listening intently, only to run into a sign. A sign that stops both of us in our tracks. The sign the kid led us to.

Four lines are written on a board blocking the hall. The boy is nowhere to be seen although the click of a door sounds in the far-off distance.

Leave the boy.
All those who made a deal with Walsh can enter.
Everyone else leave now.
Or the girl dies.

"What happened?" Carter questions in a hushed demand as he comes up behind me. My heart's racing, my palms are sweaty. He knew. Marcus knew and let us come.

"You have to go," I answer him as I take in a deep inhale, feeling my pulse pump harder. I can't lift my eyes from the sign. "Or the girl dies."

She can't die. Bethany needs her.

"He knew we were coming," I speak loud enough for all of them to hear as they make their way into the space. "Get them out," I tell Sebastian. "Get everyone out!" I have to raise my voice so Sebastian can hear.

"He wants us to know he knows and to admit it," Seth speaks out loud, referring to the deal with Walsh.

"Admit it in front of our men," Carter adds, looking behind him at the men lined up and ready to fight beside us. Ready to die for us.

"I couldn't give two shits who knows." My hiss of a mutter grabs his attention and I look him in the eyes and tell my brother, "I promised Bethany I'd bring her sister back." The thumping in my chest rages. "Even if I have to go in alone."

"I'm here, Jase," Seth speaks up, reminding me I'm not alone.

Carter speaks before I can answer, "Then do it." He doesn't let go of me, he grips my arm and forces me to stand there a second longer. "Don't get yourself killed." He says it like it's a demand, but it's drenched with emotion.

"And to think, I was expecting you to tell me you love me," I joke back in a deadpan voice even though dread consumes me. It's just to ease the tension and hurt that riddle every muscle inside of me at the thought of Jenny being dead already and Marcus being one step ahead as usual. Merely toying with us.

"That too," Carter adds.

With a farewell grip on his shoulder, I look him in the eyes and tell him, "I'll try not to be stupid."

"Go," he tells me and shares a glance with Sebastian. With a nod of his head, Sebastian starts to lead the men back.

"I'll see you when it's through," I answer Carter as he walks off without looking back.

"You should go too," I tell Seth as the place empties. "Go with them."

"What are you talking about?" His voice is low with disbelief.

"You stay back. In case it's a setup." I can feel chills flowing down my skin at the thought of Marcus being more prepared than we are. He's the one who made the rules to this game. He knows it better than anyone. He sets himself up to win.

"I'm the one who needs to go in. I'm the one who brought us all here." A cold sweat breaks out across my shoulders and down my back before taking over my entire body as I stare down the barren hall. It feels like my death sentence. I'm a fool to think otherwise, but I have to go in. I can't leave her here. I can't and I won't.

"It says 'all,'" Seth says as he looks me in the eyes, defying me and referring to the sign that blocks the path. "I'm not letting you go in there alone." Disregarding my orders he takes a step forward, pushing the sign to the side, into the dimly lit hall and I yank him back, fisting the thin white cotton of his shirt.

Time passes with both of us waiting for the other, knowing what we're walking into and looking it in the eyes anyway.

"Are you sure?" I ask him.

"We're in this together. I have to admit, I didn't really care for

Marcus before, but now I hate the fucker." He offers me a hint of a smirk and a huff of humor leaves me. Patting his back, I grip my gun with both hands. He readies his and I nod.

"We get her and we get out."

"Got it," he says then nods and we go in together.

The thumping in my chest gets harder listening to Seth's pace picking up to match mine as we move down the dark hall, the smell of soil and rust filling my lungs as we move.

"You have a strong family," Seth comments with something that sounds like longing.

"We're close," I answer him and he glances at me, but doesn't say another word.

"Let's not die today. I'd like to go back to them."

CHAPTER
19

Bethany

I CAN'T GET THIS FEELING OUT OF THE PIT OF MY STOMACH.
Sitting and waiting. Sitting and waiting. I don't like sitting and fucking waiting around.

Everyone you love will die before you. My mother's voice has kept me company for more hours than I can count. Warning me. I let myself fall and it feels like I've been delivered a death sentence. Why did I let myself fall? Why did he have to keep me from running?

The thump of the book falling from my hand down to the floor scares the shit out of me. My nerves are messier than ever; they're worse than a necklace tangled at the bottom of a luggage case on a bumpy road trip.

I force myself to read The Coverless Book. I read every page in it. I read about Emmy feeling better and the two of them getting married in secret. I read about them falling in love and sharing their first time together.

Then a new sentence started as he watched her lie down, but I don't know how it ends. I stared at the last page for the longest time, not understanding. It's half a sentence, mid-thought from Jacob about how he'd do anything for her. Someone cut the pages out. Lots of them. It looks like there's at least twenty missing that I can spot. So much for reading to distract me.

I know there's more to the story. It can't be cut short like that. The moment the thought hits me, I'm drenched in the nightmare of my sister crying on the floor. Telling me she just wanted them to have a happy ending.

"Jenny," I breathe her name, staring at the clock and wanting Jase to come back with her.

I can't sit here and do nothing.

With nothing to distract me, my mind goes to the worst of places. Pacing and staring into the fire as the smell of leather envelops me.

Dropping my hands to my knees, I feel the flames as my hair hits my face. It's the waiting that kills me. I can't sleep without seeing my mother remind me that *everyone I love will die before me*. I can't think without wondering if Jase has found Jenny and all the things she may have had to endure. I don't know who she'll be when he finds her. *If* he finds her.

This isn't a way to live, waiting and in fear.

Are you there? I text Laura and wait. I'm exhausted from barely sleeping, but there's no way I can sleep now.

I'm scared, I message her again, needing to tell someone. She doesn't text me back though. She could be working; she could be sleeping. I don't know. I don't know anything anymore.

"Fuck this," I say then toss the book down on the table and make my way out of the room. The hall seems longer than it has before as I head for the grand staircase and the hidden door beneath it.

My pulse pounds in my temples as I place my hand on the scanner to open it. It takes a long moment. "Please open," I whisper as the jitters flow through me.

It does, the large door slides aside seamlessly, presenting me with a dark kitchen until I turn the lights on.

It's empty and quiet. The whole world is sleeping while mine crumbles around me. A sudden chill overwhelms me and a split second later the click of the heater makes me jump.

"Carter," I call out as I walk deeper into the kitchen. My feet pad on the floor and that's the only sound other than my racing heart. Something's wrong. I can feel it in my bones.

Wrapping my arms around myself I make my way to the other hall that the kitchen leads to. It's quiet and dark.

"Anyone," I call out and my voice strays from me, receiving no answer. "I don't want to be alone right now." It's a hard feeling to accept, when you open yourself up to love and then feel fate toying with taking them from you. "I don't want to be alone anymore."

"Bethany?" a voice calls out just as I turn on my heel to walk away.

"Daniel?" I question, fairly sure it's him and not Jase's other brother. Someone's here at least. "Were you sleeping? I'm sorry, I hope I didn't wake you up." The sentences tumble from my mouth as he makes his way into the kitchen, also in bare feet and gray pajama bottoms with a white t-shirt tight over his chest. He has to pull it the rest of the way down as he stops at the counter.

"No, you're fine, I was just lying down with Addison but not sleeping." There are bags under his eyes, so I know he's tired. "You okay?"

"Are you?" I ask him, feeling the anxiousness grip my throat.

His expression softens to a knowing look. "It's hard. Moments like this can be difficult," he admits and just to hear someone else say what I feel is a slight relief.

"I don't know how to be okay right now." Gripping the tips of my fingers to have something to hold, I watch as he pulls out a wine glass and then heads to the cellar.

"Do you like white or red?" he asks and I swallow a small laugh at the implication that the answer is to drink. "Red."

It's quiet as he opens the bottle, the dim light from outside glinting off the torn metal wrapper.

"I don't know what I can do to help." I emphasize the last word as he gently pushes the glass toward me and then pours one for himself.

He doesn't answer me; instead he takes a drink and so I do the same, sipping on the decadent wine and feeling guilty that I can.

"I just have a bad feeling," I finally confess. "It won't leave me alone and I'm afraid."

Daniel's still quiet, but he nods in understanding. I start to wonder if he'll speak at all until he says, "Let him do what he knows how to do, what he's good at."

"That doesn't--"

"Yes it does. You want to be involved," he says then looks me in the eyes and that's when I see the remorse in his. "You want to be there in case something happens." His voice drops as he tells me, "I know that feeling."

"I'm sorry."

"Don't be. I get to be here with Addison. Don't be sorry for me. There's nothing in this situation to be guilty or sorry or resentful over." He leans forward on the bar before looking over his shoulder down the empty hall. "We do what we're needed to do," he says with resolve.

"I don't know what I'm needed to do," I admit to him, feeling the weight lift, knowing that's the core of my problem in so many ways.

"When he brings your sister back, you take care of her. You're good at that, aren't you?"

The thought of Jenny being here soon forces me to brace myself on the counter.

"I heard that's what you do," Daniel prods, waiting for me to look back at him and I nod.

"Take care of her when she comes back, because that's something no one else can do. Let Jase do what he does and you do what you do."

"Even if I'm scared?" I question him in a whisper.

"Can I tell you a secret?" he asks and again I nod.

"We all are. Anyone who tells you they're not is lying. We live in a world where there's plenty to be afraid of. It's okay to be scared sometimes, but have hope. Have faith. Jase knows what he's doing."

CHAPTER
20

Jase

WITH SINGLE BULBS SWINGING SLIGHTLY AND CREAKING AS THEY DO from the high ceilings, the hall is dim. The rocking of the water can be felt in the aged corridors.

"How old is this place?" Seth murmurs his question as he gently kicks the first steel door open. Without a light in the small ten-by-ten room, it's hard to look in every corner. The rustling of Seth's shirt as he pulls out a small flashlight and clicks it on gets my attention. The heat of worry, of restlessness, is dulled by my conditioned response to chaos, *stay calm*. Always calm and alert. Or else death is sure to come for you.

He brings the light to his gun, both hands holding the pair steady and revealing an empty room inside. There's only a mattress on the floor and nothing else.

The same with the next room and the next.

Rows of doors, mostly open, line each side of the hall and we go through each one. Every door we open that reveals nothing but rumpled blankets and makeshift beds leaves me with the dreadful thought that we're too late… that when we push the next door open wider, it'll reveal a girl on the floor, no longer breathing.

"We can't be too late." The fear disguises itself as a hushed request.

"She's here," Seth reassures me beneath his breath as he turns the knob of the next door, and lets it creak open, revealing another barren room. "Why else would he do this?"

My gaze moves instinctively to him. "Why does Marcus do anything?"

"If you want to beat him, you have to think like him. Why this place? Why the boy? Why the sign?" He pauses to make sure I've heard.

"Why her in the first place?" I add to the pile of questions.

I count the remaining rooms, four of them, two on each side. Three open, one closed.

My mind travels to deceit. Wondering if he already took her away. Wondering if Marcus locked the two of us in here in her place. "If his intention was so easily known, he wouldn't be who he is."

With the slow creak of the next steel door, rusted on the bottom edge, I hear Marcus's rough laugh in my memory and an icy sensation flows over my skin. Unforgiving, cruel.

We betrayed him first. I can already hear his excuse. We came onto his territory; we stole from him. The only question is: what are the consequences?

"Empty too," Seth whispers. The next room and the next prove the same.

Prepared to be left with nothing but more questions and curses hissed beneath our breath, I place my hand on the final closed door and turn the knob, but it doesn't move.

Seth and I share a glance in the silence as I try again and then quietly shake my head. *Locked.*

Hope thrums in my chest as my pulse races and I take one step back and then another.

"On the count of three?" Seth asks, backing up with me. Nodding, I tell him, "Kick it in."

One.

Two.

Three.

My muscles scream as I slam my boot against the door as hard as I can along with Seth, the two of us putting everything we have against the steel lock with the last hope of seeing Jennifer behind it.

The door slams open to reveal darkness and then a shriek. My eyes can't adjust fast enough, although I think I see her small form just before I hear the *bang!*

The heat of a gun going off, the metal against my skin, singeing my shirt and filling the air with the smell of metallic powder is disorienting but familiar. Adrenaline surges in my veins and I'm quick to push forward, not knowing if the bullet hit me, grazed me, or if I was spared from the shot. Anger, fear, and the need to survive all war inside of me to come out on top as I shove myself forward, closer to the gun and whoever's holding it.

Bang! It goes off again, the shot hitting the ceiling with a pop of steel breaking that joins the crackling of the plaster that falls from above my head.

My body hurtles forward, landing on top of the small woman who's desperate to cling to the gun. She fires it again as I grip the barrel, forcing it away from me just in time to send the shot wide and feeling the burning hot metal as I rip it from her hands and toss it away. It thuds on the floor as she turns under me, desperate to get it back.

"Jennifer!" I scream out her name and hear Seth cuss behind me.

She screams and kicks wildly, fighting like her life depends on it.

"Stop!" The command is torn from me with equal parts demand and desperation. Seth moves to the side, kicking the gun farther out of reach. "Stop fighting," I grit out as her heel hits my ribs and she scrambles on the dirt floor.

The impact to my ribs leaves me seething, the pain rocketing through me as I clench my teeth and hold on to her.

"I don't want to hurt you."

"Calm down," Seth demands lowly, and it comes with the faint sound of a gun being cocked. That gives her pause. "I don't want to hurt you either," he says calmly.

Jenny stops moving, stops fighting and her gaze moves to Seth in the darkness. I can barely see him, but I can see the glint of the gun.

Time moves slowly as I back away from her to stand and while I do, Seth lifts his gun the second she looks at him. He uncocks it. "I didn't want to do that," he admits to her, swallowing thickly. "Just calm down. We're here to help you."

It's only then that I can take a good look at her.

What's most alarming is how disoriented Jennifer is. She's not skin and bones like I thought she'd be. Even through the grime that covers her skin, she has weight to her that lets me know she's been eating. Her eyes though are dark with lack of sleep and fear drives every half step she takes as she backs away, trying to get away from us, but knowing the wall is behind her.

With her gaze darting from me, to the gun, to Seth, she crouches down and stares up at us, ready to scream and fight.

"We're here to help you." I keep my voice low as I speak. The ringing in my ears from the gun she just fired has dulled. All I can hear now is her ragged breathing.

Seth tells her calmly, lowering himself down with both hands in the air, "We're here to save you."

I do the same, raising my hands and letting her know, "We're not here to hurt you."

With wild eyes full of disbelief, she shakes her head, letting us know she doesn't believe us.

"I'm not leaving without you," I tell her and the thin girl shoves her weight against me and her ragged nails scratch down my neck. Seething in the slight pain and more pissed than anything, I snatch her wrists and hold her close. "Calm down."

"You're not taking me," she screams out. Even held close, she doesn't stop fighting. It's useless though. She has to know it, but she doesn't stop. Kicking out and wriggling to get away, she never lets up. Pressing her against the wall, I'm careful not to hurt her, just to keep her as still as I can until she can calm down.

"We're taking you to your sister." Seth has the common sense to bring up Bethany.

"Bethany asked us to save you," I tell her and add, "I told her I'd bring you back."

For the second time she stills, but I don't trust it. "To save me? Bethany?"

The mere mention of Bethany paralyzes her. With a gasp and then harsh intakes, Jennifer trembles and her body wracks with sobs. She tries to fight it, writhing in my embrace in an effort to cover her cries, but she breaks down instead. No longer fighting us, instead she wars with herself.

"It's okay," I say and rock her, but my eyes move to the gun on the floor and Seth's quick to take it.

"Where is she?"

Keeping my voice soft and soothing, I answer her. "We'll take you to her."

"Right now, okay?" Seth adds sympathetically, the way someone speaks to a lost child. I pull back slightly, giving Jennifer more space and taking my time to release her, still ready to pin her down again if I need to so she doesn't attack either of us or hurt herself in the process.

"We're going now; we'll take you right to her." The second I release her fully, her arms wrap around herself. Her sweater, once a light cream color judging by its appearance, is dirtied with brown.

"The note said it was time," she murmurs and looks away from us, rocking back and forth.

"Time for what?" Seth questions and I watch her. Her wide eyes are corrupted with fear and regret.

"It just said it was time and there was the gun. I thought…" she trails off as the tears come back and the poor girl's body wracks with a dry heave. She braces herself with both palms on the ground.

"It's okay," I comfort her, rubbing her back and wondering how Bethany is going to react. How she'll be after seeing her after so long.

"What happened?" I have to ask. It's the first time I'm able to look around and the room is the same as the rest. My stomach drops low when she tells me she doesn't remember everything, but she's been in this room for as long as she can remember since she's left.

"This is where he kept you? Marcus put you in here?"

"I asked him to," she admits and her voice cracks. "I just don't remember why or what happened."

"We'll have a doctor come," I tell her, petting her hair and noting that it's clean. It's been washed recently.

"Did he touch you?" I ask her, needing to know what Marcus did. It's the only thought that comes to mind as I stare at the mattress on the floor.

With her disheveled blonde hair a matted mess down her back, she stares down at herself as if seeing her appearance for the first time. She shakes her head and answers in a tight voice, "He didn't." She's quick to add with a hint of desperation, "I want to see a doctor." "I need to know that I'm better."

"Better?"

Her dull eyes lift to meet mine and a chill threatens to linger on my skin, the room getting colder every second we stay here. "He said he'd help me get better if I helped him."

"What did you have to do?" Seth asks, but I cut her off before she can reply.

"We need to get out of here. Come with us," I urge her, feeling a need to get out as quickly as we can. The longer we stay here, the more we talk in Marcus's territory, the more tangled this problem will get.

I usher her to the door, reaching out for her, but she's quick to jump back, smacking her body against the cinder block wall although she doesn't seem to notice. She yells in the way a child does when they're scared and they need an excuse to keep them from having to walk down a dark hallway. "Wait."

Tears leak from the corners of her eyes and their path leaves a clean line down her mucky skin. "Is Bethany okay?" Her voice cracks and her expression crumbles as she holds herself tighter, but her eyes plead with me, wanting to know that everything's all right. "Tell me Bethany's okay... please?"

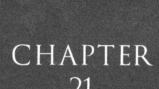

CHAPTER
21

Bethany

TO KNOW SOMETHING IS ONE THING. IT'S A PIECE OF A THOUGHT, A fact, a quote. It stays in your head and that's all it will ever be. A nonphysical moment in your mind.

But to *see* it—or to see someone—to feel them, smell them, hear them call out your name… There is no replacement for what it does to you. How it changes you. It's not a piece of knowledge. That's life. Making new memories and sharing them with others. There is no way to feel more alive than to do just that.

Than to hold your crying sister, collapsed in your arms as tightly as you can hold her as she cries your name over and over again.

As I breathe in her hair, the faint smell of dirt clings to her, but so do childhood memories and a desperate need to hold on to her. To never let her go again. In any sense of the word.

"I'm so sorry," she murmurs, her breath warm in the crook of my neck as I hug her tighter to me, shaking my head. As if there's no room for apologies.

I don't want to tell her I'd given up. I don't want to tell her what's happened. I want to go back. Back to the very beginning and fight for her and never stop. If only time and memories worked like that.

"Are you okay?" I barely speak the question before a rustling behind her, toward the doorway to the guest bedroom catches my attention.

Jase is hovering, watching us and I wish he'd come in closer to hear. Jenny needs all the help she can get.

Jase clears his throat and speaks before Jenny can. "The doctor is on his way. She's having some minor--"

"I can't remember," my sister cuts Jase off. My gaze moves from his to hers although she won't look me in the eyes.

"I know I left, I know where I was, but the days... I don't remember, Bethy." Her shoulders hunch as her breathing becomes chaotic. The damage has been done. Whatever that damage may be.

"Hey, hey." Keeping my voice as soft and even as I can, I grip her hand and wait for her eyes to meet mine. "It's okay." The words are whispered, but they're true.

"You're here now. You're safe." Jase's voice is stronger, more confident and I thank the Lord for that.

"You remember me, and that's all that matters," I say without thinking. Instantly, I regret it.

"Mom didn't remember us." Jenny's words are lifeless on her tongue.

Digging my teeth into my lower lip, I watch Jase stalk to the corner of the room and take a seat on the edge of the guest bed. The room is still devoid of anything but simple furniture and curtains. It's exactly the same as it was when I was first here, only weeks ago.

It's only been short of a month, and yet so much has changed in the strongest of ways.

"You'll remember the days, or you won't. But it's because of what happened to you. Not because of you," I speak carefully, keeping in mind that Jenny's scared, and that I need to be strong for her.

Even though I feel like crumbling beside her.

Her eyes turn glossy as she sobs, "I'm so sorry I left. I'm sorry I ever left."

"I'm here," is all I can say. Over and over, I pet her hair to calm her and shush her all the while.

Jase is quiet, but there. If I need him, he's there. Gratitude is something I've never felt to this degree before. My life will be dedicated to making him feel the same.

A shower calms my sister. Maybe it's the comfort of the heat, or maybe it's washing away what she does remember. With both of us in the bathroom, her drying off and getting dressed and me staring at the door so as not to watch, I ask her, "What did Marcus do to you?"

The fear creeps up and then consumes me. Imagination is an awful thing and I wish I could stop it.

"I don't remember everything," she confesses. "I know I feel…" she trails off to swallow thickly and I prepare for the worst. Picking under my nails and steeling my composure, I ready myself with what to say back, putting all the right words in order to make her feel like she's all right now, as if there were ever such a combination.

"I feel healthier. More with it. I haven't had a… a need to."

"To what?"

"To take a hit." Her answer comes out tight and I turn to see her staring at me as strength and sorrowful memories are worn on her expression. "I feel better."

She breaks our gaze, maybe from the shame of what used to be, I don't know. I return to looking ahead as she dresses in a pair of my pajama pants and a t-shirt.

Better.

My bottom lip wobbles and I can't help it. I can't help how tense I feel. *Better.*

Of all the things, that's a word I would never have known would come from her.

"I don't know at what cost. The idea of him scares me, even if I don't remember. I know I changed my mind. I changed the deal."

"Even if you don't remember what someone said or what they did to you, you always remember how they made you feel."

The towel drops to the floor as she blurts out, "Marcus scares me, Bethany. He scares the hell out of me."

"Do you remember anything that he did?" I ask her again, this time beneath my breath. All she gives me is a shake of her head.

"I don't know. I don't think he's going to let me walk away though."

The conviction in my voice is enough to break the fixation of her fear. "Then he'll have to fight me to get to you."

With her glancing at the knob, I open the door and cool air greets us. It feels colder without her answering me. She heads out first and after looking at Jase, still in the chair, his phone in his hand she apologizes to him.

"What did you do?" I ask her as Jase tells her it's all right.

"I shot him," she tells me, and I can't help the huff of a laugh that leaves me, although it's short and doesn't carry much humor.

"What's so funny?" She stares at me as if I'm crazy.

"She shot me when she first saw me too," Jase answers for me.

Jenny doesn't answer; she doesn't respond although she nods in recognition. The bed creaks in protest as she sits on the end of it.

"Can we have a minute?" I ask Jase. "I just need to talk to her," I reason with him, but it's unneeded.

With a single nod, he moves to leave and I'm quick to close the distance between us and hug him from behind. He's so much taller and it's awkward at first, but he turns to face me and I rest my cheek against his chest, breathing in his scent and hugging him tighter. "Thank you," I whisper and feel the warmth of my air mix with his body heat.

There's something about the way he holds me back, his strong hand running soothing circles on my skin while his other arm braces and supports me. I could stand here forever, just holding him. But Jenny needs me.

I kiss his chest and he kisses my hair before we say goodbye.

I don't know what Jenny's seen or what she thinks as she's staring out of the window.

The bed dips as I sit down cross-legged behind her, watching Jenny intently and telling her that I'm here for her.

"I miss Mom," is all she says for the longest time. Other than her constant apologies. Sorry for letting me think she was missing and then that she was dead. She didn't think it would happen like this.

After every apology, I tell her it's all right, because truly it is. I only ever wanted her back. This doesn't happen in real life. You don't get to wish for your loved ones to come back and then they do.

"I'm just happy you're here." This time when I tell her, I reach my hand forward, palm upturned and she takes it.

"Me too," she tries to say, but her words are choked.

I struggle to find something else to talk about. Something to distract her, to make her feel better. Life has slowed down since she's left.

Slowed down and sped up, a whirlwind of nothing but Jase Cross for me. And I'm not ready to share that story with her yet. It's too closely tied to me mourning her.

"Did you read the book?" she asks in the quiet air. Nothing else can be heard but the owls from outside the windows and far off in the forest. They're relentless as the sky turns dark and the end of winter makes its exit known.

"I did," I answer her and before I can tell her what I thought, she speaks.

"I hated the ending. I'm sorry, I ripped it out." I almost tell her I know. I almost say the words as she does. "I wanted them to have a happily ever after."

My blood turns to ice as the memory of her sobbing on the floor while she ripped out the pages comes back to me. *It was only a dream*, I remind myself. Only a dream. It didn't really happen. But yet, the question, the question asking her if she did that is right there, waiting to be spoken.

A different one creeps out in its place. There was a line I could never forget. "Why did you cross out 'I hate you for giving me hope?'"

"It wasn't me," she answers me and the chill seeps deeper into my bones. "It was Mom. Mom left it for you. I don't know why she pulled off the cover, but I hated the ending, so I ripped out the pages."

Goosebumps don't appear then vanish, instead they come and stay as I remember the dream. My sister and Mom did always look so alike.

"When she died there was that stack of books. This one had a post-it on it instead of a cover. She left it for you, but I took it."

"Why?" I don't know how I can speak when as we sit here, all I can see is the woman in my terrors.

"She said, 'Only you would understand, Bethany.' It pissed me off," my sister admits. "I took it and wanted to read it. I had to know why... why it was always you."

The eerie feeling that's been coming and going comes over me again, clawing for attention and I can barely stand not to react to it.

Bringing my knees into my chest, I try to avoid it, to shake it off. "What was the ending?" I ask her although I already know. It was some kind of tragedy.

"She died," Jenny says and her voice is choked. "That night, their first and only night, she died because she was really sick and there was no way to save her." My sister's shoulders heave as she sobs.

"It's okay." I try to reassure her that it's only a book, but both of us know it's so much more. It's the last words our mother left us.

"Her mother killed herself. The last ten pages is the mother facing Miss Caroline and telling her she hated her for giving her any hope and making her wait longer to end it all."

"That's awful," I comment.

Jenny sucks in a deep steadying breath and says, "The book is awful. It's all about how the ones you love aren't supposed to die before you."

Chills play down my shoulders, like a gentle touch. "What?"

I hear my mother's voice. *Everyone you love will die before you.*

"That was the point, that the greatest tragedy is watching everyone you love die before you do," my sister tells me with disgust. "I hate the book. I hate that Mom left it. I hate even more that she said you'd understand. You don't, do you?" Her eyes beg me to agree with her and I do.

"I hate it too. Mom wasn't well." I use the excuse, but her words keep coming back to me. She thought my life was a tragedy. She hadn't met Jase though. She couldn't have known my life would take this turn. "She's wrong," I say more to myself than to Jenny, but she nods in agreement.

"Even if they die," she whispers before staring out of the window, "you still got to love them."

"Do you ever feel like she's with us?" I ask my sister, feeling the eyes of someone watching us, but not daring to look to my left, toward the bathroom. No one's there, I already know that. But still, something inside of me doesn't want me to look.

"All the time. I can't sleep because of it."

The cold evaporates, the uneasiness settles. It's only me and Jenny and I'll be strong for her.

"We'll get you on a good sleep schedule. I promise everything will be all right." I would give her all the promises in the world right now to keep her safe. Safe from Marcus and the world beyond these doors. Safe from herself and the memories that haunt her.

"I think I know why," Jenny says offhandedly as if she didn't hear me, still staring out of the window.

"Why what?"

"Why she crossed it out..." She doesn't give me the answer until she realizes I'm staring at her, desperate for a reason. "It didn't belong there. Hope is the best thing you can give someone, second to love. If it wasn't there... the mom wouldn't have killed herself."

It's quiet for a long time. The memories of my sister hurting herself stare me in the face, daring me to mention them and beg Jenny to realize there's so much hope.

I cower at the thoughts, mostly because she squeezes my hand, and I'd like to think it's because she already knows.

"If I had known it was a tragedy, I wouldn't have read it," I admit to her and then question why my mother would think I'd understand this book better than my sister. Why she would leave that book just for me? She wasn't well though so there's no reasoning there.

"That's what you have when there's no hope... tragedy." Jenny's comment doesn't go unheard and I let the statement sit before speaking out loud.

Not really to her, more to myself.

"Hope is the opposite of tragedy. It's a glimmer of light in utter darkness. It isn't a long way of saying goodbye. It's knowing you never have to say it, because whoever's gone, is still with you. Always. That's what hope is."

"They really are. They're always with us," she remarks.

"That's what makes it hard to say goodbye."

"You don't have to say goodbye," she says softly, as if she's considered this a million times over.

"Then how can you ever get over it?" I ask her genuinely, thoughts of her disappearance, of Mom being laid to rest playing in my mind. "How do you get over the loneliness and the way you miss them all the time?"

"Get over it?" she asks with near shock—as if she's never thought of it that way—and I nod without conscious reason.

"How?"

"You can never get over it. Whether you say goodbye or not. Loss isn't something you get over." My sister isn't indignant, or hurt. She's simply matter of fact and the truth of it, I've never dared to consider. She looks me dead in the eyes and asks with nothing but compassion, "So why say goodbye? Why do it, when they're still here and you'll never get over it? Never."

CHAPTER
22

Jase

"I just need to know…" Bethany's voice is desperate, a sound I'm not used to hearing from her unless she's under me. She hasn't laid down since I told her it's time to go to bed. I don't know how long it's been since she's slept. Instead, she sits wrapped in the covers, staring at the door.

"She's all right." My words intertwine with the sound of the comforter rustling as I lean closer to her and wrap my arm around her waist. I pull her closer to me, making her lean slightly so I can kiss her hair, but I don't move her. She'll move when she's ready. I can wait for that.

I'll wait for her.

"Tell me you'll protect her." She swallows hard after blurting out the words. Her eyes are wide and glossy. "Please. I'll do anything." As she speaks her last word cracks and the only thing I can hear is her thumping heart, running like mad in her chest.

"Of course I will. She's family now."

"Family?" she questions me as if it's a foreign word.

"Bricks, cailín tine. I was serious when I said it, and serious about marrying you… even if you aren't ready."

"You really are bringing bricks and not just to fence me in, huh?" I have to laugh at her playful response. More than that, I love that she smiles. Even if it's gentle and small, it's there.

It falls quickly, though, as her gaze moves behind me to the door.

With one arm resting over her midsection and her other hand cradling her elbow, Jenny looks lost and uncertain as she clears her throat.

"Are you okay?" Bethany's quick to question and rise from the bed.

"Sorry," she answers and almost turns to leave, but Bethany stops her. "Wait. What's wrong?"

I stay where I am. Observing and waiting. Waiting for Bethany to tell me what's needed. Whatever it is, I'll be ready.

"I didn't mean to intrude."

"You weren't," Bethany assures her. I have forever with Bethany, so forever can wait a moment.

"Can... can we talk?" Jenny asks Bethany, although she looks hesitantly at me.

"Of course." If Bethany is aware of Jenny's objection toward me listening, she doesn't show it. Instead she drags the bench at the end of the bed closer to the chair by the dresser and pats it, welcoming her to sit.

"If you want me to go," I speak up, "I can grab you something to eat while you two talk?"

Jenny's gaze flicks between the two of us before she shakes her head. "You've already given me dinner, and a place to sleep... and clothes." She goes on and the baggy long-sleeve shirt pools around her thin wrist. "I don't need anything else."

As I stand to go the bathroom and busy myself so they have some semblance of privacy, Jenny adds, "Thank you." A tight smile and a nod is given to Jenny, but Bethany reaches for my hand and squeezes it before I can walk away.

I nearly think she wants me to stay, but she releases me with a *thank you*.

My hand is still warm from her touch when I turn on the faucet. Even over the sound of the water splashing in the sink, I can hear Jenny asks her questions about me.

Does she trust me?

What is she doing with me?

And finally, does she love me?

All of which are answered with many words, but the first of them each time is yes.

"You led him to me," Bethany informs her sister and I remember the first time I saw her. Across the bar, my fiery girl, picking a fight with whoever she could because she was hurting and needed help. Fighting is all either of us knew.

I scrub my face, feeling the roughness along my jaw and listen intently even though I hadn't planned on eavesdropping.

"The only clues you gave me before you left were The Red Room and the Cross brothers. So I went there, searching for you."

Opening the cabinet to get my razor and shaving cream, I grab the bottle of pills and stare at them until they fall from my hand into the bottom of the trashcan beneath the sink. The inhale I take is deep and cathartic, but it doesn't stop the twisted hurt that will always come when I think about that time in my life. I don't need the constant reminder though.

Gripping my razor, I use the back of my hand to close the cabinet door. Jenny's reflection is clear in the mirror. A disturbed look plays on her face when she tells Bethany, "Marcus told me to. He said to make sure you heard me say it."

Staring down at the rippling water, I listen to her explain that she's sorry. She's sorry for everything.

I don't shave. I don't move, other than bracing one hand on each side of the sink and staring down, wondering what Marcus planned, how he thought ahead and what he thought would happen.

It's not until Jenny says good night and I feel Bethany's hand on my back that I bring myself to look at Bethany in the mirror.

"You okay?" she whispers against my back and I almost tell her that I'm fine. Instead I answer, "I hate hearing his name."

"Marcus?" she asks and I nod.

"Seth will find him," she answers me and plants a small kiss on my back through my white t-shirt when I turn off the faucet.

She watches me as I dry my face and thanks me for giving her sister space.

The smile on my lips falters until she reaches out, grabbing my hand and kissing it.

"Isn't that what a man is supposed to do?" I toy with her. "Kneel and kiss the back of a lady's hand."

A glimmer of surprise filters in her eyes as she says, "I thought it's what ladies did to the knights? I thought they kissed the back of their hands when they saved them."

Even though I'm still, she moves, pushing herself between me and the sink and reaching up to kiss me. It's always the same with her. The first is quick and teasing and then she gives me what I need, deep and slow. As I groan into her mouth, she lets out a soft sigh of affection and balls my shirt in her fist, bringing me closer to her.

"So needy," I tell her, my voice low and playful before tugging her bottom lip between my teeth and then letting her go.

I move my hands from her hips to her ass and pick her up, loving the gasp and then the squeal she gives me when I toss her on our bed.

The air heats as I kick off my pants and watch her right herself on the bed, her gaze wandering down my body until I climb on the bed to join her.

With both of her hands in my hair and mine bracing me on the bed as I lean over her, forcing her to lie down, she kisses me with soft, quick kisses all over my lips. I smile as she does it, short pecks moving in a clockwise motion.

I lift my head to look down at her, to joke about what she's done. I stop myself though; there's nothing but seriousness in her gaze.

"Thank you for saving me, Jase."

"You saved me too, you know," I tell her as I pull my shirt off, knowing damn well she has.

She stares at me for an awkward moment and then looks down with a huff. "I don't know what to say."

Confusion takes over. "What do you mean?"

"I don't know what would mean more right now. That I love you. Or that I don't love you."

The short huff of a laugh leaves me with relief. *Thank fuck.*

"Let's stick with I love you from now on."

"Then I love you, Jase Cross. I love you with everything in me."

CHAPTER
23

Bethany

GOOD THINGS DON'T COME OFTEN. NOT FOR ME. NOT FOR MOST people. I'm aware of that. I get it. Life isn't meant to be a garden of roses.

I'm used to the thorns. I would even say I like them. They're predictable, when nothing else is.

The sound of the printer in Jase's office that isn't an office makes me jump. It's louder than I anticipated, and I anxiously look to the doorway.

He should be here soon.

Jenny's tucked away in her room. Some days are better than others, but overall she's better. She's better than she has been in a very long time. If only she could remember what happened over the past few months, I think she'd be like my old sister again. Or at least who that girl was supposed to be.

Before the paper can fall to the tray, I catch it and lift it up to look at the certificate. It's so simple and not as expensive as I thought it would be.

It's merely a sheet of paper with ink on it. But then again so are books, and they can be wielded like weapons. They can destroy people; they can give them hope too.

"There you are." Jase's deep voice greets me with a sensual need. I can already feel his warmth before he wraps his arms around my waist and pulls me into his chest. The paper clings to my front as I keep it from his prying eyes.

"What are you hiding from me?" he questions.

"No hiding anything anymore. Isn't that the deal?" I remind him, peeking around to not just see him, but to steal a quick kiss as well. I love it when he smirks at me.

With a lift of his chin he tells me, "Then show it."

I do so willingly, listening to the paper crinkle and watching his dark eyes as he reads each line.

"Marriage certificate?" It's a sin that he looks so handsome, even when he's confused.

"It's a certificate to get a marriage certificate. Like a gift card. I didn't know you could get one of these. You have to be there for it to actually be done and all," I explain to him. I thought this would be the best way to tell him that I want to marry him.

As he steps back, snagging the paper from me and then looking between it and me, nerves flow through every part of me.

"My answer is yes." In my mind, when I decided I'd do this, I said it confidently, playfully even, but the way the words came out now was hurried and with an anxiousness to hear his response.

Which he still hasn't given me.

"At least I answered you quickly," I tell him and pretend like my hands aren't trembling.

"You want to do this?" he asks me, his shoulders squared as he lowers the paper to the leather sofa and closes the space between us.

Reaching up to adjust the collar of his pressed white shirt, I tell him easily, as if he's said yes, "I don't want a big wedding."

"Are you proposing to me?" he finally says with a grin and the playfulness and the charm are obvious. This is the man I love.

Nodding, I fight back the prick at the back of my eyes and tell him, "I am. Are you saying yes?"

"I already asked you, though. You don't get to ask me now." He walks circles around me, making me spin slowly.

"You aren't exactly good at it, so I figured I should give it a shot." I'm just as playful with him as he is me, nipping his bottom lip and then kissing him. He deepens it, stopping where he is and splaying his hands against my lower back and shoulder.

When he breaks the kiss, he stares down at me. "Why?" he asks me, toying with me and my emotions instead of just ending it quickly.

"You have no mercy," I joke with him. "Are you not saying yes?" I can't even voice the word no right now.

He only stares down at me, waiting for a response with a smug look on his face.

"When I'm sad, I want you to be there because then I feel less sad. When I'm happy, I want you there because I want you happy with me. I just want you there... and I want to be there for you. If you'll let me." Tears form but I blink them away.

"I'll let you," he whispers ruggedly as he lowers his lips to the dip in my throat, giving me a chance to breathe easy. And to breathe him in.

"That's not how you say 'yes,' Jase. Or how you make a girl feel secure," I tease him although my words are still a bit unsteady. He pulls back to look at me, both of his hands still on me as I add, "When she prints out a marriage certificate, you're supposed to say yes."

"What if I gave her something else instead?" he asks, reaching into his pocket. "What if it was a tit for tat and I asked her a question to answer her question." My eyes turn watery as he gets down on his knee and pulls out a small black velvet box.

"I have something for you."

I can barely speak. "Jase."

"I love the way you say my name," he tells me, holding the box in one hand and my left hand in his other.

"I realized when I asked you to marry me, I probably should have done it better. I thought you'd be more willing to say 'yes' if there was something in it for you. I didn't think about a ring or feel like a ring would be enough."

Tears are warm as they fall down my face and I sniffle before telling Jase, "You are enough, Jase. It baffles me how you don't see that." I have to sniffle again before I can tell him that I'll remind him of it every day for as long as he lives if that's what it takes.

"Will you marry me?" he finally asks, opening the box. I don't have time to even look at what's inside. I need to touch him more than look at his surprise. I need to hold him and for him to hold me.

"I love you, Jase." I breathe against his shoulder, letting my tears fall to the thin white fabric.

"Say yes, first," he answers in what should be a playful voice, but feels nervous.

"A million times yes. It's always been yes."

Sometimes you meet someone, although maybe *meet* isn't quite the right word. You don't even have to say hello for this to happen. You simply pass by them and everything in your world changes forever. Chills flow from where you imagine he'd kiss you in the crook of your neck, moving all the way down with only a single glance.

I know you know what I'm referring to. The moment when something inside of you ignites to life, recognizing the other half that's been gone for far too long.

It burns hot, destroying any hope that it's only a coincidence, and that life will go back to what it was. These moments are never forgotten.

That's only with a single glance.

I can tell you what a single touch will do. It will consume you and everything you thought you knew.

I felt all of this with Jase Cross, with every flicker of the flames that roared inside of me. I knew he'd be my downfall, and I was determined to be his just the same.

He deserves as much. To have every brick in his guarded walls brought to the ground and be left to turn into something more. I want nothing between us. Nothing but us. Even if that means this world will collapse around us and become a chaos I never imagined.

So long as I'm with him, so long as his touch is within reach, I would give everything else up.

That's the part that scared me in that first moment.

Somewhere deep inside of me I knew I would be his.

And I'll do it again and again. In this life and the next.

CHAPTER
24

Jase

You're welcome for your gift.
It was mine to give all along.

M ARCUS'S HANDWRITING STARES BACK AT ME UNTIL I CRUMPLE THE small parchment into my hand.

He's had a hand in the details, but he's slipping. More of his intention is showing. It's contradictory and changes on a whim, but he's falling. I can feel it.

One small token won't save him from the consequences of his actions. Our enemies will fall one by one, as they should. Their names will be carved in stone long before I allow anyone I love to meet the same fate.

He's the one who chose to be our enemy. A gift won't change that.

Balling up the note, I think back on everything that's happened. Not just to me, but also to my brothers and to Sebastian. It all comes down to the simple fact that we found irresistible attractions. And all the while, Marcus knew. He used them against us. Each and every one of us.

Sometimes when people are in pain they push love away. Tossing the paper into the metal trashcan outside the old brick building, I think of Sebastian and how much he tried to resist.

Pain makes people go to extremes they know are wrong. Carter is proof of that. Sometimes all life will give you is only a tragedy, but if you have someone to love, someone to hold on to, like Daniel and Addison had each other, then life will go on.

We are only men. Not invincible heroes.

And Marcus is just the same.

He's in pain like all of us. In fear like we've all been in. The answer to finding him, to bringing him to his knees lies in the one thing we've given into that he hasn't.

The girl Officer Walsh can't get over. The girl who ties him and Marcus together...

That girl will make Marcus fall. I know she will.

Seth will find her. *He must.*

"What's wrong?" Bethany's voice carries through the warmth of the April sunshine as her heels click on the sidewalk. Slipping her hand into the pocket of her jacket, she looks up at me and I can't resist brushing the hair from her face to cup her chin in my hand.

Before I can lean down to kiss her, she grips my dress shirt at the buttons, fisting the fabric in her hands and bringing her lips to mine. Desire ignites and the burn from it diminishes any other thought, any other need.

That's how it happens. It's how love conquers. Boldly, without fear, and with a ruling flame that nothing can tame.

Her lips soften the second they meet mine. Her body presses against my own as well. With a hand on the small dip at her waist I pull her closer to me, leaving nothing between us.

It's only when she pulls back that I even dare to breathe.

"I want to kiss you like that forever," she whispers against my lips with her eyes still closed. When they open, she peeks up at me through her lashes and adds, "I want to take my kisses from you every damn day."

A low groan of approval rumbles up my chest as she twines her fingers through mine.

"Now tell me what's wrong."

"A little demanding, aren't you, cailín tine?" A pang of nervousness worms its way between us. Before it can do any damage, I tell her, "I'm considering Marcus's next move." I resist telling her the second piece, but only for a split second. With her lips parted to answer me, I cut her off with, "And ours."

She doesn't let go of my hands, but she takes a half step back, letting her head nod. Intensity, curiosity, even fear swirl in her gaze. All the while, I wait for what she'll say, what she'll do.

"If you need me I'm here," she finally answers.

"All I need is for you to follow me," I tell her and lower my lips to hers. Nipping her bottom lip, the small bit of tension wanes. She may not be involved in what I do, but she'll stay with me.

I know she will. Because she loves me and she knows how deeply I love her.

Moving my hand around her waist, I'll make sure she never forgets, never questions what I feel for her.

She won't go a day without knowing. Her head rests against my arm as we walk, her one hand holding mine, the other on top of our clasped hands.

"It's all going to be all right," she tells me, although she stares ahead, noting the *Rare Books* sign in the window which causes her brow to furrow.

The smell of old books is unique, and it engulfs us as we walk deeper into the aisle. The full shelves of worn and previously read books make rows, but the one shelf at the very back is the one she needs to see.

"What are we doing here?" she questions and lifts her gaze to mine, but I only squeeze her hand in response.

"Jase," Bethany pushes for more, practically hissing my name although her steps have picked up with a giddiness she can't hide, making me chuckle at her impatience.

When I come to a stop in front of the shelves, she brushes against me and steps forward. I watch her reaction to seeing the wall of thin cream pages.

"They don't have covers?" she whispers and reaches out, her fingers trailing down the fronts of them.

I watch as she swallows, her throat tensing and her lips turning down.

"These are the books with no covers. No titles. They're only stories."

Her eyes glaze over, as I'm sure the Coverless Book comes back to her, a gift from her mother and so much more. We may forget words or details, but the way we feel never leaves our memories. I know that book scarred her in a way I can't imagine although I'm not sure why.

"I wanted to get you another one. A different story to take its place."

"We drove hours and hours to get a book?" she questions silently, her eyes beseeching me to explain why.

"This is the only place I found on the East Coast that carried unknown books-"

"I don't want to read another tragedy," she says and cuts me off. "I don't want to risk it."

"You're going to want to though, cailín tine."

A second passes and I swear I can hear her heart beating, waiting in limbo for more.

"These books all came from one person's home years ago. She collected stories that made her feel loved."

Bethany turns her attention back to the books, back to the stories I want her to read.

"I brought you here because they call this the aisle of hope."

CHAPTER
25

Seth

WITH HER LEGS CROSSED LIKE THAT, HER RED SKIRT RIDES UP higher. It draws my eye and as she clears her throat, noticing my wandering gaze, I let the smirk appear on my lips before carelessly covering it with my hand.

It's been too long since I've been this close to her, face to face. Too many years since she's sought me out.

My stubble is rough beneath my fingertips; it'll leave small scratches against her soft skin when I ravage her with the hunger I've had for so long.

"Did you hear what I said?" Laura asks. When she got into my car with Bethany, I could feel the waves of apprehension hidden in the silence, the lust that roared back to life when Bethany left us. And we made a deal.

"You said you wanted an exchange. You want to change the details of our deal."

Her doe eyes beg me to consider, and they hold a vulnerability that her tense curves fail to deliver. She grips both arms of the chair across from me as her chest rises and falls with a quickened pace. She can't hide the fear of coming back to this life. *Of coming back to me.*

As her bottom lip slips between her teeth, I note that she can't hide the desire either.

"I've wanted this for too long to consider your proposal," I tell her, spreading my legs wider and leaning forward in my office chair in the back room of the bar. My elbows rest on my knees as I lean closer to her, only inches away as I whisper, "You know what I want."

"I can give you something you want more," she speaks clearly, although her last words waver when her gaze drifts to my lips.

Lies. There's nothing I want more.

I would have told her that and meant it with every bone in my body, but then she tells me, "I can give you Marcus."

ABOUT THE AUTHOR

Thank you so much for reading my romances. I'm just a stay at home mom and avid reader turned author and I couldn't be happier.

I hope you love my books as much as I do!

More by Willow Winters
www.willowwinterswrites.com/books

CPSIA information can be obtained
at www.ICGtesting.com
Printed in the USA
LVHW041040260722
724433LV00001B/20

9 781950 862597